"A total revelation... the book is balan[ced between the] real-life abolitionist and feminist Sara[h Grimké and her han]d-maiden Handful, who nearly leaps off every page."
—ESSENCE

"*The Invention of Wings* isn't just the story of a friendship that defies an oppressive society.... It's a much more satisfying story of two people discovering together that their lives are worth the fight."
—ENTERTAINMENT WEEKLY

"A story of empowerment and self-expression in the face of brutal, institutionalized, racial subjugation... An utterly absorbing work of fiction."
—THE SEATTLE TIMES

"Unforgettable... it isn't easy, but Handful will invent her own wings, and so will Sarah. And to their engrossing stories, by turns shocking and thrilling and moving, Kidd brings her own kind of magic."
—TAMPA BAY TIMES

PENGUIN BOOKS

THE INVENTION OF WINGS

Sue Monk Kidd's first novel, *The Secret Life of Bees*, spent more than one hundred weeks on the *New York Times* bestseller list, has sold more than six million copies in the United States, was turned into an award-winning major motion picture, and has been translated into thirty-six languages. It has been nominated for and received numerous awards both here and abroad. Her second novel, *The Mermaid Chair*, was a number-one *New York Times* bestseller and adapted into a television movie. She is also the author of several acclaimed memoirs, including the *New York Times* bestseller *Traveling with Pomegranates*, written with her daughter, Ann Kidd Taylor. She lives in Florida.

Sue Monk Kidd

THE INVENTION OF WINGS

Penguin Books

PENGUIN BOOKS
Published by the Penguin Group
Penguin Group (USA) LLC
375 Hudson Street
New York, New York 10014

USA | Canada | UK | Ireland | Australia | New Zealand | India | South Africa | China
penguin.com
A Penguin Random House Company

First published in the United States of America by Viking Penguin,
a member of Penguin Group (USA) LLC, 2014
Published in Penguin Books 2015

Copyright © 2014 by Sue Monk Kidd, Inc.
Penguin supports copyright. Copyright fuels creativity, encourages diverse voices, promotes free speech, and creates a vibrant culture. Thank you for buying an authorized edition of this book and for complying with copyright laws by not reproducing, scanning, or distributing any part of it in any form without permission. You are supporting writers and allowing Penguin to continue to publish books for every reader.

THE LIBRARY OF CONGRESS HAS CATALOGED THE
HARDCOVER EDITION AS FOLLOWS:
Kidd, Sue Monk.
The invention of wings : a novel / Sue Monk Kidd.
pages cm
ISBN 978-0-670-02478-0 (hc.)
ISBN 978-0-14-312170-1 (pbk.)
1. Grimké, Sarah Moore, 1792–1873—Fiction. 2. Antislavery movements—Fiction. 3. Feminists—South Carolina—Fiction. 4. Women's rights.—Fiction. I. Title.
PS3611.I44I58 2014
813'.6—dc23   2013028185

Printed in the United States of America
1 3 5 7 9 10 8 6 4 2

Set in Garamond Premier Pro
Designed by Francesca Belanger

This is a work of fiction. Names, characters, places, and incidents either are the product of the author's imagination or are used fictitiously, and any resemblance to actual persons, living or dead, businesses, companies, events, or locales is entirely coincidental.

*To Sandy Kidd
with all my love*

THE INVENTION OF WINGS

PART ONE

November 1803–February 1805

Hetty Handful Grimké

There was a time in Africa the people could fly. Mauma told me this one night when I was ten years old. She said, "Handful, your granny-mauma saw it for herself. She say they flew over trees and clouds. She say they flew like blackbirds. When we came here, we left that magic behind."

My mauma was shrewd. She didn't get any reading and writing like me. Everything she knew came from living on the scarce side of mercy. She looked at my face, how it flowed with sorrow and doubt, and she said, "You don't believe me? Where you think these shoulder blades of yours come from, girl?"

Those skinny bones stuck out from my back like nubs. She patted them and said, "This all what left of your wings. They nothing but these flat bones now, but one day you gon get 'em back."

I was shrewd like mauma. Even at ten I knew this story about people flying was pure malarkey. We weren't some special people who lost our magic. We were slave people, and we weren't going anywhere. It was later I saw what she meant. We could fly all right, but it wasn't any magic to it.

The day life turned into nothing this world could fix, I was in the work yard boiling slave bedding, stoking fire under the wash pot, my eyes burning from specks of lye soap catching on the wind. The morning was a cold one—the sun looked like a little white button stitched tight to the sky. For summers we wore homespun cotton dresses over our drawers, but when the Charleston winter showed up like some lazy girl in November or January, we got into our sacks—these thickset coats made of heavy yarns. Just an old sack with sleeves. Mine was a cast-off and trailed to my ankles. I couldn't say how many unwashed bodies had worn it before me, but they had all kindly left their scents on it.

Already that morning missus had taken her cane stick to me once cross my backside for falling asleep during her devotions. Every day, all us slaves, everyone but Rosetta, who was old and demented, jammed in the dining room before breakfast to fight off sleep while missus taught us short Bible verses like "Jesus wept" and prayed out loud about God's favorite subject, *obedience*. If you nodded off, you got whacked right in the middle of God said this and God said that.

I was full of sass to Aunt-Sister about the whole miserable business. I'd say, "Let this cup pass from me," spouting one of missus' verses. I'd say, "Jesus wept cause he's trapped in there with missus, like us."

Aunt-Sister was the cook—she'd been with missus since missus was a girl—and next to Tomfry, the butler, she ran the whole show. She was the only one who could tell missus what to do without getting smacked by the cane. Mauma said watch your tongue, but I never did. Aunt-Sister popped me backward three times a day.

I was a handful. That's not how I got my name, though. Handful was my basket name. The master and missus, they did all the proper naming, but a mauma would look on her baby laid in its basket and a name would come to her, something about what her baby looked like, what day of the week it was, what the weather was doing, or just how the world seemed on that day. My mauma's basket name was Summer, but her proper name was Charlotte. She had a brother whose basket name was Hardtime. People think I make that up, but it's true as it can be.

If you got a basket name, you at least had something from your mauma. Master Grimké named me Hetty, but mauma looked on me the day I came into the world, how I was born too soon, and she called me Handful.

That day while I helped out Aunt-Sister in the yard, mauma was in the house, working on a gold sateen dress for missus with a bustle on the back, what's called a Watteau gown. She was the best seamstress in Charleston and worked her fingers stiff with the needle. You never saw such finery as my mauma could whip up, and she didn't use a stamping pattern. She hated a book pattern. She picked out the silks and velvets her own self at the market and made everything the Grimkés had—window curtains, quilted petticoats, looped panniers, buckskin pants, and these done-up jockey outfits for Race Week.

I can tell you this much—white people lived for Race Week. They had one picnic, promenade, and fancy going-on after another. Mrs. King's party was always on Tuesday. The Jockey Club dinner on Wednesday. The big fuss came Saturday with the St. Cecilia ball when they strutted out in their best dresses. Aunt-Sister said Charleston had a case of the grandeurs. Up till I was eight or so, I thought the grandeurs was a shitting sickness.

Missus was a short, thick-waist woman with what looked like little balls of dough under her eyes. She refused to hire out mauma to the other ladies. They begged her, and mauma begged her too, cause she would've kept a portion of those wages for herself—but missus said, I can't have you make anything for them better than you make for us. In the evenings, mauma tore strips for her quilts, while I held the tallow candle with one hand and stacked the strips in piles with the other, always by color, neat as a pin. She liked her colors bright, putting shades together nobody would think—purple and orange, pink and red. The shape she loved was a triangle. Always black. Mauma put black triangles on about every quilt she sewed.

We had a wooden patch box for keeping our scraps, a pouch for our needles and threads, and a true brass thimble. Mauma said the thimble would be mine one day. When she wasn't using it, I wore it on my fingertip like a jewel. We filled our quilts up with raw cotton and wool thrums. The best filling was feathers, still is, and mauma and I never passed one on the ground without picking it up. Some days, mauma would come in with a pocketful of goose feathers she'd plucked from mattress holes in the house. When we got desperate to fill a quilt, we'd strip the long moss from the oak in the work yard and sew it between the lining and the quilt top, chiggers and all.

That was the thing mauma and I loved, our time with the quilts.

No matter what Aunt-Sister had me doing in the yard, I always watched the upstairs window where mauma did her stitching. We had a signal. When I turned the pail upside down by the kitchen house, that meant everything was clear. Mauma would open the window and throw down a taffy she stole from missus' room. Sometimes here came a bundle of cloth scraps—real nice calicos, gingham, muslin, some import linen. One time, that true brass thimble. Her favorite thing to take was scarlet-red thread. She would wind it up in her pocket and walk right out the house with it.

The yard was over busy that day, so I didn't have hope for a taffy falling from the clear blue. Mariah, the laundry slave, had burned her hand on charcoal from the iron and was laid up. Aunt-Sister was on a tear about the backed-up wash. Tomfry had the men fixing to butcher a hog that was running and screeching at the top of its lungs. Everyone was out there, from old Snow the carriage driver all the way down to the stable mucker, Prince. Tomfry wanted to get the killing over quick cause missus hated yard noise.

Noise was on her list of slave sins, which we knew by heart. Number one: stealing. Number two: disobedience. Number three: laziness. Number four: noise. A slave was supposed to be like the Holy Ghost—don't see it, don't hear it, but it's always hovering round on ready.

Missus called out to Tomfry, said keep it down, a lady shouldn't know where her bacon comes from. When we heard that, I told Aunt-Sister, missus didn't know what end her bacon went in and what end it came out. Aunt-Sister slapped me into yesterday.

I took the long pole we called a battling stick and fished up the bedcovers from the wash pot and flopped them dripping on the rail where Aunt-Sister dried her cooking herbs. The rail in the stable was forbidden cause the horses had eyes too precious for lye. Slave eyes were another thing. Working the stick, I beat those sheets and blankets to an inch of their lives. We called it fetching the dirt.

After I got the wash finished, I was left idle and pleased to enjoy sin number three. I followed a path I'd worn in the dirt from looping it ten, twelve times a day. I started at the back of the main house, walked past the kitchen house and the laundry out to the spreading tree. Some of the branches on it were bigger round than my body, and every one of them curled like ribbons in a box. Bad spirits travel in straight lines, and our tree didn't have one un-crooked place. Us slaves mustered under it when the heat bore down.

Mauma always told me, don't pull the gray moss off cause that keeps out the sun and everybody's prying eyes.

I walked back past the stable and carriage house. The path took me cross the whole map of the world I knew. I hadn't yet seen the spinning globe in the house that showed the rest of it. I poked along, wishing for the day to get used up so me and mauma could go to our room. It sat over the carriage house and didn't have a window. The smell of manure from the stable and the cow house rose up there so ripe it seemed like our bed was stuffed with it instead of straw. The rest of the slaves had their rooms over the kitchen house.

The wind whipped up and I listened for ship sails snapping in the harbor cross the road, a place I'd smelled on the breeze, but never seen. The sails would go off like whips cracking and all us would listen to see was it some slave getting flogged in a neighbor-yard or was it ships making ready to leave. You found out when the screams started up or not.

The sun had gone, leaving a puckered place in the clouds, like the button had fallen off. I picked up the battling stick by the wash pot, and for no good reason, jabbed it into a squash in the vegetable garden. I pitched the butternut over the wall where it splatted in a loud mess.

Then the air turned still. Missus' voice came from the back door, said, "Aunt-Sister, bring Hetty in here to me right now."

I went to the house, thinking she was in an uproar over her squash. I told my backside to brace up.

Sarah Grimké

My eleventh birthday began with Mother promoting me from the nursery. For a year I'd longed to escape the porcelain dolls, tops, and tiny tea sets strewn across the floor, the small beds lined up in a row, the whole glut and bedlam of the place, but now that the day had come, I balked at the threshold of my new room. It was paneled with darkness and emanated the smell of my brother—all things smoky and leather. The oak canopy and red velvet valance of the bedstead was so towering it seemed closer to the ceiling than the floor. I couldn't move for dread of living alone in such an enormous, overweening space.

Drawing a breath, I flung myself across the door sill. That was the artless way I navigated the hurdles of girlhood. Everyone thought I was a plucky girl, but in truth, I wasn't as fearless as everyone assumed. I had the temperament of a tortoise. Whatever dread, fright, or bump appeared in my path, I wanted nothing more than to drop in my tracks and hide. *If you must err, do so on the side of audacity.* That was the little slogan I'd devised for myself. For some time now, it had helped me to hurl myself over door sills.

That morning was full of cold, bright wind pouring off the Atlantic and clouds blowing like windsocks. For a moment, I stood just inside the room listening to the saber-fronds on the palmettos clatter around the house. The eaves of the piazza hissed. The porch swing groaned on its chains. Downstairs in the warming kitchen, Mother had the slaves pulling out Chinese tureens and Wedgwood cups, preparing for my birthday party. Her maid Cindie had spent hours wetting and fastening Mother's wig with paper and curlers and the sour smell of it baking had nosed all the way up the stairs.

I watched as Binah, the nursery mauma, tucked my clothes into the heavy old wardrobe, recalling how she used a fire poke to rock Charles' cradle, her cowrie shell bracelets rattling along her arms while she terrified us with tales of the Booga Hag—an old woman who rode about on a broom and sucked the breath from bad children. I would miss Binah. And sweet Anna, who slept with her thumb in her mouth. Ben and Henry, who jumped like banshees until their mattresses erupted with geysers of goose feathers, and little Eliza, who had a habit of slipping into my bed to hide from the Booga's nightly reign of terror.

Of course, I should've graduated from the nursery long ago, but I'd been forced to wait for John to go away to college. Our three-storied house was one of the grandest in Charleston, but it lacked enough bedrooms, considering how . . . well, fruitful Mother was. There were ten of us: John, Thomas, Mary, Frederick, and myself, followed by the nursery dwellers—Anna, Eliza, Ben, Henry, and baby Charles. I was the middle one, the one Mother called *different* and Father called *remarkable,* the one with the carroty hair and the freckles, whole constellations of them. My brothers had once traced Orion, the Dipper, and Ursa Major on my cheeks and forehead with charcoal, connecting the bright red specks, and I hadn't minded—I'd been their whole sky for hours.

Everyone said I was Father's favorite. I don't know whether he preferred me or pitied me, but he was certainly *my* favorite. He was a judge on South Carolina's highest court and at the top of the planter class, the group Charleston claimed as its elite. He'd fought with General Washington and been taken prisoner by the British. He was too modest to speak of these things— for that, he had Mother.

Her name was Mary, and there ends any resemblance to the mother of our Lord. She was descended from the first families of Charleston, that little company of Lords that King Charles had sent over to establish the city. She worked this into conversations so tirelessly we no longer made the time or effort to roll our eyes. Besides governing the house, a host of children, and fourteen slaves, she kept up a round of social and religious duties that would've worn out the queens and saints of Europe. When I was being forgiving, I said that my mother was simply exhausted. I suspected, though, she was simply mean.

When Binah finished arranging my hair combs and ribbons on the lavish

Hepplewhite atop my new dressing table, she turned to me, and I must have looked forsaken standing there because she clucked her tongue against the roof of her mouth and said, "Poor Miss Sarah."

I did so despise the attachment of *Poor* to my name. Binah had been muttering *Poor Miss Sarah* like an incantation since I was four.

It's my earliest memory: arranging my brother's marbles into words. It is summer, and I am beneath the oak that stands in the back corner of the work yard. Thomas, ten, whom I love above all the others, has taught me nine words: SARAH, GIRL, BOY, GO, STOP, JUMP, RUN, UP, DOWN. He has written them on a parchment and given me a pouch of forty-eight glass marbles with which to spell them out, enough to shape two words at a time. I arrange the marbles in the dirt, copying Thomas' inked words. *Sarah Go. Boy Run. Girl Jump.* I work as fast as I can. Binah will come soon looking for me.

It's Mother, however, who descends the back steps into the yard. Binah and the other house slaves are clumped behind her, moving with cautious, synchronized steps as if they're a single creature, a centipede crossing an unprotected space. I sense the shadow that hovers over them in the air, some devouring dread, and I crawl back into the green-black gloom of the tree.

The slaves stare at Mother's back, which is straight and without give. She turns and admonishes them. "You are lagging. Quickly now, let us be done with this."

As she speaks, an older slave, Rosetta, is dragged from the cow house, dragged by a man, a yard slave. She fights, clawing at his face. Mother watches, impassive.

He ties Rosetta's hands to the corner column of the kitchen house porch. She looks over her shoulder and begs. *Missus, please. Missus. Missus. Please.* She begs even as the man lashes her with his whip.

Her dress is cotton, a pale yellow color. I stare transfixed as the back of it sprouts blood, blooms of red that open like petals. I cannot reconcile the savagery of the blows with the mellifluous way she keens or the beauty of the roses coiling along the trellis of her spine. Someone counts the lashes—is it Mother? *Six, seven.*

The scourging continues, but Rosetta stops wailing and sinks against the porch rail. *Nine, ten.* My eyes look away. They follow a black ant traveling the far reaches beneath the tree—the mountainous roots and forested mosses, the endless perils—and in my head I say the words I fashioned earlier. *Boy Run. Girl Jump. Sarah Go.*

Thirteen. Fourteen . . . I bolt from the shadows, past the man who now coils his whip, job well done, past Rosetta hanging by her hands in a heap. As I bound up the back steps into the house, Mother calls to me, and Binah reaches to scoop me up, but I escape them, thrashing along the main passage, out the front door, where I break blindly for the wharves.

I don't remember the rest with clarity, only that I find myself wandering across the gangplank of a sailing vessel, sobbing, stumbling over a turban of rope. A kind man with a beard and a dark cap asks what I want. I plead with him, *Sarah Go.*

Binah chases me, though I'm unaware of her until she pulls me into her arms and coos, "Poor Miss Sarah, poor Miss Sarah." Like a decree, a proclamation, a prophecy.

When I arrive home, I am a muss of snot, tears, yard dirt, and harbor filth. Mother holds me against her, rears back and gives me an incensed shake, then clasps me again. "You must promise never to run away again. *Promise me.*"

I want to. I try to. The words are on my tongue—the rounded lumps of them, shining like the marbles beneath the tree.

"Sarah!" she demands.

Nothing comes. Not a sound.

I remained mute for a week. My words seemed sucked into the cleft between my collar bones. I rescued them by degrees, by praying, bullying and wooing. I came to speak again, but with an odd and mercurial form of stammer. I'd never been a fluid speaker, even my first spoken words had possessed a certain belligerent quality, but now there were ugly, halting gaps between my sentences, endless seconds when the words cowered against my lips and people averted their eyes. Eventually, these horrid pauses began to come and go according to their own mysterious whims. They might plague me for weeks and then remain away months, only to return again as abruptly as they left.

The day I moved from the nursery to commence a life of maturity in John's staid old room, I wasn't thinking of the cruelty that had taken place in the work yard when I was four or of the thin filaments that had kept me tethered to my voice ever since. Those concerns were the farthest thing from my mind. My speech impediment had been absent for some time now—four months and six days. I'd almost imagined myself cured.

So when Mother swept into the room all of a sudden—me, in a paroxysm of adjustment to my surroundings, and Binah, tucking my possessions here and there—and asked if my new quarters were to my liking, I was stunned by my inability to answer her. The door slammed in my throat, and the silence hung there. Mother looked at me and sighed.

When she left, I willed my eyes to remain dry and turned away from Binah. I couldn't bear to hear one more *Poor Miss Sarah*.

Handful

Aunt-Sister took me to the warming kitchen where Binah and Cindie were fussing over silver trays, laying them full of ginger cake and apples with ground nuts. They had on their good long aprons with starch. Off in the drawing room, it sounded like bees buzzing.

Missus showed up and told Aunt-Sister to peel off my nasty coat and wash my face, then she said, "Hetty, this is Sarah's eleventh birthday and we are having a party for her."

She took a lavender ribbon from the top of the pie safe and circled it round my neck, tying a bow, while Aunt-Sister peeled the black off my cheeks with her rag. Missus wound more ribbon round my waist. When I tugged, she told me in a sharp way, "Stop that fidgeting, Hetty! Be still."

Missus had done the ribbon too snug at my throat. It felt like I couldn't swallow. I searched for Aunt-Sister's eyes, but they were glued on the food trays. I wanted to tell her, *Get me free of this, help me, I need the privy.* I always had something smart to say, but my voice had run down my throat like a kitchen mouse.

I danced on one leg and the other. I thought what mauma had told me, "You be good coming up on Christmas cause that when they sell off the extra children or else send them to the fields." I didn't know one slave master Grimké had sold, but I knew plenty he'd sent to his plantation in the back country. That's where mauma had come from, bearing me inside her and leaving my daddy behind.

I stopped all my fidget then. My whole self went down in the hole where my voice was. I tried to do what they said God wanted. Obey, be quiet, be still.

Missus studied me, how I looked in the purple ribbons. Taking me by the arm, she led me to the drawing room where the ladies sat with their dresses fussed out and their china teacups and lacy napkins. One lady played the tiny piano called a harpsichord, but she stopped when missus gave a clap with her hands.

Every eye fixed on me. Missus said, "This is our little Hetty. Sarah, dear, she is your present, your very own waiting maid."

I pressed my hands between my legs and missus knocked them away. She turned me a full circle. The ladies started up like parrots—*happy birthday, happy birthday*—their fancy heads pecking the air. Miss Sarah's older sister, Miss Mary, sat there full of sulk from not being the center of the party. Next to missus, she was the worst bird in the room. We'd all seen her going round with *her* waiting maid, Lucy, smacking the girl six ways from Sunday. We all said if Miss Mary dropped her kerchief from the second floor, she'd send Lucy jumping out the window for it. Least I didn't end up with that one.

Miss Sarah stood up. She was wearing a dark blue dress and had rosy-colored hair that hung straight like corn silk and freckles the same red color all over her face. She took a long breath and started working her lips. Back then, Miss Sarah pulled words up from her throat like she was raising water from a well.

When she finally got the bucket up, we could hardly hear what she was saying. "......... I'm sorry, Mother...... I can't accept."

Missus asked her to say it over. This time Miss Sarah bellowed it like a shrimp peddler.

Missus' eyes were frost blue like Miss Sarah's, but they turned dark as indigo. Her fingernails bore into me and carved out what looked like a flock of birds on my arm. She said, "Sit down, Sarah dear."

Miss Sarah said, "... I don't need a waiting maid ... I'm perfectly fine without one."

"That is quite enough," missus said. How you could miss the warning in that, I don't know. Miss Sarah missed it by a mile.

"... Couldn't you save her for Anna?"

"Enough!"

Miss Sarah plopped on her chair like somebody shoved her.

The water started in a trickle down my leg. I jerked every way I could to get free of missus' claws, but then it came in a gush on the rug.

Missus let out a shriek and everything went hush. You could hear embers leap round in the fireplace.

I had a slap coming, or worse. I thought of Rosetta, how she threw a shaking fit when it suited her. She'd let the spit run from her mouth and send her eyes rolling back. She looked like a beetle-bug upside down trying to right itself, but it got her free of punishment, and it crossed my mind to fall down and pitch a fit myself the best I could.

But I stood there with my dress plastered wet on my thighs and shame running hot down my face.

Aunt-Sister came and toted me off. When we passed the stairs in the main hall, I saw mauma up on the landing, pressing her hands to her chest.

That night doves sat up in the tree limbs and moaned. I clung to mauma in our rope bed, staring at the quilt frame, the way it hung over us from the ceiling rafters, drawn tight on its pulleys. She said the quilt frame was our guarding angel. She said, "Everything gon be all right." But the shame stayed with me. I tasted it like a bitter green on my tongue.

The bells tolled cross Charleston for the slave curfew, and mauma said the Guard would be out there soon beating on their drums, but she said it like this: "Bugs be in the wheat 'fore long."

Then she rubbed the flat bones in my shoulders. That's when she told me the story from Africa her mauma told her. How the people could fly. How they flew over trees and clouds. How they flew like blackbirds.

Next morning mauma handed me a quilt matched to my length and told me I couldn't sleep with her anymore. From here on out, I would sleep on the floor in the hall outside Miss Sarah's bed chamber. Mauma said, "Don't get off your quilt for nothin' but Miss Sarah calling. Don't wander 'bout. Don't light no candle. Don't make noise. When Miss Sarah rings the bell, you make haste."

Mauma told me, "It gon be hard from here on, Handful."

Sarah

I was sent to solitary confinement in my new room and ordered to write a letter of apology to each guest. Mother settled me at the desk with paper, inkwell, and a letter she'd composed herself, which I was to copy.

"... ... You didn't punish Hetty, did you?" I asked.

"Do you think me inhuman, Sarah? The girl had an accident. What could I do?" She shrugged with exasperation. "If the rug cannot be cleaned, it will have to be thrown out."

As she walked to the door, I struggled to pry the words from my mouth before she exited. "... ... Mother, please, let me... ... let me give Hetty back to you."

Give Hetty back. As if she was mine after all. As if owning people was as natural as breathing. For all my resistance about slavery, I breathed that foul air, too.

"Your guardianship is legal and binding. Hetty is yours, Sarah, there is nothing to be done about it."

"... ... But—"

I heard the commotion of her petticoats as she crossed the rug back to me. She was a woman the winds and tides obeyed, but in that moment, she was gentle with me. Placing a finger under my chin, she tilted my face to hers and smiled. "Why must you fight this? I don't know where you get these alien ideas. This is our way of life, dear one, make your peace with it." She kissed the top of my head. "I expect all eighteen letters by the morning."

The room filled with an orange glow that lit the cypress panels, then melted into dusk and shadows. In my mind, I could see Hetty clearly—the confused, mortified look on her face, her hair braids cocked in every direction, the disgraceful lavender ribbons. She was puny in the extreme, a year younger than I, but she looked all of six years old. Her limbs were stick and bone. Her elbows, the curves of two fastening pins. The only thing of any size about her was her eyes, which were colored a strange shade of gold and floated above her black cheeks like shiny half-moons.

It seemed traitorous to ask forgiveness for something I didn't feel sorry for in the least. What I regretted was how pathetic my protest had turned out. I wanted nothing more than to sit here unyielding through the night, for days and weeks if need be, but in the end I gave in and wrote the damnable letters. I knew myself to be an odd girl with my mutinous ideas, ravenous intellect, and funny looks, and half the time I sputtered like a horse straining at its bit, qualities in the female sex that were not endearing. I was on my way to being the family pariah, and I feared the ostracism. I feared it most of all.

Over and over I wrote:

> *Dear Madame,*
> *Thank you for the honor and kindness you bestowed upon me by attending my eleventh birthday tea. I regret that though I have been well-taught by my parents, my behavior on this occasion was exceedingly ill-mannered. I humbly beg your pardon for my rudeness and disrespect.*
> *Your Remorseful Friend,*
> *Sarah Grimké*

I climbed the preposterous height to the mattress and had only just settled when a bird outside my window began to trill. First, a stream of pelting whistles, then a soft, melancholic song. I felt alone in the world with my alien ideas.

Sliding from my perch, I stole to the window where I shivered in my white woolen gown, gazing along East Bay, past the dark rooftops toward the harbor. With hurricane season behind us, there were close to a hundred topsails moored out there, shimmering on the water. Plastering my cheek against the frigid pane, I discovered I had a partial view of the slave quarters above the carriage house where I knew Hetty to be spending her last night with her mother. Tomorrow she would take up her duties and sleep outside my door.

It was then I had a sudden epiphany. I lit a candle from the dwindling coals in the fire, opened my door, and stepped into the dark, unheated passageway. Three dark shapes lay on the floor beside the bedroom doors. I'd never really seen the world beyond the nursery at night and it took a moment to realize the shapes were slaves, sleeping close by in case a Grimké rang his bell.

Mother wished to replace the archaic arrangement with one that had recently been installed in the house of her friend, Mrs. Russell. There, buttons were pressed that rang in the slaves' quarters, each with a special chime. Mother was bent on the innovation, but Father thought it wasteful. Though we were Anglicans, he had a mild streak of Huguenot frugality. There would be ostentatious buttons in the Grimké household over his dead body.

I crept barefooted down the wide mahogany stairs to the first floor where two more slaves slept, along with Cindie, who sat wide awake with her back against the wall outside my parents' chamber. She eyed me warily, but didn't ask what I was doing.

I picked my way along the Persian rug that ran the near-length of the main passage, turned the knob to Father's library, and stepped inside. An ornately framed portrait of George Washington was lit with a scrim of moonlight coming through the front window. For almost a year, Father had looked the other way as I'd slipped beneath Mr. Washington's nose to plunder the library. John, Thomas, and Frederick had total reign over his vast trove—books of law, geography, philosophy, theology, history, botany, poetry, and the Greek humanities—while Mary and I were officially forbidden to read a word of it. Mary didn't seem to care for books, but I . . . I dreamed of them in my sleep. I loved them in a way I couldn't fully express even to Thomas. He pointed me to certain volumes and drilled me on Latin declensions. He was the only one who knew my desperation to acquire a true education, beyond the one I received at the hands of Madame Ruffin, my tutor and French nemesis.

She was a small, hot-tempered woman who wore a widow's cap with strings floating at her cheeks, and when it was cold, a squirrely fur cloak and tiny fur-lined shoes. She was known to line girls up on the Idle Bench for the smallest infraction and scream at them until they fainted. I despised her, and her "polite education for the female mind," which was composed of needlework, manners, drawing, basic reading, penmanship, piano, Bible, French, and enough arithmetic to add two and two. I thought it possible I might die from tracing teensy flowers on the pages of my art tablet. Once I wrote in the margin, "If I should die of this horrid exercise, I wish these flowers to adorn my coffin." Madame Ruffin was not amused. I was made to stand on the Idle Bench, where she ranted at my insolence, and where I forced myself not to faint.

Increasingly, during those classes, longings had seized me, foreign, torrential aches that overran my heart. I wanted to know things, to become someone. *Oh, to be a son!* I adored Father because he treated me almost as if I *were* a son, allowing me to slip in and out of his library.

On that night, the coals in the library's fireplace lay cold and the smell of cigar smoke still pooled in the air. Without effort, I located Father's *South Carolina Justice of the Peace and Public Laws,* which he himself had authored. I'd thumbed through it enough to know somewhere in the pages was a copy of a legal manumission document.

Upon finding it, I took paper and quill from Father's desk and copied it:

> *I hereby certify that on this day, 26 November 1803, in the city of Charleston, in the state of South Carolina, I set free from slavery, Hetty Grimké, and bestow this certificate of manumission upon her.*
>
> Sarah Moore Grimké

What could Father do but make Hetty's freedom as legal and binding as her ownership? I was following a code of law he'd fashioned himself! I left my handiwork atop the backgammon box on his desk.

In the corridor, I heard the tingle of Mother's bell, summoning Cindie, and I broke into a run back upstairs that blew out the flame on my candle.

My room had turned even colder and the little bird had ceased its song. I crept beneath the stack-pile of quilts and blankets, but couldn't sleep for excitement. I imagined the thanksgiving Hetty and Charlotte would heap on me. I imagined Father's pride when he discovered the document, and

Mother's annoyance. *Legal and binding, indeed!* Finally, overcome with fatigue and satisfaction, I drifted to sleep.

When I woke, the bluish tint of the Delft tiles around the hearth gleamed with light. I sat up into the quietness. My ecstatic burst of the night before had drained away, leaving me calm and clear. I couldn't have explained then how the oak tree lives inside the acorn or how I suddenly realized that in the same enigmatic way something lived inside of me—the woman I would become—but it seemed I knew at once who she was.

It had been there all along as I'd scoured Father's books and constructed my arguments during our dinner table debates. Only the past week, Father had orchestrated a discussion between Thomas and me on the topic of exotic fossilized creatures. Thomas argued that if these strange animals were truly extinct, it implied poor planning on God's part, threatening the ideal of God's perfection, therefore, such creatures must still be alive in remote places on earth. I argued that even God should be allowed to change his mind. "Why should God's perfection be based on having an unchanging nature?" I asked. "Isn't flexibility more perfect than stasis?"

Father slapped his hand on the table. "If Sarah was a boy, she would be the greatest jurist in South Carolina!"

At the time, I'd been awed by his words, but it wasn't until now, waking up in my new room, that I saw their true meaning. The comprehension of my destiny came in a rush. *I would become a jurist.*

Naturally, I knew there were no female lawyers. For a woman, nothing existed but the domestic sphere and those tiny flowers etched on the pages of my art book. For a woman to aspire to be a lawyer—well, possibly, the world would end. But an acorn grew into an oak tree, didn't it?

I told myself the affliction in my voice wouldn't stop me, it would compel me. It would make me strong, for I would have to be strong.

I had a history of enacting small private rituals. The first time I took a book from Father's library, I'd penned the date and title—February 25, 1803, *Lady of the Lake*—on a sliver of paper that I wedged into a tortoise-shell hair clip and wore about surreptitiously. Now, with dawn gathering in bright tufts across the bed, I wanted to consecrate what was surely my greatest realization.

I went to the armoire and took down the blue dress Charlotte had sewed for the disastrous birthday party. Where the collar met, she'd stitched a large silver button with an engraved *fleur de lis*. Using the hawk bill letter opener John had left behind, I sawed it off. Squeezing it in my palm, I prayed, *Please, God, let this seed you planted in me bear fruit.*

When I opened my eyes, everything was the same. The room still bore patches of early light, the dress lay like a blue heap of sky on the floor, the silver button was clutched in my palm, but I felt God had heard me.

The sterling button took on everything that transpired that night—the revulsion of owning Hetty, the relief of signing her manumission, but mostly the bliss of recognizing that innate seed in myself, the one my father had already seen. *A jurist.*

I tucked the button inside a small box made of Italian lava rock, which I'd received one Christmastime, then hid it at the back of my dressing drawer.

Voices came from the corridor mingled with the *clink-clank* of trays and pitchers. The sound of slaves in their servitude. The world waking.

I dressed hurriedly, wondering if Hetty was already outside my door. As I opened it, my heart picked up its pace, but Hetty wasn't there. The manumission document I'd written lay on the floor. It was torn in two.

Handful

My life with Miss Sarah got off on a bad left foot.

When I got to her room that first morning, the door hung open and Miss Sarah was sitting in the cold, staring at the blank wall. I stuck my head in and said, "Miss Sarah, you want me to come in there?"

She had thick little hands with stubby fingers and they went up to her mouth and spread open like a lady's fan. Her eyes were pale and spoke plainer than her mouth. They said, *I don't want you here*. Her mouth said, "...... Yes, come in...... I'm pleased to have you for my waiting maid." Then she slumped in her chair and went back to what she was doing before. Nothing.

A ten-year-old yard slave who hadn't done nothing but chores for Aunt-Sister never got inside the house much. And never to the top floors. What such a room! She had a bed big as a horse buggy, a dressing table with a looking glass, a desk for holding books and more books, and lots of padded chairs. The chimney place had a fire screen embroidered with pink flowers I knew came from mauma's needle. Up on the mantel were two white vases, pure porcelain.

I looked everything over, then stood there, wondering what to do. I said, "Sure is cold."

Miss Sarah didn't answer, so I said louder, "SURE IS COLD."

This snapped her from her wall-staring. "...... You could lay a fire, I guess."

I'd seen it done, but seeing ain't doing. I didn't know to check the flue, and here came all this smoke swarming out like chimney bats.

Miss Sarah started throwing open windows. It must've looked like the house was burning cause out in the yard Tomfry yelled, *"Fire, fire."*

Then everybody took it up.

I grabbed the basin of water in the dressing room used for freshening up and hurled it on the fire, which didn't do nothing but cause the smoke to double up. Miss Sarah fanned it out the windows, looking like a ghost through all the black clouds. There was a jib door in her room that opened to the piazza, and I ran to get it open, wanting to shout to Tomfry we didn't have a fire, but before I could yank it free, I heard missus flying round the house hollering for everybody to get out and take an armload.

After the smoke thinned to a few floating cobwebs, I followed Miss Sarah to the yard. Old Snow and Sabe had already bridled up the horses and pulled the carriages to the back in case the whole yard went down with the house. Tomfry had Prince and Eli toting buckets from the cistern. Some neighbor men had showed up with more buckets. Folks feared a fire worse than the devil. They kept a slave sitting all day up in the steeple on St. Michael's, watching the rooftops for fire, and I worried he'd see all this smoke, ring the church bell, and the whole brigade show up.

I ran to mauma who was bunched with the rest of 'em. The stuff they thought worth saving was heaped in piles by their feet. China bowls, tea caddies, record books, clothes, portraits, Bibles, brooches, and pearls. Even a marble bust was sitting out there. Missus had her gold-tip cane in one hand and a silver cigar holder in the other.

Miss Sarah was trying to cut through the frantics to tell Tomfry and the men there wasn't a fire to throw their water on, but by the time she dragged the words out of her mouth, the men had gone back to hauling water.

When it got worked out what'd happened, missus went into a fury. "Hetty, you incompetent fool!"

Nobody moved, not even the neighbor men. Mauma moved over and tucked me behind her, but missus jerked me out front. She brought the gold-tip cane down on the back of my head, worst blow I ever got. It drove me to my knees.

Mauma screamed. So did Miss Sarah. But missus, she raised her arm like she'd go at me again. I can't describe proper what came next. The work yard, the people in it, the walls shutting us in, all that fell away. The ground rolled out from under me and the sky billowed off like a tent caught in the wind. I was in a space to myself, somewhere time can't cross. A voice called steady in my head, *Get up from there. Get up from there and look her in the face. Dare her to strike you. Dare her.*

I got on my feet and poked my face at her. My eyes said, *Hit me, I dare you.* Missus let her arm drop and stepped back.

Then the yard was round me again and I reached up and felt my head. A lump was there the size of a quail egg. Mauma reached over and touched it with her fingertip.

The rest of that God-forsook day every woman and girl slave was made to drag clothes, linens, rugs, and curtains from every room upstairs out to the piazza for airing-out. Everyone but mauma and Binah showered me with looks of despising. Miss Sarah came up there wanting to help and started hauling with the rest of us. Every time I turned round, she was looking at me like she'd never seen me before in her life.

Sarah

I took meals alone in my room for three full days as a protest against owning Hetty, though I don't think anyone much noticed. On the fourth day, I swallowed my pride and arrived in the dining room for breakfast. Mother and I hadn't spoken of the doomed manumission document. I suspected she was the one who'd torn it into two even pieces and deposited them outside my room, thereby having the Last Word without uttering a syllable.

At the age of eleven, I owned a slave I couldn't free.

The meal, the largest of the day, had long been under way—Father, Thomas, and Frederick had already left in pursuit of school and work, while Mother, Mary, Anna, and Eliza remained.

"You are late, my dear," Mother said. Not without a note of sympathy.

Phoebe, who assisted Aunt-Sister and looked slightly older than myself, appeared at my elbow, emanating the fresh odors of the kitchen house—sweat, coal, smoke, and an acrid fishiness. Typically, she stood by the table and swished the fly brush, but today she slid a plate before me heaped with sausages, grit cake, salted shrimp, brown bread, and tapioca jelly.

Attempting to lower a quivery cup of tea beside my plate, Phoebe deposited it on top my spoon, causing the contents to slosh onto the cloth. "Oh missus, I sorry," she cried, whirling toward Mother.

Mother blew out her breath as if all the mistakes of all the Negroes in the world rested personally upon her shoulders. "Where is Aunt-Sister? Why, for heaven's sake, are you serving?"

"She showing me how to do it."

"Well, see that you learn."

As Phoebe rushed to stand outside the door, I tried to toss her a smile.

"It's nice of you to make an appearance," Mother said. "You are recovered?"

All eyes turned on me. Words collected in my mouth and lay there. At such moments, I used a technique in which I imagined my tongue like a slingshot. I drew it back, tighter, tighter. "... . . . I'm fine." The words hurled across the table in a spray of saliva.

Mary made a show of dabbing her face with a napkin.

She'll end up exactly like Mother, I thought. *Running a house congested with children and slaves, while I—*

"I trust you found the remains of your folly?" Mother asked.

Ah, there it was. She had confiscated my document, likely without Father knowing.

"What folly?" Mary said.

I gave Mother a pleading look.

"Nothing you need concern yourself with, Mary," she said, and tilted her head as if she wanted to mend the rift between us.

I slumped in my chair and debated taking my cause to Father and presenting him with the torn manumission document. I could think of little else for the rest of the day, but by nightfall, I knew it would do no good. He deferred to Mother on all household matters, and he abhorred a tattler. My brothers never tattled, and I would do no less. Besides, I would've been an idiot to rile Mother further.

I countered my disappointment by conducting vigorous talks with myself about the future. *Anything is possible, anything at all.*

Nightly, I opened the lava box and gazed upon the silver button.

Handful

Missus said I was the worst waiting maid in Charleston. She said, "You are *abysmal*, Hetty, *abysmal*."

I asked Miss Sarah what *abysmal* means and she said, "Not quite up to standard."

Uh huh. I could tell from missus' face, there's bad, there's worse, and after that comes abysmal.

That first week, beside the smoke, I spilled lamp oil on the floor leaving a slick spot, broke one of those porcelain vases, and fried a piece of Miss Sarah's red hair with a curling tong. Miss Sarah never tattled. She tugged the rug over to cover the oily place, hid the broke porcelain in a storeroom in the cellar, and cut off her singed hair with the snuffer we used to snip the candle wick.

Only time Miss Sarah rang her bell for me was if missus was headed our way. Binah and her two girls, Lucy and Phoebe, always sang out, "The cane tapping. The cane tapping." Miss Sarah's warning bell gave me some extra lead on my rope, and I took it. I would rove down the hallway to the front alcove where I could see the water in the harbor float to the ocean and the ocean roll on till it sloshed against the sky. Nothing could hold a glorybound picture to it.

First time I saw it, my feet hopped in place and I lifted my hand over my head and danced. That's when I got true religion. I didn't know to call it religion back then, didn't know Amen from what-when, I just knew something came into me that made me feel the water belonged to me. I would say, that's my water out there.

I saw it turn every color. It was green one day, then brown, next day yellow as cider. Purple, black, blue. It stayed restless, never ceasing. Boats coming and going on top, fishes underneath.

I would sing these little verses to it:

Cross the water, cross the sea
Let them fishes carry me.
If that water take too long,
Carry me on, Carry me on.

After a month or two, I was doing more things right in the house, but even Miss Sarah didn't know some nights I left my post by her door and watched the water all night long, the way it broke silver from the moon. The stars shining big as platters. I could see clean to Sullivan's Island. I pined for mauma when it was dark. I missed our bed. I missed the quilt frame guarding over us. I pictured mauma sewing quilts by herself. I would think about the gunny sack stuffed with feathers, the red pouch with our pins and needles, my pure brass thimble. Nights like that, I hightailed it back to the stable room.

Every time mauma woke and found me in bed with her, she had a fit, saying all the trouble there would be if I got caught, how I already lived too far out on missus' bad side.

"Ain't nothin' good gon come from you wandering off like this," she said. "You got to stay put on your quilt. You do that for me, you hear me?"

And I'd do it for her. Least for a few days. I'd lay on the floor in the hall, trying to stay warm in the draft, twisting round in search of the softest floorboard. I could make do with that misery and take my solace from the water.

Sarah

On a bleary morning in March, four months after the calamity of my eleventh birthday, I woke to find Hetty missing, her pallet on the floor outside my room crumpled with the outline of her small body. By now, she would've been filling my basin with water and telling me some story or other. It surprised me that I felt her absence personally. I missed her as I would a fond companion, but I fretted for her, too. Mother had already taken her cane to Hetty once.

Finding no trace of her in the house, I stood on the top step by the back door, scanning the work yard. A thin haze had drifted in from the harbor, and overhead the sun glinted through it with the dull gold of a pocket watch. Snow was in the door of the carriage house, repairing one of the breeching straps. Aunt-Sister straddled a stool by the vegetable garden, scaling fish. Not wishing to rouse her suspicions, I ambled to the porch of the kitchen house where Tomfry was handing out supplies. Soap to Eli for washing the marble steps, two Osnaburg towels to Phoebe for cleaning crystal, a coal scoop to Sabe for re-supplying the scuttles.

As I waited for him to finish, I let my eyes drift to the oak in the back left corner. Its branches were adorned with tight buds, and though the tree bore little resemblance to its summer visage, the memory of that long-ago day returned: sitting straddle-legged on the ground, the hot stillness, the green-skinned shade, arranging my words with marbles, *Sarah Go—*

I looked away to the opposite side of the yard, and it was there I saw Hetty's mother, Charlotte, walking beside the woodpile, bending now and then to pick up something from the ground.

Arriving behind her unseen, I noticed the tidbits she scavenged were small, downy feathers. ".. . . . . Charlotte—"

She jumped and the feather between her fingers fluttered off on the sea wind. It flitted to the top of the high brick wall that enclosed the yard, snagging in the creeping fig.

"Miss Sarah!" she said. "You scared the jimminies out of me." Her laugh was high-pitched and fragile with nerves. Her eyes darted toward the stable.

"… … I didn't mean to startle you … I only wondered, do you know where—"

She cut me off, and pointed into the woodpile. "Look way down 'n there."

Peering into a berth between two pieces of wood, I came face to face with a pointy-eared brown creature covered with fuzz. Only slightly bigger than a hen's chick, it was an owl of some sort. I drew back as its yellow eyes blinked and bore into me.

Charlotte laughed again, this time more naturally. "It ain't gon bite."

"… … It's a baby."

"I came on it a few nights back. Poor thing on the ground, crying."

"… … Was it … hurt?"

"Naw, just left behind is all. Its mauma's a barn owl. Took up in a crow's nest in the shed, but she left. I'm 'fraid something got her. I been feeding the baby scraps."

My only liaisons with Charlotte had been dress fittings, but I'd always detected a keenness in her. Of all the slaves Father owned, she struck me as the most intelligent, and perhaps the most dangerous, which would turn out to be true enough.

"… … I'll be kind to Hetty," I said abruptly. The words—remorseful and lordly—came out as if some pustule of guilt had disgorged.

Her eyes flashed open, then narrowed into small burrs. They were honey colored, the same as Hetty's.

"… … I never meant to own her … I tried to free her, but … I wasn't allowed." I couldn't seem to stop myself.

Charlotte slid her hand into her apron pocket, and silence welled unbearably. She'd seen my guilt and she used it with cunning. "That's awright," she said. "Cause I know you gon make that up to her one these days."

The letter M clamped on to my tongue with its little jaws. "......... M-m-make it up?"

"I mean, I know you gon hep her any way you can to get free."

"...... Yes, I'll try," I said.

"What I need is you swearing to it."

I nodded, hardly understanding that I'd been deftly guided into a covenant.

"You keep your word," she said. "I know you will."

Remembering why I'd approached her in the first place, I said, "... I've been unable to find—"

"Handful gon be at your door 'fore you know it."

Walking back to the house, I felt the noose of that strange and intimate exchange pull into a knot.

Hetty appeared in my room ten minutes later, her eyes dominating her small face, fierce as the little owl's. Seated at my desk, I'd only just opened a book I'd borrowed from Father's library, *The Adventures of Telemachus*. Telemachus, the son of Penelope and Odysseus, was setting out to Troy to find his father. Without questioning her earlier whereabouts, I began to read aloud. Hetty plopped onto the bed-steps that led to the mattress, rested her chin in the cup of her hands, and listened through the morning as Telemachus took on the hostilities of the ancient world.

Wily Charlotte. As March passed, I thought obsessively about the promise she'd wrung from me. Why hadn't I told her Hetty's freedom was impossible? That the most I could ever offer her was kindness?

When it came time to sew my Easter dress, I cringed to think of seeing her again, petrified she would bring up our conversation by the woodpile. I would rather have impaled myself with a needle than endured more of her scrutiny.

"I don't need a new dress this Easter," I told Mother.

A week later, I stood on the fitting box, wearing a half-sewn satin dress. On entering my room, Charlotte had hastened Hetty off on some contrived mission before I could think of a way to override her. The dress was a light shade of cinnamon, remarkably similar to the tone of Charlotte's skin, a likeness I noted as she stood before me with three straight pins wedged between her lips. When she spoke, I smelled coffee beans, and knew she'd been chewing them. Her words squeezed out around the pins in twisted curls of sounds. "You gon keep that word you gave me?"

To my disgrace, I used my impediment to my advantage, struggling more than necessary to answer her, pretending the words fell back into the dark chute of my throat and disappeared.

Handful

On the first good Saturday, when it looked like spring was staying put this time, missus took Miss Sarah, Miss Mary, and Miss Anna off in the carriage with the lanterns on it. Aunt-Sister said they were going to White Point to promenade, said all the women and girls would be out with their parasols.

When Snow drove the carriage out the back gate, Miss Sarah waved, and Sabe, who was dandied up in a green frock coat and livery vest, was hanging off the back, grinning.

Aunt-Sister said to us, "What yawl looking at? Get to work cleaning, a full spit and shine on their rooms. Make hay while the mice away."

Up in Miss Sarah's room, I spread the bed and scrubbed the gloom on the looking glass that wouldn't come off with any kind of ash-water. I swept up dead moths fat from gnawing on the curtains, wiped down the privy pot, and threw in a pinch of soda. I scrubbed the floors with lime soap from the demijohn.

Wore out from all that, I did what we call shilly-shally. Poking round up to no good. First, I looked to see was any slave in the passage way—some of them would as soon tell on you as blink. I shut the door and opened Miss Sarah's books. I sat at her desk and turned one page after another, staring at what looked like bits and pieces of black lace laid cross the paper. The marks had a beauty to them, but I didn't see how they could do anything but confuddle a person.

I pulled out the desk drawer and rooted all through her things. I found a piece of unfinished cross stitch with clumsy stitches, looked like a three-year-old had done it. There was some fine, glossy threads in the drawer wrapped on wood spools. Sealing wax. Tan paper. Little drawings with ink smudges. A long brass key with a tassel on it.

I went through the wardrobe, touching the frocks mauma'd made. I nosed through the dressing table drawer, pulling out jewelry, hair ribbons, paper fans, bottles and brushes, and finally, a little box. It glistened dark like my skin when it was wet. I pushed up the latch. Inside was a big silver button. I touched it, then closed the lid the same slow way I'd closed her wardrobe, her drawers, and her books—with my chest filling up. There was so much in the world to be had and not had.

I went back and opened up the desk drawer one more time and stared at the threads. What I did next was wrong, but I didn't much care. I took the plump spool of scarlet thread and dropped it in my dress pocket.

The Saturday before Easter we all got sent to the dining room. Tomfry said things had gone missing in the house. I went in there thinking, *Lord, help me.*

There wasn't nothing worse for us than some little old piece of nonsense disappearing. One dent-up tin cup in the pantry or a toast crumb off missus' plate and the feathers flew. But this time it wasn't a piece of nonsense, and it wasn't scarlet thread. It was missus' brand new bolt of green silk cloth.

There we were, fourteen of us, lined up while missus carried on about it. She said the silk was special, how it traveled from the other side of the world, how these worms in China had spun the threads. Back then, I'd never heard such craziness in my life.

Every one of us was sweating and twitching, running our hands in our britches pockets or up under our aprons. I could smell the odors off our bodies, which was nothing but fear.

Mauma knew everything happening out there over the wall—missus gave her passes to travel to the market by herself. She tried to keep the bad parts from me, but I knew about the torture house on Magazine Street. The white folks called it the *Work* House. Like the slaves were in there sewing clothes and making bricks and hammering horseshoes. I knew about it before I was eight, the dark hole they put you in and left you by yourself for weeks. I knew about the whippings. Twenty lashes was the limit you could get. A white man could buy a bout of floggings for half a dollar and use them whenever he needed to put some slave in the right frame of mind.

Far as I knew, not one Grimké slave had gone to the Work House, but that morning, every one of us in the dining room was wondering is this the day.

"One of you is guilty of thieving. If you return the bolt of cloth, which is what God would have you do, then I will be forgiving."

Uh huh.

Missus didn't think we had a grain of sense.

What were any of us gonna do with emerald silk?

The night after the cloth vanished, I slipped out. Walked straight out the door. I had to pass by Cindie outside missus' door—she was no friend to mauma, and I had to be wary round her, but she was snoring away. I slid into bed next to mauma, only she wasn't in bed this time, she was standing in the corner with her arms folded over her chest. She said, "What you think you doing?"

I never had heard that tone to her voice.

"Get up, we going back to the house right now. This the last time you sneaking out, the last time. This ain't no game, Handful. There be misery to pay on this."

She didn't wait for me to move, but snatched me up like I was a stray piece of batting. Grabbed me under one arm, marched me down the carriage house steps, cross the work yard. My feet didn't hardly touch the ground. She dragged me inside through the warming kitchen, the door nobody locked. Her finger rested against her lips, warning me to stay quiet, then she tugged me to the staircase and nodded her head toward the top. *Go on now.*

Those stair steps made a racket. I didn't get ten steps when I heard a door open down below, and the air suck from mauma's throat.

Master's voice came out of the dark, saying, "Who is it? Who is there?"

Lamplight shot cross the walls. Mauma didn't move.

"Charlotte?" he said, calm as could be. "What are you doing in here?"

Behind her back, mauma made a sign with her hand, waving at the floor, and I knew she meant me to crouch low on the steps. "Nothing, massa Grimké. Nothing, sir."

"There must be some reason for your presence in the house at this hour. You should explain yourself now to avoid any trouble." It was almost kind the way he said it.

Mauma stood there without a word. Master Grimké always did that to her. *Say something.* If it was missus standing there, mauma could've spit out three, four things already. Say Handful is sick and you're going to see about her. Say Aunt-Sister sent you in here to get some remedy for Snow. Say you can't sleep for worrying about their Easter clothes, how they gonna fit in the morning. Say you're walking in your sleep. Just say *something*.

Mauma waited too long, cause here came missus out from her room. Peering over the step, I could see she had her sleeping cap on crooked.

I have knots in my years that I can't undo, and this is one of the worst—the night I did wrong and mauma got caught.

I could've showed myself. I could've given the rightful account, said it was me, but what I did was ball up silent on the stair steps.

Missus said, "Are you the pilferer, Charlotte? Have you come back for more? Is this how you do it, slipping in at night?"

Missus roused Cindie and told her to fetch Aunt-Sister and light two lamps, they were going to search mauma's room.

"Yessum, yessum," said Cindie. Pleased as a planter punch.

Master Grimké groaned like he'd stepped in a dog pile, all this nasty business with women and slaves. He took his light and went back to bed.

I followed after mauma and them from a distance, saying words a ten-year-old shouldn't know, but I'd learned plenty of cuss at the stables listening to Sabe sing to the horses. *God damney, god damney, day and night. God damney, god damney, all them whites.* I was working myself up to tell missus what'd happened. *I left my place beside Miss Sarah's door and sneaked out to my old room. Mauma brought me back to the house.*

When I peered round the door jam into our room, I saw the blankets torn off the bed, the wash basin turned over, and our flannel gunny sack dumped upside down, quilt-fillings everywhere. Aunt-Sister was working the pulley to lower the quilt frame. It had a quilt-top on it with raw edges, bright little threads fluttering.

Nobody looked at me standing in the doorway, just mauma whose eyes always went to me. Her lids sank shut and she didn't open them back.

The wheels on the pulley sang and the frame floated down to that squeaky music. There on top of the unfinished quilt was a bolt of bright green cloth.

I looked at the cloth and thought how pretty. Lamplight catching on every wrinkle. Me, Aunt-Sister, and missus stared at it like it was something we'd dreamed.

Missus gave us an earful then about how hard it was for her to visit discipline on a slave she'd trusted, but what choice did she have?

She told mauma, "I will delay your punishment until Monday—tomorrow is Easter and I do not want it marred by this. I will not send you *off* for punishment, and you should be grateful for that, but I assure you your penalty will match your crime."

She hadn't said *Work House*, she'd said *off*, but we knew what *off* meant. Least mauma wasn't going there.

When missus finally turned to me, she didn't ask what was I doing out here or send me back to Miss Sarah's floorboards. She said, "You may stay with your mother until her punishment on Monday. I wish her to have some consolation until then. I am not an unfeeling woman."

Long into that night, I slobbered out my sorrow and guilt to mauma. She rubbed my shoulders and told me she wasn't mad. She said I never should've snuck out of the house, but she wasn't mad.

I was about asleep when she said, "I should've sewed that green silk inside a quilt and she never would've found it. I ain't sorry for stealing it, just for getting caught."

"How come you took it?"

"Cause," she said. "Cause I could."

Those words stuck with me. Mauma didn't want that cloth, she just wanted to make some trouble. She couldn't get free and she couldn't pop missus on the back of her head with a cane, but she could take her silk. You do your rebellions any way you can.

Sarah

On Easter, we Grimkés rode to St. Philip's Episcopal Church beneath the Pride of India trees that lined both sides of Meeting Street. I'd asked for a spot in the open-air Sulky with Father, but Thomas and Frederick snared the privilege, while I was stuck in the carriage with Mother and the heat. The air oozed through slits that passed for windows, blowing in thinly peeled wisps. I pressed my face against the opening and watched the splendor of Charleston sweep by: bright single houses with their capacious verandas, flower boxes bulging on row houses, clipped jungles of tropical foliage—oleander, hibiscus, bougainvillea.

"Sarah, I trust you're prepared to give your first lesson," Mother said. I'd recently become a new teacher in the Colored Sunday School, a class taught by girls, thirteen years and older, but Mother had prodded Reverend Hall to make an exception, and for once her overbearing nature had yielded something that wasn't altogether repugnant.

I turned to her, feeling the burn of privet in my nostrils. "... Yes... I studied v-very hard."

Mary mocked me, protruding her eyes in a grotesque way, mouthing, "... V-v-very hard," which caused Ben to snicker.

She was a menace, my sister. Lately, the pauses in my speech had diminished and I refused to let her faze me. I was about to do something useful for a change, and even if I hemmed and hawed my way through the entire class, so be it. At the moment, I was more concerned I had to teach it paired with Mary.

As the carriage neared the market, the noise mounted and the sidewalks began to overflow with Negroes and mulattoes. Sunday was the slaves' only day off, and they thronged the thoroughfares—most were walking to their masters' churches, required to show up and sit in the balconies—but even on regular days, the slaves dominated the streets, doing their owners' bidding, shopping the market, delivering messages and invitations for teas and dinner parties. Some were hired out and trekked back and forth to work. Naturally, they nicked a little time to fraternize. You could see them gathered at street corners, wharves, and grog shops. The *Charleston Mercury* railed against the "unsupervised swarms" and called for regulations, but as Father said, as long as a slave possessed a pass or a work badge, his presence was perfectly legitimate.

Snow had been apprehended once. Instead of waiting by the carriage while we were in church, he'd driven it about the city with no one inside—a kind of pleasure ride. He'd been taken to the Guard House near St. Michael's. Father was furious, not at Snow, but at the City Guard. He stormed down to the mayor's court and paid the fine, keeping Snow from the Work House.

A glut of carriages on Cumberland Street prevented us from drawing closer to the church. The onslaught of people who attended services only on Eastertide incensed Mother, who saw to it the Grimkés were in their pew every dull, common Sunday of the year. Snow's gravelly voice filtered to us from the driver's seat. "Missus, yawls has to walk from here," and Sabe swung open the door and lifted us down, one by one.

Our father was already striding ahead, not a tall man, but he looked imposing in his gray coat, top hat, and cravat of silk surah. He had an angular face with a long nose and profuse brows that curled about the ledge of his forehead, but what made him handsome in my mind was his hair, a wild concoction of dark, auburn waves. Thomas had inherited the rich brown-red color, as had Anna and little Charles, but it had come to me in the feeble shade of persimmons and my brows and lashes were so pale they seemed to have been skipped over altogether.

The seating arrangement inside St. Philip's was a veritable blueprint of Charleston status, the elite vying to rent pews down front, the less affluent in the back, while the pointblank poor clustered on free benches along the sides. Our pew, which Father rented for three hundred dollars a year, was a mere three rows from the altar.

I sat beside Father, cradling his hat upside down on my lap, catching a waft of the lemon oil he used to domesticate his locks. Overhead, in the upper galleries, the slaves began their babble and laughter. It was a perennial problem, this noise. They found boldness in the balcony the way they found it on the streets, from their numbers. Recently, their racket had escalated to such a degree that monitors had been placed in the balconies as deterrents. Despite them, the rumblings grew. Then, *thwack*. A cry. Parishioners swung about, glaring upward.

By the time Reverend Hall mounted the pulpit, a full-scale hubbub had broken out at the rafters. A shoe sailed over the balcony and plummeted down. A heavy boot. It landed on a lady midway back, toppling her hat and concussing her head.

As the shaken lady and her family left the sanctuary, Reverend Hall pointed his finger toward the far left balcony and moved it in a slow circle clockwise. When all was silent, he quoted a scripture from Ephesians, reciting from memory. "Slaves, be obedient to them that are your masters, with fear and trembling, in singleness of heart, as unto Christ." Then he made what many, including my mother, would call the most eloquent extemporization on slavery they'd ever heard. "Slaves, I admonish you to be content with your lot, for it is the will of God! Your obedience is mandated by scripture. It is commanded by God through Moses. It is approved by Christ through his apostles, and upheld by the church. Take heed, then, and may God in his mercy grant that you will be humbled this day and return to your masters as faithful servants."

He walked back to his chair behind the chancel. I stared down at Father's hat, then up at him, stricken, confused, stupefied even, trying to understand what I should think, but his face was a blank, implacable mask.

After the service, I stood in a small, dingy classroom behind the church while twenty-two slave children raced about in anarchy. Upon entering the dim, airless room, I'd flung open the windows only to set us adrift in tree pollen.

I sneezed repeatedly as I rapped the edge of my fan on the desk, trying to install order. Mary sat in the only chair in the room, a dilapidated Windsor, and watched me with an expression perfectly situated between boredom and amusement.

"Let them play," she told me. "That's what I do."

I was tempted. Since the reverend's homily, I had little heart for the lesson.

A pile of dusty, discarded kneeling cushions were heaped in the back corner, the needlepoint frayed beyond repair. I assumed they were for the children to sit on, as there wasn't a stick of furniture in the room other than the teacher's desk and chair. No curriculum leaflets, picture books, slate board, chalk, or adornment for the walls.

I laid the kneeling cushions in rows on the floor, which started a game of kicking them about like balls. I'd been told to read today's scripture and elaborate on its meaning, but when I finally succeeded in getting the children perched on the cushions and saw their faces, the whole thing seemed a travesty. If everyone was so keen to Christianize the slaves, why weren't they taught to read the Bible for themselves?

I began to sing the alphabet, a new little learning-ditty. A B C D E F G ... Mary looked up surprised, then sighed and returned to her state of apathy. H I J K L M N O P ... There had never been hesitation in my voice when I sang. The children's eyes glittered with attention, Q R S ... T U V ... W X ... Y and Z.

I cajoled them to sing it in sections after me. Their pronunciations were lacking. Q came out *coo*, L M as *ellem*. Oh, but their faces! Such grins. I told myself when I returned next time, I would bring a slate board and write out the letters so they could see them as they sang. I thought then of Hetty. I'd seen the disarrangement of books on my desk and knew she explored them in my absence. How she would love to learn these twenty-six letters!

After half a dozen rounds, the children sang with gusto, half-shouting. Mary plugged her ears with her fingers, but I sang full-pitch, using my arms like conductor sticks, waving the children on. I did not see Reverend Hall in the doorway.

"What appalling mischief is going on here?" he said.

We halted abruptly, leaving me with the dizzy sense the letters still danced chaotically in the air over our heads. My face turned its usual flamboyant colors.

"......... We were singing, Reverend Sir."

"Which Grimké child are you?" He'd baptized me as a baby, just as he had all my siblings, but one could hardly expect him to keep us straight.

"She's Sarah," Mary said, leaping to her feet. "I had no part in the song."

"...... I'm sorry we were boisterous," I told him.

He frowned. "We do not *sing* in Colored Sunday School, and we most assuredly do not sing the alphabet. Are you aware it is against the law to teach a slave to read?"

I knew of this law, though vaguely, as if it had been stored in a root cellar in my head and suddenly dug up like some moldy yam. All right, it was the law, but it struck me as shameful. Surely he wouldn't claim this was God's will, too.

He waited for me to answer, and when I didn't, he said, "Would you put the church in contradiction of the law?"

The memory of Hetty that day when Mother caned her flashed through my mind, and I raised my chin and glared at him, without answering.

Handful

What came next was a fast, bitter wind.

Monday, after we got done with devotions, Aunt-Sister took mauma aside. She said missus had a friend who didn't like floggings and had come up with the one-legged punishment. Aunt-Sister went to a lot of trouble to draw us a picture of it. She said they wind a leather tie round the slave's ankle, then pull that foot up behind him and hitch the tie round his neck. If he lets his ankle drop, the tie chokes his throat.

We knew what she was telling us. Mauma sat down on the kitchen house steps and laid her head flat against her knees.

Tomfry was the one who came to strap her up. I could see he didn't want any part of it, but he wasn't saying so. Missus said, "One hour, Tomfry. That will do." Then she went inside to her window perch.

He led mauma to the middle of the yard near the garden where tiny shoots had just broke through the dirt. All us were out there huddled under the spreading tree, except Snow who was off with the carriage. Rosetta started wailing. Eli patted her arm, trying to ease her. Lucy and Phoebe were arguing over a piece of cold ham left from breakfast, and Aunt-Sister went over there and smacked them both cross their faces.

Tomfry turned mauma so she was facing the tree with her back to the house. She didn't fight. She stood there limp as the moss on the branches. The scent of low tide coming from the harbor was everywhere, a rotted smell.

Tomfry told mauma, "Hold on to me," and she rested her hand on his shoulder while he bound her ankle with what looked like an old leather belt. He pulled it up behind her so she was standing on one leg, then he wound the other end of the strap round her throat and buckled it.

Mauma saw me hanging on to Binah, my lips and chin trembling, and she said, "You ain't got to watch. Close your eyes."

I couldn't do it, though.

After he got her trussed up, Tomfry moved off so she couldn't grab on to him, and she took a hard spill. Split the skin over her brow. When she hit the ground, the strap yanked tight and mauma started choking. She threw back her head and gulped for air. I ran to help her, but the *tat-tat, tat-tat* of missus' cane landed on the window, and Tomfry pulled me away and got mauma to her feet.

I closed my eyes then, but what I saw in the dark was worse as the real thing. I cracked my eyes and watched her trying to keep her leg from dropping down and cutting off her air, fighting to stay upright. She set her eyes on top of the oak tree. Her standing leg quivered. Blood from her head-cut ran down her cheek. It clung to her jaw like rain on the roof eave.

Don't let her fall anymore. That's the prayer I said. Missus told us God listened to everybody, even a slave got a piece of God's ear. I carried a picture of God in my head, a white man, bearing a stick like missus or going round dodging slaves the way master Grimké did, acting like he'd sired a world where they don't exist. I couldn't see him lifting a finger to help.

Mauma didn't fall again, though, and I reckoned God had lent me an ear, but maybe that ear wasn't white, maybe the world had a colored God, too, or else it was mauma who kept her own self standing, who answered my prayer with the strength of her limbs and the grip of her heart. She never whimpered, never made a sound except some whisperings from her lips. Later on, I asked if her whispers were for God, and she said, "They was for your granny-mauma."

When that hour passed and Tomfry loosed the strap off her neck, she fell down and curled up on the dirt. Tomfry and Aunt-Sister lifted her up by the arms and lugged her and her numb legs up the stairs of the carriage house to her room. I ran behind, trying to keep her ankles from bumping on the steps. They laid her on the bed like flopping down a sack of flour.

When we were left to our selves, I lay beside her and stared up at the quilt frame. From time to time, I said, "You want some water? Your legs hurting?"

She nodded her answers with her eyes shut.

In the afternoon, Aunt-Sister brought some rice cakes and broth off a chicken. Mauma didn't touch it. We always left the door open to get the light, and all day, noise and smells from the yard wandered in. Long a day as I ever lived.

Mauma's legs would walk again same as ever, but she never was the same inside. After that day, it seemed part of her was always back there waiting for the strap to be loosed. It seemed like that's when she started laying her cold fire of hate.

Sarah

The morning after Easter, there was still no sign of Hetty. Between breakfast and my departure for Madame Ruffin's school on Legare Street, Mother saw to it that I was shut in my room, copying a letter of apology to Reverend Hall.

> *Dear Reverend Sir,*
> *I apologize for failing in my duties as a teacher in the Colored Sunday School of our dear St. Philip's. I beg forgiveness for my reckless disregard of the curriculum and ask your forgiveness for my insolence toward you and your holy office.*
> *Your Remorseful and Repentant Soul,*
> *Sarah Grimké*

No sooner had I signed my name than Mother whisked me to the front door where Snow waited with the carriage, Mary already inside. Typically, Mary and I met the carriage out back, while Snow tarried, making us late.

"Why has he come to collect us at the front?" I asked, to which Mother replied I should be more like my sister and not ask tedious questions.

Snow turned and looked at me, and a kind of foreboding leaked from him.

The whole day seemed strung upon a thin, vibrating wire. When I met with Thomas that afternoon on the piazza for my studies—my *real* studies—my unease had reached a peak.

Twice weekly, we delved into Father's books, into points of law, Latin, the history of the European world, and recently, the works of Voltaire. Thomas insisted I was too young for Voltaire. "He's over your head!" He was, but naturally I'd flung myself into the Sea of Voltaire anyway and emerged with nothing more than several aphorisms. "Every man is guilty of all the good he didn't do." Such a notion made it virtually impossible to enjoy life! And this, "If God did not exist, man would have to invent him." I didn't know whether Reverend Hall had invented his God or I'd invented mine, but such ideas tantalized and disturbed me.

I lived for these sessions with Thomas, but seated on the joggling board that day with the Latin primer on my lap, I couldn't concentrate. The day was full of torpid warmth, of the smell of crabs being trolled from the ginger waters of the Ashley River.

"Go on. Proceed," said Thomas, leaning over to tap the book with his finger. "Water, master, son—nominative case, singular and plural."

"... ... *Aqua, aquae ... Dominus, domini ... Filius, filii..* ... . Oh, Thomas, something is wrong!" I was thinking of Hetty's absence, Mother's behavior, Snow's glumness. I'd sensed a moroseness in all of them—Aunt-Sister, Phoebe, Tomfry, Binah. Thomas must've felt it, too.

"Sarah, you always know my mind," he said. "I thought I'd concealed it, I should've known."

"... What is it?"

"I don't want to be a lawyer."

He'd misread my intent, but I didn't say so—this was as riveting a secret as he'd ever revealed to me.

"... Not a lawyer?"

"I've never wanted to be a lawyer. It goes against my nature." He gave me a tired smile. "*You* should be the lawyer. Father said you would be the greatest in South Carolina, do you remember?"

I remembered the way one remembers the sun, the moon, and the stars hanging in the sky. The world seemed to rush toward me, sheened and beautiful. I looked at Thomas and felt confirmed in my destiny. I had an ally. A true, unbending ally.

Running his hands through the waves of his hair, torrential like Father's, Thomas began to pace the length of the piazza. "I want to be a minister," he said.

"I'm less than a year from following John to Yale, and I'm treated as if I can't think for myself. Father believes I don't know my own mind, but I *do* know."

"He won't allow you to study theology?"

"I begged for his blessing last evening and he refused. I said, 'Don't you care that it's God's own call I wish to answer?' And do you know what he said to that? 'Until God informs *me* of this call, you will study the law.'"

Thomas plopped into a chair, and I went and knelt before him, pressing my cheek against the back of his hand. His knuckles were prickly with heat bumps and hair. I said, "If I could, I would do anything to help you."

As the sun lowered over the back lot, Hetty was still nowhere to be seen. Unable to contain my fears any longer, I planted myself outside the window of the kitchen house, where the female slaves always congregated after the last meal of the day.

The kitchen house was their sanctum. Here, they told stories and gossiped and carried on their secret life. At times, they would break into song, their tunes sailing across the yard and slipping into the house. My favorite was a chant that grew rowdier as it went:

> *Bread done broken.*
> *Let my Jesus go.*
> *Feet be tired.*
> *Let my Jesus go.*
> *Back be aching.*
> *Let my Jesus go.*
> *Teeth done fell out.*
> *Let my Jesus go.*
> *Rump be dragging.*
> *Let my Jesus go.*

Their laughter would ring out abruptly, a sound Mother welcomed. "Our slaves are happy," she would boast. It never occurred to her their gaiety wasn't contentment, but survival.

On this evening, though, the kitchen house was wrapped in a pall. Heat and smoke from the oven glugged out the window, reddening my face and neck. I caught glimpses of Aunt-Sister, Binah, Cindie, Mariah, Phoebe, and Lucy in their calico dresses, but heard only the clunk of cast iron pots.

Finally, Binah's voice carried to me. "You mean to say she ain't eat all day?"

"Not one thing," Aunt-Sister said.

"Well, I ain't eating neither if they strap *me* up like they done her," Phoebe said.

A cold swell began in my stomach. *Strapped her up? Who? Not Hetty, surely.*

"What she think would happen if she pilfer like that?" I believed that voice to be Cindie's. "What'd she say for herself?"

Aunt-Sister spoke again. "She won't talk. Handful up there in bed with her, talking for both of 'em."

"Poor Charlotte," said Binah.

Charlotte! They'd strapped her up. What did that mean? Rosetta's melodic keening rose in my memory. I saw them bind her hands. I saw the cowhide split her back and the blood-flowers open and die on her skin.

I don't remember returning to the house, only that I was suddenly in the warming kitchen, ransacking the locked cupboard where Mother kept her curatives. Having unlocked it often to retrieve a bromide for Father, I easily found the key and removed the blue bottle of liniment oil and a jar of sweet balm tea. Into the tea, I dropped two grains of laudanum.

As I stuffed them into a basket, Mother entered the corridor. "What, pray tell, are you doing?"

I threw the question back at her. "...... What did *you* do?"

"Young lady, hold your tongue!"

Hold my tongue? I'd held the poor, tortured thing the near whole of my life.

"...... What did you do?" I said again, almost shouting.

She drew her lips tight and yanked the basket from my arm.

An unknown ferocity took me over. I wrenched the basket back from her and strode toward the door.

"You will not set foot from this house!" she ordered. "I forbid it."

I stepped through the back door into the soft gloom, into the terror and thrill of defiance. The sky had gone cobalt. Wind was coursing in hard from the harbor.

Mother followed me, shrieking, "I forbid it." Her words flapped off on the breezes, past the oak branches, over the brick fence.

Behind us, shoes scraped on the kitchen house porch, and turning, we saw Aunt-Sister, Binah, Cindie, all of them shadowed in the billowy dark, looking at us.

Mother stood white-faced on the porch steps.

"I'm going to see about Charlotte." I said. The words slid effortlessly over my lips like a cascade of water, and I knew instantly the nervous affliction in my voice had gone back into hibernation, for that was how it had happened in the past, the debility gradually weakening, until one day I opened my mouth and there was no trace of it.

Mother noticed, too. She said nothing more, and I trod toward the carriage house without looking back.

Handful

When dark fell, mauma started to shake. Her head lolled and her teeth clattered. It wasn't like Rosetta and her fits, where all her limbs jerked, it was like mauma was cold inside her bones. I didn't know what to do but pat her arms and legs. After a while, she grew still. Her breathing drew heavy, and before I knew it, I drifted off myself.

I started dreaming and in that dream I was sleeping. I slept under an arbor of thick green. It was bent perfect over me. Vines hung round my arms. Scuppernongs fell alongside my face. I was the girl sleeping, but at the same time I could see myself, like I was part of the clouds floating by, and then I looked down and saw the arbor wasn't really an arbor, it was our quilt frame covered in vines and leaves. I went on sleeping, watching myself sleeping, and the clouds went on floating, and I saw inside the thick green again. This time, it was mauma herself inside there.

I don't know what woke me. The room was quiet, the light gone.

Mauma said, "You wake?" Those were the first words she'd said since Tomfry strapped her.

"I'm awake."

"Awright. I gon tell you a story. You listening, Handful?"

"I'm listening."

My eyes had got used to the dark, and I saw the door still propped wide to the hallway, and mauma beside me, frowning. She said, "Your granny-mauma come from Africa when she was a girl. 'Bout same as you now."

My heart started to beat hard. It filled up my ears.

"Soon as she got here, her mauma and daddy was taken from her, and that same night the stars fell out the sky. You think stars don't fall, but your granny-mauma swore it."

Mauma tarried, letting us picture how the sky might've looked.

"She say everything over here sound like jibber jabber to her. The food taste like monkey meat. She ain't got nothin' but this little old scrap of quilt her mauma made. In Africa, her mauma was a quilter, best there is. They was Fon people and sewed appliqué, same like I do. They cut out fishes, birds, lions, elephants, every beast they had, and sewed 'em on, but the quilt your granny-mauma brought with her didn't have no animals on it, just little three-side-shapes, what you call a triangle. Same like I put on my quilts. My mauma say they was blackbird wings."

The floor creaked in the hallway and I heard somebody out there breathing high and fast, the way Miss Sarah breathed. I eased up on my elbow and craned my neck, and there she was—her shadow blotted on the hall window. I lowered myself back to the mattress and mauma went on telling her story with Miss Sarah listening in.

"Your granny-mauma got sold to some man for twenty dollars, and he put her in the fields near Georgetown. They eat boiled black-eye peas in the morning, and if you ain't done eating in ten minutes time, you don't get no more that day. Your granny-mauma say she always eat too slow.

"I never did know my daddy. He was a white man named John Paul, not the massa, but his brother. After I come, we got sold off. Mauma say I be the fair side of brown, and everybody know what that mean.

"We got bought by a man near Camden. He kept mauma in the fields and I stay out there with her, but nights she teach me everything she knows 'bout quilts. I tore up old pant legs and dress tails and pieced 'em. Mauma say in Africa they sew charms in their quilts. I put pieces of my hair down inside mine. When I got twelve, mauma start braggin' to the Camden missus, how I could sew anything, and the missus took me to the house to learn from their seamstress. I got better 'n she was in a hurry."

She broke off and shifted her legs on the bed. I was afraid that was all she had to say. I never had heard this story. Listening to it was like watching myself sleep, clouds floating, mauma bent over me. I forgot Miss Sarah was out there.

I waited, and finally she started back telling. "Mauma birthed my brother while I was sewing in the house. She never say who his daddy was. My brother didn't live out the year.

"After he die, your granny-mauma found us a spirit tree. It's just a oak tree, but she call it a Baybob like they have in Africa. She say Fon people keep a spirit tree and it always be a Baybob. Your granny-mauma wrapped the trunk with thread she begged and stole. She took me out there and say, 'We gon put our spirits in the tree so they safe from harm.' We kneel on her quilt from Africa, nothing but a shred now, and we give our spirits to the tree. She say our spirits live in the tree with the birds, learning to fly. She told me, 'If you leave this place, go get your spirit and take it with you.' We used to gather up leaves and twigs from round the tree and stick 'em in pouches to wear at our necks."

Her hand went to her throat like she was feeling for it.

She said, "Mauma died of a croup one winter. I was sixteen. I could sew anything there was. 'Bout that time the massa got in money-debt and sold off every one of us. I got bought by massa Grimké for his place in Union. Night 'fore I left, I went and got my spirit from the tree and took it with me.

"I want you to know, your daddy was good as gold. His name was Shanney. He work in massa Grimké's fields. One day missus say I got to come sew for her in Charleston. I say awright, but bring Shanney, he my husband. She say Shanney a field slave, and maybe I see him sometime when I back for a visit. You was already inside me, and nobody knew. Shanney die from a cut on his leg 'fore you a year old. He never saw your face."

Mauma stopped talking. She was done. She went to sleep then and left the story bent perfect over me.

Next morning when I eased out of bed headed for the privy, I bumped into a basket sitting by the door. Inside it was a big bottle of liniment and some medicine-tea.

That day I went back to tending Miss Sarah. I slipped into her room while she was reading one of her books. She was shy to bring up what happened to mauma, so I said, "We got your basket."

Her face eased. "Tell your mother I'm sorry for her treatment, and I hope she'll feel better soon," and it wasn't any toil in her words.

"That mean a lot to us," I said.

She laid the book down and came where I was standing by the chimney place and put her arms round me. It was hard to know where things stood. People say love gets fouled by a difference big as ours. I didn't know for sure whether Miss Sarah's feelings came from love or guilt. I didn't know whether mine came from love or a need to be safe. She loved me and pitied me. And I loved her and used her. It never was a simple thing. That day, our hearts were pure as they ever would get.

Sarah

Spring turned to summer, and when Madame Ruffin suspended classes until the fall, I asked Thomas to expand our private lessons on the piazza.

"I'm afraid we have to stop them altogether," he said. "I have my own studies to consider. Father has ordered me to undertake a systematic study of his law books in preparation for Yale."

"I could help you!" I cried.

"Sarah, Sarah, quite contra-rah." It was the phrase he used when his refusal was foregone and final.

He had no idea the extent I'd enmeshed him in my plans. There was a string of barrister firms on Broad Street, from the Exchange to St. Michael's, and I pictured the two of us partnered in one of them with a signboard out front, *Grimké and Grimké*. Of course, there would be an out-and-out skirmish with the rank and file, but with Thomas at my side and Father at my back, nothing would prevent it.

I bore down on Father's law books every afternoon myself.

In the mornings, I read aloud to Hetty in my room with the door bolted. When the air cooked to unbearable degrees, we escaped to the piazza, and there, sitting side by side in the swing, we sang songs that Hetty composed, most of them about traveling across water by boat or whale. Her legs swung back and forth like little batons. Sometimes we sat before the windows in the second-floor alcove and played Lace the String. Hetty always seemed to have a stash of red thread in her dress pocket and we spent hours passing it through our upstretched fingers, creating intricate, bloodshot mazes in the air.

Such occupations are what girls do together, but it was the first occasion for either of us, and we carried them out as covertly as possible to avoid Mother putting an end to them. We were crossing a dangerous line, Hetty and I.

One morning while Charleston turned miserably on the brazier of summer, Hetty and I lay flat on our stomachs on the rug in my room while I read aloud from *Don Quixote*. The week before, Mother had ordered the mosquito nettings out of storage and affixed above the beds in anticipation of the bloodsucking season, but having no such protection, the slaves were already scratching and clawing at their skin. They rubbed themselves with lard and molasses to draw out the itch and trailed its *eau de cologne* through the house.

Hetty dug at an inflamed mosquito bite on her forearm and frowned at the book pages as if they were some kind of irresolvable code. I wanted her to listen to the exploits of the knight and Sancho Panza, but she interrupted me repeatedly, placing her finger on some word or other, asking, "What does that one say?" and I would have to break off the story to tell her. She'd done the same thing recently as we read *The Life and Strange Surprizing Adventures of Robinson Crusoe of York,* and I wondered if, perhaps, she was merely bored with the antics of men, from the shipwrecked to the chivalrous.

As I sent my voice into dramatic lilts and accents, trying to lure her back into the tale, the room grew dark, tinctured with an approaching storm. Wind blew through the open window, coming thick with the smell of rain and oleander, swirling the veils of the mosquito net. I stopped reading, as thunder broke and rain splatted across the sill.

Hetty and I leapt up in unison and drew down the pane, and there, swooping low in the yellow gloom, was the young owl that Charlotte and Hetty had fed faithfully through the spring. It had grown out of its fledgling ways, but it had not vacated its residence in the woodpile.

I watched it fly straight toward us, arcing across George Street and gliding over the work yard wall, its comical barn owl face strikingly visible. As the bird disappeared, Hetty went to light the lamp, but I was fixed there. What came to me was the day at the woodpile when Charlotte first showed me the bird, and I remembered the oath I'd made to help Hetty become free, a promise impossible to fulfill and one that continued to cause me no end of guilt, but it suddenly rang clear in me for the first time: Charlotte said I should help Hetty get free *any way I could.*

Turning, I watched her carry the lantern to my dressing table, light swilling about her feet. When she set it down, I said, "Hetty, shall I teach you to read?"

Equipped with an elementary primer, two blue-back spellers, a slate board, and lump of chalk, we began daily lessons in my room. Not only did I lock the door, I screened the keyhole. Our tutorials went on throughout the morning for two or more hours. When we ended them, I wrapped the materials in a swath of coarse cloth, known as Negro cloth, and tucked the bundle beneath my bed.

I'd never taught anyone to read, but I'd been tutored in copious amounts of Latin by Thomas and subjected to enough of Madame to devise a reasonable scheme. As it turned out, Hetty had a knack. Within a week, she could write and recite the alphabet. Within two, she was sounding out words in the spellers. I'll never forget the moment when she made the magical connection in her mind and the letters and sounds passed from nonsense into meaning. After that, she read through the primer with growing proficiency.

By page forty, she had a vocabulary of eighty-six words. I recorded and numbered each one she mastered on a sheaf of paper. "When you reach a hundred words," I promised her, "we'll celebrate with a tea."

She began to decipher words on apothecary labels and food jars. "How do you spell *Hetty*?" she wanted to know. "How do you spell *water*?" Her appetite to learn was voracious.

Once, I glimpsed her in the work yard writing in the dirt with a stick and I raced into the yard to stop her. She'd scrawled W-A-T-E-R with exact penmanship for the entire world to see.

"What are you doing?" I said, rubbing the letters away with my foot. "Someone will see."

She was equally exasperated with me. "Don't you think I got my own foot to rub out letters, if somebody comes along?"

She conquered her hundredth word on the thirteenth of July.

We held her celebratory tea the next day on the hipped roof of the house, hoping to catch sight of the Bastille Day festivities. We had a sizeable French population from St. Domingo, a French theatre, and a French finishing school on every corner. A French hair-dresser frizzed and powdered Mother and her friends, regaling them with accounts of the guillotining of Marie Antoinette, which he claimed to have witnessed. Charleston was British to the soles of its feet, but it observed the destruction of the Bastille with as much zeal as our own independence.

We climbed into the attic with two china cups and a jar of black tea spiked with hyssop and honey. From there, we mounted a ladder that led to a hatch in the roof. Thomas had discovered the secret opening at thirteen and taken me up to wander among the chimneys. Snow spotted us as he drove Mother home from one of her charity missions, and without a word to her, he'd climbed up and retrieved us. I'd not ventured here since.

Hetty and I nestled into one of the gullies on the south side with our backs against a slope. She claimed never to have drunk from a china cup and gulped quickly, while I sipped slowly and stared at the hard blue pane over our heads. When the populace marched in procession along Broad Street, they were too far away for us to see, but we heard them singing the *Hymne des Marseillois*. The bells of St. Philip's chimed and there was a salute of thirteen guns.

Birds had been loitering on the roof, and scatterings of feathers were here and there. Hetty tucked them into her pockets, and something about this created a feeling of tenderness in me. Perhaps I was a little drunk on hyssop and honey, on the novelty of being girls together on the roof. Whatever it was, I began telling Hetty confidences I'd kept only with myself.

I told her I was accomplished at eavesdropping, that I'd stood outside Charlotte's room the night she was punished and heard the story she told.

"I know," she said. "You not so good at snooping as you think."

I spilled every possible secret. My sister Mary despised me. Thomas had been my only friend. I'd been dismissed as an unfit teacher of slave children, but she shouldn't worry, it was not due to incompetence.

As I went on, my revelations turned grave. "I saw Rosetta being whipped one time," I told her. "I was four. That was when the trouble with my speech began."

"It seems like you're talking all right now."

"It comes and goes."

"Was Rosetta hurt bad?"

"I think it was very bad."

"What'd she do wrong?"

"I don't know. I didn't ask—I couldn't speak afterward, not for weeks."

We turned taciturn, leaning back and gazing at the crenulated clouds. Talk of Rosetta had sobered us more than I'd intended, far too much for a tea celebrating a hundred-word vocabulary.

Hoping to restore the mood, I said, "I'm going to be a lawyer like my father." I was surprised to hear myself blurt this out, the crown jewel of secrets, and feeling suddenly exposed, I added, "But you can't tell anyone."

"I don't have nobody to tell. Just mauma."

"Well, you can't even tell her. Promise me."

She nodded.

Satisfied, I thought of the lava box and my silver button. "Do you know how an object can stand for something entirely different than its purpose?" She looked at me blankly, while I tried to think of a way to explain. "You know my mother's cane, for instance—how it's meant to help her walk, but we all know what it stands for."

"Whacking heads." After a pause, she added, "A triangle on a quilt stands for a blackbird wing."

"Yes, that's what I mean. Well, I have a stone box in my dresser with a button inside. A button is meant for fastening clothes, but this one is beautiful, just plain uncommon, so I decided to let it stand for my desire to be a lawyer."

"I know about the button. I didn't touch it, I just opened the box and looked at it."

"I don't mind if you hold it," I told her.

"I have a thimble and it stands for pushing a needle and keeping my fingertip from turning sore, but I could let that stand for something else."

When I asked her what, she said, "I don't know, 'cept I wanna sew like mauma."

Hetty got into the spirit. She retold the entire story I'd overheard her mother tell that night about her grandmother coming from Africa, appliquéing quilts with the triangles. When Hetty talked about the spirit tree, her voice took on a reverential tone.

Before we went back down the hatch, Hetty said, "I took a spool of thread from your room. It was laying in your drawer no use to anybody. I'm sorry, I can bring it back."

"Oh. Well, go ahead and keep it, but please Hetty, don't steal anymore, even little things. You could land in terrible trouble."

As we descended the ladder, she said, "My real name is Handful."

Handful

Mauma came down with a limp. When she was in her room or in the kitchen house for meals, she didn't have any trouble, but the minute she stepped in the yard, she dragged her leg like it was a dead log. Aunt-Sister and them watched her go lame and shook their heads. They didn't like that kind of trick and didn't mind saying it. Mauma told them, "After you get *your* one-legged punishment, you can say all you want. Till then, you best shut up."

After that, they stayed clear of her. Stopped talking if she showed up, started back when she left. Mauma said it was a hateful shun.

Her eyes burned with anger all the time now. Sometimes she turned her blackened stare on me. Sometimes she turned it to cleverness. One day I found her at the foot of the stairs, explaining to missus she had a hard time climbing up to do her sewing, and for that matter, a hard time climbing the carriage house steps to her room. She said, "But I gon make out somehow, don't worry." Then while missus and me watched, she pulled on the bannister and dragged herself to the top, calling on Jesus the whole way.

Next we know, missus had Prince clear out a big room in the cellar, on the side of the house that backed up to the work yard wall. He moved mauma's bed in there and all her stuff. Took the quilt frame down from her old ceiling and nailed it on the new one. Missus said mauma would do all the sewing in her room from here out and had Prince bring down the lacquer sewing table.

The cellar room was large as three slave rooms put together. It was bright whitewash and had its own tiny window near the ceiling, but looking through it, you didn't see clouds in the sky, you saw bricks in the wall. Mauma made it a calico curtain anyway. She got hold of some pictures of sailing ships from a cast-off book and tacked them on the wall. A painted rocking chair turned up in there, along with a beat-up toilet table she covered with Ticklingburg cloth. On top, she set empty colored bottles, a box of candles, a cake of tallow, and a tin dish piled with coffee beans for her chewing pleasure. Where she got all this hoard, I don't know. Along the wall shelf, she laid out our sewing stuff: the patch box, the pouch with needles and thread, the sack of quilt stuffing, pin cushion, shears, tracing wheel, charcoal, stamping papers, measuring ribbons. Sitting off by themselves was my brass thimble and the red thread I stole from Miss Sarah's drawer.

Once mauma got the place fixed like a palace, she asked Aunt-Sister could they all come give a prayer for her "poor sorry room." One evening here came the lot of them all too glad to see how poor and sorry it was. Mauma offered each of them a coffee bean. She let them look to their hearts' content, then showed them how the door locked with an iron slide bolt, how she had her own privy pot under the bed, which it fell to me to empty, considering how cripple she was. She made a lot over the wooden cane missus had given her for getting round.

When Aunt-Sister left mauma's party, she spit on the floor outside the door, and Cindie came behind her and did the same thing.

Best thing was, I could get to the new room without leaving the house. More nights than not, I crept down the two flights from Sarah's room, side-stepping the creaks. Mauma loved that lock on her door. If she was in her room, you could be sure it was latched, and if she was sleeping, I had to pound my knuckles sore till she roused.

Mauma didn't care anymore about me leaving my post. She'd snatch open her door, yank me in, and bolt it back. Under the covers, I'd ask her to tell me about the spirit tree, wanting more detail of it, every leaf, branch, and nest. When she thought I was sleeping, she got up and paced the room, humming a quiet sound through her lips. Those nights, something dark and heedless was loose in her.

By day, she sat in her new room and sewed. Miss Sarah let me go down every afternoon and stay till suppertime. A little air might fuss round mauma's window, but it was like a smelter in there most of the time. Mauma would say, "Get yoself busy." I learned baste, gather, pleat, shire, gore, and gusset.

Every stitch there is. I learned to do a button hole and a shank. Cut a pattern from scratch without stamping powder.

That summer, I turned eleven years, and mauma said the pallet I slept on upstairs wasn't fit for a dog. We were supposed to be working on the next ration of slave clothes. Every year the men got two brown shirts and two white, two pants, two vests. Women got three dresses, four aprons, and a head scarf. Mauma said all that could wait. She showed me how to cut black triangles each one big as the end of my thumb, then we appliquéd two hundred or more on red squares, a color mauma called oxblood. We sewed on tiny circles of yellow for sun splatter, then cranked down the quilt frame and pieced everything together. I hemmed on the homespun backing myself, and we filled the inside with all the batting and feathers we had. I cut a plug of my hair and plug of mauma's and put them inside for charms. It took six afternoons.

Mauma had stopped stealing and taken up safer ways to do harm and wreckage. She'd forget, so-call forget, that missus' sleeves were basted loose, and one of them would pop open at church or somewhere. Mauma had me sew on buttons without knots, and they would fall off missus' bosom on the first wear-round. Everybody with an ear could hear missus shout at mauma for her laziness, and mauma cry out, "Oh, missus, pray for me, I wants to do better."

I can't say what all mischief mauma did, just what I saw, and that was plenty. She "accidently" broke whatever piece of china or table figurine was sitting round. Flipped it over and kept walking. When she saw the tea trays Aunt-Sister left in the warming kitchen for Cindie to take up, she would drop whatever bit of nastiness she could into the teapot. Dirt off the floor, lint off the rug, spit from her mouth. I told Miss Sarah, stay clear of the tea trays.

Day before the storm came, a still feeling weighed on the air. You felt like you were waiting, but you didn't know what for. Tomfry said it was a hurricane and batten down. Prince and Sabe closed the house shutters, stored the work yard tools in the shed, and fastened up the animals. Inside, we rolled up carpets on the first floor and moved the fragiles from near the windows. Missus had us bring the food rations inside from the kitchen house.

It came in the night while I was in bed with mauma. The wind screamed and threw limbs against the house. So many palm trees rattled in the dark, mauma and I had to shout to hear each other. We sat in the bed and watched the rain pitch against the high window and pour in round the edges. Floodwater washed under the door. I sang my songs loud as I could to take my mind from it.

> *Cross the water, cross the sea,*
> *Let them fishes carry me.*
> *If that water take too long,*
> *Carry me on, Carry me on.*

When the storm finally passed, we swung our legs onto the floor and the water cut circles above our ankles. Mauma's so-call poor sorry room had turned into a poor sorry room.

At low tide next day, the floodwater drew back and everyone got called to the cellar to shovel out the mud. The work yard was a mess of sticks and broken palm fans, water pails and horse feed, the door off the privy, whatever the wind had grabbed and dropped. A piece of ship sail was hung in the branches of the spreading tree.

Once we got mauma's room cleaned up, I went out to see the sail in the tree. It waved in the breeze, making a strange sight. Beneath the branches, the ground was a wet slate of clay. Taking a stick, I wrote BABY BOY BLUE BLOW YOUR HORN HETTY, digging the letters deep in the starchy mud, pleased at my penmanship. When Aunt-Sister called me to the kitchen house, I smeared over the words with the toe of my shoe.

The rest of the day, the sun shone down and dried out the world.

Next morning while me and mauma were in the dining room waiting for devotions, Miss Mary came hurrying down the hallway with missus trotting behind her. Headed for the back door.

Mauma leaned on her cane, said, "Where they tearing off to?"

Looking from the window, we saw Lucy, Miss Mary's waiting maid, under the tree and the sail still caught in the branches. We saw Miss Mary lead missus cross the yard right to where Lucy stood looking at the ground, and a hot feeling came up from my stomach and spread over my chest.

"What they looking at?" mauma said, watching how the three of them tipped from their waists and studied the dirt.

Then Lucy ran full-tilt back toward the house. Drawing close, she yelled, "Handful! Handful! Missus say come out here right now."

I went, full-knowing.

My words, straight from the speller, were baked in the clay. The smear-over of mud from my shoe had crackled and thinned away, leaving the deep crevice of the letters.

BABY BOY BLUE BLOW YOUR HORN HETTY.

Sarah

Two days after a September hurricane sent tidewater over East Bay all the way to Meeting Street, Binah knocked on my door before breakfast, her eyes filled with fear and consolation, and I knew some catastrophe had fallen.

"Has someone died? Is Father—"

"No, ain't nobody die. Your daddy, he want you in the library."

I'd never been summoned like this and it caused an odd, plummeting sensation in my legs, so much so I dipped a little at the knees while walking back to the Hepplewhite to inspect the ivory ribbon I'd been tying in my hair.

"What's happened?" I asked, tugging the bow, smoothing my dress, letting my hand rest for a moment across my jittery stomach.

I could see her reflection in the glass. She shook her head. "Miss Sarah, I can't say what he want, but it ain't help to poke."

Placing her hand at the small of my back, she nudged me from the room, past Handful's new quilt lying in the hallway, its mass of triangles pinioned on the floor. We walked down the stairs, pausing outside the library door. Abstaining from her Poor Miss Sarahs, Binah said instead, "Listen to Binah now. Don't be crying, and don't be running away. Buck yourself up now."

Her words, meant to steady me, unnerved me further. As I tapped on the door, the airy feeling returned to the back of my knees. He sat at his desk with his hair oiled and combed back smooth and didn't look up, intent on a stack of documents.

When he lifted his face, his eyes were hardened. "You have disappointed me, Sarah."

I was too stunned to cry or run away, the two things Binah had warned against. "I would never knowingly disappoint you, Father. I only care to—"

He thrust out his palm. "I have brought you here to listen. Do not speak."

My heart beat so ferociously my hands went to either side of my ribs to keep them from unhinging.

"It has been brought to my attention that your slave girl has become literate. Do not think to deny it, as she wrote a number of words on the muddy ground in the yard and even took care to sign her name."

Oh Handful, no! I looked away from his harsh, accusing eyes, trying to arrange things into perspective. Handful had been careless. We'd been found out. But my disbelieving mind could not accept that Father, of all people, believed her ability to read was an unpardonable offense. He would chastise me as he must, undoubtedly at Mother's urging. Then he would soften. In the depths of his conscience, he understood what I'd done.

"How do you suppose she acquired this ability?" he asked calmly. "Did it descend upon her one day out of the blue? Was she born with it? Did she teach her own ingenious self to read? Of course, we know how the girl came to read—you taught her. You defied your mother, your father, the laws of your state, even your rector, who expressly admonished you about it."

He rose from his leather chair and walked toward me, stopping at arm's reach, and when he spoke again, some of the hostility had left his voice. "I've asked myself how you are able to disobey with such ease and disregard. I fear the answer is you are a coddled girl who does not understand her place in the world, and that is partly my own fault. I've done you no favors with my lenience. My indulgence has given you the idea you can transgress a serious boundary such as this one."

Feeling the chill of some new and different terror, I dared to speak, and felt my throat clench in the familiar old way. I squeezed my eyes and forced out my thought. "......... I'm sorry, Father...... I meant no harm."

"No harm?"

He hadn't noticed the return of my stammer. He paced about the stuffy room and lectured me, while Mr. Washington gazed serenely from the mantel. "You think there's no detriment in a slave learning to read? There are sad truths in our world, and one is that slaves who read are a threat. They would be abreast of news that would incite them in ways we could not control. Yes, it's unfair to deprive them, but there's a greater good here that must be protected."

"......... But Father, it's wrong!" I cried.

"Are you so impudent as to challenge me even now? When you left the document on my desk freeing your slave girl, I should have brought you to your senses then and there, but I cosseted you. I thought by tearing the fool thing in two and returning it to you, you would understand we Grimkés do not subvert the institutions and laws by which we live, even if we don't agree with them."

I felt confused and very stupid. Father had torn up my manumission paper. *Father.*

"Do not mistake me, Sarah, I will protect our way of life. I will not tolerate sedition in this family!"

When I'd espoused my anti-slavery views during those dinner table debates, Father beaming and spurring me on, I'd thought he prized my position. I'd thought he *shared* my position, but it hit me suddenly that I'd been the collared monkey dancing to his master's accordion. Father had been amusing himself. Or perhaps he'd encouraged my dissenting opinion only because it gave the rest of them a way to sharpen their own opposing views. Perhaps he'd tolerated my notions because the debates had been a pitying oral exercise to help a defective daughter speak?

Father crossed his arms over his white shirt and stared at me from beneath the unclipped hedge of his brows. His eyes were clear and brown and empty of compassion, and that's when I first saw my father as he really was—a man who valued principle over love.

"You have quite literally committed a crime," he said and resumed his pacing, making a wide, slow orbit around me. "I will not punish you accordingly, but you must learn, Sarah."

"From now on, you are denied entrance to this room. You shall not cross this threshold at any time, day or night. You are denied all access to the books here, and to any other books wherever they might be, except for those Madame Ruffin has allotted for your studies."

No books. God, please. My legs gave way then, and I went onto my knees.

He kept circling. "You will study nothing but Madame's approved subjects. No more Latin sessions with Thomas. You will not write it, speak it, or compose it in your head. Do you understand?"

I lifted my hands, palms up, as high as my head, molding myself into the shape of a supplicant. "......... Father, I beg you ... P-please, don't take books from me ... I can't bear it."

"You have no need of books, Sarah."

"...... F-f-father!"

He strode back to his desk. "It causes me distress to see your misery, Sarah, but it's *fait accompli*. Try not to take it so hard."

From the window came the rumble of drays and carriages, the cries of slave vendors on the street—the old woman with the basket atop her head who squawked, "Red ROSE to-may-TOES." The din of commerce went on without regard. Opening the library door, I saw Binah had waited. She took my hand and led me up the stairs to the doorway of my room. "I get you some breakfast and bring it up here on a tray," she said.

After she left, I peered beneath the bed where I'd kept the slate board, spellers, and primer. They were gone. The books on my desk were gone, too. My room had been scoured.

It was not until Binah returned with the tray that I thought to ask, "...... Where's Handful?"

"Oh, Miss Sarah, that just it. She 'bout to get her own punishing out back."

I have no memory of my feet grazing the stairs.

"It just one lash," Binah cried, racing behind me. "One lash, missus say. That be all."

I flung open the back door. My eyes swept the yard. Handful's skinny arms were tied to the porch rail of the kitchen house. Ten paces behind her, Tomfry held a strap and stared at the ground. Charlotte stood in the wheel ruts that cut from the carriage house to the back gate, while the rest of the slaves clustered beneath the oak.

Tomfry raised his arm. "No!" I screamed. *"Nooooo!"* He turned toward me, hesitating, and relief filled his face.

Then I heard Mother's cane tap the glass on the upstairs window, and Tomfry lifted his tired eyes toward the sound. He nodded and brought the lash down across Handful's back.

Handful

Tomfry said he tried not to put much force in it, but the strike flayed open my skin. Miss Sarah made a poultice with Balm of Gilead buds soaked in master Grimké's rum, and mauma handed the whole flask to me and said, "Here, go on, drink it, too." I don't hardly remember the pain.

The gash healed fast, but Miss Sarah's hurt got worse and worse. Her voice had gone back to stalling and she pined for her books. That was one wretched girl.

It'd been Lucy who ran tattling to Miss Mary about my lettering under the tree, and Miss Mary had run tattling to missus. I'd judged Lucy to be stupid, but she was only weak-willed and wanting to get in good with Miss Mary. I never did forgive her, and I don't know if Miss Sarah forgave her sister, cause what came from all that snitching turned the tide on Miss Sarah's life. Her studying was over and done.

My reading lessons were over, too. I had my hundred words, and I figured out a good many more just using my wits. Now and then, I said my ABCs for mauma and read words to her off the picture pages she'd tacked on her wall.

One day I went to the cellar and mauma was making a baby gown from muslin with lilac bands. She saw my face and said, "That's right, *another* Grimké coming. Sometime this winter. Missus ain't happy 'bout it. I heard her tell massa, that's it, this the last one."

When mauma finished hemming the little gown, she dug in the gunny sack and pulled out a short stack of clean paper, a half full inkwell, and a quill pen, and I knew she'd stole every one of these things. I said, "Why you keep doing this?"

"I need you to write something. Write, 'Charlotte Grimké has permission for traveling.' Under that, put the month, leave off the day, and sign Mary Grimké with some curlicue."

"First off, I don't know how to write *Charlotte*. I don't know the word *permission* either."

"Then, write, 'This slave is allowed for travel.'"

"What you gonna do with it?"

She smiled, showing me the gap in her front teeth. "This slave gon travel. But don't worry, she always coming back."

"What you gonna do when a white man stops you and asks to see your pass and it looks like some eleven-year-old wrote it?"

"Then you best write it like you ain't some eleven-year-old."

"How you plan on getting past the wall?"

She looked up at the window near the ceiling. It wasn't big as a hat box. I didn't see how she could wriggle through it, but she would grease herself with goose fat if that's what it took. I wrote her pass cause she was bent on hell to have it.

After that, least one or two afternoons a week, she took off. Stayed gone from middle of the afternoon till past dark. Wouldn't say where she went. Wouldn't say how she got in and out of the yard. I worked out her escape path in my head, though. Outside her window, it wasn't but a couple of feet between the house and the wall, and I figured once she squeezed through the window, she would press her back against the house and her feet against the wall and shimmy up and over, dropping to the ground on the other side.

Course, she had to find another way back in. My guess was the back gate where the carriage came and went. She never came back till it was good and dark, so she could climb it and nobody see. She always made it before the drums beat for curfew. I didn't wanna think of her out there hiding from the City Guard.

One afternoon, while me and mauma were finishing up the slave clothes for the year, I laid out my reasoning, how she went out the window in daylight and came back over the gate at dark. She said, "Well, ain't you smart."

In the far back of my head, I could see her with the strap tied on her ankle and round her neck, and I filled up and started begging. "Don't do it no more. Please. All right? You gonna get yourself caught."

"I tell you what, you can help me—if somebody here find me missing, you sit the pail next to the cistern where I can see it from the back gate. You do that for me."

This scared me worse. "And if you see it, what you gonna do—run off? Just leave me?" Then I broke down.

She rubbed my shoulders the way she always liked to do. "Handful, child. I would soon die 'fore I leave you. You know that. If that pail sit by the cistern, that just help me know what's coming, that's all."

When their social season was starting off again, and me and mauma couldn't keep up with all the gowns and frocks, she up and hired herself out without permission. I learned it one day after the supper meal, while we were standing in the middle of the work yard. Miss Sarah had been in one of her despairs all day, and I thought the worst things I had to fret over was how low she got and mauma slipping out the window. But mauma, she pulled a slave badge out from her pocket. If some owner hired his slave out, he had to buy a badge from the city, and I knew master Grimké hadn't bought any such. Having a fake badge was worse than having missus' green silk.

I took the badge and studied it. It was a small square of copper with a hole poked through the top so you could pin it to your dress. It was carved with words. I sounded them out till it finally came clear what I was saying. "Domes-tic . . . Do-mes-tic. Ser-vant. *Domestic Servant!*" I cried. "Number 133. Year 1805. Where'd you get this?"

"Well, I ain't been out there grogging and lazing round this whole time—I been finding work for myself."

"But you got more work here than we can see to."

"And I don't make nothin' from it, do I?" She took the badge from me and dropped it back in her pocket.

"One of the Russell slaves name Tom has his own blacksmith shop on East

Bay. Missus Russell let him work for hire all day and she don't take but three-quarter of what he make. He made this badge for me, copied it off a real one."

I had the mind of an eleven-year-old, but I knew right off this blacksmith wasn't just some nice man doing her a favor. Why was he putting himself in danger to make a fake badge for her?

She said, "I gon be making bonnets and dresses and quilts for a lady on Queen Street. Missus Allen. I told her my name was Pearl, and I belong to massa Dupré on the corner of George and East Bay. She say to me, 'You mean that French tailor?' I say, 'Yessum, he can't fill my time no more with work, so he letting me out for hire.'"

"What if she checks on your story?"

"She an old widow, she ain't gon check. She just say, 'Show me your badge.'"

Mauma was proud of her badge and proud of herself.

"Missus Allen say she pay me by the garment, and her two daughters need clothes and coverings for they children."

"How you gonna get all this extra work done?"

"I got you. I got all the hours of the night."

Mauma burned so many candles working in the dark, she took to swiping them from whatever room she happened on. Her eyes grew down to squints and the skin round them wrinkled like drawing a straight stitch. She was tired and frayed but she seemed better off inside.

She brought home money and stuffed it inside the gunny sack, and I helped her sew day and night, anytime I didn't have duties drawing Miss Sarah's baths, cleaning her room, keeping up with her clothes and her privy pot. When we got the widow's orders done, mauma would squirm out the window and carry the parcels to her door where she got more fabric for the next batch. Then she would wait till dark and sneak over the back gate. All this dangerous business got natural as the day was long.

One afternoon during a real warm spell in January, missus sent Cindie to the basement to fetch mauma, something about rosettes falling off her new empire waist dress, and course, mauma was gone over the wall. She didn't lock the door while she was out cause she knew missus would have Prince saw the door off its hinges if she didn't answer, and how was she gonna explain an empty room behind a locked door?

News of a missing slave flies like brush fire. When I heard the news, my heart dropped to my knees. Missus used her bell and gathered everybody in the yard, up near the back door. She laid her hands on top of her big pregnant belly and said, "If you know Charlotte's whereabouts, you are duty bound to tell me."

Not a peep from anybody. Missus cast her eyes on me. "Hetty? Where is your mother?"

I shrugged and acted stumped. "I don't know, missus. Wish I did know."

Missus told Tomfry to search the kitchen house, laundry, carriage house, stable, storage shed, privy, and slave rooms. She said comb every nook in the yard, look down the chute where Prince sent hay from the loft to the horses' trough. If that didn't turn up mauma, she said Tomfry would go through the house, the piazza, and the ornament garden, top to bottom.

She rang her bell, which meant go back to work. I hurried to mauma's room to check the gunny sack. All her money was still at the bottom under the stuffing. Then I crept back outside and set the pail next to the cistern. The sun was coming down the sky, turning it the color of apricots.

While Tomfry did his searching high and low, I took up my spot in the front alcove on the second floor to wait. At the first shade of dark, lo-to-behold, I looked down through the window and there was mauma turning the corner. She marched straight to the front door and knocked.

I tore down the stairs and got to the door the same time as Tomfry.

When he opened it, mauma said, "I gon give you half of a dollar if you get me back in there safe. You owe me, Tomfry."

He stepped out onto the landing, me beside him, and closed the door. I threw my arms round mauma. She said to him, "Quick now, what it gon be?"

"They ain't nowhere to put you," he said. "Missus had me search every corner."

"Not the rooftop," I said.

Tomfry made the coast clear, and I led mauma to the attic and showed her the ladder and the hatch. I said, "When they come, you say it was so warm you came out here to see the harbor and lay down and fell asleep."

Meantime, Tomfry went and explained to missus how he forgot about the rooftop when he was searching, how he knew for a fact Charlotte had been up there one time before.

Missus waited at the foot of the attic steps with her cane, huffing from climbing the stairs, big as she was. I lurked behind her. I was trembling with nerves.

Mauma came down the ladder, shivering, telling this cockamamie story I'd come up with. Missus said, "I did not think you were as naturally dumb as the rest, Charlotte, but you have proved me wrong. To fall asleep on the roof! You could have rolled off onto the street. *The roof?* You must know such a place is completely off-limits."

She raised her cane and brought it down cross the back of mauma's head. "See yourself to your room, and tomorrow morning after devotions, you are to sew the rosettes back on my new dress. Your sloppiness with the needle has only worsened."

"Yessum," mauma said, hurrying to the stairs, waving me in front of her. If missus noticed how mauma didn't have her cane or her limp, she didn't say so.

When we reached the cellar, mauma shut the door and threw the lock. I was winded, but mauma's breath was steady. She rubbed the back of her head. She set her jaw. She said, "I is a 'markable woman, and you is a 'markable girl, and we ain't never gon bow and scrape to that woman."

Sarah

The idea of a new sibling didn't strike me as happy news. Shut away in my room, I absorbed it with grim resignation. When pregnant, Mother's mood became even fouler, and who among us would welcome that? My real dismay came when I took paper and pen and worked out the arithmetic: Mother had spent ten of the last twenty years pregnant. *For pity sake!*

Soon to be twelve, I was on the cusp of maidenhood, and I wanted to marry—truly, I did—but such numbers petrified me. Coming, as they did, so soon after my books being taken away, quite soured me on the female life.

Since Father's dressing-down, I hadn't left the four walls of my room except for meals, Madame Ruffin's class three mornings a week, and church on Sunday. Handful kept me company, asking questions to which she didn't care to know the answer, asking only to animate me. She watched me make feeble attempts at embroidery and write stories about a girl abandoned to an island in the manner of Robinson Crusoe. Mother ordered me to snap from my inwardness and misery, and I did try, but my despair only grew.

Mother summoned our physician, Dr. Geddings, who after much probing decided I suffered from severe melancholy. I listened at the door as he told Mother he'd never witnessed a case in someone so young, that this kind of lunacy occurred in women after childbirth or at the withdrawal of a woman's menses. He declared me a high-strung, temperamental girl with predilections to hysteria, as evidenced by my speech.

Shortly after Christmas, I passed Thomas' door and glimpsed his trunk open on the floor. I couldn't bear his leaving, but it was worse knowing he was going off to New Haven to pursue a dream I myself had, but would never realize. Consumed with envy for his dazzling future, I fled to my room where I sobbed out my grief. It gushed from me in black waves, and as it did, my despondency seemed to reach its extremity, its farther limit, passing over into what I can only now call an anguished hope.

All things pass in the end, even the worst melancholy. I opened my dresser and pulled out the lava box that held my button. My eyes glazed at the sight of it, and this time I felt my spirit rise up to meet my will. I would not give up. I would err on the side of audacity. That was what I'd always done.

My audacious erring occurred at Thomas' farewell party, which took place in the second-floor withdrawing room on Twelfth Night. During the past week, I'd caught Father smiling at me across the dining table, and I'd interpreted his Christmas gift—a print of Apollo and the Muses—as an offering of love and the end of his censure. Tonight, he conversed with Thomas, Frederick, and John, who was home from Yale, all of them in black woolen topcoats and striped vests of various colors, Father's flaxen. Seated with Mary at the Pembroke table, I watched them and wished to know what they debated. Anna and Eliza, who'd been allowed at the festivities, sat on the rug before the fire screen, clutching their Christmas dolls, while Ben pitted his new wooden soldiers in battle, shouting "Charge!" every few seconds.

Mother reclined against the red velvet of her rosewood Récamier, which had been brought up from her bedroom. I'd observed five of Mother's gestations, and clearly this was her most difficult. She'd enlarged to mammoth proportions. Even her poor face appeared bloated. Nevertheless, she'd created an elaborate fete. The room blazed with candles and lamplight, which reflected off mirrors and gilt surfaces, and the tables were laid with white linen cloths and gold brocade runners in keeping with the colors of the Epiphany. Tomfry, Snow, and Eli served, wearing their dark green livery, hauling in trays of crab pies, buttered shrimps, veal, fried whiting, and omelet soufflé.

My prodigal appetite had returned, and I occupied myself with eating and listening to the whirr of bass voices across the room. They conversed about the reelection of Mr. Jefferson, whether Mr. Meriwether Lewis and Mr. William Clark had any chance of reaching the Pacific coast, and most tantalizing, what the abolition of slavery in the Northern states, most recently in New Jersey, boded for the South. *Abolition by law?* I'd never heard of it and craned to get every snippet. Did those in the North, then, believe God to be sided against slavery?

We finished the meal with Thomas' favorite sweet, macaroons with almond ice, after which Father tapped a spoon against his crystal goblet and silenced the room. He wished Thomas well and presented him with *An Abridgement of Locke's Essay Concerning Human Understanding*. Mother had allowed Mary and me to each have half a flute of wine, my inaugural taste, and I gazed at the book in Thomas' hand with a downy feeling between my ears.

"Who will send Thomas off with a tribute?" Father said, scanning the faces of his sons. Firstborn John tugged on the hem of his vest, but it was I, the sixth-born child and second daughter, who leapt to my feet and made a speech.

"... ... Thomas, dear brother, I shall miss you.. ..... I wish you God's speed with your studies . . ." I paused and felt an upwelling of courage. "One day I intend to follow in your footsteps.. ..... To become a jurist."

When Father found his tongue, his tone was full of amusement. "Did my ears deceive? Did you say you would follow your brother to the bar?" John twittered, and Fredrick laughed outright. Father looked at them and smiled, continuing, "Are there female jurists now? If so, little one, do enlighten us."

Their hilarity burst forth, and I saw Thomas, too, was laughing.

I tried to answer, not fully comprehending the depth of their derision, that his question was for the benefit of my brothers alone.

"... ... Would it not be a great accomplishment if *I* should be the first?"

At that, Father's fun turned into annoyance. "There will be no *first*, Sarah, and if such a preposterous thing did occur, it will be no daughter of mine."

Still, I went on stupidly, blindly. "... ... Father, I would make you proud. I would do anything."

"Sarah, stop this nonsense! You shame yourself. You shame us all. Where did you ever get the notion you could study the law?"

I fought to stand there, to hold on to what felt like some last dogged piece of myself. "... ... You said I would be the greatest jurist—"

"I said if you were a boy!"

My eyes flitted to Anna and Eliza, who gazed up at me, and then to Mary, who would not meet them.

I turned to Thomas. "...... Please...... do you remember... you said *I* should be the jurist?"

"Sarah, I'm sorry, but Father is right."

His words finished me.

Father made a gesture with his hand, dismissing the matter, and the band of them turned from me and resumed their conversation. I heard Mother say my name in a quiet way. She no longer reclined, but sat upright, her face bearing a commiserate look. "You may go to your room," she said.

I slinked away like some scraped-out soul. On the floor beside my door, Handful was coiled into her red squares and black triangles. She said, "I put on your lamp and stoked the fire. You need me to help with your dress?"

"... No, stay where you are." My words sounded flat with hurt.

She studied me, uncertain. "What happened, Miss Sarah?"

Unable to answer, I entered my room and closed the door. I sat on the dresser stool. I felt strange and hollow, unable to cry, unable to feel anything but an empty, extinguished place in the pit of my stomach.

The knock at my door moments later was light, and thinking it was Handful, I gathered the last crumbs of my energy and called out, "... I have no need of you."

Mother entered, swaying with her weight. "I took no joy in seeing your hopes quashed," she said. "Your father and brothers were cruel, but I believe their mockery was in equal portion to their astonishment. A lawyer, Sarah? The idea is so outlandish I feel I have failed you bitterly."

She placed her palm on the side of her belly and closed her eyes as if warding off the thrust of an elbow or foot. The gentleness in her voice, her very presence in my room revealed how distressed she was for me, and yet she seemed to suggest their unkindness was justified.

"Your father believes you are an anomalous girl with your craving for books and your aspirations, but he's wrong."

I looked at her with surprise. The hauteur had left her. There was a lament in her I'd never seen before. "Every girl comes into the world with varying degrees of ambition," she said, "even if it's only the hope of not belonging body and soul to her husband. I was a girl once, believe it or not."

She seemed a stranger, a woman without all the wounds and armature the years bring, but then she went on, and it was Mother again. "The truth," she said, "is that every girl must have ambition knocked out of her for her own good. You are unusual only in your determination to fight what is inevitable. You resisted and so it came to this, to being broken like a horse."

She bent and put her arms around me. "Sarah darling, you've fought harder than I imagined, but you must give yourself over to your duty and your fate and make whatever happiness you can."

I felt the puffy skin of her cheek, and I wanted both to cling to her and shove her away. I watched her go, noticing she hadn't closed the door when she'd entered. Handful would've heard everything. The thought comforted me. There's no pain on earth that doesn't crave a benevolent witness.

As Handful appeared, regarding me with her large, soulful eyes, I took the lava box from my dresser, removed the silver button, and dropped it into the ash bin by the fire, where it disappeared beneath the gray and white soot.

The following day, the withdrawing room was cleared for mother's lying-in. She'd birthed her last six children there, surrounded by Binah, Aunt-Sister, Dr. Geddings, a hired wet nurse, and two female cousins. It seemed unlikely she would grant me a visit, but a week before her labor began, she allowed me in to see her.

It was a frosty morning in February. The sky was bunched with winter clouds, and the fireplaces throughout the house crackled and hissed. In the withdrawing room, the fire provided the only light. Mother, who was a week from her fortieth birthday, was sprawled on her Récamier, looking perfectly miserable.

"I hope you have no trouble to speak of, for I have no strength to deal with it," she said through swollen lips.

"... . . . I have a request."

She raised herself slightly and reached for her cup on the tea table. "Well then, what is it? What is this request that cannot wait?"

I'd come prepared with a speech, feeling resolute, but now my head swam with anxiety. I closed my eyes and wondered how I could make her understand.

"...... I'm afraid you'll refuse me without thought."

"For heaven's sake, why should I do that?"

"...... Because my wish is out of the ordinary...... I wish to be godmother to the new baby."

"Well, you're correct—it's out of the ordinary. It's also out of the question."

I'd expected this. I knelt beside her. "...... Mother, if I have to beg, I will ... I've lost everything precious to me. What I thought to be the purpose of my life, my hope for an education, books, Thomas ... Even Father seems lost to me now ... Don't deny me this, please."

"But Sarah, the baby's godmother? Of all things. It's not some frippery. The religious welfare of the child would be in your hands. You're twelve. What would people say?"

"... I'll make *the child* the purpose of my life ... You said I must give up ambition ... Surely the love and care of a child is something you can sanction ... Please, if you love me—" Lowering my head to her lap, I cried the tears I'd not been able to cry the night of Thomas' farewell or since.

Her hand cupped the back of my head, and when I finally composed myself, I saw that her eyes were moist. "All right then. You'll be the baby's godmother, but see to it you do not fail him." I kissed her hand and slipped from the room, feeling, oddly, that I'd reclaimed a lost part of myself.

Handful

I twined red thread round the trunk of the spreading tree till every last bit had come off the spool. Mauma watched. It was all me and my idea to make us a spirit tree like her mauma had made, and I could tell she was just humoring. She clutched her elbows and blew fog with her breath. She said, "You 'bout got it? It's cold as the blue moon out here."

It was cold as Charleston could get. Sleet on the windows, blankets on the horses, Sabe and Prince chopping firewood daylight to dark. I gave mauma a look and spread my red-and-black quilt on the ground. It made a bright spot laying under the bare limbs.

I said, "First, we got to kneel on this and give our spirits to the tree. I want us to do it the way you said granny-mauma did."

She said, "Awright, let's do it then."

We dropped on our knees and stared at the tree trunk with our coat sleeves touching. The ground was hard-caked, covered with acorns, and the cold seeped through the squares and triangles. A quietness came down on us, and I closed my eyes. Inside my coat pocket, my fingertips stroked Miss Sarah's silver button. It felt like a lump of ice. I'd plucked it from the ash can after she cast it off. I felt bad she had to give up her plan, but that didn't mean you throw out a perfect good button.

Mauma shifted her knees on the quilt. She wanted to make the spirit tree quick, and I wanted to make the minutes last.

I said, "Tell it again how you and granny-mauma did it."

"Awright. What we did was get down like this on the quilt and she say, 'Now we putting our spirits in the tree so they safe from harm, so they live with the birds, learning to fly.' Then we just give our spirits to it."

"Did you feel it when it happened?"

She pulled her headscarf over her cold ears and tried to bottle up her smile. She said, "Let me see if I can remember. Yeah, I felt my spirit leave from right here." She touched the bone between her breasts. "It leave like a little draft of wind, and I look up at a branch and I don't see it, but I know my spirit's up there watching me."

She was making all this up. It didn't matter cause I didn't see why it couldn't happen that way now.

I called out, "I give my spirit to the tree."

Mauma called out the same way. Then she said, "After your granny-mauma make our spirit tree, she say, 'If you leave this place, you go get your spirit and take it with you.' Then she pick up acorns, twigs, and leaves and make pouches for 'em, and we wear 'em round our neck."

So me and mauma picked up acorns and twigs and yellow crumbles of leaves. The whole time, I thought about the day missus gave me as a present to Miss Sarah, how mauma told me, *It gon be hard from here on, Handful.*

Since that day a year past, I'd got myself a friend in Miss Sarah and found how to read and write, but it'd been a heartless road like mauma said, and I didn't know what would come of us. We might stay here the rest of our lives with the sky slammed shut, but mauma had found the part of herself that refused to bow and scrape, and once you find that, you got trouble breathing on your neck.

PART TWO

February 1811–December 1812

Sarah

Sitting before the mirror in my room, I stared at my face while Handful and six-year-old Nina wove my ponytail into braids with the aim of looping them into a circlet at the nape of my neck. Earlier I'd rubbed my face with salt and lemon-vinegar, which was Mother's formula for removing ink spots. It had lightened my freckles, but not erased them, and I reached for the powder muff to finish them off.

It was February, the height of Charleston's social season, and all week, a stream of calling cards and invitations had collected on the waiting desk beside the front door. From them Mother had chosen the most elegant and opportune affairs. Tonight, a waltzing party.

I'd entered society two years ago, at sixteen, thrust into the lavish round of balls, teas, musical salons, horseraces, and picnics, which, according to Mother, meant the dazzling doors of Charleston had flung open and female life could begin in earnest. In other words, I could take up the business of procuring a husband. How highborn and moneyed this husband turned out to be would depend entirely on the allure of my face, the delicacy of my physique, the skill of my seamstress, and the charisma of my tête-à-tête. Notwithstanding my seamstress, I arrived at the glittery entrance like a lamb to slaughter.

"Look at this mess you've gone and made," Handful said to Nina, who'd tangled the lock of hair assigned to her into what we commonly referred to as a rat's nest. Handful raked the brush through it at no small expense to my scalp, then divided the strands into three even pieces, and pronounced two of them to be rabbits and one of them a log. Nina, who'd gone into a pout at having her braid confiscated, perked up at the prospect of a game.

"Watch now," Handful told her. "This rabbit goes under the log, and this rabbit goes over the log. You make them hop like that all the way down. See, that's how you make a plait—hop over, hop under."

Nina took possession of the rabbits and the log and created a remarkably passable braid. Handful and I oohed and ahhed as if she'd carved a Florentine statue.

It was a winter evening like so many others that passed in quiet predictability: the room flushed with lamplight, a fire nesting on the grate, an early dark flattening against the windows, while my two companions fussed over me at the dresser.

My sister and godchild, Angelina—Nina for short—already bore the oval face and graceful features with which our older sister Mary had been blessed. Her eyes were brown and her hair and lashes dark as the little stone box in which I'd once kept my button. My precious Nina was strikingly beautiful. Better yet, she had a lively intellect and showed signs of being quite fearless. She believed she could do anything, a condition I took pains to foster despite the disaster that had come from my *own* fearless believing.

My aspiration to become a jurist had been laid to rest in the Graveyard of Failed Hopes, an all-female establishment. The sorrow of it had faded, but regret remained, and I'd taken to wondering if the Fates might be kinder to a *different* girl. Throughout my childhood, a framed sketch of the Three Fates had hung prominently at the top of the stairs, where they went about their business of spinning, measuring, and cutting the thread of life, all the while keeping an eye on my comings and goings. I was convinced of their personal animosity toward me, but that didn't mean they would treat my sister's thread the same way.

I'd vowed to Mother that Nina would become the purpose of my life, and so she was. In her, I had a voice that didn't stammer and a heart that was unscathed. It's true I lived a portion of my life through hers, and yes, I blurred the lines of self for both of us, but there was no one who loved Nina more than I did. She became my salvation, and I want to think I became hers.

She'd called me Mother from the time she could talk. It came naturally, and I didn't discourage it, but I did have the good sense to keep her from doing it in front of Mother. From the days Nina was in her crib, I'd proselytized her about the evils of slavery. I'd taught her everything I knew and believed, and though Mother must have had some idea I was molding her in my own image, she had no idea to what extent.

With her braid complete, Nina climbed into my lap and began her usual pleading. "Don't go! Stay with me."

"Oh, I have to, you know that. Binah will tuck you in." Nina's lip fluted out, and I added, "If you don't whine, I'll let you pick out the dress I wear."

She fairly leapt from my knees to the wardrobe, where she chose the most luxuriant costume I had, a maroon velvet gown with three satin chevrons down the front, each with an agraffe of chipped diamonds. It was Handful's own magnificent creation. At seventeen, she was a prodigy with the needle, even more so than her mother. She now sewed most of my attire.

As Handful stretched on tiptoe to retrieve the dress, I noticed how undeveloped she was—her body lithe and skinny as a boy's. She didn't reach five feet and never would. But as small as she was, it was still her eyes that drew attention. I'd once heard a friend of Thomas' refer to her as the pretty, yellow-eyed Negress.

We weren't as close as we'd been as girls. Perhaps it was due to my absorption with Nina, or to Handful's extra duties as the apprentice seamstress, or maybe we'd simply reached an age when our paths naturally began to diverge. But we *were* friends, I told myself.

As she passed the fireplace with the dress in her arms, I noticed the frown that seemed permanently etched in her features, as if by narrowing her enormous eyes she felt less of the world could reach her. It seemed she'd begun to feel the boundaries of her life more keenly, that she'd arrived at some moment of reckoning. The past week, Mother had denied her a pass to the market for some minor, forgettable reason, and she'd taken it hard. Her market excursions were the acme of her days, and trying to commiserate, I'd said, "I'm sorry, Handful, I know how you must feel."

It seemed to me I *did* know what it felt to have one's liberty curtailed, but she blazed up at me. "So we just the same, me and you? That's why you the one to shit in the pot and I'm the one to empty it?"

Her words stunned me, and I turned toward the window to hide my hurt.

I heard her breathing in fury before she fled the room, not to return the rest of the day. We hadn't spoken of it again.

She helped me now step into the gown and slide it over my corset, which I'd laced as loosely as possible. I was of average build, and didn't think it necessary to obstruct my breathing. After fastening me in, Handful pinned a black mantilla of *poult-de-soie* to the crown of my head and Nina handed me my black lace fan. Flicking it open, I swanned about the room for them.

Mother entered at the moment I pirouetted, trampling on my hemline and pitching forward—the picture of grace. "I hope you can refrain from this kind of clumsiness at Mrs. Alston's," she said.

She stood, buttressed by her cane. At forty-six, her shoulders were already rounding into an old lady's stoop. She'd been warning me of the travail of spinsterhood for a year now, elaborating on the sad, maiden life of her aunt Amelia Jane. She likened her to a shriveled flower pressed between the pages of a forgotten book, as if this might scare some poise and beauty into me. I feared that Mother was about to embark again on her aunt's desiccated existence, but she asked, "Didn't you wear this gown only two nights ago?"

"I did, but—" I looked at my baby sister perched on the dresser stool, and gave her a smile. "Nina chose it."

"It's imprudent to wear it again so soon." Mother seemed to be speaking solely to herself, and I took the opportunity to ignore her.

Her gaze fell on Angelina, her last child. She made a summoning gesture, her hand scooping at the air for several seconds before she spoke. "Come along, I will see you to the nursery."

Nina didn't move. Her eyes turned to me, as if I were the higher authority and might override the command. It was not lost on Mother. "Angelina! I said come. Now!"

If I'd been a thorn in Mother's side, Angelina would be the whole briar patch. She shook her head, as well as her shoulders. Her entire frame oscillated defiantly on the stool, and knowing very well what she was doing, she announced, "I want to stay here with Mother!"

I braced for Mother's outburst, but it didn't come. She pushed her fingers into her temples, moved them in a circle, and made a sound that was part groan, part sigh, part accusation. "I've been seized by a malicious headache," she said. "Hetty, fetch Cindie to my chamber."

With a roll of her eyes, Handful obeyed, and Mother departed after her, the dull tap of her cane receding along the corridor.

I knelt before Nina, sinking down into my skirt, which billowed out in such a way I must have appeared like a stamen in some monstrous red bloom. "How often have I told you? You mustn't call me Mother unless we're alone."

Nina's chin trembled visibly. "But you're my mother." I let her cry into the velvet of my dress. "*You* are, *you* are, *you* are."

The upstairs drawing room in Mrs. Alston's house on King Street was lit to an excessive brightness by a crystal chandelier that blazed like a small inferno from the ceiling. Beneath it, a sea of people danced the schottische, their laughter drowning out the violins.

My dance program was bare except for Thomas, who'd written in his name for two sets of the quadrille. He'd been admitted to the bar the year before and opened a practice with Mr. Langdon Cheves, a man I couldn't help but feel had taken my place, just as I'd taken Mother's. Thomas had written to me from Yale, remorseful for ridiculing my ambition on the night of his farewell, but he wouldn't budge from his position. We'd made peace, nevertheless, and in many ways he was still a demi-god to me. I looked about the room for him, knowing he would be attached to Sally Drayton, whom he was soon to marry. At their engagement party, Father had declared that a marriage between a Grimké and a Drayton would bring forth "a new Charleston dynasty." It had irked Mary, who'd entered into a suitable engagement, herself, but one without any regal connotations.

Madame Ruffin had suggested I use my fan to advantage, concealing my "strong jaw and ruddy cheeks," and I did so obsessively out of self-consciousness. Positioning the fan over the lower half of my face, I peered over its scalloped edge. I knew many of the young women from Madame Ruffin's classes, St. Philip's, or the previous social season, but I couldn't claim a friendship with any of them. They were polite enough to me, but I was never allowed into the warmth of their secrets and gossip. I think my stammer made them uneasy. That, and the awkwardness I seemed to feel in their presence. They were wearing a new style of head-turban the size of settee cushions made from heavy brocades and studded with pins, pearls, and little palettes on which the face of our new president, Mr. Madison, was painted, and their poor heads appeared to wobble on their necks. I thought they looked silly, but the beaux swarmed about them.

Night after night, I endured these grand affairs alone, revolted by what *objets d'art* we were and contemptuous of how hollow society had turned out to be, and yet inexplicably, I was filled with a yearning to be one of them.

The slaves moved among us with trays of custard and Huguenot tortes, holding doors, taking coats, stoking fires, moving without being seen, and I thought how odd it was that no one ever spoke of them, how the word *slavery* was not suitable in polite company, but referred to as *the peculiar institution*.

Turning abruptly to leave the room, I plowed headlong into a male slave carrying a crystal pitcher of Dragoon punch. It created a magnificent explosion of tea, whiskey, rum, cherries, orange slices, lemon wedges, and shards of glass. They spilled across the rug, onto the slave's frock coat, the front of my skirt, and the trousers of a tall young man who was passing by at the moment of the collision.

In those first seconds of shock, the young man held my gaze, and I reflexively lifted my hand to my chin as if to cover it with my fan, then realized I'd dropped my fan in the commotion. He smiled at me as sound rushed back into the room, gasps and thin cries of alarm. His composure calmed me, and I smiled back, noticing he had a tiny polyp of orange pulp on his cheek.

Mrs. Alston appeared in a swishing, silver-gray dress, her head bare except for a small jeweled headband across her curling bangs. With aplomb, she inquired if anyone had suffered injury. She dismissed the petrified slave with her hand and summoned another to clean the wreckage, all the while laughing softly to put everyone at ease.

Before I could make an apology, the young man spoke loudly, addressing the room. "I beg your forgiveness. I fear I am an awkward lout."

"But it was not you—" I began.

He cut me off. "The fault is completely mine."

"I insist you think no more of it," Mrs. Alston said. "Come, both of you, and we'll get you dried off." She escorted us to her own chamber and left us in the care of her maid, who dabbed at my dress with a towel. The young man waited, and without thinking, I reached out and brushed the pulp from his cheek. It was overtly forward of me, but I wouldn't consider that until later.

"We make a drowned pair," he said. "May I introduce myself? I'm Burke Williams."

"Sarah Grimké."

The only gentleman who'd ever shown interest in me was an unattractive fellow with a bulging forehead and raisin eyes. A member of the Jockey Club, he'd escorted me about the New Market Course at the culmination of Race Week last year, and afterward deposited me in the ladies' stand to watch the horses on my own. I never saw him again.

Mr. Williams took the towel and blotted his pants, then asked if I would like some air. I nodded, dazed that he'd asked. His hair was blond, mottled with brown, something like the light sands on the beach at Sullivan's Island, his eyes were greenish, his chin broad, and his cheeks faintly chiseled. I became aware of myself staring at him as we strolled toward the balcony off the drawing room, behaving like a fool of a girl, which, of course, I was. He was aware of it. I saw a smile pull about his mouth, and I silently berated myself for my transparency, for losing my precious fan, for slipping into the solitary darkness of the balcony with a stranger. *What was I doing?*

The night was cold. We stood by the railing, which had been festooned with pine wreaths, and stared at the figures moving past the windows inside the room. The music whirred behind the panes. I felt very far away from everything. The sea wind rose and I began to shiver. My stammer had been in hibernation for almost a year, but last winter it had showed up on the eve of my coming out and remained throughout my first season, turning it into a perdition. I shook now as much from fear of its return as from the frigid air.

"You're chilled," he said, removing his coat and draping it about me in gentlemanly fashion. "How is it we've not been introduced until now?"

Williams. I didn't recognize his family name. Charleston's social pyramid was ruthlessly defended by the aristocratic planters at the top—the Middletons, Pinckneys, Heywards, Draytons, Smiths, Manigaults, Russells, Alstons,

Grimkés, and so on. Below them dwelled the mercantile class, wherein a little social mobility was sometimes possible, and it occurred to me that Mr. Williams was from this secondary tier, having slipped into society through an opportune crevice, or perhaps he was a visitor to the city.

"Are you visiting here?" I asked.

"Not at all, my family's home is on Vanderhorst. But I can read your thoughts. You're trying to place my family. *Williams, Williams, wherefore art thou Williams?*" He laughed. "If you're like the others, you're worried I'm an artisan or a laborer, or worse, an *aspirer*."

I caught my breath. "Oh, I didn't mean—I'm not concerned with that sort of thing."

"It's all in jest—I can see you're not like the others. Unless, of course, you're off-put to learn my family runs the silversmith shop on Queen Street. I'll inherit it one day."

"I'm not off-put, I'm not at all," I said, then added, "I've been in your shop."

I didn't say that shopping for silver irked me no end, as did most everything I was forced to do as a wife-in-training. Oh, the days Mother had forced me to hand Nina over to Binah and sit with Mary, doing handwork samplers, hoop after hoop of white-on-white, cross stitch, and crewel, and if not handwork, then painting, and if not painting, then visitations, and if not visitations, then shopping in the somber shops of silversmiths, where my mother and sister swooned over a sterling nutmeg grater, or some such.

I'd fallen silent, uneasy with where our conversation had led, and I turned toward the garden, looking down into the faded black shadows. The pear trees were bare, their limbs spread open like the viscera of a parasol. Stretching into the darkness beyond, the single houses, double houses, and villas were lined up in cramped, neat rows which ran toward the tip of the peninsula.

"I see I've offended you," he said. "I intended to be charming, but I've been mocking instead. It's because my station is an awkward topic for me. I'm ill at ease with it."

I turned back to him, astonished that he'd been so free with his thoughts. I hadn't known a young man to display this kind of vulnerability. "I'm not offended. I'm—charmed like you said."

"I thank you, then."

"No, I should be the one to thank you. The clumsiness in the drawing room—that was mine. And you—"

"I could claim I was trying to be gallant, but in truth, I wanted to impress you. I'd been watching you. I was about to introduce myself when you whirled about and it rained punch."

I laughed, more startled than amused. Young men did not watch me.

"You created a brilliant spectacle," he was saying. "Don't you think?"

Regrettably, we were veering into the hazards of flirting. I'd always been feeble at it.

"Yes. I-I try."

"And do you create these spectacles often?" he asked.

"I try."

"You've succeeded well. The ladies on the dance floor recoiled with such shock I thought a turban might sail off and injure someone."

"Ah, but—the injury would've been laid at *your* feet, not mine. I mean, it was you who claimed responsibility for the whole thing." *Where had that come from?*

He bowed, conceding.

"We should return to the party," I told him, peeling his coat from my shoulders, wanting to end the banter on a high note, but worried, too, we might be missed.

"If you insist, but I would rather not share you. You're the loveliest lady I've met this season."

His words seemed gratuitous, and for an instant, I didn't quite trust them. But why couldn't I be lovely to him? Perhaps the Fates at the top of the stairs had changed their minds. Perhaps he'd looked past my plainness and glimpsed something deeper. Or, perhaps I was not as plain as I thought.

"May I call on you?" he asked.

"You want to call on me?"

He reached for my hand and pulled it to his lips. He kissed it, not removing his eyes from mine, pressing the heat and smoothness of his lips onto my skin. His face seemed strangely concentrated, and I felt the warmth from his mouth move up my arm into my chest.

Handful

The day mauma started sewing her story quilt, we were sitting out by the spirit tree doing handwork. We always did the trouble-free work there—hems, buttons, and trimmings, or the tiny stitches that strained your eyes in a poor-lit room. The minute the weather turned fair, we'd spread a quilt on the ground and go to town with our needles. Missus didn't like it, said the garments would get soiled. Mauma told her, "Well, I need the outdoor air to keep going, but I'll try and do without it." Right after that, mauma's quota fell off. Nobody was getting much of anything new to wear, so Missus said, "All right then, sew outside, but see to it my fabrics stay clean."

It was early in the springtime, and the tree buds were popping open while we sat there. Those days I did a lot of fretting and fraying. I was watching Miss Sarah in society, how she wore her finery and going whichever way she pleased. She was wanting to get a husband soon and leave. The world was a Wilton carpet stretched out for her, and it seemed like the doors had shut on me, and that's not even right—the doors never had opened in the first place. I was getting old enough to see they never would.

Missus was still dragging us into the dining room for devotions, preaching, "Be content with your lot, for this is of the Lord." I wanted to say, *Take your lot and put it where the sun don't shine.*

The other thing was Little Nina. She was Miss Sarah's own sister, more like a daughter to her. I loved Nina, too, you couldn't help it, but she took over Miss Sarah's heart. That was how it should be, but it left a hole in mine.

That day by the tree, me and mauma had the whole kit and comboodle of our sewing stuff lined up on the tree roots—threads, needle bags, pin cushions, shears, and a small tin of beeswax we used to grease our needles. A waxed needle would almost glide through the cloth by itself, and I got where I hated to sew without the smell of it. I had the brass thimble on my finger, finishing up a dressing table cover for missus' bedchamber, embroidering it with some scuppernong vines going round the edges. Mauma said I'd outshined her with my sewing—I didn't use a tracing wheel like her, and my darts lay perfect every time.

Back two years, when I'd turned fifteen, missus said, "I'm making you our apprentice seamstress, Hetty. You are to learn all you can and share in the work." I'd been learning from mauma since I could hold a needle, but I guess this made me official, and it spread some of the burden off mauma over to me.

Mauma had her wooden patch box beside her, plus a stack of red and brown quilt squares, fresh-cut. She rooted through the box and came up with a scrap of black cloth. I watched her cut three figures purely by eye. No hesitation, that's the trick. She pinned the shapes on a red square, and started appliquéing. She sat with her back rounded, her legs straight out, her hands moving like music against her chest.

When we'd made our spirit tree, I'd sewed a pouch for each of us out of old bed ticking. I could see hers peeking out from her dress collar, plumped with little pieces of the tree. I reached up and gave mine a pat. Beside the tree charms, mine had Miss Sarah's button inside it.

I said, "So what kind of quilt you making?"

"This a story quilt," she said, and that was the first time I heard of one. She said her mauma made one, and her mauma before her. All her kin in Africa, the Fon people, kept their history on a quilt.

I left off my embroidery and studied the figures she was sewing—a man, a woman, and a little girl between them. They were joined at the hands. "Who're they supposed to be?"

"When I get it all done, I tell you the story square by square." She grinned, showing the big space between her teeth.

After she stitched on the three people, she free-cut a tiny quilt top with black triangles and sewed it at the girl's feet. She cut out little shackles and chains for their legs, then, a host of stars that she sewed all round them. Some stars had tails of light, some lay on the ground. It was the story of the night her mauma—my granny-mauma—got sold and the stars fell.

Mauma worked in a rush, needing to get the story told, but the more she cut and stitched, the sadder her face turned. After a while her fingers slowed down and she put the quilt square away. She said, "This gon take a while, I guess." Then she picked up a half-done quilt with a flower appliqué. It was milk-white and rose-pink, something sure to sell. She worked on it lackluster. The sun guttered in the leaves over our heads, and I watched the shadows pass over her.

For the sake of some gossip, I told her, "Miss Sarah met a boy at one of her parties, and he's all she wants to talk about."

"I got somebody like that," she said.

I looked at her like her head had fallen off. I set down the embroidery hoop, and the white dresser cover flopped in the dirt. "Well, who is he, where'd you get him?"

"Next trip to the market, I take you to see him. All I gon say is: he a free black, and he one of a kind."

I didn't like she'd been keeping things from me. I snapped at her. "And you gonna marry Mr. One of a Kind Free Black?"

"No, I ain't. He already married."

Course he was.

Mauma waited through my pique, then said, "He come into some money and bought his own freedom. He cost a fortune, but his massa have a gamble debt, so he only pay five hundred dollars for hisself. And he still have money after that to buy a house at 20 Bull Street. It sit three blocks from where the governor live."

"How'd he get all this money?"

"Won it in the East Bay Street lottery."

I laughed out loud. "*That's* what he told you? Well, I reckon this is the luckiest slave that ever lived."

"It happen ten years ago, everybody know 'bout it. He buy a ticket, and his number come up. It happen."

The lottery office was down the street from the market, near the docks. I'd passed it myself when mauma took me out to learn the shopping. There was always a mish-mash of people getting tickets: ship captains, City Guard, white laborers, free blacks, slaves, mulattoes, and creoles. There'd be two, three men in silk cravats with their carriages waiting.

I said, "How come *you* don't buy a ticket?"

"And waste a coin on some fancy chance?"

For the last five years, every lick of strength mauma had left from sewing for missus had gone toward her dollar bill collection. She'd been hired out steady since I was eleven, but it wasn't on the sly anymore, and thank you kind Jesus for that. Her counterfeit badge and all that sneaking out she'd done for the better part of a year had put white hair on my head. I used to pull it out and show it to her. I'd say, "Look what you're doing to me." She'd say, "Here I is, saving up to buy us freedom and you worrying 'bout hair."

When I was thirteen, missus had finally given in and let mauma hire out. I don't know why. Maybe she got tired of saying the word *no*. Maybe it was the money she wanted—mauma could put a hundred dollars a year in missus' pocket—but I know this much, it didn't hurt when mauma made missus a patchwork quilt for Christmas that year. It had a square for each of her children made from some remnant of theirs. Mauma told her, "I know this ain't nothing much, but I sewed you a memory quilt of your family so you can wrap up in it after they gone." Missus touched each square: "Why, this is from the dress Mary wore to her coming out . . . This is Charles' baptism blanket . . . My goodness, this is Thomas' first riding shirt."

Mauma didn't waste a breath. She asked missus right then to hire her out. A month later she was hired legal to sew for a woman on Tradd Street. Mauma kept twenty cents on the dollar. The rest went to missus, but I knew mauma was selling underhand on the side—frilled bonnets, quilt tops, candlewick bedcovers, all sorts of wears that didn't call for a fitting.

She had me count the money regular. It came to a hundred ninety dollars. I hated to tell her her money-pile could hit the roof, but that didn't mean missus would sell us, specially to ourselves.

Thinking about all this, I said, "We sew too good for missus to let us go."

"Well if she refuse us, then our sewing gon get real bad, real fast."

"What makes you think she wouldn't sell us to somebody else for spite?"

Mauma stopped working and the fight seemed to almost leave her. She looked tired. "It's a chance we has to take, or else we gon end up like Snow."

Poor Snow, he'd died one night last summer. Fell over in the privy. Aunt-Sister tied his jaw to keep his spirit from leaving, and he was laid out on a cooling board in the kitchen house for two days before they put him in a burial box. The man had spent his whole life carrying the Grimkés round town. Sabe took his place as the coachman and they brought some new boy from their plantation to be the footman. His name was Goodis, and he had one lazy eye that looked sideways. He watched me so much with that eye mauma'd said, "That boy got his heart fix on you."

"I don't want him fixing his heart on me."

"That's good," she'd said. "I can't buy nobody's freedom but mine and yours. You get a husband, and he on his own."

I tied off a knot and moved the embroider hoop over, saying to myself, *I don't want a husband and don't plan on ending up like Snow on a cooling board in the kitchen house either.*

"How much will it take to buy the both of us?" I asked.

Mauma rammed the needle in the cloth. She said, "That's what you gon find out."

Sarah

I'd never been inclined to keep a diary until I met Burke Williams. I thought by writing down my feelings, I would seize control over them, perhaps even curb what Reverend Hall called "the paroxysms of carnality."

For what it's worth, charting one's passion in a small daybook kept hidden in a hatbox inside a wardrobe does not subdue passion in the least.

> *20 February 1811*
> *I had imagined romantic love to be a condition of sweet utopia, not an affliction! To think, a few weeks ago, I thought my starved mind would be my worst hardship. Now my heart has its own ordeal. Mr. Williams, you torment me. It's as if I've contracted a tropical fever. I cannot say whether I wish to be cured.*

My diary overflowed with this sort of purple outburst.

> *3 March*
> *Mr. Williams, why do you not call? It's unfair that I must wait for you to act. Why must I, as a female, be at your disposal? Why can't I send a calling note to you? Who made up these unjust rules? Men, that's who. God devised women to be the minions. Well, I quite resent it!*

> *9 March*
> *A month has passed, and I see now what transpired between Mr. Williams and my naïve self on the balcony was a farce.*

He has toyed with me shamelessly. I knew it even then! He is a fickle-hearted cad, and I would no sooner speak to him now than I would speak to the devil.

When I was not engaged in aerating my feelings, or caring for little Nina, or fending off Mother's attempts to draw me into my dutiful female tasks, I was foraging among the invitations and calling cards left on the desk by the front door. When Nina napped in the afternoon, I had Handful wheel the copper bathtub into my room and fill it with buckets of blistering water from the laundry.

This copper tub was a modern wonder imported from France by way of Virginia, and it was the talk of Charleston. It sat on noisy little wheels and traveled room to room like a portable dipping cart. You *sat* in it. You did not stand over a basin and pat water on yourself—no, you were quite immersed! To top it off, one side of the tub possessed a vent that could be opened to release the used water. Mother instructed the slaves to trundle the tub onto the piazza near the rail and discharge the bathwater over the side. The waterfalls splattering into the garden alerted neighbors the hygienic Grimkés had been bathing again.

When a note with scratchy penmanship arrived at the house shortly before noon on the ides of March, I swooped upon it before Mother.

15 March
Burke Williams compliments Sarah Grimké, requesting the
pleasure of her company tomorrow night. If he can serve her in
any way in the meantime, he would be honored.
        P.S. Please excuse the borrowed paper.

I stood still for several moments, then placed the note back on the pile, thinking, *Why should anyone care if the paper is borrowed,* and then the stupefaction wore off. Caught in a sudden swell of elation, I ascended the stairs to my room, where I danced about like some tipsy bird. I'd forgotten Handful and Nina were there. They'd spread the doll tea set on the floor beneath the window, and when I turned, I saw them staring at me, holding tiny cups of pretend-tea in the air.

"You must've heard from that boy," Handful said. She was the only one who knew of his existence.

"What boy?" Nina asked, and I was forced to tell her about Mr. Williams, too. At this moment Mother would be dispatching an acceptance while singing Glory be to God in the Highest. She would be so jubilant with allelujahs, it would not occur to her to wonder at his credentials.

"Will you get married like Thomas?" Nina asked. His wedding was two and a half months away and a reference point for everything.

"I do believe I will," I told her, and the idea seemed altogether plausible. I would not be a pressed flower in a book after all.

We'd expected Mr. Williams at 8:00 P.M., but at ten past, he was still absent. Mother's neck was splotched red with patches of insult, and Father, who'd joined Mother and me in the drawing room, held his watch in his hand. The three of us sat as if waiting for a funeral procession to pass. I feared he wouldn't appear at all, and if he did, that our visit would be cut short. By custom, the slave's curfew—9:00 in the winter, 10:00 in the summer—cleared gentlemen callers from the drawing rooms. When the City Guard beat drums to summon the slaves off the streets, the suitors would rise on cue.

He rapped on the front door at a quarter past the appointed hour. When Tomfry ushered him into the room, I lifted my fan—an extravagant nosegay of hen feathers—and my parents rose with cool civility and offered him the Duncan Phyfe chair that flanked the right side of the fireplace. I'd been relegated to the chair on the left, which meant we were separated by the fire screen and forced to crane our necks for a glimpse of one another. A pity—he looked more handsome than I remembered. His face had bronzed with sun and his hair was longer, curling behind his ears. Detecting the scent of lime-soap drifting from his direction, my insides convulsed involuntarily—a full-blown paroxysm of carnality.

After the excuses and the trivialities, Father got right to the point. "Tell us, Mr. Williams, what is it that your father does?"

"Sir, my father owns the silver shop on Queen Street. It was founded by my great-grandfather and is the largest silver shop in the South."

He spoke with unconcealed pride, but the stiff silence that had preceded his arrival descended again. A Grimké daughter would marry a son of the planter class who would study law, medicine, religion, or architecture in order to occupy himself until he inherited.

"A shop, you say?" Mother asked, giving herself time to absorb the blow.

"That's correct, madame."

She turned to Father. "A silver shop, John."

Father nodded, and I read his thought: *Merchant*. It rose in the air above his forehead like a dark condensation.

"We've frequented the shop often," I said, beaming as if those occasions had been the highlight of my life.

Mother came to my aid. "Indeed we have. It's a lovely shop, John."

Mr. Williams slid forward in his chair and addressed Father. "Sir, my grandfather's wish was to provide our city with a silver shop that would live up to the one your own grandfather, John Paul Grimké, owned. I believe it was on the corner of Queen and Meeting, wasn't it? My grandfather thought him to be the greatest silversmith in the country, greater than Mr. Revere."

Oh, the adroitness of this man! I twisted in my chair the better to see him. In the guise of a compliment, he'd let it be known he was not the only one in the room descended from the merchant class. Of course, the difference was that John Paul Grimké had parlayed the success of his shop into cotton ventures and large land holdings in the low country. He'd been ambitious and prudent, and toiled his way into Charleston aristocracy. Nevertheless, Mr. Williams had landed his punch.

Father eyed him steadily and spoke two words. "I see."

I think he did see, too. In that moment, he saw Mr. Williams quite well.

Tomfry served Hyson tea and biscuits, and the conversation turned back to trivialities, an interlude cut short when the curfew drums began. Mr.

Williams rose, and I felt a sudden deflation. To my wonder, Mother entreated him to visit again, and I saw one of Father's luxuriant eyebrows lift.

"May I see him to the door?" I asked.

"Of course, dear, but Tomfry will accompany you."

We trailed Tomfry from the room, but once past the door, Mr. Williams stopped and placed his hand on my arm. "You look enchanting," he whispered, drawing his face close to mine. "It would ease my regret in leaving, if you favored me with a lock of your hair."

"My hair?"

"As a token of your affection."

I lifted the hen feathers to cover the heat in my face.

He pressed a white handkerchief into my hand. "Fold the lock inside my kerchief, then toss it over the fence to George Street. I'll be there, waiting." With that titillating directive, he gave me a grin, *such* a grin, and strode toward the door, where Tomfry waited uncomfortably.

Returning to the drawing room to face my parents' evaluations, I halted outside the door, realizing they were speaking about me.

"John, we must face reason. He may be her only chance."

"You think our daughter so poor a marriage prospect she can draw no better than *that*?"

"His family is not poor. They are reasonably well-to-do."

"But Mary, it is a mercantile family."

"The man is a suitor, and he is likely the best she can do."

I fled to my room, chagrined, but too preoccupied with my clandestine mission to be wounded. Having lit the lamps and turned down the bed, Handful was bent over my desk, frowning and picking her way through the poem *Leonidas,* which was an almost unreadable ode to men and their wars. As always, she wore a pouch about her neck filled with bark, leaves, acorns, and other gleanings from the oak in the work yard.

"Quickly," I blurted. "Take the shears from my dresser and cut off a lock of my hair."

She squinted at me without moving a muscle. "Why do you wanna do something like that?"

"Just do it!" I was a wreck of impatience, but seeing how my tone miffed her, I explained the reason.

She cut a whorl as long as my finger and watched me secret it inside the handkerchief. She followed me downstairs to the ornamental garden where I glimpsed him through the palisade fence, a shadowed figure, leaning against the stuccoed brick wall of the Dupré house across the street.

"That him?" Handful asked.

I shushed her, afraid he would hear, and then I flung the amorous bundle over the fence. It landed in the crushed shell that powdered the street.

The next day Father announced we would depart immediately for Belmont. Because of Thomas' upcoming nuptials, it'd previously been decided Father would journey to the upcountry plantation alone this spring, and now suddenly the entire family was thrown into a frenzied mass exodus. Did he think no one understood it had everything to do with the unsuitable son of a silversmith?

I penned a hurried letter, which I left for Tomfry to post.

> *17 March*
>
> *Dear Mr. Williams,*
>
> *I am sorry to inform you that my family will leave Charleston in the morning. I will not return until the middle of May. Leaving in such an impromptu manner prevents me saying farewell in person, which I much regret. I hope I might welcome you again to our home on East Bay as soon as I return to civilization. I trust you found your handkerchief and its contents, and keep them close.*
>
> *With Affectionate Regards, I am*
> *Sarah Grimké*

The seven weeks of my separation from Mr. Williams were a cruel agony. I busied myself with the establishment of a slave infirmary on the plantation, installing it in a corner of the weaving house. It had once been a sickbay, years before, but had fallen into dereliction, and Peggy, the slave who did the weaving, had taken to storing her carded wool on the infirmary's old cot. Nina helped me scrub the corner and assemble an apothecary of medicine, salves, and herbs that I begged or blended myself in the kitchen house. It didn't take long for the sick and ailing to show up, so many the overseer complained to Father that my healing enterprise interfered with field production. I expected Father to shut our doors, but he left me to it, though not without instructing me on the numberless ways the slaves would abuse my efforts.

It was Mother who nearly ended the operation. Upon discovering I'd spent the night in the infirmary in order to care for a fifteen-year-old with childbirth fever, she shut the infirmary for two days, before finally relenting. "Your behavior is woefully intemperate," she said, and then treading too closely to the truth, added, "I suspect it's not compassion that drives you as much as the need to distract your mind from Mr. Williams."

My afternoons were frittered away with needlework and teas or painting landscapes with Mary while Nina played at my feet, all of which took place in a stuffy parlor with poorly lit windows draped in velvet swags the color of Father's port. My one respite was striking out alone on a high-spirited black stallion named Hiram. The horse had been given to me when I was fourteen, and since he didn't fall into the category of slave, slave owner, or handsome beau, I was left to love him without complication. Whenever I could steal away from the parlor, Hiram and I galloped at splendiferous speeds into a landscape erupting with the same intractable wildness I felt inside. The skies were bright cerulean, teeming with ferocious winds, spilling mallards and fat wood drakes from the clouds. Up and down the lanes, the fences were lit with yellow jasmine, its musk a sweet, choking smoke. I rode with the same drunk sensuality with which I had reclined in the copper tub, riding till the light smeared, returning with the falling dark.

Mother allowed me to write to Mr. Williams only once. Anything more, she insisted was *woefully intemperate*. I received no letter in return. Mary heard nothing from her intended either and claimed the mail to be atrocious, therefore I didn't overly fret, but quietly and daily I wondered whether Mr. W.

and his grin would be there when I returned. I placed my hope in the bewitching properties contained in the lock of my red hair. This wasn't so different than Handful placing her faith in the bark and acorns she wore around her neck, but I wouldn't have admitted it.

I'd thought little of Handful during my incarceration at Belmont, but on the day before we left, the fifteen-year-old slave I'd nursed appeared, cured of childbirth fever, but now with boils on her neck. Seeing her, I understood suddenly that it wasn't only miles that separated Handful and me. It wasn't any of those things I'd told myself, not my preoccupation with Nina, or Handful's duties, or the natural course of age. It was some other growing gulf, one that had been there long before I'd left.

Handful

Late in the afternoon, after the Grimkés had gone off to their plantation and the few slaves left on the premise were in their quarters, mauma sent me into master Grimké's library to find out what me and her would sell for. She stood lookout for Tomfry. I told her, don't worry about Tomfry, the one you have to watch for is Lucy, Miss Come-Look-at-the-Writing-Under-the-Tree.

A man had come last winter and written down everything master Grimké owned and what it was worth. Mauma had been there while he wrote down the lacquer sewing table, the quilt frame, and every one of her sewing tools in a brown leather book he'd tied with a cord. She said, "If we in that book, then it say what our price is. That book got to be in the library somewhere."

This seemed like a tolerable idea till I closed the door behind me, then it seemed like a damn fool one. Master Grimké had books in there the likes you wouldn't believe, and half of them were brown leather. I opened drawers and rummaged the shelves till I found one with a cord. I sat at the desk and opened it up.

After I got caught for the crime of reading, Miss Sarah stopped teaching me, but she set out books of poems—that was all she got to read now—and she'd say, "It doesn't take long to read a poem. Just close the door, and if there's a word you can't make out, point to it, and I'll whisper it to you." I'd learned a legion of words this way, *legion* being one of them. Some words I learned couldn't be worked into a conversation: *heigh-ho; O hither; alas; blithe and bonny; Jove's nectar*. But I held on to them just the same.

The words inside the leather book weren't fit for poems. The man's writing looked like scribble. I had to crack every word one by one and pick out the sound the way we cracked blue crabs in the fall and picked out the meat till our fingers bled. The words came lumps at a time.

City of Charleston, to wit . . . We the undersigned . . . To the best of our judgment, . . . the personal inventory . . . Goods and chattels . . .

2 Mahogany card tables . . . 20.50.
General Washington picture and address . . . 30.
2 Brussels carpets & cover . . . 180.
Harpsichord . . . 29.

I heard footsteps in the passage. Mauma said she'd sing if I needed to hit out for cover, but I didn't hear anything and went back to running my finger down the list. It went for thirty-six pages. Silk this and ivory that. Gold this, silver that. But no Hetty and no Charlotte Grimké.

Then I turned the last page and there were all us slaves, right after the water trough, the wheelbarrow, the claw hammer, and the bushel of flint corn.

Tomfry, 51 yrs. Butler, Gentleman's Servant . . . 600.
Aunt-Sister, 48 yrs. Cook . . . 450.
Charlotte, 36 yrs. Seamstress . . . 550.

I read it two times—Charlotte, my mauma, her age, what she did, what she sells for—and I felt the pride of a confused girl, pride mauma was worth so much, more than Aunt-Sister.

Binah, 41 yrs. Nursery Servant . . . 425.
Cindie, 45 yrs. Lady's Maid . . . 400.
Sabe, 29 yrs. Coachman, House Servant . . . 600.
Eli, 50 yrs. House Servant . . . 550.
Mariah, 34 yrs. Plain Washer, Ironer, Clear Starcher . . . 400.

Lucy, 20 yrs. Lady's Maid . . . 400.
Hetty, 16 yrs. Lady's Maid, Seamstress . . . 500.

My breath hung high in my chest. *Five hundred dollars!* I ran my finger over the figure, over the dregs of dried ink. I marveled how they'd left off *apprentice,* how it said seamstress full and clear, how I was worth more than every female slave they had, beside mauma. *Five hundred dollars.* I was good on figures and I added me and mauma together. We were a thousand fifty dollars' worth of slaves. I was blinkered like a horse and I smiled like this made us somebody and read on to see what the rest were valued.

Phoebe, 17 yrs. Kitchen Servant . . . 400.
Prince, 26 yrs. Yard Servant . . . 500.
Goodis, 21 yrs. Footman, Stable Mucker, Yard Servant . . . 500.
Rosetta, 73 yrs. Useless . . . 1.

I put the book back, then went out and told mauma what I found out. A thousand fifty dollars. She sank on the bottom step of the stairs and held on to the bannister. She said, "How I gon raise all that much money?"

It would take ten years to come up with that much. "I don't know," I told her. "Some things can't be done—that's all."

She got up and headed for the basement, talking with her back to me. "Don't be telling me—*can't be done.* That's some god damney white talk, that's what that is."

I lugged myself up the stairs and went straight for the alcove. Next to the tree out back, this was my chosen spot, up here where I could see the water. With the house empty, I was the only one upstairs, and I stayed by the window till all the light bled from the sky and the water turned black. *Cross the water, cross the sea, let them fishes carry me.* The songs I used to sing back when I first belonged to Miss Sarah still came to me, but I didn't feel like the water would take me much of anywhere.

I said under my breath, *Five hundred dollars.*

Goods and chattel. The words from the leather book came into my head. We were like the gold leaf mirror and the horse saddle. Not full-fledge people. I didn't believe this, never had believed it a day of my life, but if you listen to white folks long enough, some sad, beat-down part of you starts to wonder. All that pride about what we were worth left me then. For the first time, I felt the hurt and shame of just being who I was.

After a while, I went down to the cellar. When mauma saw my raw eyes, she said, "Ain't nobody can write down in a book what you worth."

Sarah

Our caravan of two carriages, two wagons, and seventeen people returned to Charleston in May on the high crest of spring. Rains had left the city rinsed and clean, scented with newly flowering myrtle, privet, and Chinese tallow. The bougainvillea had advanced en masse over garden gates, and the sky was bright and creamed with thin, swirling clouds. I felt exultant to be back.

As we lumbered through the back gate into an empty work yard, Tomfry hurried from the kitchen house at an old man's trot, calling, "Massa, you back early." He had a napkin stuffed at his collar and looked anxious, as if we'd caught him in the dilatory act of eating.

"Only by a day," Father said, climbing from the Barouche. "You should let the others know we're here."

I squirmed past everyone, leaving even Nina behind, and broke for the house where I pillaged the calling cards on the desk, and there it was—the borrowed paper.

3 May

Burke Williams requests Sarah Grimké's company on a (chaperoned) horseback outing at Sullivan's Island, upon her return to Charleston.
Yours, most truly.

I let out an exhale, behemoth in nature, and ascended the stairs.

I remember very clearly coming to a full halt on the second-floor landing and gazing curiously at the door to my room. It alone was shut, while the others stood open. I walked toward it uncertainly, with a vague sense of portent. I paused with my hand over the knob for a second and cocked my ear. Hearing nothing, I turned the knob. It was locked.

I gave the knob a second determined try, and then a third and fourth, and that's when I heard the tentative voice inside.

"That you, mauma?"

Handful? The thought of her inside my room with the door locked was so incongruent I could not immediately answer back.

She called out, "Coming." Her voice sounded exasperated, reluctant, breathy. There was the sound of water splashing, a key thrust into the lock. *Click. Click.*

She stood in the doorway dripping wet, naked but for a white linen towel clutched around her waist. Her breasts were two small, purple plums protruding from her chest. I couldn't help gazing at her wet, black skin, the small compact power of her torso. She'd unloosed her braids, and her hair was a wild corona around her head, shimmering with beaded water.

She stepped backward and her mouth parted. Behind her, the wondrous copper tub sat in the middle of the room, filled with water. Vapor was lifting off the surface, turning the air rheumy. The audacity of what she'd done took my breath. If Mother discovered this, the consequences would be swift and dire.

I moved quickly inside and closed the door, my instinct even now to protect her. She made no attempt to cover herself. I glimpsed defiance in her eyes, in the way she wrested back her chin as if to say, *Yes, it's me, bathing in your precious tub.*

The silence was terrible. If she thought my reserve was due to anger, she was right. I wanted to shake her. Her boldness seemed like more than a frolic in the tub, it seemed like an act of rebellion, of usurpation. What had possessed her? She'd violated not only the privacy of my room and the intimacy of our tub, she'd breached my trust.

I didn't recognize how my mother's voice ranted inside me.

Handful started to speak, and I was terrified of what she would say, fearful it would be hateful and justifying, yet oddly, I feared an expression of shame and apology just as much. I stopped her. "Please. Don't say anything. At least do that for me, say nothing."

I turned my back while she dried herself and pulled on her dress. When I looked again, she was tying a kerchief around her hair. It was pale green, the same color as the tiny discolored patches on the copper. She bent to mop the puddles from the floor, and I saw the scarf darkening as it soaked the dampness.

She said, "You want me to empty the water out now or wait?"

"Let's do it now. We can't have Mother wander in and find it."

With effort, I helped her roll the sloshing tub through the jib door onto the piazza, close to the rail, hoping the family was inside now and wouldn't hear the gush of water. Handful yanked open the vent and it spilled in a long, silver beak over the side. I seemed to taste it in my mouth, the tang of minerals.

"I know you're angry, Sarah, but I didn't see any harm with me being in the tub, same as you."

Not *Miss* Sarah, but Sarah. I would never again hear her put Miss before my name.

She had the look of someone who'd declared herself, and seeing it, my indignation collapsed and her mutinous bath turned into something else entirely. She'd immersed herself in forbidden privileges, yes, but mostly in the belief she was worthy of those privileges. What she'd done was not a revolt, it was a baptism.

I saw then what I hadn't seen before, that I was very good at despising slavery in the abstract, in the removed and anonymous masses, but in the concrete, intimate flesh of the girl beside me, I'd lost the ability to be repulsed by it. I'd grown comfortable with the particulars of evil. There's a frightful muteness that dwells at the center of all unspeakable things, and I had found my way into it.

As Handful began to shove the vessel back across the piazza, I tried to speak. "...... Wait...... I'll...... help..."

She turned and looked at me, and we both knew. My tongue would once again attempt its suicide.

Handful

Missus sent me and mauma to the market for some good cotton to make a dress for Nina. She was growing out from everything. Missus said, get something pastel this time and see about some homespun for Tomfry and them to have new vests.

The market was a row of stalls that ran all the way from East Bay to Meeting and had whatever under the sun you wanted. Missus said the place was a vulgar bazaar, that was her words. The turkey buzzards wandered round the meat stands like regular customers. They had to keep a man in there with a palm branch to shoo them. Course, they flew to the roofs and waited him out, then came on back. The smells in there would knock you down. Ox tails, bullock hearts, raw pork, live chickens, cracked oysters, blue crabs, fish, and more fish. The sweet peanut cakes didn't stand a chance. I used to go round holding my nose till mauma got some eucalyptus leaves to rub over my top lip.

The slave sellers, what they called higglers, were shouting their wares, trying to out-do each other. The men sang out, "Jimmie" (that's what we called the male crabs), and the women sang back, "Sook" (those were the females). "Jimmieeee . . . Soooook . . . Jimmieeee . . . Soooook." You needed something for your nose *and* your ears.

It was September, and I still hadn't laid eyes on the man mauma had told me about, the lucky free black who won the money to buy his freedom. He had a carpenter shop out back of his house, and I knew every time she was let out for hire or sent to the market without me, she was dallying with him. One, two times a week, she came back smelling like wood shavings, the back of her dress saw-dusted.

That day, when we got to the piece good stalls, I started saying how he was made-up. "Awright then," mauma said. She grabbed up the first pastel she saw and some drab brown wool and we headed outside with our baskets loaded. A block down, they were selling slaves right on the street, so we crossed the other way toward King. I patted the pass inside my dress pocket three times and checked to see did mauma still have her badge fastened on her dress. Out in the streets, I always had the bad feeling of something coming, some meanness gathering. On Coming Street, we spotted a guard, couldn't have been old as me, stop an old man who got so nervous he dropped his travel pass. The guard stepped on it, having his fun.

We walked in a hurry, outpacing the carriages. Mauma didn't use her wooden cane anymore except special occasions. Those came along when she needed a letup from missus. She'd tell her, "Looks like the cure I prayed for my leg has worn off. I just need to rest up and pray for a few days." Out came the cane.

Mauma's free black man lived at 20 Bull. It was a white frame single house, had black shudders with the paint flecking off and scruffy bushes round the porch. She shook the powder shell from the street off her hemline and said, "If I stand here, he see me and come right out."

"So we're supposed to stand here till he looks out the window?"

"You want me to go up there and knock on the door? If his wife come, you want me to say, 'Tell your husband his girlfriend out here?'"

"How come you're fooling with somebody who has a wife anyway?"

"They not married legal, she his free-wife. He got two more of 'em, too. All mulatto."

As she said the word, *mulatto,* he stepped from the house and stood on the porch looking at us. A bull of a man. I wanted to say, *Well he sure does live on the right street*. He was thickset and solid with a big chest and large forehead.

When he came over, mauma said to him, "This my girl, Handful."

He nodded. I could see he was stern, and proud. He said, "I'm Denmark Vesey."

Mauma sidled up to him and said for my benefit, "Denmark is a country next to France, and a real fine one, too." She smiled at him in a way I had to look away from.

He slid his hand up the side of her arm, and I eased off down the street. If they wanted to carry on, all right, but I didn't have to stand there and watch it.

In the coming year, we'd make this visit to 20 Bull more times than I care to tell. The two lovebirds would go in his workshop, and I'd sit outside and wait. After they were done, he'd come out and talk. And he could talk, Lord, could that man talk. Denmark the man never had been to Denmark the country, just the Danish Islands. To hear him tell it, though, he'd been everywhere else. He'd traveled the world with his owner Captain Vesey, who sailed a slave ship. He spoke French, Danish, Creole, Gullah, and the King's English. I heard him speak every one of these tongues. He came from the Land of Barbados and liked to say Charleston didn't trust slaves from there, cause they'd slit your throat. He said Charleston wanted saltwater blacks from Africa who knew rice planting.

The worst troubling thing he told me was how his neighbor down the street—a free black named Mr. Robert Smyth—owned three slaves. Now what you supposed to do with something like that? Mr. Vesey had to take me to the man's house to meet the slaves before I allowed any truth to it. I didn't know whether this Mr. Smyth was behaving like white people, or if it just showed something vile about all people.

Denmark Vesey read the Bible up and down. Give him five minutes and he'd tell you the story of Moses leading slaves from Egypt. He'd have the sea parting, frogs falling from the sky, firstborn baby boys stabbed in their beds. He mouthed a Bible verse from Joshua so many times, it still comes to me in full. *They utterly destroyed all that were in the city, both man and woman, both young and old.* The man was head-smart and reckless. He scared the wits out of me.

The two of us had a clash the first day we met. Like I said, I'd eased off down the street to let them know I didn't have a need to see their urges. The street was busy, everybody from free blacks to the mayor and the governor lived on it, and when a white woman came along, walking in my path, I did the common thing you do—I stepped to the side to let her pass. It was the law, you were supposed to give way on the street, but here came Denmark Vesey charging down to where I stood with fury blowing from his nostrils, and mauma looking panic right behind him. He yanked me by the arm, yelled, "Is this the sort of person you want to be? The kind that steps aside? The kind that grovels in the street?"

I wanted to say, *Get your hand off me, you don't know nothing about me, I bathe in a copper tub, and you're standing here and stink to heaven.* The air round my head turned thick and my throat tightened on it. I managed to say, "Let me go."

Behind him, mauma said, a little too sweet for my taste, "Take your hand off her."

He dropped his grip. "Don't let me see that from you again." Then he smiled. And mauma, she smiled, too.

We walked home without a word between us.

Inside the Grimké house, the door to the library was open. The room was empty, so I went in and spun the globe. It made a screech sound. Like a nail on a slate board. Binah said that sound was the devil's toenail. I looked over all the countries on the globe, round the whole earth. Denmark wasn't next to France, it was up by Prussia, but looking at it, I knew why mauma chose him. He'd been places, and he was going places, and he set her alight with the notion she'd go places, too.

Sarah

Nina came up with the idea that my speech infirmity might be cured by kneading my tongue, a process typically applied to dough. The child was nothing if not pioneering. She'd listened to my tortured sentences throughout the summer and into the fall and came to believe the ornery protuberance in my mouth could be molded in a way that caused words to plump and rise as effortless as yeast. She was six and a half.

Once Nina was seduced by a problem, she wouldn't give up until she'd improvised a solution and acted on it, and these solutions of hers could be outlandish, but also wondrously imaginative. Not wishing to dampen this fascinating proclivity of hers, I stuck out my tongue and allowed her to grasp it with what I hoped to be a clean drying towel.

This experiment was being performed on the second-floor piazza—me, sitting on the swing, neck craned, mouth open, eyes bulging—the vision of a voracious baby bird awaiting her worm, though to any observer, I'm sure it appeared the worm was being extracted rather than deposited.

An autumn sun was climbing over the harbor, spilling like yolk onto the clouds. From the corner of my watering eye, I could see the sheen of it angling sharply toward Sullivan's Island. Mr. Williams and I had cantered along that island's shoreline on horseback in what had turned out to be a sullen affair. Fearing my freshly returned stammer would cause him to abandon the courtship, I'd barely opened my mouth. Nevertheless, he'd continued to call—there'd been five occasions since I'd returned from Belmont last May. I expected each one to be the last. The boundary of feeling between Nina and me was permeable to a fault, and I believe my fear had become Nina's. She seemed uncommonly determined to cure me.

Grasping my tongue, she pressed and pulled. In return, it flailed like the tentacle of an octopus.

She sighed. "Your tongue is being implacable."

Implacable! Where did the little genius get these words? I was teaching her to read, as I'd once taught Handful, but I was sure I'd never introduced the word *implacable*.

"And you are holding your breath," she added. "Let it out. Try to loosen yourself."

Very bossy she was, too. Already she possessed more authority and self-assurance than I. "... I'll try," I said, though perhaps what really happened was an accidental not-trying. I closed my eyes and breathed, and in my mind, I saw the bright water in the harbor and then the image of Handful's bathwater streaming over the side of the piazza like a falling ribbon, and I felt my tongue unknot and grow tranquil beneath Nina's fingers.

I don't know how long she persisted with her efforts. I quite lost myself in the flow of water. Finally she said, "Repeat after me: *Wicked Willy Wiggle*."

"Wicked Willy Wiggle," I said, without a trace of stutter.

This odd interlude on the piazza brought me not a cure, but the nearest thing to a cure I would ever find, and it had nothing to do with Nina's fanciful tongue kneading. It had somehow to do with breathing and repose and the vision of water.

So it would be from now on—whenever my stints of stammering came, I would close my eyes and breathe and watch Handful's bathwater. I would see it pouring down and down, and opening my eyes, I would often speak with ease, sometimes for hours.

In November my nineteenth birthday came and went without acknowledgement except Mother's reminder at breakfast that I'd reached a prime marriageable age. There were weekly dress fittings in preparation for the winter season, providing practically the only contact I had with Handful. She spent her days sewing in Charlotte's room in the cellar or beneath the oak when the weather was mild. Her forbidden bath all those months ago still hung leaden between us, though Handful didn't seem the least bit shamed by my discovery of it. Rather the opposite, she was like someone who'd risen to her full measure. During the fittings, Handful sang as she pinned me into half-made dresses. Standing on the fitting box, turning slow rotations, I wondered if she sang to avoid conversation. Whatever motivated her, I was relieved.

Then, one day in January, I noticed my father and older brothers huddled in the library with the door agape. The first icing of the winter had come in the night and glazed the city, and Tomfry had set the fireplaces ablaze. From where I stood in the main passage, I could see Father rubbing his hands before the flames, while Thomas, John, and Frederick gestured and flitted like moths in the light around his shoulders. Frederick, who'd recently returned from Yale and followed Thomas to the bar, slammed his fist into the palm of his hand. "How dare they, how *dare* they!"

"We'll mount a defense," Thomas said. "You mustn't worry, Father, we won't be defeated, I promise you that."

Someone had wronged Father? I drew as close to the door as I dared, but I could make little sense of the discussion. They spoke of an outrage, but didn't name it. They vowed a defense, but against what? Through the gap in the door, I watched them move to the desk, where they closed ranks around a document. They pointed at various passages, jabbing it with their fingers, debating in low, purposeful tones. The sight of them roused my ravenous old hunger to take my place in the world, too, to have my part matter. How many years had elapsed since I threw away the silver button?

I moved from the door, suddenly flush with anger. I was sorry for Father. He'd been wronged in some way, but here they all were ready to move heaven and earth to right it, and their wives, their mother, their sisters had no rights, not even to their own children. We couldn't vote or testify in a court, or make a will—of course we couldn't, we owned nothing to leave behind! Why didn't the Grimké men assemble in *our* defense?

My anger dissipated, but my ignorance went on for another week. During those interminable days, Mother stayed in her chamber with a headache and even Thomas refused my queries, saying it was Father's matter to disclose, not his. As it turned out, I would learn the news at a parlor concert held at one of the plantations northwest of the city.

Mary and I arrived on the plantation as the afternoon turned gray with twilight, our carriage met by a bevy of peacocks that strolled about the grounds for no reason other than ornamentation. They created a beautiful blue shimmer in the fading light, but I found them a sad spectacle, the way they made little rushes at the air, going nowhere.

The concert was already under way when I reached the parlor door. Burke slipped from his seat and greeted me with unusual warmth. He looked dashing in his long cerise vest and silk suit. "I was worried you weren't coming," he whispered and led me quickly to the empty chair beside his. As I slipped off the emerald jacket that Handful had so wondrously crafted, he placed a letter upon my lap. I raised my brows to him as if to ask whether I should break the seal and read it while Miss Parodi and the harpsichord vied for the room. "Later," he mouthed.

It was unconventional to pass a note in this manner, and my mind fretted throughout the program at what it might contain. When Mrs. Drayton, Thomas' mother-in-law, played the final piece on the harp, we adjourned to the dining room where the table was spread with a Charlotte Russe dessert and a selection of French wines, brandy, and Madeira, of which I couldn't partake for all my apprehension. Burke gulped a brandy, then maneuvered me toward the front door.

". . . Where are we going?" I asked, unsure of the propriety.

"Let's take a stroll."

We stepped onto the porch beneath the palladium fanlight and gazed at the sky. It was purple, almost watery-looking. The moon was rising over the tree line. I couldn't, however, think of anything but the letter. I pulled it from my purse and ripped the seal.

My Dearest Darling,

I beg the privilege of becoming your most attached and devoted fiancé. My heart is yours.

I await your answer.

Burke

I read it once, then again, mildly disoriented, as if the letter he'd slipped to me earlier had been swapped for this one that had nothing at all to do with me. He seemed entertained by my confusion. He said, "Your parents will want you to wait and give your answer after you've consulted with them."

"I accept your proposal," I said, smiling at him, overwhelmed with a queer mixture of jubilation and relief. I would be married! I would not end up like Aunt Amelia Jane.

He was right, though, Mother would be horrified I'd answered without her say-so, but I didn't doubt my parents' response. After swallowing their disapproval, they would seize upon the miracle of Burke Williams' proposal like it was the cure for a dread disease.

We walked along the carriage way, my arm looped in his. A little tremor was running rib to rib to rib inside of me. Abruptly, he steered me off the path toward a camellia grove. We disappeared into the shadows that hung in swaths between the huge, flowering bushes, and without preamble, he kissed me full on the mouth. I reared back. "... Why ... why, you surprise me."

"My Love, we're engaged now, such liberties are allowed."

He drew me to him and kissed me again. His fingers moved along the edge of my décolletage, brushing my skin. I didn't entirely surrender, but I allowed Burke Williams a great amount of freedom during that small peccadillo in the camellia grove. When I mustered myself finally, pulling from his embrace, he said he hoped I didn't hold his ardor against him. I did not. I adjusted my dress. I tucked vagrant pieces of hair back into my upswept coif. *Such liberties are allowed now.*

As we walked back to the house, I fixed my eyes on the path, how it was riddled with peacock excrement and pebbles shining in the moon's light. This marriage, it would be life-enough, wouldn't it? Surely. Burke was speaking about the necessity of a long engagement. A year, he said.

As we drew near the porch, a horse whinnied, and then a man stepped from the front door and lit his pipe. It was Mr. Drayton, Thomas' father-in-law.

"Sarah?" he said. "Is that you?" His eyes shifted to Burke and back to me. A lock of my hair fluttered guiltily at my shoulder. "Where've you been?" I heard the reproof, the alarm. "Are you all right?"

"... I am ... we are engaged." My parents weren't yet informed, and I'd heralded the news to Mr. Drayton, whom I barely knew, hoping it would excuse whatever his mind imagined we were doing out there.

"We took a quick turn in the night air," Burke said, trying, it seemed, to bring some normalcy to the moment.

Mr. Drayton was no fool. He gazed at me, plain Sarah, returning from a "turn in the night" with a startlingly handsome man, looking flushed and slightly unkempt. "Well, then, congratulations. Your happiness must be a welcome respite for your family given this recent trouble of your father's."

Was Father's trouble common knowledge, then?

"Has some misfortune fallen upon Judge Grimké?" Burke asked.

"Sarah hasn't told you?"

"... I suppose I've been too distressed to speak of it," I said. "... But please, sir, inform him on my behalf. It would be a service to me."

Mr. Drayton took a draught from his pipe and blew the spicy smoke into the night. "I regret to say the judge's enemies seek to remove him from the court. Impeachment charges have been brought."

I let my breath out. I couldn't imagine a greater humiliation for our father.

"On what grounds?" Burke asked, properly outraged.

"They say he has grown biased and overly righteous in his judgments." He hesitated. "They charge incompetence. Ah, but it is all politics." He waved his hand dismissively, and I watched the bowl of his pipe flare in the small wind.

Any flicker of gladness I might've hoped for from my family about my engagement, any retribution I might've feared for accepting the proposal without permission, was swallowed by Father's trial. Mother's reaction to my announcement was simply, "Well done, Sarah," as if reviewing one of my embroidery samplers. Father did not respond at all.

Throughout the winter, he sequestered in the library day and night with Thomas, Frederick, and Mr. Daniel Huger, a lawyer friend of Father's who was known for legally eviscerating his opponents. My hearing was almost preternatural, cultivated by years of unsanctioned listening, and I caught scraps of conversation while sitting at the card table in the main passage, pretending to read.

John, you've received no money, no favors. You are accused of nothing that rises to the level of high crimes.

Isn't a charge of incompetence bad enough? They accuse me of being biased! The streets and the papers are full of it. I'm ruined, regardless.

Father, you have friends in the legislative chamber!

Don't be a fool, Thomas, what I have are enemies. Scheming bastards from the upcountry, seeking the bench for themselves.

They cannot possibly get a two-thirds majority.

Make meat of them, Daniel, do you hear me? Feed them to the dogs.

When the trial was heard that spring in the House of Representatives in Columbia, Mr. Huger assailed Father's enemies with a vengeance, laying bare their political conniving with such force Father was acquitted in a single day, but the vote was ominously close, and he returned to Charleston, vindicated, but dirtied.

At fifty-nine, Father was suddenly a very old man. His face had turned haggard and his clothes baggy as if he'd wilted inside them. A tremor appeared in his right hand.

As the months passed, Burke paid courting calls to me weekly in the withdrawing room, where we were allowed unchaperoned visits. He filled these rendezvous with the same fever and excess we'd shared in the camellia grove, and I complied, drawing lines the best I could. I counted it God's miracle we weren't discovered, though I'm sure our invisibility was not due to God, but to the family's distraction. Father continued to shuffle and shrivel and tuck his hand in his pocket to hide its shake. He turned into a recluse of a man. And I, I turned into a Jezebel of a woman.

Handful

Mauma couldn't sleep. She was up fussing round the cellar room like usual. She didn't know the meaning of the words *quiet as a mouse*.

I was laying in the straw bed we'd always slept in, wondering what was on her mind this time. I'd stopped sleeping on the floor outside Sarah's room a long time back, just decided it on my own, and nobody said a word about it, not even missus. During those years, her meanness was hit and miss.

Mauma dragged the chair over to the high-up window so she could crane her neck and see a piece of sky beyond the wall. I watched how she sat there and studied it.

Most of her waking nights, she would light the lamp and sew her story quilt. She'd been working on those quilt squares bits at a time for more than two years. "If there a fire and I ain't here, that's what you get," she'd say. "You save the squares cause they pieces of me same like the meat on my bones."

I pestered her all the time wanting to see the squares she'd finished, but she held firm. Mauma loved a good surprise. She wanted to unveil her quilt like they did marble statues. She had put her history on a quilt like the Fon people, and she meant to show it all at once, not piecemeal.

The day before, she'd told me, "You wait. I'm 'bout ready to roll down the frame and start quilting it all together."

She kept the squares locked in a wood trunk she'd dragged from the storeroom in the basement. The trunk had a bad, musty smell to it. Inside we'd found mold, dead moth-eggs, and a little key. She cleaned the trunk with linseed oil, then locked the squares inside, wrapped in muslin. I guessed she locked our freedom money in there too, cause right after that the bills disappeared from the gunny sack.

Last time I'd counted, she'd saved up four hundred dollars even.

Laying in bed now, I did the numbering in my head—we needed six hundred fifty more dollars to buy the both of us.

I broke the quiet. "Is this how you gonna be all night—sit in the dark and stare up at a hole in the wall?"

"It's something to do. Go on back to sleep."

Go back to sleep—that was a lot of useless.

"Where do you keep the key to the chest?"

"Is that how *you* gon be? Lay there figurin' how to peek at my quilt? The key hid on the back of nowhere."

I let it be, and my mind drifted off to Sarah.

I didn't care for this Mr. Williams. The only thing he'd ever said to me was, "Remove yourself hastily." I'd been building a fire in the drawing room so the man could get himself warm, and that's what he had to say, *Remove yourself hastily.*

I couldn't see Sarah married to him any more than I could see myself married to Goodis. He still trailed after me, wanting you know what. Mauma said, tell him, go jump in the lake.

Yesterday, Sarah had asked, "When I marry, would you come with me to live?"

"Leave mauma?"

Real quick, she'd said, "Oh, you don't have to ... I just thought ... Well, I'll miss you."

Even though we didn't have that much to say to each other anymore, I hated to think about us parting. "I reckon I'll miss you, too," I told her.

Cross the room, mauma said, "How old you reckon I is?" She never did know her age for sure, didn't have a record. "Seems I had you when I'm 'bout the same old as you now, and you nineteen. What that make me?"

I counted it in my head. "You're thirty-eight."

"That ain't too old," she said.

We stayed like that a while, mauma staring at the window, mulling over her age, and me laying in the bed wide awake now, when she cried out, "Look,

Handful! Look a here!" She leapt to her feet, bouncing on her knees. "There go 'nother one!"

I bolted from the bed.

"The stars," she said. "They falling just like they done for your granny-mauma. Come on. Hurry."

We yanked on our shoes and sack coats, snatched up an old quilt, and were out the door, mauma tearing cross the work yard, me two steps behind.

We spread the quilt on the ground out in the open behind the spirit tree and lay down on top of it. When I looked up, the night opened and the stars poured down.

Each time a star streaked by, mauma laughed low in her throat.

When the stars stopped falling and the sky went still, I saw her hands rub the little mound of her belly.

And I knew then what it was she wasn't too old for.

Sarah

"Sarah, you should sit down. Please."

That was how Thomas began. He gestured toward the two chairs beside the window that overlooked the piazza, but it was I alone who sat.

It was half past noon, and here was my brother, the *au courant* of Charleston barristers, interrupting his lawyering to speak with me in the privacy of my room. His face was pale with what I took to be dread.

Naturally, my mind went to Father. One could scarcely look at him these days without worrying about him, this thin, hollowed-out man with the uncertain gait and erratic hand. Despite that, there'd been some improvement lately, enough that he'd returned to his duties on the bench.

Just the week before, I'd come upon Father laboring along the main passage with his cane. It had conjured up an old Sunday School image from our catechism of Lazarus hobbling from the tomb with his shroud cleaving to his ankles. Father's left hand was shaking as if waving to a passerby, and before he saw me, he grabbed it violently, trying to subdue it. Noticing me, he said, "Oh, Sarah. God is ruthless to the aged." I walked with him to the back door, moving with a corresponding slowness that only called attention to his feebleness.

"So tell me, when will you marry?" It was the only question anyone ever asked me now, but coming from Father, it brought me to a standstill. I'd been promised to Burke since last February, and not once had Father even mentioned it. I hadn't blamed him for missing the engagement party, which Thomas and Sally had graciously hosted—he'd been bedridden then—but there'd been so many months of silence since.

"I don't know," I answered. "Burke is waiting on his father to assign the business over to him. He wants to be in the proper position."

"Does he?" His tone was sardonic, and I made no attempt to answer.

It was difficult now to remember those times when Father had let me plunder his books and basked in my speeches. There'd been a kind of invisible cord running between us then, and I tried to think exactly when it'd been broken. The day he forbade me books? Thomas' farewell party, when he hurled his vicious words? *You shame yourself. You shame us all. Where did you get the notion that you could study the law?*

"I remind you, Sarah, there is no divorce law in our state," he was saying. "Once you are married, the contract is indissoluble. You are aware of this?"

"Yes, Father, I know."

He nodded with what seemed like bleak acceptance.

That was where my mind alighted in those final moments before Thomas delivered his news, upon Father and my last encounter with him, upon his frailty.

"You've always been my favorite sister," Thomas said. "You know that. In truth, you've been the favorite of all my siblings."

He paused, stalling, gazing through the window across the piazza into the garden. I watched a drop of perspiration slide to his temple and cling in the net of wrinkles that was already forming. A strange resignation settled on me. *Whatever it is, it has already happened.*

". . . Please, I'm not as fragile as you might think. Tell me plainly."

"You're right. I will simply say it. I'm afraid Burke Williams has misrepresented himself to you. It has come to my attention that he has other female acquaintances."

Without considering the hidden entendre, I said, "Surely, that's not a crime."

"Sarah, these acquaintances—they're also his fiancées."

I knew suddenly what he said was true. So many things made sense now. The delay in naming a marriage date. The incessant trips he made to visit family or conduct business. The curious fact that someone so full of looks and charm had settled on me.

My eyes filled. Thomas dug for his handkerchief and waited while I dabbed them dry.

"How did you learn of this?" I asked, composed, no doubt protected by the recoil of shock.

"Sally's cousin Franny in Beaufort wrote to say she'd attended a soirée there and seen Burke openly courting a young woman. She didn't approach him, of course, but she did discreetly question the young woman, who told her Burke had recently proposed."

I looked down at my lap, trying to absorb what he'd said. "But why? Why would he do this? I don't understand."

Thomas sat and took my hands. "He's one of those men who prey on young ladies. We hear of this kind of thing now. There's a fast-set of young men acquiring fiancées in order to—" He paused. "To lure women into sexual liaisons. They assure the women that given the promise of wedlock, such compromises are acceptable." He could barely look at me. "I trust he didn't take advantage—"

"No," I said. "He did not."

Thomas exhaled with relief that embarrassed me in its extravagance.

"... You said fiancées. Beside the acquaintance in Beaufort, there's another?"

"Yes, I believe she lives in Savannah."

"And how did you learn of *this* one? Not another cousin, I hope."

He gave me a weak smile. "No, this one I heard of from Burke himself. I confronted him last evening. He admitted to both young ladies."

"You confronted him? But why didn't you let me—"

"I wanted to spare you the pain and disgrace. Both of our parents agreed you should be left out of it. There's no reason for you to see him again. I've broken the engagement on your behalf."

How could you? He'd usurped any chance I had for personal retribution. In that moment, I felt more enraged by Thomas' babyish protection than by Burke's cruelty. I sprang to my feet and stood with my back to him, almost gagging on mouthfuls of jumbled, scathing words.

"I know how you must feel," he said behind me. "But it's better this way."

He knew *nothing* of how I felt. I wanted to shout at him for uttering so arrogant a claim, but when I whirled about, I saw his eyes were filled with tears and I forced myself to speak with civility. "... I would like to be alone. Please."

He stood. "There's one more thing. You'll need to withdraw from public for a brief time. Mother believes three weeks will be sufficient for the talk to die down. Then you can return to society."

He left me by the window, engulfed with anger and mortification, and with nowhere to hurl it except at myself. How could I have fallen prey to such a lascivious person? Was I so besotted, so needy, so blind that I imagined he loved *me*? I could see myself in the glare of the window, the flushed, round face, Father's long nose, the pale eyes, the mis-colored hair. I'd clipped a piece of that hair for him. He must have laughed at that.

I went to my desk and retrieved the letter with his proposal of marriage. I didn't read it again, I tore it into as many pieces as I could manage. The tatters fell onto the desktop and the rug and the folds of my skirt.

It was the time of year when migrating crows wheeled across the sky, thunderous flocks that moved like a single veil, and I heard them, out there in the wild chirruping air. Turning to the window, I watched the birds fill the sky before disappearing, and when the air was still again, I watched the empty place where they had been.

Handful

Sarah was up in her room with her heart broke so bad, Binah said you could hear it jangle when she walked. Her brother, Thomas, hadn't even got his hat on to leave before the whole house knew what happened. Mr. Williams had himself two more fiancées. *Now* who has to remove himself hastily?

Come teatime that day, missus said to Tomfry, "Sarah will not be receiving visitors for the next three weeks. Explain to any callers that she is indisposed. *Indisposed,* Tomfry. That's the word I would like you to use."

"Yessum."

Missus saw me hovering. "Quit dawdling, Hetty, and take a tray to Sarah's room."

I fixed it, but I knew she wouldn't touch a bite. I got the hyssop tea she liked, thinking of us when we were little, how we drank it on the roof, her telling me about the silver button and the big plan she had. I'd worn that button in my neck pouch almost every day since she'd tossed it away.

I slipped into the warming kitchen, slid off the pouch, and dug the button out. It was full of tarnish. Looked like a big shriveled grape. I studied it a minute, then I got out the polish and rubbed it till it gleamed.

Sarah was sitting at her desk, writing in a notebook. Her eyes were so raw from crying I didn't know how she could see to write. I set the tray in front of her. I said, "Look what's on the tea saucer."

She hadn't laid eyes on the button in all these years, but she knew right off what it was. "How did . . . Why, Handful, you saved it?"

She didn't touch it. Only stared.

I said, "Awright then, there it is," and went to the door.

Sarah

The following morning, despite my protests, Mother sent Nina off to spend the day with one of the little Smith girls, whose family lived a block or so from the Work House. During Nina's last visit there, she'd heard screams floating on the breezes and had leapt up in alarm, scattering jackstones across the piazza. At the time, my sister knew nothing of Charleston's torture chamber—I'd tried to protect her from it—but the Smith boys had no such scruples. They informed her that the cries she heard came from a slave in the whipping room, describing it for her in lurid detail. Apparently there was a crane with pulleys by which the slaves' bound hands were drawn over their heads, while their feet were chained to a plank. The boys told her of other horrors, too, which she reported to me through sobs, stories about the splitting of ears and the removal of teeth, about spiked collars and some sort of birdcage contraption that was locked over a slave's head.

I'd assured Nina she wouldn't have to go back. But now, with Father's career in dire straits, Mother was not above using a seven-year-old to make an inroad with the politically powerful Smiths.

The rain began to fall not long after Nina left, a torrent coming at the peak of high tide, turning the streets into canals of mud. By early afternoon, after the storm had blown out to sea, I could bear it no longer. I put on Mary's old black riding hat with the veils and slipped out the back door, determined to collect my sister no matter the cost.

Sabe wasn't in the stable, only Goodis, which seemed just as well as I felt I could trust him more. "I just the footman, I ain't meant to drive the carriage," he told me. It took some doing, but I convinced him it was an errand of great urgency, and off we set in the new cabriolet.

The city was abuzz that day with talk of an astral event—a comet storm, it was said. Even sensible people like Father and Thomas had been speaking about the apocalypse, but I knew my scandal with Burke was being discussed in parlors throughout Charleston with more fervor than the end of the world. The cabriolet was new enough, however, to be unfamiliar on the streets, and with its hood up and Mary's hat on, I didn't see how I could be recognized. With any luck, Mother would never know I'd broken my seclusion.

Feeling anxious about Nina, I closed my eyes and imagined scooping her into my arms. Then there was a terrible jolt, and the carriage came to a shuddering stop on Coming Street, the right wheel sunk into a mud hole.

Goodis coaxed the horse with the whip, then climbed down and tugged at the bridle and collar. The mare, known for her keen spirit of revenge, jerked her head and stepped backward, sinking the carriage further. I heard Goodis quietly curse.

He went to the rear of the carriage and shoved, causing it to rock forward a little, but nothing more. "Stay put where you is," he told me. "I gon get us some help."

As he lumbered off, I surveyed the street. Despite the sogginess, there were ladies out strolling, men huddled in conclaves, Negro hawkers carrying troughs of shrimp and baskets of French coconut patties. I reached up nervously and touched the veil at my face, and it was at that moment I glimpsed Charlotte, walking toward Bull Street.

She picked her way like a ropewalker, moving along a narrow shelf of grass that ran beside a brick wall. She wore her red bandana low on her forehead and carried a basket bulging with cloth, unaware of me or of the finely dressed woman with white skin who approached her on the same grassy ledge from the opposite direction. One of them would be forced to turn around and retrace her steps all the way back to where the brick wall began, or else yield way by stepping off into the muddy roadway. Face-offs of this sort played out on the streets so regularly a city ordinance had been passed requiring slaves to give deference. Had the slave been anyone other than Charlotte—had it been Binah, Aunt-Sister, Cindie, even Handful—I wouldn't have worried so much, but Charlotte.

The two women stopped a few feet apart. The white woman lifted her parasol and tapped Charlotte's arm. *Move along now. Off with you.*

I didn't detect the slightest movement in Charlotte. She seemed to solidify as she stood there. The woman's umbrella thumped at her again: *Shoo. Shoo.*

They exchanged words I didn't understand, their voices rising, turning into jagged antlers over their heads. I looked around frantically for Goodis.

A man wearing a City Guard uniform reined his horse in the middle of the street. "Step aside, Negress," he yelled. He climbed from his horse, handing the reins to a slave boy who'd wandered up pulling a dray.

Before the guard could reach the scene, Charlotte swung her basket. It moved in an arc, spilling what I realized were bonnets, then crashing against the woman's arm, knocking her sideways. The mud in the street was like pudding, viscous and pale-brown as tapioca, and when the woman landed, perfectly seated, it made a little wave on either side of her.

I leapt from the carriage and ran toward them with no thought of what I might do. The guardsman had seized Charlotte by the arms, assisted by another man whom he'd enlisted. They dragged her down the street, while she spit and clawed.

I chased them all the way to Beaufain where the men commandeered a wagon and forced her into the back, pushing her flat onto her stomach. The guardsman sat atop her. The driver snapped the reins, the horses jerked, and I could only stand there spattered with the pudding from the street.

I swept back the veils on my hat and screamed her name. *"Charlotte!"*

Her eyes found me. She did not make a sound, but held my gaze as the wagon rolled away.

Handful

Mauma disappeared two days after we watched the stars fall.

We were standing in the work yard near the back gate. She had the red scarf on her head and wore her good dress, the one dyed indigo. Her apron was pressed to a crisp. She'd oiled her lips and borrowed Binah's cowrie shell bracelets to dress up her wrists. In the sunlight her skin had a gold luster and her eyes shined like river rocks. That's how I see her now in my dreams, with the look she had then. Almost happy.

She pinned on her slave badge, full of haste. She'd got permission to deliver her fresh-made bonnets, but I knew before the last one left the basket, she'd be obliging that man, Mr. Vesey.

I said, "Be sure your badge is on good."

Mauma hated my pestering. "It on there, Handful. It ain't goin' nowhere."

"What about your pouch?" I couldn't see the bulge of it under her dress like usual. I kept both of our pouches fresh with scraps from our tree, and I meant for her to wear it, what with me going to all that trouble and her needing all the protection she could get. She fished it up from her bosom. Her fingers had faded smudges on them from the charcoal powder she'd used to trace designs on her bonnets.

I wanted to say more to her. *Why're you wearing the good dress with all that mud out there? When are you planning on telling me about the baby? Now we got to buy freedom for the three of us?* But I shoved all this to the side for later.

I lingered while Tomfry unlocked the back gate and let her out. After she stepped through to the alley, she turned round and looked at me, then walked on off.

After mauma left that day, I did everything usual. Cut sleeves and collars for the men slaves to have work shirts, got busy on missus' splashers, these squares of cloth you tack up behind the washstands cause Lord forbid you get a drop of water on the wall. Each and every one had to be embroidered to the hilt.

Middle of the afternoon, I went out to the privy. The sun had stayed put, and the sky was blue as cornflowers. Aunt-Sister was in the kitchen house baking whole apples with custard poured round them, what's called a bird nest pudding, and that whole smell was in the air. I was on my way back inside, relishing the sweet air after being in the latrine, when the carriage came flying through the gate with Sarah and Nina, both of them looking scared to pieces. And look who was driving. Goodis. When it rolled to a stop, their feet hit the ground running. They passed me without a word and struck for the house. The little gray traveling cape I'd sewed Nina flapped behind her like a dove wing.

Goodis gave me a long look of pity before he tugged the horse inside the stable.

When the long shadows started, I sat on the porch steps to the kitchen house and watched the gate for mauma. Cross the yard, Goodis held vigil with me in the stable door, whittling on a piece of wood. He knew something I didn't.

The apple-eggs were still in the air when Aunt-Sister and Phoebe cleaned up and blew out the lamps. The dark came, and no moon.

Sarah found me hunched on the steps. She sat down close next to me. "... Handful," she said. "... I wanted to be the one to tell you."

"It's mauma, ain't it?"

"She got in a dispute with a white lady ... The lady wanted her to give way on the street. She prodded your mother with an umbrella, and ... you know your mother, she wouldn't stand aside. She ... she struck the lady." Sarah sighed into the dark, and took hold of my hand. "The City Guard was there. They took her away."

All this time I'd been waiting for her to say mauma was dead. Hope came back into me. "Where is she?"

Sarah looked away from me then. "... That's what I've been trying to discover... We don't know where she is... They were taking her to the Guard House, but when Thomas went to pay the fine, he was told Charlotte had managed to wrestle free... Apparently, she ran off... They said the Guard chased her, but lost her in the alleys. They're out there looking for her now."

All I could hear was breathing—Sarah, Goodis cross the yard, the horses in the stable, the creatures in the brush, the white people on their feather beds, the slaves on their little pallets thin as wafers, everything breathing but me.

Sarah walked with me to the basement. She said, "Would you like some warmed tea? I can put a little brandy in it."

I shook my head. She wanted to draw me to her for solace, I could tell, but she held back. Instead, she laid her hand gentle on my arm and said, "She'll come back."

I said those words all night long.

I didn't know how to be in the world without her.

Sarah

Charlotte's disappearance brought a severe and terrible mercy, for not once throughout the harrowing weeks that followed Burke's betrayal was I uncertain which event was tragic and which was merely unfortunate.

Someone—Mother, Father, perhaps Thomas—placed an ad in the *Charleston Mercury*.

> **Disappeared, Female Slave**
>
> Mulatto. Wide space between upper front teeth. Occasional limp. Answers to the name of Charlotte. Wearing red scarf and dark blue dress. A seamstress of skill and value. Belongs to Judge John Grimké. Large reward for her return.

The appeal brought no response.

Each day I watched from the back window in my room as Handful walked a repetitive circuit in the work yard. Sometimes she walked the entirety of the morning. Never varying her path, she started at the back of the house, moved toward the kitchen house, past the laundry, cut over to the oak tree, where she touched the trunk as she passed, then back to the house by way of the stable and carriage house. Upon reaching the porch steps, she would simply begin again. It was a circumambulation of such precise, ritualistic grief no one interfered. Even Mother left her to walk a rut of anguish into the yard.

I didn't much mourn the loss of Burke or the demise of our wedding. I felt little heartbreak. Was that not strange? I did cry buckets, but mostly from the shame of it all.

I didn't break my seclusion again. Instead, I took refuge in it.

Almost daily I received notes of concern in flowery scripts. I was being prayed for by everyone imaginable. It was hoped my reputation wouldn't suffer too much. Did I know that Burke had vacated the city and was staying indefinitely with his uncle in Columbia? Wasn't it a shame that his mother had taken ill with apoplexy? How was my own mother bearing up? I was missed at tea, but my absence was commended. I shouldn't despair, for surely a young man would come forth who wouldn't be put off by my disgrace.

I wrote rants and rebukes in my diary, then tore them out and burned them along with all the supercilious notes. Gradually, the lava in me subsided and there remained only a young woman whose life course had been demolished. Unlike Handful, I had no notion what path to walk.

One month after Charlotte's disappearance, a frigid wind brought down most of the leaves on the oak. Handful still walked obsessively each morning, but only a quick loop or so now. The week before, Mother had put a stop to her unremitting march and sent her back to her duties. The high social season with its quota of gowns awaited—all the sewing now fell to Handful. Charlotte was gone. No one believed she was coming back.

I'd managed to stretch my three weeks of seclusion into four, but on this day, my reprieve ended. Mother had ordered me back to my duties, as well: procuring a husband. She'd informed me that a rowboat traversing the Atlantic might eventually be rescued by a passing ship, but *only* if the rowboat bravely set out upon the water—this, her hapless metaphor of my marital prospects. My sister Mary arrived with similar encouragement. "Lift your chin, Sarah. Behave as if nothing has happened. Be gay and act assured. You'll find a husband, God willing."

God willing. How strangely that strikes me now.

On the evening my solitude ended, I shoved myself out into the public domain by attending a lecture at the Second Presbyterian Church delivered by the Reverend Henry Kollack, a famed preacher. Those were not the waters Mother had in mind. The Episcopal Church might pass for society, but certainly not the Presbyterians with their revivalism and shouts for repentance—but she didn't object. I was at least rowing, wasn't I?

Sitting in a pew beside the devout friend who'd invited me, I scarcely listened at first. Words—*sin, moral degradation, retribution*—flitted in and out of my awareness, but at some point during that hour, I became morbidly engrossed.

The reverend's eyes found me—I can't explain it. Nor did he look away as he spoke. "Are you not sick of the frivolous being you have become? Are you not mortified at your own folly, weary of the ballroom and its gilded toys? Will you not give up the vanities and gaieties of this life for the sake of your soul?"

I felt utterly spoken to, and in the most direct and supernatural way. How could he know what lay inside me? How did he know what I was only that moment able to see myself?

"God calls you," he bellowed. "God, your beloved, begs you to answer."

The words ravished me. They seemed to break down some great artifice. I sat on the pew quietly shaken while Reverend Kollack looked at me now without focus or interest, and perhaps it had been so all along, but it didn't matter. He'd been God's mouthpiece. He'd delivered me to the precipice where one's only choice was between paralysis or abandon.

With the reverend praying a long, earnest prayer for our souls, I took my leap. I vowed I would not return to society. I would not marry, I would never marry. Let them say what they would, I would give myself to God.

Two weeks later, on my twentieth birthday, I entered the drawing room, where the family had gathered to offer me well wishes, accompanied by Nina, who clung to my hand. Seeing that I'd chosen to wear one of my simpler dresses and no jewelry, Mary smiled at me sadly as if I wore the costume of a nun. I gathered Mother had confided my religious conversion to my sisters, perhaps to my father and brothers, as well.

Aunt-Sister had baked my favored dessert, a two-tiered election cake, filled with currants and sugar. Such cakes were molded on a board with yeast and left to rise, if they *so elected,* and this one had done so with majesty. Nina pranced about it impatiently until Mother signaled Aunt-Sister to cut the slices.

Father was seated with my brothers, who were engaged in a debate of some sort. Edging to the fringes, I determined that Thomas had evoked their wrath by promoting a program known as colonization. From what I could gather, the term had little to do with the British occupation of the last century and everything to do with the slaves.

"... What's this concept?" I asked, and they turned to me as if a housefly had pried through a slat in the shutters and was buzzing wantonly about.

"It's a new and advanced idea," Thomas answered. "Despite what any of you believe, it will soon expand into a national movement. Mark my words."

"But what *is* it?" I said.

"It proposes we free the slaves and send them back to Africa."

Nothing had prepared me for so radical a scheme. "... Why, that's preposterous!"

My reaction took them by surprise. Even Henry and Charles, now thirteen and twelve, gaped at me. "Christ preserve us," said John. "Sarah is against it!"

He assumed I'd outgrown my rebellions and become like the rest of them—a guardian of slavery. I couldn't fault him for it. When was the last time any of them had heard me speak out against the peculiar institution? I'd been wandering about in the enchantments of romance, afflicted with the worst female curse on earth, the need to mold myself to expectations.

John was laughing. A fire raged on the grate and Father's face was bright and sweating. He wiped at it and joined the mirth.

"Yes, I *am* against colonization," I began. There was no falter now in my throat. I forced myself to keep on. "I'm against it, but not for the reason you think. We should free the slaves, but they should remain here. As equals."

An odd intermezzo ensued during which no one spoke. There'd been mounting talk from certain clergy and pious women about treating slaves with Christian sympathy, and now and then some rare soul would speak of freeing the slaves altogether. But equality, ludicrous!

By law, a slave was three-fifths of a person. It came to me that what I'd just suggested would seem paramount to proclaiming vegetables equal to animals, animals equal to humans, women equal to men, men equal to angels. I was upending the order of creation. Strangest of all, it was the first time thoughts of equality had entered my head, and I could only attribute it to God, with whom I'd lately taken up and who was proving to be more insurrectionary than law-abiding.

"My goodness, did you learn this from the Presbyterians?" Father asked. "Are *they* saying slaves should live among us as equals?" The question was sarcastic, meant for my brothers and for the moment itself, yet I answered him.

"No, Father, *I'm* saying it."

As I spoke, a rush of pictures spilled through my mind, all of them Handful. She was tiny, wearing the lavender bow on her neck. She was filling the house with smoke. She was learning to read. She was sipping tea on the roof. I saw her taking her lash. Wrapping the oak with stolen thread. Bathing in the copper tub. Sewing works of pure art. Walking bereaved circles. I saw everything as it was.

Handful

Mauma was gone sure as I'm sitting here and I couldn't do a thing but walk the yard trying to siphon my sorrow. The sorry truth is you can walk your feet to blisters, walk till kingdom-come, and you never will outpace your grief. Come December, I stopped all that. I halted in my track by the woodpile where we used to feed the little owl way back then, and I said out loud, "Damn you for saving yourself. How come you left me with nothing but to love you and hate you, and that's gonna kill me, and you know it is."

Then I turned round, went back to the cellar room, and picked up the sewing.

Don't think she wasn't in every stitch I worked. She was in the wind and the rain and the creaking from the rocker. She sat on the wall with the birds and stared at me. When darkness fell, she fell with it.

One day, before they started the Days of Christmas in the house, I looked at the wood trunk on the floor, shoved behind mauma's gunny sack.

I said, "Now, where'd you go and put the key?"

I had got where I talked to her all the time. Like I would say, I didn't hear her talk back, so I hadn't lost my sanities. I turned the room upside down and the key was nowhere. It could've been in her pocket when she went missing. We had an axe in the yard shed, but I hated to chop the trunk apart. I said, "If I was you, where would I hide the key that locked up the only precious things I had?"

I stood there a while. Then, I lifted my eyes to the ceiling. To the quilt frame. The wheels on the pulley were fresh with oil. They didn't make a peep when I brought the frame down. *Sure enough.* The key was laying in a groove along one of the boards.

Inside the trunk was a fat bundle wrapped in muslin. I peeled back the folds and you could smell mauma, that salty smell. I had to take a minute to cry. I held her quilt squares against me, thinking how she said they were the meat on her bones.

There were ten good-size squares. I spread them out cross the frame. The colors she'd used outdid God and the rainbow. Reds, purples, oranges, pinks, yellows, blacks, and browns. They hit my ears more than my eyes. They sounded like she was laughing and crying in the same breath. It was the finest work ever to come from mauma's hands.

The first square showed her mauma standing small, holding her mauma and daddy's hands and the stars falling round them—that was the night my granny-mauma got sold away, the night the story started.

The rest was a hotchpotch, some squares I could figure, some I couldn't. There was a woman hoeing in the fields—I guessed her to be my granny-mauma, too—wearing a red head scarf, and a baby, my mauma, was laying in the growing plants. Slave people were flying in the air over their heads, disappearing behind the sun.

Next one was a little girl sitting on a three-leg stool appliquéing a quilt, red with black triangles, some of the triangles spilling on the floor. I said, "I guess that's you, but it could be me."

Fourth one had a spirit tree on it with red thread on the trunk, and the branches were filled with vultures. Mauma had sewed a woman and baby boy on the ground—you could tell it was a boy from his privates. I figured they were my granny-mauma when she died and her boy that didn't make it. Both were dead and picked bloody. I had to walk out in the cold air after that one. You come from your mauma, you sleep in the bed with her till you're near twenty years grown, and you still don't know what haunches in the dark corners of her.

I came back inside and studied the next one—it had a man in the field. He had a brown hat on, and the sky was full of eyes sitting in the clouds, big yellow eyes and red rain falling from the lids. *That man is my daddy, Shanney,* I said to myself.

One after that was mauma and a baby girl stretched on the quilt frame. I knew that girl was me, and our bodies were cut in pieces, bright patches that needed piecing back. It made my head sick and dizzy to look at it.

Another square was mauma sewing a wild purple dress covered with moons and stars, only she was doing it in a mouse-hole, the walls bent over her.

Going picture to picture, felt like I was turning pages in a book she'd left behind, one that held her last words. Somewhere along the way, I stopped feeling anything, like when you lay on your arm wrong and wake up and it's pins and needles. I started looking at the appliqués that had taken mauma two years to sew like they didn't have any belonging to me, cause that was the only way I could bear to see them. I let them float by like panes of light.

Here was mauma with her leg hitched up behind her with a strap, standing in the yard getting the one-legged punishment. Here was another spirit tree same like the other one, but it was ours, and it didn't have vultures, only green leaves and a girl underneath with a book and a whip coming down to strike her.

Last square was a man, a bull of a man with a carpenter apron on—Mr. Denmark Vesey—and next to him she'd stitched four numbers big as he was: 1884. I didn't have a notion what that meant.

I went straight to stitching. Hell with missus and her gowns. All that day and far in the night, I pieced mauma's squares together with the tiny stitches you can't barely see. I sewed on the lining and filled the quilt with the best padding we'd saved and the whole collection of our feathers. Then I took shears to my hair and cut every bit of it off my head, down to a scalp of fuzz. I loosed the cut hair all through the stuffing.

That's when I remembered about the money. Eight years, saving. I went over and looked down in the trunk and it was empty as air. Four hundred dollars, gone same as mauma. And I'd run out of places to look. I couldn't draw a breath.

⚯

Next day, after I'd slept a little, I sewed the layers of the quilt together with a tacking stitch. Then I wrapped the finish quilt round me like a glory cloak. I wore it out into the yard where Aunt-Sister was bundled up chopping cane sugar, and she said, "Girl, what you got on you? What'd you do to your head?"

I didn't say nothing. I walked back to the tree with my breath trailing clouds, and I wrapped new thread round the trunk.

Then the noise came into the sky. The crows were flying over and smoke from the chimneys rising to meet them.

"There you go," I said. "There you go."

PART THREE

October 1818–November 1820

Handful

Some days I'd be coming down East Bay and catch sight of a woman with cinnamon skin slipping round a corner, a snatch of red scarf on her head, and I'd say, *There you are again.* I was twenty-five years old and still talking to her.

Every October on the anniversary-day of mauma going missing, us slaves sat in the kitchen house and reminisced on her. I hated to see that day come dragging round.

On the six-year mark, Binah patted my leg and said, "Your mauma gone, but we still here, the sky ain't fall in yet."

No, but every year one more slat got knocked out from under it.

That evening, they dredged up stories on mauma that went on past supper. Stealing the bolt of green cloth. Hoodwinking missus with her limp. Wrangling the cellar room. Getting herself hired out. That whole Jesus-act she did. Tomfry told about the time missus had him search the premise and mauma was nowhere on it, how we slipped her in the front door to the roof, then trumped up that story about her falling asleep there. Same old tales. Same laughing and slapping.

Now that she was gone, they loved her a lot better.

"You sure do have her eyes," Goodis said, looking at me moon-face like he always did.

I did have her eyes, but the rest of me had come from my daddy. Mauma said he was an undersize man and blacker than the backside of the moon.

On my sake, they left out the stories of her pain and sorrow. Nothing about what might've happened to her. Every one of them, even Goodis, believed she'd run and was living the high life of freedom somewhere. I could more easy believe she'd been on the roof all this time, sleeping.

Outside the day was fading off. Tomfry said it was time to light the lamps in the house, but nobody moved, and I felt the ache for them to know the real woman mauma was, not just the cunning one, but the one smelted from iron, the one who paced the nights and prayed to my granny-mauma. Mauma had yearned more in a day than they felt in a year. She'd worked herself to the bone and courted danger, searching for something better. I wanted them to know that woman. That was the one who wouldn't leave me.

I said, "She didn't run off. I can't help what you think, but she didn't run."

They just sat there and looked at me. You could see the little wheels turning in their heads: *The poor misled girl, the poor misled girl.*

Tomfry spoke up, said, "Handful, think now. If she didn't run off, she got to be dead. Which-a-one you want us to believe?"

No one had put it to me that straight before. Mauma's story quilt had slaves flying through the sky and slaves laying dead on the ground, but in my way of reckoning, mauma was lost somewhere between the two. Between flyaway and dead-and-gone.

Which-a-one? The air was stiff as starch.

"Not neither one," I told them and got up from there and left.

In my room, I laid down on the bed, on top of the story quilt, and stared at the quilt frame still nailed to the ceiling. I never lowered it anymore, but I slept under mauma's stories every night except summers and the heat of autumn, and I knew them front, back, and sideways. Mauma had sewed where she came from, who she was, what she loved, the things she'd suffered, and the things she hoped. She'd found a way to tell it.

After a while, I heard footsteps overhead—Tomfry, Cindie, Binah up there lighting lamps. I didn't have to worry with Sarah's lamp anymore. I just had sewing duties now. Some time ago, Sarah had given me back to missus, official on paper. She said she didn't want part in owning a human person. She'd come special to my room to tell me, so nerve-racked she couldn't hardly get the words up. "... ... I would've freed you if I could ... but there's a law ... It doesn't allow owners to easily free slaves anymore ... Otherwise, I would have ... you know that ... don't you?"

After that, it was plain as the freckles on her face—the only way I was getting away from missus was drop dead, get sold, or find the hid-place mauma had gone. Some days I mooned over the money mauma'd saved—it never had turned up. If I could find that fortune, I could try and buy my freedom from missus like we'd planned on. Least I'd have a chance—a horse-piss of a chance, but it would be enough to keep me going.

Six years gone. I rolled over on the bed, my face to the window. I said, "Mauma, what happened to you?"

When the new year came round, I was in the market getting what Aunt-Sister needed when I overheard the slave who cleaned the butcher stall talking about the African church. This slave's name was Jesse, a good, kind man. He used to take the leftover pig bladders and fill them with water for the children to have a balloon. I didn't usually pay him any mind—he was always wagging his tongue, putting *Praise the Lord* at the end of every sentence—but this day, I don't know why it was, I went over there to hear what he was saying.

Aunt-Sister had told me to hurry back, that it looked like sleet coming, but I stood there with the raw smell hanging in the air while he talked about the church. I found out the proper name was African Methodist Episcopal Church, and it was just for coloreds, slaves and free blacks together, and it was meeting in an empty hearse house near the black burial ground. Said the place was packed to the rafters every night.

A slave man next to me, wearing some worn-out-looking livery, said, "Since when is the city so fool-trusting to let slaves run their own church?"

Everybody laughed at that, like the joke was on Charleston.

Jesse said, "Well, ain't that the truth, Praise the Lord. There's a man at the church who's always talking 'bout Moses leading the slaves from Egypt, Praise the Lord. He say, Charleston is Egypt all over again. Praise the Lord."

My scalp pricked. I said, "What's the man's name?"

Jesse said, "Denmark Vesey."

For years, I'd refused to think of Mr. Vesey, how mauma had sewed him on the last square on her story quilt. I didn't like the man being on it, didn't like the man period. I'd never thought he knew anything about what happened to her, why would he, but standing there, a bell rang in my head and told me it was worth a try. Maybe then I could put mauma to rest.

That's when I decided to get religion.

First chance I got, I told Sarah I was burdened down with the need for deliverance, and God was calling me to the African church. I dabbed at my eyes a little.

I was cut straight from my mauma's cloth.

Next day, missus called me to her room. She was sitting by the window with her Bible laid open. "It has come to my attention you wish to join the new church that has been established in the city for your kind. Sarah informs me you want to attend nightly meetings. I'll allow you to go twice a week in the evenings and on Sunday, as long as it doesn't interfere with your work or cause problems of any sort. Sarah will prepare your pass."

She looked at me through her little glasses. She said, "See to it you don't squander the favor I'm granting you."

"Yessum." For measure, I added, "Praise the Lord."

Sarah

I couldn't imagine why Nina and I had been summoned to the first-floor drawing room—that was never a good thing. We entered to find the very corpulent Reverend Gadsden seated on the yellow silk settee, and beside him, Mother, squeezed way over to one side, gripping her cane as if she might bore it into the floor. Glancing at Nina, who, at fourteen, was taller than I was, I noticed her eyes flash beneath their thick, dark lashes. She gave her chin a tiny defiant yank upward, and for a moment, I felt a passing bit of pity for the reverend.

"Close the door behind you," Mother said. Down the passageway, Father was in his room, too ill now to work. Dr. Geddings had ordered quiet, and for weeks, the slaves had padded about, speaking in whispers, careful not to rattle a tray for fear of their lives. When one's physician prescribes quiet as a remedy, along with a syrup made from horseradish root, he has clearly given up.

I took my seat on the twin settee beside Nina, facing the pair of them. The accusation against me would be failing as Nina's godmother. As usual.

This past Sunday, my sister had refused confirmation into St. Philip's Church, and it wasn't even that as much as the way she'd done it. She'd made a pageant of it. When the other youths left their chairs on the dais and went to the altar rail for the bishop to lay his hands on their sweet heads, Nina remained pointedly in her seat. Our entire family was there, except for Father, and I watched with a confused mix of embarrassment and pride as she sat with her arms crossed, her dark hair gleaming around her shoulders and a tiny circle of red blazing on each of her cheeks.

The bishop walked over and spoke to her, and she shook her head. Mother went stiff as a piece of wrought iron on the pew beside me, and I felt the air in the church clotting around our heads. There was more coaxing by the bishop, more obstinacy by Nina, until he gave up and continued the service.

I'd had no inkling what she planned, though perhaps I should have—this was Nina, after all. She was full of fiery opinions and mutinous acts. Last winter, she'd scandalized her classroom by taking off her shoes because the slave boy, who cleaned the slate boards, was barefooted. I'd lost count of the letters of apology Mother had ordered her to write. Rather than submit, she would sit before the blank paper for days until Mother relented. On *her* eleventh birthday, Nina had refused her human present with such vehemence, Mother had given up out of sheer weariness.

Even if I'd tried to prevent Nina's display at church that day, she would've pointed out that I, too, had spurned the Anglicans. Well, I had, but I'd done so to embrace the Presbyterians, whereas Nina would've spurned the Presbyterians, too, given half a chance. She hated them for what she called their "gall and wormwood."

If there was a wedge between my sister and me, it was religion.

Over the last several years, it seemed my entire life had been possessed of swings between asceticism and indulgence. I'd banished society in the aftermath of Burke Williams, yes, but I'd been a chronic backslider, succumbing every season to some party or ball, which had left me empty and sickened, which had then sent me crawling back to God. Nina had often found me on my knees, weeping as I prayed, begging forgiveness, engaged in one of my excruciating bouts of self-contempt. "Why must you be like this?" she would shout.

Why, indeed.

Mr. Williams had been shaken from the lap of Charleston like a soiled napkin. He was married now to his cousin, keeping shop in his uncle's dry goods store in Columbia. I'd put him behind me long ago, but I hadn't been able to make peace with living here in this house till the end of my days. I had Nina, but not for much longer. As charismatic and beautiful as she was, she would be wooed by a dozen men and leave me here with Mother. It was the ubiquitous truth at the center of everything, and it had driven me to my backsliding. But there could be no more of that—at twenty-six I would be too old for the coming season. It was truly over, and I felt lost and miserable, galled and wormwood-ed, and there was nothing to be done about it.

Here in the drawing room, Reverend Gadsden looked reluctant and uncomfortable. He kept pursing and unpursing his lips. Nina sat erect beside me, as if to say, *All right, let the castigation begin,* but under the cover of our skirts, she reached for my hand.

"I'm here today because your mother asked me to reason with you. You gave us all a shock yesterday. It's a grave thing to reject the church and her sacraments and salvation..."

He went on with his jabber, while Nina's hand sweated into mine.

She saw my private agonies, but I saw hers, too. There was a place inside of her where it had all broken. The screams she'd heard coming from the Work House still inhabited her, and she would wake some nights, shouting into the dark. She put up an invincible show, but underneath I knew her to be bruised and vulnerable. After Mother's scathing reprimands, she would vanish into her room for hours, emerging with her eyes bloodshot from weeping.

The reverend's kind but tedious speech had been floating in and out of my awareness. "I must point out," I heard him say, "that you are placing your soul in jeopardy."

Nina spoke for the first time. "Pardon me, Reverend Sir, but the threat of *hell* will not move me."

Mother sank her eyes closed. "Oh, Angelina, for the love of God."

Nina had used the word *hell*. Even I was a little shocked by it. The rector sat back with resignation. He was done.

Naturally, Mother was not. "Your father lies gravely ill. Surely you know it's his wish that you be confirmed into the church. It could well be his last wish. Would you deny him that?"

Nina squeezed my hand, struggling to hold on to herself.

"... Should she deny her conscience or her father?" I said.

Mother drew back as if I'd slapped her. "Are you going to sit there and encourage your sister's disobedience?"

"I'm encouraging her to be true to her own scruples."

"*Her* scruples?" The skin at Mother's neck splotched like beetroot. She turned to the reverend. "As you see, Angelina is completely under Sarah's sway. What Sarah thinks, Angelina thinks. What Sarah scruples, she scruples. It's my own fault—I chose Sarah to be her godmother, and to this day, she leads the child astray."

"Mother!" Nina exclaimed. "I think for myself."

Mother shifted her calm, pitiless gaze from the reverend to Nina and uttered the question that would always lie between us. "Just so I'm not confused, when you said 'Mother' just now, were you referring to me, or to Sarah?"

The rector squirmed on the settee and reached for his hat, but Mother continued. "As I was saying, Reverend, I'm at a loss of how to undo the damage. As long as the two of them are under the same roof, there's small hope for Angelina."

As she escorted the reverend to the door, rain broke loose outside. I felt Nina slump slightly against me, and I pulled her to her feet and we slipped behind them up the stairs.

In my room, I turned back the bed sheet and Nina lay down. Her face seemed stark and strange against the linen pillow. Rain was darkening the window, and she stared at it with her eyes gleaming, her back rising and falling beneath my hand.

"Do you think Mother will send me away?" she asked.

"I won't allow it," I told her, though I had no idea how to stop such a thing if Mother took it in her head to banish my sister. A rebellious girl could easily be sent off to a boarding school or deported to our uncle's plantation in North Carolina.

Handful

"Didn't my Lord deliver Daniel?" Denmark Vesey shouted.

The whole church answered, "Now he's coming for me."

Must've been two hundred of us packed in there. I was sitting in the back, in the usual spot. Folks had started leaving it free for me, saying, "That's Handful's place." Four months I'd been sitting there and hadn't learned a thing about mauma, but I knew more than missus about the people God had delivered.

Abraham, Moses, Samson, Peter, Paul—Mr. Vesey went down the list, chanting their names. Everybody was on their feet, clapping, and waving in the air, shouting, "Now he's coming for me," and I was smack-dab in the middle of them, doing the little hopping dance I used to do in the alcove when I was a girl singing to the water.

Our reverend was a free black man named Morris Brown, and he said when we got worked up like this, it was the Holy Ghost that had got into us. Mr. Vesey, who was one of his four main helpers, said it wasn't the Holy Ghost, it was hope. Whatever it was, it could burn a hole in your chest.

The heat in the church was awful. While we shouted, sweat drenched our faces and clothes, and some of the men got up and opened all the windows. The fresh air flowed in and the shouting flowed out.

When Mr. Vesey ran out of people in the Bible for God to deliver, he went along the benches calling names.

Let my Lord deliver Rolla.

Let my Lord deliver Nancy.

Let my Lord deliver Ned.

If he called your name, you felt like it would fly straight to heaven and hit God between the eyes. Reverend Brown said, be careful, heaven would be whatever you picture it. His picture was Africa before the slaving—all the food and freedom you wanted and not a white person to blight it. If mauma was dead, she would have a big fine house somewhere and missus for her maid.

Mr. Vesey, though, he didn't like any kind of talk about heaven. He said that was the coward's way, pining for life in the hereafter, acting like this one didn't mean a thing. I had to side with him on that.

Even when I was singing and hopping like this, part of me stayed small and quiet, noticing everything he said and did. I was the bird watching the cat circle the tree. Mr. Vesey had white wooly nubs in his hair now, but beside that, he looked like before. Wore the same scowl, had the same knife blades in his eyes. His arms were still thick and his chest big as a rain barrel.

I hadn't mustered the nerve to talk to him. People feared Denmark Vesey. I'd started telling myself the joke was on me—maybe I'd come to the African church for the Lord, after all. What'd I think I could learn about mauma anyway?

Nobody heard the horses outside. Mr. Vesey had a new chant going—*Joshua fought the battle of Jericho, and the walls came tumbling down*. Gullah Jack, his right-hand man, was beating a drum, and we were stomping the floor. *Jericho. Jericho*.

Then the doors busted open, and Gullah Jack's hands stopped pounding, and the song died away. We looked round, confused, while the City Guard spread along the walls and in the aisle, one at every window, four barring the door.

The head guard marched down front with a paper in one hand and a musket gun in the other. Denmark Vesey said with his booming voice, "What's the meaning of this? This is the house of the Lord, you have no business here."

The guard looked like he couldn't believe his luck. He took the butt of the gun and rammed it in Mr. Vesey's face. A minute ago, he'd been shouting Jericho, and now he was on the floor with a shirt full of blood.

People started screaming. One of the guards fired into the rafters, sending wood crumbs and smoke swirling down. The inside of my ears pounded, and when the head man read the warrant, he sounded like he was at the bottom of a dry well. He said the neighbors round the church found us a nuisance. We were charged with disorderly conduct.

He stuffed the paper in his pocket. "You'll be removed to the Guard House and sentenced in the morning with due and proper punishment."

A sob drifted from a woman on the far side, and the place came alive with fear and murmuring. We knew about the Guard House—it was where they held the lawbreakers, black and white, till they figured out what to do with them. The whites ones stayed till their hearings, and the black ones till their owners paid the fine. You just prayed to God you didn't have a stingy master, cause if he refused to pay, you went to the Work House to work off the debt.

Outside, the moon looked weak in the sky. They gathered us in four herds and marched us down the street. A slave sang, *Didn't my Lord deliver Daniel?* and a guard told him to hush up. It was quiet from then on except for the clopping horses and a little baby tied on its mother's back that whimpered like a kitten. I craned my neck for Mr. Vesey, but he wasn't anywhere to see. Then I noticed the dark wet spatter-drops on the ground, and I knew he was on up ahead.

We spent the night on the floor in a room filled with jail cells, men and women crammed in together, all of us having to pee in the same bucket in the corner. One woman coughed half through the night and two men got in a shove-fight, but mostly we sat in the dark and stared with flat eyes and dozed in and out. One time, I came awake, hearing that same little baby mewing.

At first light, a guard with hair scruffing his shoulders brought a pail of water with a dipper and we took turns drinking while our stomachs rumbled for food. After that, we were left to wonder what was coming. One man in our cell had been picked up by the Guard six times and he told us the facts and figures. The fine was five dollars, and if your master didn't pay, you got twelve lashes at the Work House, or worse, you got the treadmill. I didn't know what the treadmill was and he didn't say, just told us to beg for the whip. Then he lifted his shirt, and his back was grooved like the hide of an alligator. The sight brought bile to my throat. "My massa never pay," he said.

The morning stretched out and we waited, and then waited some more. All I could think about was the man's back, where they'd put Mr. Vesey, how his bashed face was holding up. Heat cooked the air and the smell turned sour and the baby started bawling again. Somebody said, "Why don't you feed the child?"

"I can't raise no milk," its mauma said, and another woman with stains on her dress front said, "Here, give me the baby. Mine's back home and all this milk with nobody to suck it." She pulled out her brown bosom, clear milk leaking from the nipple, and the baby latched on.

When the long-hair guard came back, he said, "Listen for your name. If I call it out, you're free to leave and go home to whatever awaits you."

We all got to our feet. I said to myself, *Never has been a Grimké slave sent to the Work House. Never has.*

"Seth Ball, Ben Pringle, Tinnie Alston, Jane Brewton, Apollo Rutledge . . ." He read the names till it was just me and the scarred man and the mauma with the baby and a handful of others. "If you're still here," he said, "your owner has decided the Work House will put you in a wholesome frame of mind."

A man said, "I'm a free black, I don't have an owner."

"If you've got the papers that say that, then you can pay the fine yourself," the guard told him. "If you can't pay it on the spot, then you're going to the Work House with the rest."

I felt genuine confused. I said, "Mister. Mister? You left off my name. It's Hetty. Hetty Grimké."

He answered me with the thud of the door.

―⸺~⸺―

The treadmill was chomping and grinding its teeth—you could hear it before you got in the room. The Work House man led twelve of us to the upper gallery, poking us along with a stick. Denmark Vesey came behind me with the side of his face swollen so bad his eye was shut. He was the only one of us with shackles on his hands and feet. He took shuffle-steps, and the chain dragged and rattled.

When he tripped on the stairs, I said over my shoulder, "Be careful now." Then I whispered, "How come you didn't pay the fine? Ain't you supposed to have money?"

"Whatever they do to the least of them, they do it unto me," he said.

I thought to myself, *Mr. Vesey fancies himself like Jesus carrying the cross, and that's probably cause he doesn't have five dollars on him for the fine.* Knowing him, though, he could've been throwing his lot with the rest of us. The man was big-headed and proud, but he had a heart.

When we got to the gallery and looked over the rail at the torment waiting for us, we just folded up and sat down on the floor.

One of the overseers fastened Mr. Vesey's chain to an iron ring and told us to watch the wheel careful so we'd know what to do. The mauma with the baby on her back said to him, "Who gon watch my baby while I down there?"

He said, "You think we got people to tend your baby?"

I had to turn from her, the way her head dropped, the baby looking wide-eye over her shoulder.

The treadmill was a spinning drum, twice as tall as a man, with steps on it. Twelve scrambling people were climbing it fast as they could go, making the wheel turn. They clung to a handrail over the top of it, their wrists lashed to it in case their grip slipped. The mill groaned and the corn cracked underneath. Two black-skin overseers paced with cowhides—cat o'nine tails, they called them—and when the wheel slowed, they hit the backs and legs of those poor people till you saw pink flesh ripple.

Mr. Vesey's good eye studied me. "Don't I know you from somewhere?"

"From the church."

"No, somewhere else."

I could've spit the truth out, but we were both in Daniel's lion's den, and God had left us to it. I said, "Where's all that delivering God's supposed to do?"

He snorted. "You're right, the only deliverance is the one we get for ourselves. The Lord doesn't have any hands and feet but ours."

"That doesn't say much for the Lord."

"It doesn't say much for us, either."

A bell rang down below and the jaws on the wheel stopped chewing. The overseers loosed the people's wrists and they climbed down a ladder to the floor. Some of them were so used-up they had to be dragged off.

The overseer unlocked Mr. Vesey from the floor ring. "Get on your feet. It's your turn."

Sarah

Handful's mangled foot was propped on a pillow, and Aunt-Sister was laying a plantain leaf across the wound. From the smell that drifted in the air, I knew her injury had been freshly plastered with potash and vinegar.

"Miss Sarah's here now," Aunt-Sister said. Handful's head rolled side to side on the mattress, but her eyes stayed closed. She'd been heavily sedated with laudanum, the apothecary already come and gone.

I blinked to keep tears away—it was the sight of her lying there maimed, but some of my anguish came from guilt. I didn't know she'd been arrested, that Mother had decided to let her suffer the consequences in the Work House. I hadn't even missed Handful's presence. This would never have happened if I hadn't returned Handful's ownership to Mother. I'd known Handful would be worse off with her, and I'd given her back anyway. That awful self-righteousness of mine.

Sabe had brought Handful home in the carriage while I'd been away at Bible study. *Bible study.* I felt shame to think of myself, probing verses in the thirteenth chapter of Corinthians—*Though I have all knowledge and all faith, and have not charity, I am nothing.*

I forced myself to look across the bed at Aunt-Sister. "How bad is it?"

She answered by peeling back the green leaf so I could see for myself. Handful's foot was twisted inward at an unnatural angle and there was a gash running from her ankle to the small toe, exposing raw flesh. A row of bright blood beaded through the poultice. Aunt-Sister dabbed it with a towel before smoothing the leaf back in position.

"How did this happen?" I asked.

"They put her on the treadmill, say she fell off and her foot went under the wheel."

A sketch of the newly installed monstrosity had appeared in the *Mercury* recently with the caption, *A More Resourceful Reprimand.* The article speculated it would earn five hundred dollars profit for the city the first year.

"The apothecary say the foot ain't broken," Aunt-Sister said. "The cords that hold the bones are torn up, and she gon be cripple now, I can tell from looking at it."

Handful moaned, then muttered something that came out slurred and indistinguishable. I took her hand in mine, startled by how slight it felt, wondering how her foot hadn't crumbled to dust. She looked small lying there, but she was no longer childlike. Her hair was cut ragged an inch from her head. Little sags drooped beneath her eyes. Her forehead was pleated with frown-lines. She'd aged into a tiny crone.

Her lids fluttered, but didn't open, as she attempted again to speak. I bent close to her lips.

"Go away," she hissed. *"Go. Away."*

Later I would tell myself her mind was addled with opiates. She couldn't have known what she was saying. Or perhaps she'd been referring to her own desire to go away.

Handful didn't leave her room for ten days. Aunt-Sister and Phoebe carried her meals and tended her foot, and Goodis always seemed to linger by the back steps, waiting for news, but I stayed away, fearing her words had been for me after all.

The ban on Father's study had never been lifted and I rarely set foot there, but while Handful convalesced, I slipped in and took two books—*Pilgrim's Progress* by Bunyan and Shakespeare's *The Tempest,* a sea adventure I thought she would especially like—and left them at her door, knocking and hurrying away.

On the morning Handful emerged, we Grimkés were having breakfast in the dining room. There were only four children who hadn't yet married or gone off to school: Charles, Henry, Nina, and of course myself, the red-headed maiden aunt of the family. Mother was seated at the head of the table with the hinged silk screen directly behind her, its hand-painted jasmine all but haloing her head. She turned to the window, and I saw her mouth part in surprise. There was Handful. She was crossing the work yard toward the oak, using a wooden cane too tall for her. She maneuvered awkwardly, thrusting herself forward, dragging her right foot.

"She's walking!" cried Nina.

I pushed back my chair and left the table with Nina chasing after me.

"You're not excused!" Mother called.

We didn't so much as turn our heads in her direction.

Handful stood beneath the budding tree on a patch of emerald moss. There were drag marks in the dirt from her foot, and I found myself stepping over them as if they were sacrosanct. As we approached, she began to wind fresh red thread around the trunk. I couldn't imagine what this odd practice meant. It'd been going on, though, for years.

Nina and I waited while she pulled a pair of shears from her pocket and cut away the faded old thread. Several pink strands clung to the bark, and as she plucked at them, her cane slipped and she grabbed the tree to catch herself.

Nina picked up the cane and handed it to her. "Does it hurt?"

Handful looked past Nina at me. "Not all that much now."

Nina squatted unselfconsciously to inspect the way Handful's foot pigeoned inward, the odd hump that had formed across the top of it, how she'd fitted a shoe over it by trimming the opening and leaving off the lace.

"I'm sorry for what happened," I said. "I'm so sorry."

"I read what I could of the books you brought. They gave me something to do beside lay there."

"Can I touch your foot?" Nina asked.

"Nina," I said, then suddenly understood—here was the nightmare she'd dreamed about since she was a child, here was the hidden horror of the Work House.

Maybe Handful understood, too, her need to confront it. "I don't mind," she said.

Nina traced her finger along a crusting scar that flamed across Handful's skin. Silence jelled around us, and I looked up at the leaves feathering on the branches like little ferns. I could feel Handful looking at me.

"Is there anything you need?" I asked.

She laughed. *"There anything I need?* Well, let's see now." Her eyes were hard as glass, burning yellow.

She'd borne a cruelty I couldn't imagine, and she'd come through it scathed, the scar much deeper than her disfigured foot. What I'd heard in her ruthless laugh was a kind of radicalizing. She seemed suddenly dangerous, the way her mother had been dangerous. But Handful was more considering and methodical than her mother ever was, and warier, too, which made it more worrying. A wave of prescience washed over me, a hint of darkness coming, and then it was gone. I said to her, "I just meant—"

"I know what it is you meant," she said, and her tone had mellowed. The anger in her face left, and I thought for a moment she might cry, a sight I'd never witnessed, not even when her mother disappeared.

Instead, she turned and made her way toward the kitchen house, her body listing heavily to the left. The determination in her pained me almost as much as her lameness, and it wasn't until Nina wrapped her arm around my waist and tugged that I realized I was listing with her.

Some days later, Cindie knocked at my door with a note, ordering me to the first-floor piazza, where Mother retreated most afternoons to catch the breezes. It was unusual for her to write out her summons, but Cindie had grown abnormally forgetful, wandering into rooms unable to recall why she was there, bringing Mother a hairbrush instead of a pillow, an array of queer errors that I knew would soon convince Mother to replace her with someone younger.

As I made my way down the stairs, it occurred to me for the first time she might also replace Handful, whose resourcefulness and ability to walk to the market for fabric and supplies was now in question. I paused on the landing, the portrait of the Fates leering, as always, and my stomach gave a lurch of dread. Could this be the reason Mother had summoned me?

Though it was early in May, the heat had moved in with its soaking humidity. Mother sat in the swing and tried to cool herself with her ivory fan. She didn't wait for me to sit. "We've seen no progress in your father's condition for over a year. His tremors are growing worse by the day and there's no more that can be done for him here."

"What are you telling me? Is he—"

"No, just listen. I've spoken with Dr. Geddings and we're in agreement—the only course left is to take him to Philadelphia. There's a surgeon there of renown, a Dr. Philip Physick. I wrote to him recently and he has agreed to see your father."

I lowered myself into a porch chair.

"He will go by ship," she said. "It will be an exacting trip for him, and it's likely he'll have to remain up north through the summer, or as long as it takes to find a cure, but the plan has brought him hope."

I nodded. "Well, yes, of course. He should do everything possible."

"I'm pleased you feel that way. You'll be the one to accompany him."

I leapt to me feet. "Me? Surely you can't mean I'm to take Father to Philadelphia by myself. What about Thomas or John?"

"Be reasonable, Sarah. They cannot leave their professions and families so easily."

"And I can?"

"Do I need to point out you have no profession or family to care for? You live under your father's roof. Your duty is to him."

Caring for Father week after week, possibly for months, all alone in a faraway place—I felt the life drain out of me.

"But I can't leave—" I was going to say, *I can't leave Nina,* but thought better of it.

"I will see to Nina, if that's what you're concerned about."

She smiled, such a rare thing. The memory of being in the drawing room with the rector swept back to me: Mother's cold stare as I defended Nina's right to follow her conscience. I hadn't taken her warning seriously enough: *As long as the two of you are under the same roof, there is little hope for Angelina. . . .* It hadn't been Nina whom Mother meant to remove. It had been I.

"You leave in three days," she said.

Handful

Mauma pretended a limp, and I got the real one. I used her old wood cane, but it came up to my chest—more like a crutch than a cane.

One day when the rain poured and Goodis couldn't work the garden, he said to me, "Gimme that cane."

"What for?"

"Just give it here," he said, so I did.

The rest of the day, he sat in the stable and whittled. When he came back, he had the cane clasped behind his back. He said, "I sure hope you like rabbits."

Not only had the man trimmed off the bottom end to make it the right size, he'd carved the handle into a rabbit head. It had a round, speckled nose, big eyes, and two long ears going straight back. He'd even notched the wood to look like fur.

I said, "I like rabbits *now*."

That was one of the kindliest things ever done for me. One time I asked him how he got his name, and he said his mauma gave it to him when he was ten cause he was the goodest one of her children.

I could travel with the cane like nobody's business. Cindie saw me coming to the kitchen house for supper that night and said I was springing cross the yard like a rabbit. I had to laugh at that.

The day after Cindie praised me, they took her off somewhere and we never saw her again. Aunt-Sister said her mind had worn out, that missus had sent her off with Thomas to their plantation, where she'd live out her days. Thomas, he was the one taking care of the plantation now, and sure enough, he came back with a new maid for missus named Minta.

God help the girl.

Cindie getting sent off like that put a scare in all of us. I went back to my sewing duties faster than you could *say* the word *rabbit*. I showed missus how I could go up the stairs. I climbed sure and steady, and when I got to the top, she said, "Well done, Hetty. I'm sure you know how much it grieved me to send you to the Work House."

I nodded to let her know what a heavy burden this must've been for her.

Then she said, "Sadly, these things become necessary at times, and you do seem to have profited. As for your foot . . . well, I regret the accident, but look at you. You're getting about fine."

"Yessum." I gave her a curtsy from the top step, thinking what Mr. Vesey said one time at church: *I have one mind for the master to see. I have another mind for what I know is me.*

I heard a *tap-tap* on my door one afternoon late, and Sarah stood there with her freckle face white as an eggshell. I'd been working on master Grimké's pants—missus had sent a slew of them down, said they were hanging off him too big. When Sarah came in, I was hobbling round the cutting table, spreading out a pair of britches to see what I could do. I set the shears down.

". . . I only want to say . . . Well, I have to go away . . . Up north. I . . . I don't know when I'll be able to return."

She was talking with the pauses back in her voice, telling me about the doctor in Philadelphia, her having to nurse her daddy, being parted from Nina, all the miseries of packing that waited for her. I listened and thought to myself, *White folks think you care about everything in the world that happens to them, every time they stub their toe.*

"That's a millstone for you," I told her, "I'm sorry," and the minute it left my mouth, I knew it was coming from the true mind that was me, not the mind for the master to see. I *was* sorry for her. Sarah had jimmied herself into my heart, but at the same time, I hated the eggshell color of her face, the helpless way she looked at me all the time. She was kind to me and she was part of everything that stole my life.

". . . You take care of yourself while I'm gone," she said.

Watching her walk to the door, I made up my mind. "Remember how you asked me a while ago if I needed anything? Well, I need something."

She turned back and her face had brightened. "Of course... whatever I can do."

"I need a signed note."

"... What kind of note?"

"One that gives me permission to be on the street. In case somebody stops me out there."

"Oh." That was all she said for a minute. Then, "... Mother doesn't want you going out, not for a while... She has designated Phoebe to do the marketing. Besides, they closed the African church—there won't be anything to attend."

I could've told you the church was doomed, but it was a blow to hear it. "I still need a pass, though."

"... Why? Where do you need to go?... It's dangerous, Handful."

"I spent most of my life getting and doing for you and never have asked for a thing. I got places to go, they're my own business."

She raised her voice at me. The first time. "... And how do you propose to get off the property?"

Looking down on us was the little window mauma used to climb through. It was sitting high up, letting in the only light in the room. I said to myself, *If mauma can do it, I can do it. I'll do it lame, blind, and backward, if I have to.*

I didn't spell out my ways for her. I nodded at a piece of paper on the shelf beside a pen and a pot of ink. I said, "If you can't see fit to write me this pass for safe passage, I'll have to write it myself and sign your name."

She took a deep breath and stared at me for a moment, then she went over and dipped the pen in the ink.

First time I squeezed through the window and went over the wall, Sarah had been gone a week. The worst part was when I had to flop myself over the top of the bricks with nothing but the white oleander for cover. I had the rabbit cane and a thick burlap bundle tied on my back that made me cumbersome, and when I dropped to the ground, I landed on my bad foot. I sat there till the throb wore off, then I slipped out from the trees to the street, just one more slave doing some white person's bidding.

I chose this day cause missus had a headache. We lived for her headaches. When they came, she took to bed and left us to our blessed selves. I tried not to think how I'd get back inside the yard. Mauma had waited for dark and crawled over the back gate and that was the best remedy, but it was summertime and dark came late, giving plenty of time for folks to wonder where I was.

One block down East Bay, I spotted one of the Guard. He looked straight at me and studied my limp. *Walk steady. Not too fast. Not too slow.* Squeezing the ears on the rabbit, I didn't breathe till I turned the corner.

It took me twice as long to get to 20 Bull. I stood cross the street and stared at the house, still in need of paint. I didn't know if Denmark Vesey had got out of the Work House or what had happened to him. Last memory I had from that hellhole was his voice shouting, "Help the girl down there, help the girl."

I hadn't let myself think about it, but standing there on the street, the memory came like a picture in a painting. *I'm up on the treadmill, gripping the bar with all the strength I got. Climbing the wheel, climbing the wheel. It never will stop. Mr. Vesey is quiet, not a grunt from him, but the rest are moaning and crying Jesus and the rawhide splits the air. My hands sweat, sliding on the bar. The knot that lashes my wrist to it comes loose. I tell myself don't look side to side, keep straight ahead, keep going, but the woman with the baby on her back is howling. The whip slashes her legs. Then the child screams. I look. I look to the side and its little head is bleeding. Red and wet. That's when the edges go black. I drop, my hands pulling free from the rope. I fall and there ain't no wings sprouting off my shoulders.*

In the front window of his house, a woman was ironing. Her back was to me, but I could see the shape of her, the lightness of her skin, the bright head scarf, her arm swinging over the cloth, and it caused a hitch in my chest.

When I got up on the porch, I heard her singing. *Way down yonder in the middle of the field, see me working at the chariot wheel.* Peering in the open window, I saw she had her hips swishing, too. *Now let me fly, now let me fly, now let me fly way up high.*

I knocked and the tune broke off. She opened the door still holding the iron, the smell of charcoal straggling behind her. Mauma always said he had mulatto wives all over the city, but the main one lived here in the house. She stuck out her chin, frowning, and I wondered did she think I was the new bride.

"Who're you?"

"I'm Handful. I came to see Denmark Vesey."

She glared at me, then down at my twisted foot. "Well, I'm Susan, his wife. What you want with him?"

I could feel the heat glowing off the iron. The woman had been hard done by and I couldn't blame her not opening the door to stray women. "All I want is to talk to him. Is he here or not?"

"I'm here," a voice said. He stood propped in the doorway behind her with his arms folded on his chest like he's God watching the world go by. He told his wife to find something to do, and her eyes trimmed down to little slits. "Take that iron with you," he said. "It's smoking up the room."

She left with it, while he eyed me. He'd lost some fat from his face. I could see the top rim of his cheek bones. He said, "You're lucky you didn't get rot in your foot and die."

"I made out. Looks like you did, too."

"You didn't come to see about my health."

He didn't wanna beat the bushes. Fine with me. My foot hurt from trudging here. I took the bundle off my back and sat down in a chair. There wasn't a frill in the room, just cane chairs and a table with a Bible on it.

I said, "I used to come here with my mauma. Her name was Charlotte."

The sneer he always wore slid off his face. "I knew I knew you from somewhere. You have her eyes."

"That's what they tell me."

"You have her gumption, too."

I squeezed the burlap bundle against my chest. "I wanna know what happened to her."

"That was a long time ago."

"Coming on seven years."

When he kept silent, I undid the burlap and spread mauma's story quilt cross the table. The squares hung nearly to the floor, bright enough to set a fire in the dark room.

People say he never smiled, but when he saw the slaves flying in the air past the sun, he smiled. He gazed at granny-mauma and the falling stars, at mauma leaving my daddy behind in the field, me and her laying in cut-up pieces on the quilt frame. He studied the spirit trees and the one-legged punishment. Didn't ask what anything meant. He knew it was her story.

I stole a look at the last square where mauma had sewed the man with the carpenter apron and the numbers 1884. I watched careful to see if he'd recognize himself.

"You think that's me, don't you?" he said.

"I know that's you, but I don't know about those numbers."

He chuckled outright. "One, eight, eight, four. That was the number on my lottery ticket. The numbers that bought my freedom."

The room was stifle hot. Sweat dribbled on my temples. *So, that's her last word, then. That's what it came to—a chance for getting free. A fancy chance.*

I folded up the quilt, wrapped it back in the burlap, and tied it on my back. I picked up my cane. I said, "She was pregnant, you know that? When she went missing, your baby went missing with her."

He didn't flinch, but I could tell he didn't know.

I said, "Those numbers never did come up for her, did they?"

Sarah

The ship ride was harrowing. We plied up the coast for nearly two weeks, sickened by heaving waves off Virginia, before finally making our way along the Delaware to Penn Landing. Arriving there, I had an impulse to bend down and kiss the solid ground. With Father almost too weak to speak, it was left to me to figure out how to retrieve our trunks and hire a coach.

As we drew close to Society Hill, where the doctor resided, the city turned lovely with its trees and steeples, its brick row houses and mansions. What struck me was how empty the streets were of slaves. The sudden realization caused a tightness inside of me to release, one I was not aware existed until that moment.

I found us lodging in a Quaker boardinghouse near Fourth Street, where Father relinquished himself to me—what he ate, what he wore, all decisions about his care. He even turned over the money pouches and ledgers. Every few days, I navigated us to the doctor's house by hired carriage, but after three weeks of seemingly futile visits, Father still couldn't walk more than a stone's throw without exhaustion and pain. He'd lost more weight. He looked absolutely desiccated.

Seated in the doctor's parlor one morning, I stared at Dr. Physick's white hair and aquiline nose, a nose very like Father's. He said, "Sadly, I can find no cause for Judge Grimké's tremors or his deterioration."

Father was not the only one who was frustrated. I, too, was weary of coming here optimistic and leaving dismayed. ". . . Surely, there must be something you can prescribe."

"Yes, of course. I believe the sea air will do him good."

"Sea air?"

He smiled. "You're skeptical, but it's quite recognized—it's known as thalassotherapy. I've known it to bring even the gravely ill back to health."

I could only imagine what Father would say to this. *Sea air.*

"My prescription," he said, "is that you take him to Long Branch for the summer. It's a small, rather isolated place on the New Jersey shore known for its sea cure. I'll send you with laudanum and paregoric. He should be outside as much as possible. Encourage him to wade in the ocean, if he's able. By fall, perhaps he'll be recovered enough to travel home."

Perhaps I would be home with Nina before September.

The doctor had said Long Branch was small, but he'd exaggerated. It was not small, it was not even miniscule; it was barely existent. There were four farmhouses, one tiny clapboard Methodist church, and a dry goods store. Neither was the place "rather isolated"; it was woefully isolated. We traveled by private coach from Philadelphia for six days, the last one bumping over a foot trail. After stopping for toiletry supplies in the dry goods, we continued a ways further to Fish Tavern, the only hotel. It was perched atop a bluff overlooking the ocean—a large, sea-weathered edifice. When the clerk informed us that prayer meetings were held in the communal dining hall after dinner, I took it as a sign God had guided us.

Father had come willingly, too willingly, it seemed. I'd felt sure he would insist on returning to South Carolina. I'd expected him to quip, "Do we not have sea-air in Charleston?" but when I'd broken the news to him there in Dr. Physick's examination room, careful to use the word *thalassotherapy,* he'd only looked at me for a long, strange moment. A shadow passed over his face, what I took to be disappointment. He said, "Let's go to New Jersey then. That's what we'll do."

That first afternoon before dusk, I brought cod soup to Father's room. When he tried to eat it, his hand quivered so violently, spoonfuls splattered onto the bed sheets. He lay back against the bedstead and let me feed him. I chattered about the squalling ocean, about the serpentine steps that led from the hotel down to the shore, almost frantic to divert us from what was happening. His mouth opening and closing like a baby bird's. Ladling in the colorless broth. The helplessness of it.

While I fed him, the crush of waves filled the room. Through the window, I could see a swatch of water the color of pewter, whipped by the wind into frothing swells. Finally, he put up his hand to let me know he'd had enough of soup and babbling both.

I placed the chamber pot on the floor nearby. "Good night, Father."

His eyes were already closed, but his hand fumbled for my forearm. "It's all right, Sarah. We will let it be what it is."

---

17 July 1819

Dear Nina,

We are settled at Fish Tavern. Mother would call the place shabby, but it was once elegant and it has character. The rooms are nearly filled with boarders, but I've met only two. They are elderly widowed sisters from New York, who come to prayer meetings each evening in the dining room. I like the younger one quite a lot.

Father commands all of my attention. We came for the sea air, but he hasn't ventured from his room. I open the window, but the squawking gulls annoy him, and he orders the window closed by noon. I'm quite devious—I leave it open a crack and tell him it's shut. It's all the more reason I must go to the dining room and pray with the sisters.

At fifteen, you are old enough that I may speak sister to sister. Father's pain grows worse. He sleeps long, fitful hours from the laudanum, and when I insist he take some exercise around the room, he leans heavily against me. I must feed him most of his meals. Still, Nina, I know there's hope! If faith moves mountains, God will rally Father soon. Each day, I sit by his bed and pray and read the Bible aloud for hours at a time. Don't be angry at me for my piety. I am Presbyterian after all. As you know, we're fond of our gall and wormwood.

I trust you're not provoking Mother too much. If possible, restrain yourself until my return. I pray Handful is well. Keep your eye out for her. If she needs protecting for any reason, do your best.

I miss your company. Perhaps I'm a bit lonely, but I have God. You may tell Mother all is well.

     Your Devoted Sister,
     Sarah

Every day at specified times, the hotel clerk raised and lowered red and white flags near the steps that led down to the beach. At nine o'clock sharp, the red flag went up, signaling the gentlemen to take possession of the shore. I would observe them thundering into the waves, racing beyond the breakers, and diving. Surfacing, they stood waist-deep, their hands on their hips, and surveyed the horizon. On the beach, they tussled or huddled together and smoked cigars. At eleven, the white flag went up, and the men climbed the stairs back to the hotel with woolen towels draped about their necks.

Then the ladies appeared. Even if I was in the midst of prayer, I would mutter a hasty Amen and fly to the window to watch them descend the stairs in their bathing dresses and oilskin caps. I'd never seen ladies bathing. Back home, women didn't go into the ocean in fanciful get-ups. There was a floating bathhouse in the harbor off East Battery with a private area for females, but Mother thought it was unseemly. Once, to my astonishment, I spotted the two elderly sisters I'd written about to Nina, moving gingerly down the steps with the others. The younger one, Althea, always took pains to inquire not only about Father, but about me. "How are you, dear? You look pallid. Are you getting outdoors enough?" When I'd glimpsed her among the bathers that day, she'd glanced back, and seeing me at the window, she'd motioned me to join them. I'd shaken my head, but nothing would've pleased me more.

The women always entered the water differently than the men, holding on to heavy ropes anchored to the shore. At times there would be a dozen of them stretched into the water, clinging to a single line, squealing and turning their backs against the spray. If Father was sleeping, I would stay at the window and watch with a lump in my chest until the white flag came down.

On the morning of August eighth, I was there at the windowsill, neglecting my prayers, when Father woke, crying my name. *"Sarah!"* Reaching his side, I realized he was still asleep. *"Sarah!"* he shouted again, tossing his head in agitation. I placed my hand on his chest to steady him, and he woke with his breath coming hard and fast.

He gazed at me with the feverish look of someone stumbling back from a nightmare. It saddened me to think I'd been part of it. During these weeks at Long Branch, Father had been kind to me. *How are you faring, Sarah? Are you eating enough? You seem weary. Put down the Bible, go for a walk.* His tenderness had shocked me. Yet he'd remained aloof, never speaking of deeper things.

I pressed a cool cloth to his forehead. "... Father, I know coming here has been a trial for you, and your progress has been . . . it has been slow."

He smiled without opening his eyes. "It's time we spoke the truth. There has been no progress at all."

"... We mustn't give up hope."

"Mustn't we?" The skin on his cheeks was as thin and sheer as a veil. "I came here to die, you must know that."

"No! I certainly don't know that." I felt aghast, even angry. It was as if the bad dream had cracked his façade, and I suddenly wished for it back. "... If you believe you're dying, then why didn't you insist we go home?"

"It will be hard for you to understand this, but the last few years at home have been difficult. It seemed a relief to be far away, to be here with you and go quietly. I felt like here I could detach more easily from the things I've known and loved my whole life."

My hand went to my mouth. I felt my eyes film over with tears.

"Sarah. My dear girl. Let's not indulge vain hopes. I don't expect to recover, nor do I want to."

His face blazed intensely now. I took his hand and gradually his expression eased, and he drifted to sleep.

He woke at three in the afternoon. The white flag had just been raised—I could see it framed in the window, snapping against the translucent sky. I held the water glass to his lips and helped him to drink. He said, "We've had our quarrels, haven't we?"

I knew what was coming and I wanted to spare him. To spare me. "It doesn't matter now."

"You've always had a strong, separate mind, perhaps even a radical mind, and I was harsh with you at times. You must forgive me."

I couldn't imagine what it cost him to say these words. "I do," I said. "And you must forgive me."

"Forgive you for what, Sarah? For following your conscience? Do you think I don't abhor slavery as you do? Do you think I don't know it was greed that kept me from following my conscience as you have? The plantation, the house, our entire way of life depended on the slaves." His face contorted and he clutched at his side a moment before going on. "Or should I forgive you for wanting to give natural expression to your intellect? You were smarter than even Thomas or John, but you're female, another cruelty I was helpless to change."

"Father, please. I have no resentment of you." It wasn't completely true, but I said it.

Giggles floated up from the beach below, tangled in the wind. "You should go outside and refresh your spirit," he said.

I protested, but he wouldn't relent. "How will you take care of me, if you don't take care of yourself? Do this for me. I'll be fine."

I meant only to wade in the surf. I removed my shoes and placed them beside the portable changing house that had been wheeled out onto the sand.

At that moment, the friendly sister, Althea, drew back the canvas and stepped out wearing a red-and-black-striped bathing gown with a peplum flounce and balloon sleeves. I wished Handful could've seen it.

"How lovely. Are you finally bathing with us?" she said.

". . . Oh, no, I don't have the attire for it."

She scrutinized my face, which must've radiated unhappiness in every direction, for she announced she'd suddenly lost the desire to bathe and it would please her enormously if I would don her dress and take a plunge. After my conversation with Father, I felt flayed open, all pulp and redness. I wanted to disappear somewhere alone, yet I looked at the rope-line of women jutting into the sea, and then beyond it at the green mountains of water, so limitless and untamed, and I accepted her offer.

She smiled when I emerged from the changing room. She had no cap, and I'd unpinned my hair, which was flaming out in the wind. She said I looked like a mermaid.

I took hold of one of the ropes and followed it into the waves, hand over fist, until I came to where the rest of the ladies stood. The water slapped our thighs, tossing us to and fro, a tiny game of Snap the Whip, and then without knowing what I was about to do, I turned loose and strode away from them. I pushed into the seething water, and when I was some distance, I dropped onto my back and floated. It was a shock to feel the water hold me. To lie in the sea while upstairs my father lay dying.

9 August 1819

> *Dear Mother,*
> *The Bible assures us that God shall wipe away every tear from our eyes . . .*

I lowered my pen. I didn't know how to tell her. It seemed strange I should be the one informing her of such news. I'd imagined her gathering us, her children, into the drawing room and saying, *Your father has gone to God.* How was it possible this had fallen to me?

Instead of the distinguished funeral he would've had in Charleston—the pomp of St. Philip's, a stately procession along Meeting Street, his coffin mounted on a flowered carriage and half the city walking behind it—instead of all that, he would be buried anonymously in the overgrown cemetery behind the tiny Methodist church we'd passed on the way here. A farm wagon would pull his casket. I would walk behind it, alone.

But I would tell Mother none of this. Nor would I tell her that at the hour of his death, I was floating free in the ocean, in a solitude I would remember all of my life, the gulls cawing over my head and the white flag flying at the top of the pole.

Handful

Missus' eyes were swollen shut from crying. It was the middle of the morning and she was in bed with her sleeping clothes on. The mosquito net was drawn round her and the curtains were pulled on the windows, but I could see her lids puffed out. Minta, the new girl, was over in the corner trying to disappear.

When missus tried to speak to me, she broke down crying. I felt for her. I knew what it was to lose a person. What I didn't know was why she'd called me to her room. All I could do was stand there and wait for her to get hold of herself.

After a few minutes, she yelled at Minta, "Are you or are you not going to bring me a hankie?"

Minta went scrambling through a drawer in the linen press, and missus turned to me. "You should start on my dress immediately. I want black velvet. With beading of some kind. Mrs. Russell had jet beads on hers. I will need a spoon bonnet with a long crepe veil down the back. And black gloves, but make them fingerless mitts because of the heat. Are you remembering this?"

"Yessum."

"It must be ready in two days. And it must be flawless, Hetty, do you understand? Flawless. Work through the night if you have to."

Seemed like she'd gotten hold of herself real tight.

She wrote me a pass for the market and sent me in the carriage with Tomfry, who was going out to purchase the mourning cards. Said it would take too much time for me to hobble all that way and back. That's how I got the first carriage ride of my life. Along the way, Tomfry said, "Wipe the grin off your face, we supposed to be grieving."

In the market, I was at the high-class stalls looking for the beads missus had to have when I came upon Mr. Vesey's wife, Susan. I hadn't seen her since the first of the summer when I'd gone to 20 Bull.

"Look what the field cat dragged up," she said. I guess she still had her dander up.

I wondered what all she knew. Maybe she'd listened in that day I'd talked to Mr. Vesey. She could know about mauma, the baby, everything.

I didn't see any sense in keeping the feud going. "I don't have a bicker with you. I won't be bothering you anymore."

That took the nettle from her. Her shoulders dipped and her face turned soft. That's when I noticed the scarf she was wearing. Red. Edges sewed with a perfect chain stitch. Little oil spots on the side. I said, "That's my mauma's head scarf."

Her lips opened like the stopper had popped from the bottle. I waited, but she stood there, with her mouth empty.

"I know that scarf," I said.

She set down her basket of cottons and took it off her head. "Go on, take it."

I ran my finger along the stitched hem, cross the creases where her hair had been. I undid the scarf on my head and tied mauma's on. Low on my forehead, the way she wore it.

"How'd you get it?" I said.

She shook her head. "I guess you ought to know. The night your mauma disappeared, she showed up at our door. Denmark said the Guard would be looking for a woman with a red scarf, so I took hers and gave her one of mine. A plain brown one that wouldn't draw notice."

"You helped her? You helped her get away?"

She didn't give any kind of answer, she said, "I do what Denmark says do." Then she sashayed off with her head stripped bare.

I sewed through that day and night and all the next day and night, and the whole time I wore mauma's scarf. The whole time I thought about her showing up at Mr. Vesey's that night, how he knew more than he was saying.

Every time I took the dress upstairs for fittings, the house would be in a tizzy getting ready for the mourners. Missus said half the city was coming. Aunt-Sister and Phoebe were baking funeral biscuits and seeing to the tea sets. Binah shrouded the paintings and mirrors with black swags and Eli was put to cleaning. Minta had the worst job, in there getting hankies and taking the brunt.

Tomfry set up master Grimké's portrait in the drawing room and fixed a table with tokens. Had his beaver top hat and stick pins and the books of law he wrote. Thomas brought over a cloth banner that said, *Gone, But Not Forgotten,* and Tomfry put that on the table, too, with a clock stopped to the hour of his death. Missus didn't know the time exact. Sarah had written he passed in the late afternoon, so missus said, just make it 4:30.

When she wasn't crying, she was fuming that Sarah hadn't had the sense to cut off a lock of master Grimké's hair and put it in the letter. It left her without anything to go in her gold mourning brooch. Another thing she didn't like was the notice that came out in the *Mercury*. It said he'd been laid to rest in the North without family or friends and this would surely be a travail to a great son of South Carolina.

I don't know how I got the dress done in time. It was the finest dress I ever made. I strung hundreds of black glass beads, then sewed the strands into a collar that looked like a spider web. I fitted it round the neck and let it drape to the bust. When missus saw it, she said the one and only kind thing I can't forget. She said, "Why, Hetty, your mother would be proud."

I went through the window and over the wall on a Sunday after the callers had quit coming by to give their condolence. It was our day off and the servants were lolling round and missus was shut away in her room. I had a short walk past the front of the house before I could feel safe, and coming round the side of it, I saw Tomfry on the front steps, haggling with the slave boy who huckstered fish. They were bent over what looked like a fifty-pound basket of flounders. I put my head down and kept going.

"Handful! Is that you?"

When I looked up, Tomfry was staring at me from the top step. He was old now, with milk in his eyes, and it crossed my mind to say, *No, I'm somebody else,* but then, he could've seen the cane in my hand. You couldn't misjudge that. I said, "Yeah, it's me. I'm going to the market."

"Who said you could go?"

I had Sarah's pass in my pocket, but seemed like he'd question that—she was still up north, waiting to sail home. I stood on the sidewalk stuck to the spot.

He said, "What you doing out here? Answer me."

Off in my head, I could hear the treadmill grind.

A shape moved at the front window. *Nina.* Then the front door opened, and she said, "What is it, Tomfry?"

"Handful out here. I'm trying to see what she's doing."

"Oh. She's doing an errand for me, that's all. Please say nothing to Mother, I don't want her bothered." Then she called down to me, "Carry on."

Tomfry went back to the fish huckster. I couldn't get my legs to move fast enough. At George Street, I stopped and looked back. Nina was still out there, watching me go. She lifted her hand and gave me a wave.

Close to 20 Bull, there was a little jug band going—three boys blowing on big jars and Gullah Jack, Mr. Vesey's man, slapping his drum. A crowd of colored folks was gathered, and two of the women started doing what we called stepping. I stopped to watch cause they were Strutting Miss Lucy. Mostly, I kept my eye on Gullah Jack. He had fat side whiskers and was bouncing on his short legs. When he finished the tune, he tucked the drum under his arm and headed down the street to Mr. Vesey's. Me, following behind.

I could see smoke from the kitchen house, and went back there and knocked. Susan let me in, saying, "Well, I'm surprised it took you this long." She said I could give her some help, the men were in the front room, meeting.

"Meeting about what?"

She shrugged. "Don't know, don't wanna know."

I helped her chop cabbages and carrots for their supper, and when she carried a bottle of Madeira to them, I trailed her. I waited outside the door, while she poured their glasses, but I could see them at the table: Mr. Vesey, Gullah Jack, Peter Poyas, Monday Gell, plus two who belonged to the governor, Rolla

Bennett and Ned Bennett. I knew every one of them from church. They were all slaves, except Mr. Vesey. Later on, he'd start calling them his lieutenants.

I slunk back into the hallway and let Susan go back to the kitchen house without me. Then I eased to the door, close as I could without getting seen.

It sounded like Mr. Vesey was divvying up all the slaves in the state. "I'll take the French Negroes on the Santee, and Jack, you take the slaves on the Sea Islands. The ones that'll be hard to enlist are the country slaves out on the plantations. Peter, you and Monday know them best. Rolla, I'm giving you the city slaves, and Ned, the ones on the Neck."

His voice dropped and I crept a little closer. "Keep a list of everybody you draft. And keep that list safe on pain of death. Tell everybody, be patient, the day is coming."

I don't know where he came from, but Gullah Jack was on top of me before I could turn my head. He grabbed me from behind and threw me into the room, my rabbit cane flying. I bounced off the wall and landed flat.

He stuck his foot on my chest, pressing me to the floor. "Who're you?"

"Take your nasty foot off me!" I spit at him and the spew fell back on my face.

He raised a hand like he was ready to strike, and from the edge of my eye, I saw Denmark Vesey pick him up by the collar and fling him half cross the room. Then he pulled me up. "You all right?"

My arms were trembling so bad I couldn't hold them still.

"Everything you heard in here, you keep to yourself," he told me.

I nodded again, and he put his arm round me to stop the shaking.

Turning to Gullah Jack and the rest of them, he said, "This is the daughter of my wife and the sister of my child. She's family, and that means you don't lay a hand on her."

He told the men to go on back to his workshop. We waited while they scraped the chairs back and eased from the room.

So, he counted mauma one of his wives. *I'm family.*

He pulled a chair for me. "Here, sit down. What're you doing here?"

"I came to find out the truth of what happened to mauma. I know you know."

"Some things are better not to know," he said.

"Well, that's not what the Bible preaches. It says if you know the truth, it'll set you free."

He circled the table. "All right, then." He closed the window so the truth would stay in the room and not float out for the world to hear.

"The day Charlotte got in trouble with the Guard, she came here. I was in the workshop and when I looked up, there she was. They'd chased her all the way to the rice mill pond, where she hid inside a sack in the millhouse. She had rice hulls all over her dress. I kept her here till dark, then I took her to the Neck, where the policing is light. I took her there to hide."

The Neck was just north of the city and had lots of tenement houses for free blacks and slaves whose owners let them "live out." Negro huts, they called them. I tried to picture one, picture mauma in it.

"I knew a free black there who had a room, and he took her in. She said when the Guard stopped searching for her, she'd go back to the Grimkés and throw herself on their mercy." He'd been pacing, but now he sat down next to me and finished up the truth quick as he could. "One night she went out to the privy in Radcliff Alley and there was a white man there, a slave poacher named Robert Martin. He was waiting for her."

A noise filled my head, a wailing sound so loud I couldn't hear. "A poacher, what's a poacher?"

"Somebody that steals slaves. They're worse than scum. We all knew this man—he had a wagon-trade in these parts. First, regular goods, then he started buying slaves, then he started stealing slaves. He hunted for them in the Neck. He'd keep his ear to the ground and go after the runaways. More than one person saw him take Charlotte."

"He took her? He sold her off somewhere?"

I was on my feet, screaming over the noise in my skull. "Why didn't you look for her?"

He took me by the shoulders and gave me a shake. His eyes were sparking like flint. He said, "Gullah Jack and I looked for two days. We looked everywhere, but she was gone."

Sarah

I made the laborious journey back to Philadelphia, where I found lodging at the same house on Society Hill where Father and I had boarded earlier, expecting to stay only until the ship sailed, but on the appointed morning—my trunk packed and the carriage waiting—something strange and unknown inside of me balked.

Mrs. Todd, who rented the room to me, tapped at my door. "Miss Grimké, the carriage—it's waiting. May I send the driver to collect the trunk?"

I didn't answer immediately, but stood at the window and stared out at the leafy vine on the picket fence, at the cobble street lined with sycamore trees, the light falling in quiet, mottled patterns, and beneath my breath I whispered, "No."

I turned to her, untying my bonnet. It was black with a small ruffle suitable for mourning. I'd purchased it on High Street the day before, maneuvering alone in the shops with no one to please but myself, then come back to this simple room where there were no servants or slaves, no immoderate furniture or filigree or gold leaf, no one summoning me to tea with visitors I didn't care for, no expectations of any kind, just this little room where I took care of everything myself, even spreading my own bed and seeing to my laundry. I turned to Mrs. Todd. ". . . I would like to keep the room a bit longer, if I may."

She looked confused. "You're not leaving as planned?"

"No, I would like to stay a while. Only a while."

I told myself it was because I wanted to grieve in private. Really, was that so implausible?

Mrs. Todd was the wife of a struggling law clerk and she clasped my hand. "You're welcome to stay as long as you wish."

I wrote a solicitous letter to Mother, explaining the unexplainable: Father had died and I wasn't coming home straight away. *I need to grieve alone.*

Mother's letter in response arrived in September. Her small, tight scrawl was thick with fury and ink. My behavior was shameful, selfish, cruel. "How could you abandon me in my darkest hour?" she wrote.

I burned her letter in the fireplace, but her words left contusions of guilt. There was truth in what she'd written. I was selfish. I'd abandoned my mother. Nina, as well. I anguished over it, but I didn't pack my trunk.

I spent my days as a malingerer. I slept whenever I was tired, often in the middle of the day. Mrs. Todd gave up on my presence at appointed meals and reserved my food in the kitchen. I would take it to my room at odd hours, then wash my own dishes. There were few books to read, but I wrote in a little journal I'd bought, mostly about Father's last days, and I practiced my scripture verses with a set of Bible flash cards. I walked up and down the streets beneath the sycamores as they turned blonde, then bronze, venturing further and further each day—to Washington Square, Philosophical Hall, Old St. Mary's, and once, quite by accident, The Man Full of Trouble Tavern where I heard shouting and crockery breaking.

One Sunday when the air was crisp and razor-cut with light, I walked ankle-deep in fallen leaves all the way to Arch Street, where I came upon a Quaker meetinghouse of such size I paused to stare. In Charleston, we had one teeny Friends House, something of a dilapidation, to which, it was said, no one came but two cantankerous old men. As I stood there, people began to stream from the central door, the women and girls clad in dismal, excoriated dresses that made us Presbyterians seem almost flamboyant. Even the children wore drab coats and grave little faces. I observed them against the red bricks, the steeple-less roof, the plain shuttered windows, and I felt repelled. I'd heard they sat in silence, waiting for someone to utter his most inward intimacies with God out loud for everyone to hear. It sounded terrifying to me.

Notwithstanding the Quakers, those days were very much like the moments I'd floated in the ocean at Long Branch beneath the white flag. A vitality inhabited those weeks, almost like a second heart beating in my chest. I'd found I could manage quite well on my own. Had it not been for Father's death, I might have been happy.

When November arrived, however, I knew I couldn't remain any longer. Winter was coming. The sea would become treacherous. I packed my trunk.

The ship was a cutter, which gave me hope of reaching Charleston in ten days. I'd booked first-class passage, but my stateroom was dark and cramped with nothing but a closet and a two-foot berth. As often as possible, I hazarded above deck to feel the cold, bracing winds, huddling with the other passengers on the lee side.

On the third morning, I woke near dawn and dressed quickly, not bothering to braid my hair. The stale, suffocating room felt like a sepulcher, and I surfaced above deck with my carrot hair flying, expecting to be alone, yet there was another already at the rail. Pulling up the hood of my cloak, I sought a spot away from him.

A tiny, white ball of moon was still in the sky, clinging to the last bit of night. Below it a thin line of blue light ran the length of the horizon. I watched it grow.

"How are thee?" a man's voice said, using the formal Quaker greeting I'd often heard in Philadelphia.

As I turned to him, strands of my hair slipped from the hood and whipped wildly about my face. "... I'm fine, sir."

He had a dramatic cleft in his chin and piercing brown eyes over which his brows slanted upward like the slopes of a tiny hill. He wore simple breeches with silver knee buckles, a dark coat, and a three-cornered hat. A lock of hair, dark as coal, tossed on his forehead. I guessed him to be some years older than I, perhaps ten or more. I'd seen him on deck before, and on the first night, in the ship's dining quarters with his wife and eight children, six boys, two girls. I'd thought then how tired she looked.

"My name is Israel Morris," he said.

Later, I would wonder if the Fates had placed me there, if they'd been the ones who'd kept me lingering in Philadelphia for three months until this particular ship sailed, though of course, we Presbyterians believed it was God who arranged propitious encounters like these, not mythological women with spindles, threads, and shears.

The mainsails were snapping and wheezing, making a great racket. I told him my name, and then we stood for a moment, gazing at the rising brightness, at the seabirds suddenly making soaring arcs in the sky. He told me his wife, Rebecca, was quarantined in their cabin tending their youngest two, who'd become sick with dysentery. He was a broker, a commission merchant, and though he was modest, I could tell he'd been prosperous at it.

In turn, I told him about the sojourn I'd made with my father and his unexpected death. The words slid fluidly off my tongue, with only an occasional stammer. I could only attribute it to the sweep and flow of water around us.

"Please, accept my sympathies," he said. "It must have been difficult, caring for your father alone. Could your husband not travel with you?"

"My husband? Oh, Mr. Morris, I'm not married."

His face flushed.

Wanting to ease the moment, I said, "I assure you, it's not a matter that concerns me much."

He laughed and asked about my family, about our life in Charleston. When I told him about the house on East Bay and the plantation in the upcountry, his lively expression died away. "You own slaves then?"

"... My family does, yes. But I, myself, don't condone it."

"Yet you cast your lot with those who do?"

I bristled. "... They are my family, sir. What would you have me do?"

He gazed at me with kindness and pity. "To remain silent in the face of evil is itself a form of evil."

I turned from him toward the glassy water. What kind of man would speak like this? A Southern gentleman would as soon swallow his tongue.

"Forgive my bluntness," he said. "I'm a Quaker. We believe slavery to be an abomination. It's an important part of our faith."

"... I happen to be Presbyterian, and while we don't have an anti-slavery doctrine like you, it's an important part of my faith, as well."

"Of course. My apologies. I'm afraid there's a zealot in me I'm at a loss to control." He pulled at the rim of his hat and smiled. "I must see about breakfast for my family. I hope we might speak again, Miss Grimké. Good day."

I thought of nothing but him for the next two days. He disturbed nearly every waking minute, and even my sleep. I was drawn to him in a deeper way than I'd been to Burke, and that's what frightened me. I was drawn to his brutal conscience, to his repulsive Quakerism, to the force of his ideas, the force of *him*. He was married, and for that I was grateful. For that, I was safe.

He approached me in the dining room on the sixth day of the voyage. The ship was scudding before a gale and we'd been banned from above deck. "May I join you?" he asked.

". . . If you like." Heat flared in my chest. I felt it travel to my cheeks, turning them to crabapples. ". . . Are your children recovered? And your wife? Has she stayed well?"

"The sickness is making its way through all of the children now, but they're recovering thanks to Rebecca. We couldn't manage a single day without her. She is—" He broke off, but when I went on gazing at him expectantly, he finished his sentence. "The perfect mother."

Without his hat, he looked younger. Thatches and sprigs of black hair waved in random directions. He had tired smudges beneath his eyes, and I imagined they were from helping his wife nurse the children, but he pulled a worn leather book from his vest, saying he'd stayed up late in the night, reading. "It's the journal of John Woolman. He's a great defender of our faith."

As the conversation turned once again to Quakerism, he opened the book and read fragments to me, attempting to educate me about their beliefs. "Everyone is of equal worth," he said. "Our ministers are female as well as male."

"Female?" I asked so many questions about this oddity, he became amused.

"Should I assume that female worth, like abolition, is also part of your personal faith?" he said.

". . . I've long wished for a vocation of my own."

"You're a rare woman."

"Some would say I'm not so much rare, as radical."

He smiled and his brows lifted on his forehead, their odd tilt deepening. "Is it possible a Quaker lurks beneath that Presbyterian skin of yours?"

"Not at all," I told him. But later, in private, I wasn't sure. To condemn slavery was one thing—that I could do in my own individual heart—but female ministers!

Throughout the few remaining days on ship, we continued our talks in the wind-pounded world above deck, as well as the dining quarters, where it smelled of boiled rice and cigars. We discussed not only the Quakers, but theology, philosophy, and the politics of emancipation. He was of the mind that abolition should be gradual. I argued it should be immediate. He'd found an intellectual companion in me, but I couldn't completely understand why he'd befriended me.

The last night aboard, Israel asked if I would come and meet his family in the dining room. His wife, Rebecca, held their youngest on her lap, a crying tot no more than three, whose red face bounced like a woodpecker against her shoulder. She was one of those slight, gossamer women, whose body seemed spun from air. Her hair was light as straw, drawn back and middle-parted with wisps falling about her face.

She patted the child's back. "Israel speaks highly of you. He says you've been kind enough to listen as he explained our faith. I hope he didn't tire you. He can be unrelenting." She smiled at me in a conspiratorial way.

I didn't want her to be so pretty and charming. "... Well, he was certainly thorough," I said, and her laughter gurgled up. I looked at Israel. He was beaming at her.

"If you return to the North, you must come and stay with us," Rebecca said, then she herded the children to their cabin.

Israel lingered a moment longer, pulling out John Woolman's journal. "Please accept it."

"But it's your own copy. I couldn't possibly take it."

"It would please me greatly—I'll get another when I return to Philadelphia. I only ask that after you read it, you write to me of your impressions." He opened the book and showed me a piece of paper on which he'd written his address.

That night, after I blew out the wick, I lay awake, thinking of the book tucked in my trunk and the address secreted inside. *After you read it, write to me.* The water moved beneath me, rushing toward Charleston into the swaying dark.

Handful

When they plan to sell you, the first thing they say is, go wash your teeth. That's what Aunt-Sister always told us. She said when the slaves got sold on the streets, the white men checked their teeth before anything else. None of us were thinking about teeth after master Grimké died, though. We thought life would go on in the same old grudgeries.

The lawyer showed up to read the will two days after Sarah got back from the North. We gathered in the dining room, every one of the Grimké children and every slave. Seemed odd to me why missus wanted us slaves here. We stood in a straight line in the back of the room, half-thinking we're part of the family.

Sarah was on one side of the table and Nina on the other. Sarah would look over at her sister with a sad smile, and Nina would glance away. Those two were in a miff.

Missus had on her nice black mourning dress. I wanted to tell her she needed to take it off and let Mariah launder it cause it had gray armpit rings. Seemed like she'd worn it every day since last August, but you couldn't tell her a thing. The woman got worse in her ways by the day.

The lawyer, his name was Mr. Huger, stood up with a handful of papers and said it was the last will and testament of John Faucheraud Grimké, drawn up last May. He read the wherefores, to wits, and hithermores. It was worse than the Bible.

Missus didn't get the house. That went to Henry, who wasn't past eighteen, but least she could stay in it till she died. "I leave her the household furniture, plate, plated ware, a carriage and two of my horses, the stock of liquors and provisions which shall be on hand at the time of my death." This went on and on. All the goods and chattels.

Then he read something that made the hairs on my arms raise. "She shall receive any six of my Negroes whom she shall choose, and the rest she will sell or disperse among my children, as she determines."

Binah was standing next to me. I heard her whisper, "Lord, no."

I looked down the row of slaves. There was just eleven of us now—Rosetta had passed on in her sleep the year before.

She shall receive any six . . . the rest she will sell or disperse. Five of us were leaving.

Minta started to sniffle. Aunt-Sister said, "Hush up," but even her old eyes darted round, looking scared. She'd trained Phoebe too good. Tomfry was getting on with age, too, and Eli's fingers were twisted like tree twigs. Goodis and Sabe were still young, but you don't need two slaves in the stable for two horses. Prince was strong and worked the yard, but he had glum spells now, sitting and staring and blowing his nose on his shirt. Mariah was a good worker, and I figured she'd stay, but Binah, she moaned under her breath cause she was the nursery mauma and there was no more children to rear.

I said to myself, *Missus will need a seamstress,* but then I noticed the black dress again. From here on out, all she'd need was a few of those to wear, and she could hire somebody for that.

All of a sudden, Sarah said, ". . . Father couldn't have meant that!"

Missus shot her a look of venom. "Your father wrote the words himself, and we'll honor his wishes. We have no choice. Please allow Mr. Huger to continue."

When he started back reading, Sarah looked at me with the same sorrowful blue eyes she'd had the day she turned eleven years old and I was standing before her with the lavender ribbon round my neck. The world was a bashed-in place and she couldn't fix it.

In December, everybody was on their last nerve waiting for missus to say who'd go and who'd stay. If I was sold, how would mauma find me if she came back?

Every night I put a hot brick in my bed to keep my feet warm and lay there thinking how mauma was alive. Out there somewhere. I wondered if the man who bought her was kind. I wondered if he'd put her in the fields. Was she doing any sewing? Did she have my little brother or sister with her? Was she still wearing the pouch round her neck? I knew she'd get back here if she could. This was where her spirit was, in the tree. This was where I was.

Don't let me be the one that has to go.

Missus didn't have Christmas that year, but she said go ahead and have Jonkonnu if you want to. That was a custom that got started a few years back brought by the Jamaica slaves. Tomfry would dress up in a shirt and pants tattered with strips of bright cloth sewed on, and a stove pipe hat on his head—what we called the Ragman. We'd traipse behind him, singing and banging pots, winding to the back door. He'd knock and missus and everybody would come out and watch him dance. Then missus would hand out little gifts to us. Could be a coin or a new candle. Sometimes a scarf or a cob pipe. This was supposed to keep us happy.

We didn't expect to feel in the mood this year, but on Jonkonnu day, here came Tomfry in the yard, wearing his shaggy outfit, and we made a lot of clatter and forgot our troubles for a minute.

Missus stepped out from the back door in the black dress with a basket of gifts, Sarah, Nina, Henry, and Charles behind her. They were trying to smile at us. Even Henry, who took after his mauma, looked like a grinning angel.

Tomfry did his jig. Twirled. Bounced. Wagged his arms. The ribbons whirled out, and when he was done, they clapped, and he took off the tall hat and rubbed the crust of gray on his scalp. Reaching in the basket, missus gave the women these nice fans made with painted paper. The men got two coins, not one.

The sky had been cast down all day, but now the sun broke free. Missus leaned on her gold-tip cane and squinted at us. She called out Tomfry's name. Then Binah. Eli. Prince. Mariah. She said, "I have something extra for you," and handed each one a jar of gargling oil.

"You've served me well," she told them. "Tomfry, you will go to John's household. Binah, you will go to Thomas. Eli, I'm sending you to Mary." Then she turned to Prince and Mariah. "I'm sorry to say you must be sold. It's not my wish, but it's necessary."

Nobody spoke. The quiet sat on us like a stone you couldn't lift.

Mariah dropped down and walked on her knees to missus, crying for her to change her mind.

Missus wiped her eyes. Then she turned and went in the house followed by her sons, but Sarah and Nina stayed behind, their faces full of pity.

The axe didn't fall on me. *Didn't my Lord deliver Handful?* The axe didn't fall on Goodis either, and I felt surprise over the relief this caused me. But there was no God in any of it. Nothing but the four of them standing there, and Mariah, still on her knees. I couldn't bear to look at Tomfry with the hat squashed under his arm. Prince and Eli, studying the ground. Binah, holding her paper fan, staring at Phoebe. A daughter she'd never see again.

Missus doled out their jobs to the ones of us left. Sabe took over for Tomfry as the butler. Goodis had the work yard, the stable, and drove the carriage. Phoebe got the laundry, and Minta and I got Eli's cleaning duties.

When the first of the year came, missus set me to work on the English chandelier in the drawing room. She said Eli hadn't shined it proper in ten years. It had twenty-eight arms with crystal shades and teardrops of cut-glass hanging down. Using the ladder and wearing white cotton gloves, I took it apart and laid it out on the table and shined it with ammonia. Then, I couldn't figure out how to put the thing back together.

I found Sarah in her room, reading a leather book. "We'll figure it out," she said. We hadn't talked much since she got back—she seemed woebegone all the time, always stuck in that same book.

After we finally got the chandelier back on the ceiling in one piece, tears flared up in her eyes. I said, "You sad about your daddy?"

She answered me the strangest way, and I knew what she said was the real hurt she'd brought back with her. "... I'm twenty-seven years old, Handful, and this is my life now." She looked round the room, up at the chandelier, and back at me. "... *This* is my life. Right here for the rest of my days." Her voice broke and she covered her mouth with her hand.

She was trapped same as me, but she was trapped by her mind, by the minds of the people round her, not by the law. At the African church, Mr. Vesey used to say, *Be careful, you can get enslaved twice, once in your body and once in your mind.*

I tried to tell her that. I said, "My body might be a slave, but not my mind. For you, it's the other way round."

She blinked at me and the tears came again, shining like cut-glass.

The day Binah left, I heard Phoebe crying all the way from the kitchen house.

Sarah

1 February 1820
Dear Israel,
How often I have thought of our conversations on board ship! I read the book you entrusted to me and my spirit was deeply kindled. There are so many things I wish to ask you! How I wish we were together again—

3 February 1820
Dear Mr. Morris,
After being away from the evils of slavery for six months, my mind burst with new horror at seeing it again on my return to Charleston. It was made all the worse upon reading the book you gave me. I have nowhere to turn but you—

10 February 1820
Dear Mr. Morris,
I trust you are well. How is your dear wife, Rebecca—

11 February 1820
Thank you, sir, for the book. I find a bewildering beauty in your Quaker beliefs—the notion there is a seed of light inside of us, a mysterious Inner Voice. Would you kindly advise me how this Voice—

I wrote to him over and over, letters I couldn't finish. Invariably, I would stop mid-sentence. I would lay down the quill, fold the letter, and conceal it with the rest at the back of my desk drawer.

It was the middle of the afternoon, the winter gloom hovering as I pulled out the thick bundle, untied the black satin ribbon, and added the letter of February 11 to the heap. Mailing the letters would only bring anguish. I was too drawn to him. Every letter he answered would incite my feelings more. And it would do no good to have him encouraging me toward Quakerdom. The Quakers were a despised sect here, regarded as anomalous, plain-dressed, and strange, a tiny cluster of jarringly eccentric people who drew stares on the street. Surely, I didn't need to invite that kind of ridicule and shun. And Mother—she would never allow it.

Hearing her cane on the pine floor outside, I snatched up the letters and yanked open the drawer, my hands fumbling with panic. The stationery cascaded into my lap and onto the rug. As I stooped to collect it, the door swung open without a knock and she stood framed in the opening, her eyes moving across my hidden cache.

I looked up at her with the black ribbon furling from my fingers.

"You're needed in the library," she said. I couldn't detect the slightest curiosity in her about the contents I'd spilled. "Sabe is packing your father's books—I need you to oversee that he does it properly."

"Packing?"

"They will be divided between Thomas and John," she said, and turning, left me.

I gathered up the letters, tied them with the ribbon, and slipped them back into the drawer. Why I kept them, I didn't know—it was foolish.

When I arrived in the library, Sabe wasn't there. He'd emptied most of the shelves, stacking the books in several large trunks, which sat open on the floor, the same floor where I'd knelt all those years ago when Father forbade me the books. I didn't want to think of it, of that terrible time, of the room stripped now, the books lost to me, always lost.

I sank into Father's chair. The clock in the main passage clicked, magnifying, and I felt the shadows gathering inside of me again, worse this time. Since returning, I'd slipped further into melancholy each day. It was the same trough of darkness I'd fallen into when I was twelve and the life had gone out of everything. Mother had summoned Dr. Geddings back then, and I feared she might do so again. Every day, I forced myself to come down for tea. I endured the visitations from her friends. I kept up my attendance at church, at Bible study, at alms meetings. I sat with Mother in the mornings, hoops of embroidery on our laps, willing the needle through the cloth. She'd given me the task of household records, and each week I sorted through the supplies, writing inventories and procurement lists. The house, the slaves, Charleston, Mother, the Presbyterians—they were the woof and warp of everything.

Nina had pulled away. She was angry at me for remaining in Philadelphia after Father died. "You don't know what it was like alone here," she'd cried. "Mother instructed me constantly in the error of my ways, everything from church to slavery to my rebellious nature. It was horrible!"

I'd been the buffer between her and Mother, and my remaining away for so long had left her exposed. "I'm sorry," I told her.

"You only wrote to me once!" Her beautiful face was contorted with hurt and resentment. *"Once."*

It was true. I'd been so enamored with my freedom up there, I hadn't bothered. "I'm sorry," I said again.

I knew in time she would forgive the selfish months I'd abandoned her, but I sensed the estrangement came from more than that. At fifteen, she needed to break away, to come out from my shadow, to understand who she was separate from me. My retreat to Philadelphia was only the excuse she needed to declare her independence.

As she fled to her room the day of our confrontation, she shouted, "Mother was right, I have no mind of my own. Only yours!"

We passed now like strangers. I let her be, but it added to my despair.

I stared at the trunks of books on the library floor, remembering the pangs I'd once had for a profession, for some purpose. The world had been such a beckoning place once.

Sabe still had not returned. I got up from my chair and rummaged nostalgically among the books, coming upon *The Sacred Biography of Jeanne d'Arc of*

France. I couldn't say how many times I'd read that wondrous little volume of Saint Joan's bravery before Father had banned me from his library. Opening it now, I gazed at a sketch of her coat of arms—two *fleurs de lis.* I'd forgotten it was there, and it made sudden sense to me why I'd latched onto the *fleur de lis* button when I was eleven. I slipped the book beneath my shawl.

That night, unable to sleep, I heard the clock downstairs bong two, then three. The rain began soon after, beating without mercy against the piazza and the windows. I climbed from the covers and lit the lantern. I would write to Israel. I would tell him how melancholy swallowed me at times, how I almost felt the grave would be a refuge. I would write yet another letter I wouldn't mail. Perhaps it would relieve me.

I pulled open the desk drawer and watched the light tumble inside it. There, as I'd left it, was my Bible and my Blackstone commentary, my stationery, ink, pen, ruler, and sealing wax, yet I didn't see the bundle of letters. I drew the lamp closer and reached my hand into the empty corners. The black ribbon was there, curled like a malicious afterthought. My letters to Israel were gone.

I wanted to scream at her. The need took hold of me with blinding violence, and I flung open my door and rushed down the stairs, clinging to the rail as my feet seemed to sweep out from under me.

I battered her door with my fist, then rattled the knob. It was locked. "... How dare you take them!" I shrieked. "How dare you. Open the door. Open it!"

I couldn't imagine what she'd thought on reading my intimate implorings to a stranger in the North. A Quaker. A man with a wife. Did she think I'd remained in Philadelphia for him?

Behind the door, I heard her call to Minta, who slept on the floor near her bed. I pounded again. "... Open it! You had no right!"

She didn't respond, but Nina's scared voice came from the stair landing. "Sister?"

Looking up, I saw her white gown glowing in the dark, Henry and Charles beside her, the three of them like wraiths.

"... Go to bed," I said.

Their bare feet slapped the floor and I heard the doors to their rooms bang shut one by one. Turning back, I lifted my fist again, but my rage had begun to recede, flowing back into the terrible place it'd come from. Limp and exhausted, I leaned my head against the door sill, hating myself.

The next morning, I couldn't get out of bed. I tried very hard, but it was as if something in me had dropped anchor. I rolled my face into the pillow. I no longer cared.

During the days that followed, Handful brought me trays of food, which I barely touched. I had no hunger for anything except sleep, and it eluded me. Some nights I wandered onto the piazza and stared over the rail at the garden, imagining myself falling.

Handful placed a gunny sack beside me on the bed one day. "Open it up," she said. When I did, the smell of char wafted out. Inside, I found my letters, singed and blackened. She'd found Minta tossing them into the fire in the kitchen house, as Mother had ordered. Handful had rescued them with a poker.

When spring came and my state of mind didn't improve, Dr. Geddings arrived. Mother seemed genuinely afraid for me. She visited my room with handfuls of drooping jonquils and spoke sweetly, saying I should come for a stroll with her on Gadsden Green, or that she'd asked Aunt-Sister to bake me a rice pudding. She brought me notes of concern from members of my church, who were under the impression I had pleurisy. I would gaze at her blankly, then look away toward the window.

Nina visited, too. "Was it me?" she asked. "Did I cause you to feel like this?"

"Oh, Nina," I said. "... You must never think that ... I can't explain what's wrong with me, but it's not you."

Then one day in May, Thomas appeared. He insisted we sit on the porch where the air was warm and weighed with the scent of lilacs. I listened as he went on heatedly about a recent compromise in Congress that had undone the ban on slavery in Missouri. "That damnable Henry Clay!" he said. "The Great Pacificator. He has started the cancer spreading again."

I had no idea what he was talking about. To my surprise, though, I felt curious. Later, I would realize that was Thomas' intention—creating a little pulley to try and tow me back.

"He's a fool—he believes letting slavery into Missouri will placate the firebrands down here, but it's only splitting the country further." He reached for the newspaper he'd brought and spread it out for me. "Look at this."

A letter had been printed on the front page of the *Mercury,* which called Clay's compromise *a fire bell in the night.*

It has awakened and filled me with terror. I consider it the knell of the Union . . . The letter was signed, *Thomas Jefferson.*

It'd been so long since I'd cared what was happening out there. Some old wrath sparked in me. Hostility toward slavery must be finding some bold new footing! Why, it sounded as if my brother himself was hostile to it.

". . . You are sided with the North?" I asked.

"I only know we can't go on blind to the sin of putting people in chains. It must come to an end."

". . . Are you freeing your slaves, then, Thomas?" Asking it was vindictive. I knew he had no such intention.

"While you were away, I founded an American colonization chapter here in Charleston. We're raising money."

". . . Please tell me you're not still hoping to buy up all the slaves and send them back to Africa?" I hadn't felt such fervor since my discussions with Israel during the voyage. My cheeks burned with it. ". . . *That* is your answer to the spreading cancer?"

"It may be a poor answer, Sarah, but I can imagine no other."

". . . Must our imaginations be so feeble as that, Thomas? If the Union dies, as our old president says, it will be from lack of imagination . . . It will be from Southern hubris, and our love of wealth, and the brutality of our hearts!"

He stood and looked down at me. He smiled. "There she is," he said. "There's my sister."

I cannot say I became my old self after that, but the melancholy gradually lifted, replaced with the jittery feeling of emerging, like a creature without a skin or a shell. I began to eat the rice puddings. I sipped tea steeped in St. John's Wort, and sat in the sun, and reread the Quaker book. I thought often of the fire bell in the night.

At midsummer, without any forethought, I took out a sheet of stationery.

19 July 1820

Dear Mr. Morris,

Forgive my long delay in writing to you. The book you gave me last November aboard ship has been my faithful companion for all this time. The Quaker beliefs beckon to me, but I do not know if I have the courage to follow them. There would be a great and dreadful cost, of that I'm certain. I ask nothing, except your counsel.

Yours Most Truly,
Sarah Grimké

I gave the letter to Handful. "Guard it carefully," I told her. "Post it yourself in the afternoon mail."

When Israel's letter arrived in return, I was in the warming kitchen, surveying the pantries and writing a list of foods needed at the market. Handful had waylaid it from Sabe when it arrived at the door. She handed it to me, and waited.

I took a butter knife from the drawer and ripped the seal. I read it twice, once to myself, then aloud to her.

10 September 1820

Dear Miss Grimké,

I was gratified to receive your letter and most especially to learn that you are swayed to the Quakers. God's way is narrow and the cost is great. I remind you of the scripture: "He that finds his life shall lose it, and he that loses his life shall find it." Do not fear to lose what needs to be lost.

I regret to say I have grave and sorrowful news to impart. My dear Rebecca passed away last January. She died of a malignant influenza soon after our return to Philadelphia. My sister, Catherine, has come to care for the children. They miss their mother, as do I, but we are comforted that our beloved wife and mother is with God.

Write to me. I am here to encourage you in your path.
Your Friend,
Israel Morris

I sat in my room at midday with my eyes closed and my fingers laced in my lap, listening for the Voice the Quakers seemed so sure was inside of us. I'd been indulging in this dubious activity since receiving Israel's letter, though I doubted the Quakers would've called it an *activity*. For them, this listening was the ultimate *inactivity*, a kind of capitulation to the stillness of one's private heart. I wanted to believe God would eventually show up, murmuring little commands and illuminations. As usual, I heard nothing.

I'd responded to Israel's letter immediately, my hand shaking so badly the ink lines had appeared rickety on the paper. I'd poured out my sympathy, my prayers, all sorts of pious assurances. Every word seemed trite, like the prattle that went on at my Bible studies. I felt protected behind it.

He'd responded with another letter and our correspondence had finally begun, consisting mostly of earnest inquires on my part and bits of guidance on his. I asked him pointedly what the Inner Voice sounded like. How will I recognize it? "I cannot tell you," he wrote. "But when you hear it, you will know."

That day the silence felt unusually dull and heavy, like the weight of water. It clogged my ears and throbbed against my drums. Fidgety thoughts darted through my mind, reminding me of squirrels loose in their trees. Perhaps I was too Anglican, too Presbyterian, too Grimké for this. I lifted my eyes to the fireplace and saw the coals had gone out.

Just a few more minutes, I told myself, and when my lids sank closed again, I had no expectations, no hope, no endeavoring—I'd given up on the Voice—and it was then my mind stopped racing and I began to float on some quiet stream.

Go north.

The voice broke into my small oblivion, dropping like a dark, beautiful stone.

I caught my breath. It was not like a common thought—it was distinct, shimmering, and dense with God.

Go north.

I opened my eyes. My heart leapt so wildly I placed a hand across my breast and pressed.

It was unthinkable. Unmarried daughters didn't go off to live unprotected on their own in a foreign place. They lived at home with their mothers, and when there was no mother, with their sisters, and when there were no sisters, with their brothers. They didn't break with everything and everyone they knew and loved. They didn't throw over their lives and their reputations and their family name. They didn't create scandals.

I rose to my feet and paced before the window, saying to myself it wasn't possible. Mother would rain down Armageddon. Voice or no Voice, she would put a swift end to it.

Father had left all his properties and the vast share of his wealth to his sons, but he hadn't forgotten his daughters. He'd left us each ten thousand dollars, and if I were frugal, if I lived on the interest, it would provide for me the rest of my life.

Beyond the window, the sky loomed large, filled with broken light, and I remembered suddenly that day last winter in the drawing room when Handful cleaned the chandelier, the allegation she'd leveled at me: *My body might be a slave, but not my mind. For you, it's the other way round.* I'd dismissed the words—what could she know of it? But I saw now how exact they were. My mind had been shackled.

I strode to my dresser and opened the drawer of my Hepplewhite, the one I never opened, the one that held the lava box. Inside it, I found the silver button Handful had returned to me some years ago. It was black with tarnish and long forgotten. I took it in my palm.

How does one know the voice is God's? I believed the voice bidding me to go north belonged to him, though perhaps what I really heard that day was my own impulse to freedom. Perhaps it was my own voice. Does it matter?

PART FOUR

September 1821–July 1822

Sarah

The house was named Green Hill. When Israel wrote, inviting me to stay with his family in the countryside of Philadelphia, I'd imagined an airy, white-frame house with a big veranda and shutters the color of pine. It was a shock to arrive at the end of spring and find a small castle made entirely of stone. Green Hill was a megalithic arrangement of pale gray rocks, arched windows, balconies, and turrets. Gazing up at it for the first time, I felt like a proper exile.

Israel's late wife Rebecca had at least made the inside of the house soft. She'd filled it with hooked rugs and floral pillows, with simple Shaker furniture and wall clocks from which little birds popped out all day and coo-cooed the hour. It was a very odd place, but I came to like living inside a quarry. I liked the way the stone façade glistened in the rain and silvered over when the moon was full. I liked how the children's voices echoed in slow spirals through the rooms and how the air stayed dim and cool in the heat of the day. Mostly, I liked how impenetrable it felt.

I took up residence in a garret room on the third floor, following months of correspondence with Israel and endless skirmishes with Mother. My tactic had been to convince her the whole thing was God's idea. She was a devout woman. If anything could trump her social obsessions, it was piety, but when I told her about the Inner Voice, she was horrified. In her mind, I'd gone the way of the lunatic female saints who'd gotten themselves boiled in oil and burned at the stake. When I finally confessed I meant to live under the roof of the man I'd written those scandalous, unsent letters to, she broke out in symptoms, cold sores to chest pain. The chest pains were real enough, as evidenced by her drawn, perspiring face, and I worried my intentions might literally kill her.

"If there's a shred of decency in you, you will not run off to live in the house of a Quaker widower," she'd shouted during our final clash.

We were in her bedchamber at the time, and I stood with my back to the window, looking at her face streaked with anger.

"... Israel's unmarried sister lives there, too," I told her for the tenth time. "... I'm simply renting a room. I'll help with the children, I'm to be in charge of the girls' lessons ... It's all very respectable. Think of me as a tutor."

"A *tutor*." She pressed the back of her hand to her forehead as if warding off some heavenly debris. "This would kill your father, if he weren't already dead."

"... Don't bring Father into this. He would want me to be happy."

"I cannot—I will not bless this!"

"... Then I'll go without your blessing." I was dazed at my boldness.

She drew back in the chair, and I knew I'd stung her. She glared at me with taut, blistering eyes. "Then *go*! But keep this sordid business of hearing voices to yourself. You're going north for your health, do you understand?"

"... And what exactly is my affliction?"

She looked toward the window and seemed to survey a piece of the saffron sky. Her silence went on for so long, I wondered if I'd been dismissed. "Coughing," she said. "We fear you have consumption."

That was the pact I made. Mother would tolerate my sojourn and refrain from severing me from the family, and I would pretend my lungs were threatened with consumption.

During the three months I'd been at Green Hill, I'd often felt dislocated and homesick. I missed Nina, and Handful was always at the edges of my mind. To my surprise, I missed Charleston, certainly not its slavery or its social castes, but the wash of light on the harbor, the salt brining the air, Birds of Paradise in the gardens with their orange heads raised, summer winds flapping the hurricane shutters on the piazzas. When I closed my eyes, I heard the bells on St Philip's and sniffed the choking sweetness of the privet hedge that fell over the city.

Mercifully, the days here had been busy. They were filled with eight forlorn children ranging from five years all the way to sixteen and the domestic chores I undertook for Israel's sister, Catherine. Even in my most severe Presbyterian moments, I'd been no match for her. She was a well-meaning woman afflicted with an incurable primness. Despite her spectacles, she had weak, watery eyes that couldn't see enough to thread a needle or measure flour. I didn't know how they'd managed before me. The girls' dresses were unevenly hemmed and we were as apt to get salt in the sponge cake as sugar.

There were long, weekly rides to the Arch Street Meetinghouse in town, where I was now a Quaker probationer, having endured the interrogation from the Council of Elders about my convictions. I had only to wait now for their decision and be on my best behavior.

Every evening, to Catherine's immense displeasure, Israel and I walked down the hill to the little pond to feed the ducks. Decked in green iridescent feathers and fancy black hoods, they were the most un-Quaker of ducks. Catherine had once compared their plumage to my dresses. "Do all Southern ladies adorn themselves in this ostentatious manner?" she'd asked. *If the woman only knew.* I'd left the most grandiose of my wardrobe behind. I'd given Nina a number of silk frocks adorned with everything from feathers to fur; a lavish lace headdress; an imported van-dyked cap; a shawl of flounced tulle; a lapis brooch; strands of pearls; a fan inlaid with tiny mirrors.

At some point, I would have to un-trim my bonnet. I would have to go through the formal divestment, getting rid of all my lovely things and resorting to gray dresses and bare bonnets, which would make me appear plainer than I already was. Catherine had already presented several of these mousy outfits to me as "encouragement," as if the sight of them encouraged anything but aversion. Fortunately, the un-trimming ritual wasn't required until my probation ended, and I had no intention of hurrying it.

When Israel and I visited the pond, we tossed crusts of bread on the water and watched the ducks paddle after them. There was a weathered rowboat turned upside down in the cattails on the far side, but we never ventured into it. We sat instead on a bench he'd built himself and conversed about the children, politics, God, and inevitably, the Quaker faith. He spoke a great deal about his wife, who'd been gone a year and a half. She could've been canonized, his Rebecca. Once, after speaking of her, his voice choked and he held my hand as we lingered silently in the deepening violet light.

In September, before summer left us, I was fathoms deep on the mattress in my room when the sound of crying broke into my slumber and I came swimming up from a dark blue sleep. The window was hinged open, and for a moment I heard nothing but the crickets in their percussion. Then it came again, a kind of whimpering.

I cracked the door to find Becky, Israel's six-year-old, swallowed in an oversized white gown, blubbering and rubbing her eyes. She not only had her mother's name, but her wilted, flaxen hair, and yet in some ways the child reminded me of myself. She had brows and lashes so light they were barely visible, giving her the same whitewashed look I wore. More than that, she chewed and mumbled her words, for which her siblings teased her unmercifully. Overhearing one of her brothers call her Mealy Mouth, I'd given him a talking-to. He avoided me nowadays, but Becky had followed me about ever since like a bear cub.

She rushed at me now, throwing herself into my arms.

"... My goodness, what's all this?"

"I dreamed about Ma Ma. She was in a box in the ground."

"... Oh, Sweet One, no. Your mother is with God and his angels."

"But I saw her in the box. I saw her." Her cries landed in wet bursts against my gown.

I cupped the back of her head, and when her tears stopped, I said, "Come on ... I'll take you back to your room."

Pulling away, she darted past me to my bed and pulled the comforter to her chin. "I want to sleep with *you*."

I climbed in beside her, an unaccountable solace washing over me as she edged close, nuzzling my shoulder. Her head smelled like the sweet marjoram leaves Catherine sewed into their pillows. As her hand fell across my chest, I noticed a chain dangling from her clamped fist.

"... What's this in your hand?"

"I sleep with it," she said. "But when I do, I dream of her."

She unfurled her fingers to reveal a round, gold-plated locket. The front was engraved with a spray of flowers, daffodils tied with a bow, and below them, a name. *Rebecca*.

"That's my name," she said.

"... And the locket, is it yours, too?"

"Yes." Her fingers curled back over it.

I'd never seen a trace of jewelry on Catherine or on Becky's older sister, but in Charleston lockets were as common on little girls as hair barrettes.

"I don't want it anymore," she said. "I want you to wear it."

"... Me? Oh, Becky, I couldn't wear your locket."

"Why?" She raised up, her eyes clouding over again.

"Because... it's yours. It has your name on it, not mine."

"But you can wear it for now. *Just for now.*"

She gave me a look of such pleading, I took it from her. "... I'll keep it for you."

"You'll wear it?"

"... I'll wear it once, if it makes you happy. But only once."

Gradually her breath grew elongated and whispery, the sound of ribbons fluttering, and I heard her mutter, "Ma Ma."

All week, Becky greeted me with a searching look at the collar of my dress. I'd hoped she would forget the episode with the locket, but my wearing it seemed to have built to an implausible height in her mind. Seeing I was without it, she would slump in disappointment.

Was it silly of me to feel wary? Wound inside the locket was a tendril of hair, Becky's, I supposed, but the vaporous color of it must've conjured memories of her mother. If seeing the necklace on me brought her some fleeting consolation, surely it harmed nothing.

I wore the locket to the girls' tutoring session on Thursday. The boys met in the classroom each morning with a male tutor who came from the city, while I instructed the two girls there in the afternoons. Israel had built a single strip of desktops and attached it to the wall, as well as a long bench. He'd installed a slate board, shelves for books, and a teacher's table that smelled of cedar. That morning I wore my emerald dress, which had seen precious little wear considering how like the ducks' feathers it was. The neckline contoured to my collar bones, where the gold locket nestled in the gully between them.

When Becky spied it, she rose on her toes, her body swelled with delight, the tiny features on her face levitating for a moment. For the next hour, she rewarded me by raising her hand whenever I asked a question, whether she knew the answer or not.

I had free rein over their curriculum, and I was determined my old adversary, Madame Ruffin, and her "education for the gentle female mind" would get nowhere near it. I meant to teach the girls geography, world history, philosophy, and math. They would read the humanities, and when I was done, know Latin better than their brothers.

I wasn't against them learning natural history, however, and after a particularly grueling lesson on longitudes and latitudes, I opened John James Audubon's *Birds of America,* a massive brown leather folio, weighing at least as much as Becky. Turning to the ruffed grouse, which was common in the woods nearby, I said, "Who can mimic its call?"

There we were, a flock of ruffed grouses at the open window, trilling and whistling, when Catherine entered the classroom and demanded to know what sort of lesson I was conducting. She'd heard our chirping as she gathered the last cucumbers in the garden. "That was quite a bit of disturbance," she said, the vegetable basket swinging on her arm, sifting crumbs of soil onto her ash-colored dress. Becky, ever alert to her aunt's annoyance, spoke before I could push out my words. "We were calling the ruffed grouse."

"Were you? I see." She looked at me. "It seemed unduly loud. Perhaps more quietly next time."

I smiled at her and she cocked her head and stepped closer, so close her dress hem brushed mine. Her eyes magnified behind the thickset lens of her glasses as she concentrated on the locket at my throat.

"What is the meaning of this?" she said.

". . . The meaning of what?"

"Take it off!"

Becky wedged herself between us. "Auntie. Auntie."

Catherine ignored her. "Your intentions have been more than clear to me, Sarah, but I had not thought you would be so bold as to wear Rebecca's locket!"

". . . Rebecca? . . . You mean, it belonged to . . ." My voice deserted me, my words adhering like barnacles at the back of my throat.

"Israel's *wife*," she said, finishing my sentence.

"Auntie?" Becky's upturned face, drowning in the waves of our gray-green skirts, made her look like a castaway. "I gave it to her."

"You did what? Well, I don't care *who* gave it to her, she shouldn't have taken it." She thrust out her palm, shoving it inches from my chin. I could hear air rasping in and out of her nostrils.

". . . . . . But I didn't . . . know."

"Give me the locket, please."

"No," Becky cried, sinking onto the rug.

I stepped back, unclasping the necklace, and placed it in Catherine's hand. As I bent to scoop Becky from the floor, her aunt pulled the child gently by her arm and maneuvered both girls from the room.

I walked calmly, slowly out the door and down the escarpment toward the pond. Before stepping into the thicket of trees, I looked back at the house. The light was still citrus and bright, but Israel would be home soon, and Catherine would be waiting for him with the locket.

Cloaked in the cedars, I pressed one hand to my stomach and one to my mouth and stood there several seconds, as if squeezing myself together. Then I straightened and followed the path to the water.

I heard the pond before I saw it—the frogs deep in their hum, the violin whir of insects. On impulse, I walked along the edge until I reached the rowboat. Sunk in the mud, it took all my strength to flip it over. I lifted out the oar and inspected the bottom for holes and rotted wood. Seeing none, I gathered up my skirt, climbed in, and paddled to the middle of the pond, an untouchable place, far from everything. I tried to think what I would say to him, worried my voice would slink off again and leave me.

I remained there a long while, lapping on the surface. Vapor curled on the water, dragonflies pricked the air, and I thought it all beautiful. I hoped Israel wouldn't send me away. I hoped the Inner Voice would not show up now, saying, *Go south.*

"Sarah!"

I jerked, causing the boat to tilt, and reached for the sides to steady it.

"What are you doing?" Israel called. He stood on the bank in his knee britches with the glinting buckles, hatless. He shaded his eyes and motioned me in with his hand.

I pulled the paddle through the water, banging the wood against the hull and made an inept, zigzag path to shore.

We sat on the bench while I did my best to explain that I'd thought the locket belonged to his daughter Rebecca, not his wife Rebecca. I told him about the evening Becky brought it to me, and while my voice clenched and spluttered, it didn't fail me altogether.

". . . I would never try to take your wife's place."

"No," he said. "No one could."

". . . I doubt Catherine would believe me, though . . . She's very angry."

"She's protective, that's all. Our mother died young and Catherine took care of me. She never married, and Rebecca, the children, and I were her only family. Your presence, I'm afraid, has flustered her. I don't think she really understands why I asked you here."

". . . I don't think I understand it either, Israel . . . Why am I here?"

"You told me yourself—God told you to leave and come north."

". . . But he didn't say, 'Go to Philadelphia, go to Israel's house.'"

He placed his hand on my arm, squeezing a little. "Do you remember the last words my Rebecca said to you on the ship? She said, 'If you come north again, you must stay with us.' I think she brought you here. For me, for the children. I think God brought you here."

I looked away from him toward the pond blotched with pollen and silt, the water bronzing in the shrinking light. When I looked back, he pulled me to him and held me against his chest, and I felt it was me he held, not his Rebecca.

Handful

I smelled the corn fritters half a block from Denmark Vesey's house, the fry-oil in the air, the sweet corn fuss coming down the street. For two years, I'd been sneaking off to 20 Bull every time I found a hole in the week to squeeze through. Sabe was a shiftless lackey of a butler and didn't watch us the way Tomfry had—we could thank missus for that much.

I'd tell Sabe we were out of thread, beeswax, buttons, or rat droppings, and he'd send me willy-nilly to the market. The rest of the time he didn't care where I was. The only thought in his head was for slurping down master Grimké's brandies and whiskeys in the cellar and messing round with Minta. They were always in the empty room over the carriage house doing just what you think they're doing. Me, Aunt-Sister, Phoebe, and Goodis would hear them all the way from the kitchen house porch and Goodis would cock his eyebrow at me. Everybody knew he'd been sweet on me since the day he got here. He'd made the rabbit cane special for me, and he would give me the last yam off his plate. Once when Sabe yelled at me for going missing, Goodis stuck a fist in his face and Sabe backed right down. I never had a man touch me, never had wanted one, but sometimes when I was listening to Sabe and Minta up in the carriage house, Goodis didn't seem so bad.

With Sarah gone, the whole place had gone to hell's dredges. With the last of the boys in college, there wasn't anybody left in the house but missus and Nina and us six slaves to keep it going. Missus stewed all the time about money. She had the lump sum master Grimké left, but she said it was a trifle of what she needed. Paint was flecking off the house and she'd sold the extra horse. She didn't eat bird nest pudding anymore, and in the slave dining room, we lived on rice and more rice.

The day I smelled the fritters, it was two days before Christmas—I remember there was a cold pinch in the air and palm wreaths tacked on the doors of the piazzas, woven fancy like hair braids. This time Sabe had sent me to carry a note from missus to the solicitor's office. Don't think I didn't read it before I handed it over.

> *Dear Mr. Huger,*
>
> *I find that my allowance is inadequate to meet the demands of living well. I request that you alert my sons as to my needs. As you know, they are in possession of properties that could be sold in order to augment my care. Such a proposal would suit better coming from a man of your influence, who was a loyal friend to their father.*
>
> *Yours Truly,*
> *Mary Grimké*

I had a jar of sorghum in my pocket that I'd swiped from the larder. I liked to bring Denmark a little something, and this would hit the spot with the fritters. He had a habit of telling whoever was hanging round his place that I was his daughter. He didn't say I was *like* a daughter, but claimed out and out I was his. Susan grumbled about it, but she was good to me, too.

I found her in her kitchen house, shoveling the corn cakes from the skillet to the plate. She said, "Where you been? We haven't seen you in over a week."

"You can't do with me and you can't do without me."

She laughed. "I can do with you all right. The one I can't do with and do without is in his workshop."

"Denmark? What's he done now?"

She snorted. "You mean beside keep women all over the city?"

It struck me best to sidestep this since mauma had been one of them. "Yeah, beside that."

A smile dipped cross her lips. She handed me the plate. "Here, take this to him. He's in a mood, is all. It's about that Monday Gell. He lost something that set Denmark off. Some sort of list. I thought Denmark was gonna kill the man."

I headed back toward the workshop knowing Monday had lost the roll of draftees he'd been collecting for Denmark out on the Bulkley farm.

For a long time now, Denmark and his lieutenants had been recruiting slaves, writing down their names in what he called the Book. Last I heard, there were more than two thousand pledged to take up arms when the time came. Denmark had let me sit there and listen while he talked about raising an army and getting us free, and the men got used to me being in there. They knew I'd keep it quiet.

Denmark didn't like the wind to blow unless he told it which way to go. He'd come up with the exact words he wanted Gullah Jack and them to say when they wooed the recruits. One day, he had me pretend like I was the slave he was courting.

"Have you heard the news?" he said to me.

"What news?" I answered. Like he told me to say.

"We're gonna be free."

"Free? Who says?"

"Come with me, and I'll show you."

That was the way he wanted it said. Then, if a slave in the city was curious enough, the lieutenant was supposed to bring him to 20 Bull to meet Denmark. If the slaves were on the plantations, Denmark would go to them and hold a secret meeting.

I'd been at the house when one of those curious slaves had showed up, and it was something I'd take to my grave. Denmark had sailed up from his chair like Elijah in his chariot. "The Lord has spoken to me," he cried out. "He said, set my people free. When your name is written in the Book, you're one of us and you're one of God's, and we'll take our freedom when God says. Let not your heart be troubled. Neither let it be afraid. You believe in God, believe also in me."

When he spoke those words, a jolt traveled through me, the same one I used to get in the alcove when I was little and thought about the water taking me somewhere, or in church when we sang about the Jericho walls crumbling and the drumsticks in my legs beat the floor. My name wasn't in the Book, just the men's, but I would've put it in there if I could. I would've written it in blood.

Today, Denmark was pegging the legs on a Scot pine table. When I stepped into the room with the fritters, he set down the claw hammer and grinned, and when I pulled out the sorghum to boot, he said, "If you aren't Charlotte all over."

Leaning on the work table to take the heft off my leg, I watched him eat for a while, then I said, "Susan said Monday lost his list."

The door to the back alley was open to let the sawdust float out and he went over, peered both ways, and closed it. "Monday is a damn fool idiot. He kept his list inside an empty feed barrel in the harness shop on Bulkley farm, and yesterday the barrel was gone and nobody knows where."

"What would happen if somebody finds it?"

He sat back on the stool and picked up the fork. "It depends. If the list rouses suspicion and gets turned over to the Guard, they'd go through the names with a whip till they found out what it was about."

That raised goose flesh on my arms. I said, "Where do you keep your names?"

He stopped chewing. "Why do you want to know?"

I was treading on the thin side of his temper, but I didn't care. "Well, are they hidden good or not?"

His eyes strayed to the leather satchel on the work table.

"They're in the satchel?" I said. "Right there for the taking?"

I said it like he was a damn fool idiot, too, but instead of lashing out, he laughed. "That satchel doesn't leave my sight."

"But if the Guard gets hold of Monday's names and comes looking for you, they'll find your list easy enough."

He got quiet and brushed the sugar dust off his mouth. He knew I was right, but didn't want to say.

The sun was stepping through the window, laying down four bright quilt squares on the floor. I stared at them while the silence hung, thinking how he'd said I was Charlotte all over, and it popped in my mind the way she'd put pieces of our hair and little charms down inside her quilts, and then I remembered the time she got caught red-handed with missus' green silk. She'd told me then, "I should've sewed that silk inside a quilt and she never would've found it."

"I know what you need to do with the list," I said.

"You do, do you?"

"You need to hide it inside a quilt. I can sew a secret pocket inside to hold it. Then you just lay the quilt on the bed in plain sight and nobody knows the difference."

He paced cross the workshop three, four times. Finally, he said, "What if I need to get to the list?"

"That's easy, I'll leave an opening in the seam big enough for your hand to slip in and out."

He nodded. "See if Susan has a quilt somewhere. Get busy."

When the new year came, Nina scrounged up five girls and started the Female Prayer Society. They met in the drawing room Wednesday mornings. I served the tea and biscuits, tended the fire, and watched the door, and from what I could tell, the last thing going on was praying. Nina was in there doing her best to introduce them to the evils of slavery.

That girl. She was like Sarah. Had the same notions, the same craving to be useful, but the two of them were different, too. Seventeen now, Nina turned every head that looked her way and she could talk the salt from the sea. Her beaux didn't last long, though. Missus said she chased them off with her opinionating.

I don't know why she didn't chase the girls off either.

During the meetings, she made hot-blooded speeches that went on till one of the girls lost the point of it and turned the talk to something else—who danced with who or who wore what at the last social. Nina would give up then, but she seemed glad to speak her mind, and missus was happy, too, thinking Nina had finally found some religion.

It was during a meeting in March that the Smith girl took umbrage. Nina was taking special care to let her know how bad her neighborhood was.

"Would you come over here, Handful?" Nina called. She turned to the girls. "See her leg? See how she drags it behind her? That's from the treadmill at the Work House. It's an abomination, and it's right under your nose, Henrietta!"

The Smith girl bristled. "Well, what was she doing at the Work House in the first place? There must be some discipline, mustn't there? What did she do?"

"What did she *do*? Haven't you heard anything I've been saying? God help us, how can you be so blind? If you want to know how Handful came to be at the Work House, she's standing right here. She's a person, ask *her*."

"I'd rather not," the girl said and tucked her skirts in round her legs.

Nina rose from her chair and came to stand beside me. "Why don't you take your shoe off and show her the kind of brutality that takes place on the same street where she lives?"

I should've minded doing it, but I always remembered that day Tomfry caught me in front of the house sneaking off to Denmark's, how Nina came to my rescue. She'd never asked where I'd gone, and the fact was, I wanted the girls to see what the Work House had done to me. I tugged off my shoe and bared the misshaped bone and the pinky-flesh scars wriggling cross my skin like earthworms. The girls pressed their fingers under their noses and blanched white as flour, but Henrietta Smith did one better. She fainted sideways in her chair.

I got the smelling salts and brought her round, but not before missus heard the uproar.

Later on that night in my cellar room, I heard a tap and opened the door to find Nina with her eyes puffed out.

"Did Mother punish you?" she asked. "I have to know."

Since master Grimké died, missus hit Minta with the gold-tip cane so much you never saw her without black bruises on her brown arms. It was no wonder she went to the carriage house with Sabe to get salved. She struck me and Phoebe with the cane, too, and had even taken to swiping Aunt-Sister, which I never thought I'd live to see. Aunt-Sister didn't take it laying down. I heard her tell missus, "Binah and the ones you sold, they the lucky ones."

Nina was saying, "I tried to tell her that I *asked* you to take off your shoe, that you didn't just volunteer—"

I stuck out my arm and showed her the welt.

"The cane?" Nina asked.

"One strike, but a good one. What'd she do to you?"

"Mostly, a lot of scolding. The girls won't be coming back for any more meetings."

"No, I didn't think so," I said. She looked so dismal I added, "Well, you tried."

Her eyes watered up and I handed her my clean head scarf. Taking it, she sank down in the rocker and buried her face in it. I didn't know how much more her eyes could take, whether she was crying over her failure with the Female Prayer Society, or Sarah leaving, or the shortfalls of people.

When she was all cried out, she went back to her room, and I lit a candle and sat in the wavy light, picturing the quilt on Denmark's bed, and inside it, the hidden pocket, and inside that, the scroll of paper with all the names. People ready to lay their lives down to get free. The day I came up with the scheme of hiding the list, Susan didn't have a single quilt in the house—she used plain wool blankets. I made a new quilt from scratch—red squares and black triangles, me and mauma's favorite, the blackbirds flying away.

Denmark believed nothing would change without blood spilled. Plopped in the rocker now, I thought about Nina, her lecturing to five spoilt white girls, and Sarah being so upset with the way her world was, she had to leave it, and while I felt the goodness in what they did, it seemed their lecturing and leaving didn't come to much when you had this much cruelty to overcome.

The retribution was coming and we'd bring it ourselves. Blood was the way. It was the only way, wasn't it? I was glad now Sarah was far away from danger, and I would have to keep Nina safe. I said to myself, *Let not your heart be troubled. Neither let it be afraid.*

Sarah

I snapped open the crisp white table cloth, unfurling it upward, watching it turn into a small ovoid cloud before it sank onto the pine needles.

"This isn't the cloth we use for picnics," Catherine said, crossing her arms over her chest.

Her criticisms of me were similar to her prayers—sacred, daily, and unsmiling. I was careful now. I taught the children, but I tried not to appear mothering. I deferred to Catherine in all household matters—if she put salt in the cake, she put salt in the cake. And Israel—I didn't so much as look at him when she was in the room.

"... I'm sorry," I told her. "... I thought you said to get the white cloth."

"It will have to be bleached and clear starched. Let's pray there's no pine sap on the ground."

God, no pine sap. Please.

It was the first day of April, which also happened to be Becky's seventh birthday and the first day all year one could actually call warm. After my first winter in the North, I had an entirely new appreciation for heat. I'd never seen snow before arriving here, and when it'd come, the Pennsylvania sky split open like a vast goose down comforter and the entire world turned to feathers. The first time it happened, I slipped outside and wandered about catching flakes in my hands and on my tongue, letting them settle into my hair, which I'd left long and flowing down my back. Returning to the house, I spotted Israel and several of the children watching me from the window, looking quite astonished. My enchantment turned to slush about the same time the snow did. We seemed stuck in a perpetual twilight. Color bled from the world, recasting the landscape into gradations of black and white, and no matter how ruthlessly the fireplaces roared, cold formed on my Charleston bones like hoarfrost.

The picnic had been my idea. Quakers didn't celebrate holidays—all days were treated equally, meant to be lived with the same simplicity—but Israel was known to hedge a bit on the children's birthdays. He was home working that day, shut in his study with invoices and ledgers and bills of exchange. Having enough sense not to go to Catherine with my whim, I'd interrupted him mid-morning.

"... Spring has come," I'd said. "Let's not squander it ... A picnic will do us all good, and you should see Becky, she's so excited to be seven ... A little celebration wouldn't hurt, would it?"

He set down the account book in his hand and gazed at me with a slow, defenseless smile. It'd been months since he'd touched me. Back in the fall he'd often held my hand or slid his arm about my waist as we walked back up the hill from the pond, but then winter came, and the walks ceased as he retreated, going off inside himself somewhere to hibernate. I didn't know what had happened until one morning in January when Catherine announced it was the second anniversary of Rebecca's death. She seemed to take morose joy in explaining how deeply her brother was mourning, even more so this winter than the one before.

"All right, have the picnic, but no birthday cake," Israel said.

"... I wouldn't dream of anything so decadent as cake," I replied, beaming, mocking him a little, and he laughed outright.

"You should come, too," I added.

His eyes veered to the locket, lying on his desk, the one with the daffodils and his wife's name engraved on it.

"Perhaps," he said. "I have a great deal of work to do here."

"... Well, try and join us. The children would like that." I left, wishing I weren't so dismayed by him at times, at how mercurial he could be, embracing one day, stand-offish the next.

Now, as I gazed down at the white cloth spread on the lawn, it wasn't even disappointment I felt, it was anger. He hadn't come.

Catherine and I laid out the contents of the basket, a dozen boiled eggs, carrots, two loaves of bread, apple butter, and a kind of soft cheese Catherine had made by boiling cream and drying it in a cloth. The children had found a thatch of mint at the woods' edge and were crushing the leaves between their fingers. The air pulsed with the smell of it.

"Oh," I heard Catherine say. She was gazing toward the house, at Israel striding toward us through the brown grass.

We ate sitting on the ground with our faces turned to the bright crater of sky. When we finished, Catherine pulled gingerbread from the basket and stacked the slices in a pyramid. "The top slice is for you, Becky," she said.

It was evident how much Catherine loved the child and all the rest of them, and I felt a sudden remorse for all my ill thoughts of her. The children grabbed the gingerbread and scattered, the boys toward the trees and the two girls off to pluck the wild flowers beginning to poke through the sod, and it was at this moment, as Catherine busied herself clearing things away, that I made a terrible mistake.

I languished, leaning back on my elbows within an arm's length of Israel, feeling that he'd returned from his long hibernation and wanting to bask in the thought of it. Catherine's back was to us, and when I looked at Israel, he had that yearning expression again, the sad, burning smile, and he dared to slide his little finger across the cloth and hook it about mine. It was a small thing, our fingers wrapped like vines, but the intimacy of it flooded me, and I caught my breath.

The sound made Catherine turn her head and peer at us over her shoulder. Israel snatched his finger from mine. Or did I snatch mine from his?

She leveled her eyes on him. "So, it is as I suspected."

"This is not your business," he told her. Getting to his feet, he smiled regretfully at me and walked back up the hill.

She didn't speak immediately, but when I tried to assist her in packing the basket, she said, "You must move out and find lodging elsewhere. It's unseemly for you to be here. I will speak to Israel about your leaving, but it would be better if you left on your own without him having to intervene."

"... He wouldn't ask me to leave!"

"We must do what propriety calls for," she said, and then surprised me by placing her hand on mine. "I'm sorry, but it's best this way."

The eleven of us sat on a single pew in the Arch Street Meetinghouse—the eight Morris children bookended by Israel on one side and by Catherine and me on the other. I thought it unnecessary that we should all be here for what was called "a meeting for worship with a concern for business." It was a business meeting, for heaven's sake, plain and simple. They occurred monthly, but I typically remained at home with the children, while Israel and Catherine attended. This time, she'd insisted we all attend.

Catherine had wasted little time in approaching Israel after the picnic, and he'd stood his ground—I would stay at Green Hill. If the locket incident had cooled the air between Catherine and me, my refusal to leave and Israel's refusal to back her had turned it bitter. I only hoped in time she would come around.

Inside the meeting room, a woman stood to convene the meeting by reading a verse from the Bible. She was the only female minister among us. She looked no more than my own age of twenty-nine, young for such an achievement. The first time I'd heard her speak in Meeting, it had been with a kind of awe. I thought of it now with a pang of jealousy. I'd made the essence of the Quaker faith my own, but so far I'd refrained from making a single utterance in Meeting.

As business began, the members brought forth a series of mind-dulling matters. Two of Israel's sons were quietly shoving at one another, and the youngest had fallen asleep. *How senseless of Catherine to drag us here,* I thought.

She rose, arranging her shawl about her small, brittle shoulders. "I'm compelled by the Spirit to bring forth a matter of concern."

I jerked my head upward, gazing at the set edge of her chin, and then at Israel on the opposite end of the row, who appeared as surprised as I was.

"I ask that we come to unity on the necessity of finding a new home for our beloved probationer, Sarah Grimké," Catherine said. "Miss Grimké is an outstanding teacher to Israel's children and a help to me with housely duties, and she is, of course, a Christian of the highest order, and it's important that no one inside or outside of our community be able to question the decorum of an unmarried woman living in the home of a widower. It pains us at Green Hill to see her leave, but it's a sacrifice we're willing to make for the greater good. We ask that you assist us in her relocation."

I stared at the unvarnished wood floor and the hem of her dress, unable almost to draw a breath.

I recall only a portion of what the members said in the aftermath of her insidious speech. I remember being hailed for my scruples and my sacrifice. I remember words like *honorable, selfless, praiseworthy, imperative.*

When the whir of voices finally faded, an elderly man said, "Are we in unity on the matter? If you stand in opposition, please acknowledge yourself."

I stand in opposition. I, Sarah Grimké. The words strained against my ribs and became lost. I wanted to refute what Catherine had said, but I didn't know where to begin. She'd ingeniously transformed me into an exemplar of goodness and self-denial. Any rebuttal I made would seem to contradict that and perhaps end my chances of being accepted into the Quaker fold. The thought of that pained me. Despite their austerity, their hair splitting, they'd put forth the first anti-slavery document in history. They'd showed me a God of love and light and a faith centered on individual conscience. I didn't want to lose them, nor did I want to lose Israel, which I would surely do, if my probation failed.

I couldn't move, not the tiniest muscle in my tongue.

Israel slid up on the pew as if he might stand and speak on my behalf, but he lingered there, balling his fist and pressing it into the palm of his hand. Catherine had put him in the same untenable position as me—he wanted to give no one a reason to question what went on in his house, especially the good people of Arch Street who were at the center of his life, who'd known and cherished Rebecca. I could understand this. Yet watching him hesitate now on the edge of his seat, I had the feeling his reluctance to speak out publicly for me stemmed from something even deeper, from some submerged, almost sovereign need to protect his love for his wife. I knew suddenly it was the same reason he hadn't declared his feelings for me privately. He cast a torturous look at me and eased back on the bench.

At the front of the room, the female minister sat on the "Facing bench" along with the other ministers, scrutinizing me, noticing the glimmers of distress I couldn't hide. Gazing back at her, I imagined she saw down to the things in my heart, things I was just coming to know myself. *He might never claim me.*

She nodded at me suddenly and stood. "I'm in opposition. I see no reason for Miss Grimké to move out. It would be a great disruption for her and a hardship for all involved. Her conduct is not in question. We should not be so concerned with outward appearances."

Taking her seat, she smiled at me, and I thought I might cry at the sight of it.

She was the only one to offer a dissent to Catherine. The Quakers decided I would depart Green Hill within the month and duly recorded it in the Minute Book.

After the meeting, Israel left quickly to bring the carriage around, but I went on sitting on the pew, trying to gather myself. I couldn't think where I would go. Would I still teach the children? As Catherine steered them toward the door, Becky looked back at me, twisting against Catherine's hands, which were fastened like a harness on her small back.

"Sarah? May I call you Sarah?" It was my defender.

I nodded. ". . . Thank you for speaking as you did . . . I'm grateful."

She thrust a folded piece of paper at me. "Here's my address. You are welcome to stay with me and my husband." She started to go, then turned back. "I'm sorry, I didn't introduce myself, did I? My name is Lucretia Mott."

Handful

In the workshop at Denmark's house, the lieutenants were standing round the work table. They were always by Denmark's side. He told them he'd set the date, two months from now, said there were six thousand names in the Book.

I was back in the corner, listening, crouched on a footstool, my usual spot. Nobody much noticed me there unless they needed something to drink. *Handful, bring the hooch water, Handful, bring the ginger beer.*

It was April and half the heat from hell had already showed up in Charleston. The men were dripping with it. "These last weeks, you need to play the part of the good slave better than ever," Denmark said. "Tell everybody to grit their teeth and obey their owners. If somebody was to tell the white folks a slave revolt is coming, we need them to laugh and say, 'Not our slaves, they're like family. They're the happiest people on earth.'"

While they talked, mauma came to my mind, and the picture I had of her was washed-out like the red on a quilt after it's boiled too many times. It'd got sometimes where I couldn't remember how her face looked, where the ridges had been on her fingers from working the needle, or what she smelled like at the end of the day. Whenever this happened, I'd go out to the spirit tree. That's where I felt mauma the sharpest, in the leaves and bark and dropping acorns.

Sitting there, I shut my eyes and tried to get her back, worried she was leaving me for good. Aunt-Sister would've said, "Let her go, it's past the time," but I wanted the pain of mauma's face and hands more than the peace of being without them.

I thought for a minute I'd slip out and go back to the spirit tree—take my chance going over the gate before dark, but Missus had caught me slipping over it last month and put a gash on my head that was just scabbing over. She'd told Sabe, "If Handful gets out again without permission, I'll have you whipped along with her." Now he had bug eyes in the back of his head.

I tried to set my mind on what the men were saying.

"What we need is a bullet mold," Denmark said. "We got muskets, but we don't have musket balls."

They went down the list of weapons. I'd known there'd be blood, but I didn't know it'd run down the streets. They had clubs, axes, and knives. They had stolen swords. They had kegs of gunpowder and slow fuses hid under the docks they meant to set off round the city and burn it to the ground.

They said a blacksmith slave named Tom was making five hundred pikes. I figured he had to be the same Tom the Blacksmith who made mauma's fake slave badge back when she'd started hiring herself out. I remembered the day she'd showed it to me. That small copper square with a pinhole at the top, said *Domestic Servant, Number 133, Year 1805*. I could see all that, but I couldn't get mauma's face to come clear.

I had a tiny jay feather down in my pocket I'd picked up on the way over here, and I pulled it out and twirled it between my fingers, just something to do, and next thing I was thinking about was the time mauma saw a bird funeral. When she was a girl, she and my granny-mauma came on a dead crow lying under their spirit tree. They went to get a scoop to bury it, and when they came back, seven crows were on the ground circling round the dead bird, carrying on, not *caw caw,* but *zeep zeep,* a high-pitch cry like a mourning chant. My granny-mauma told her, "See, that's what birds do, they stop flying and hunting food and swoop down to tend their dead. They march round it and cry. They do this so everything know: once this bird lived and now it's gone."

That story brought the bright red of mauma back to me. Her picture came perfect in my mind. I saw the yellow-parch of her skin, the calluses on her knuckles, the gold-lit eyes, and the gap in her teeth, the exact wideness of it.

"There's a bullet mold at the City Arsenal on Meeting Street," Gullah Jack said. "But getting in there—well, I don't know."

"How many guards they got?" Rolla asked.

Gullah Jack rubbed his whiskers. "Two, sometimes three. The place has the whole stockpile of weapons for the Guard, but they're not letting one of us stroll in there."

"Getting in would mean a fight," Denmark said, "and that's one thing we can't afford. Like I said, the main thing now is not to rouse suspicion."

"What about me?" I said.

They turned and looked at me like they'd forgotten I was in the room.

"What about you?" said Denmark.

"I could get in there. Nobody looks twice at a slave woman who's lame in one leg."

Sarah

As dusk hovered, I sat at the desk in my room and slit open a letter from Nina. I'd been at Green Hill almost a year, and I'd written her every month without fail, small dispatches about my life and inquiries about hers, but she'd never replied to any of them, not one, and now here was an envelope with her large calligraphy and I could only imagine the worst.

14 March 1822

Dear Sister,

I've been a poor correspondent and a poorer sister. I didn't agree with your decision to go north, and I haven't changed my mind about it, but I have behaved badly, and I hope you will forgive me.

I'm at my wit's end about our mother. She grows more difficult and violent each day. She rants that we've been left without sufficient means to live and she blames Thomas, John, and Frederick for failing to take care of her. Needless to say, they come infrequently, and Mary never comes, only Eliza. Since your departure, Mother spends most of her day shut in her room, and when she emerges, it's only to rage against the slaves. She swings her cane at them over the least thing. She recently hit Aunt-Sister for nothing more than burned loaves of bread. Last evening, she struck Handful when she spotted her climbing over the back gate. I should add that Handful was climbing into the work yard, not out of it, and when Mother asked for an explanation, Handful said she'd seen a wounded pup in the alley and gone over the gate to help the creature. She insisted she was returning from that momentary mission of mercy, but I don't think Mother believed her. I certainly didn't. Mother broke the skin over Handful's brow, which I bandaged the best I could.

I'm alarmed at Mother's escalating temper, but I also fear Handful is engaged in something dangerous that involves frequent trips over the gate. I saw her slip away from the house myself on another occasion. She refuses to speak to me about it. I doubt I can shield her if she's caught again.

I feel alone and helpless here. Please come to my aid. I beg you, come home.

Yours in need and with sisterly love,
Nina

I laid down the letter. Pushing back the chair, I went to the dormer window and stared at the darkening grove of cedars. A little swarm of fireflies was rising up from it like embers. *I feel alone and helpless here*—Nina's words, but I felt them like my own.

Earlier, Catherine had sent my trunk up from the cellar, and I busied myself now pulling belongings from the wardrobe and the desk, strewing them across the bed and onto the braided rug—bonnets, shawls, dresses, sleeping gowns, gloves, journals, letters, the little biography of Joan of Arc I'd stolen from Father's study, a single strand of pearls, ivory brushes, bottles of French glass filled with lotions and powders, and dearest of all, my lava box with the silver button.

"You didn't come down for supper." Israel stood in the doorway, peering inside, afraid, it seemed, to cross into my small, messy sanctum.

My possessions were puny by Grimké standards, but I was nevertheless embarrassed by the excess, and in particular by the woolen underwear I was holding. He fixed his eyes on the open trunk, then swung his gaze to the eaves as if the sight of my packing stung him.

". . . I had no appetite," I said.

He stepped, finally, into the disarray. "I came to say, I'm sorry. I should've spoken in the meeting. I was wrong not to. What Catherine did was unpardonable—I've told her as much. I'll go before the elders this week and make it clear I don't wish you to leave." His eyes gleamed with what I took to be anguish.

". . . It's too late, Israel."

"But it isn't. I can make them understand—"

"No!" It came out more forcefully than I intended.

He sank onto the end of my narrow bed and plowed his hand through his rampant black hair. It filled me with a sharp, almost exquisite pain to see him on the bed, there among my gowns and pearls and lava box. I thought how much I would miss him.

He stood and took my hand. "You'll still come and teach the girls, won't you? A number of people have offered to board you."

I pulled my hand away. ". . . I'm going home."

His eyes darted again to the trunk, and I watched his shoulders curve forward, his ribs dropping one onto the other. "Is it because of me?"

I paused, not knowing how to answer. Nina's letter had come just when the bottom had fallen from things, and it was true, I welcomed the excuse to leave. Was I running away from him? ". . . No," I told him. I was sure I would've left regardless, why dissect the reason?

When I recounted the contents of the letter, he said, "It's terrible about your mother, but there must be other siblings who can tend to the situation."

". . . Nina needs *me*. Not someone else."

"But it's very sudden. You should think about it. Pray about it. God brought you here, you can't deny that."

I couldn't deny it. Something good and right had brought me north, and even to this very place—to Green Hill and Israel and the children. The mandate to leave Charleston was still as radiant as the day I'd first felt it, but there was Nina's letter lying on the desk. And then there was the other matter, the matter of Rebecca.

"Sarah, we need you here. You've become indispensable to—to all of us."

". . . It's decided, Israel. I'm sorry. I'm going home to Charleston."

He sighed. "At least tell me you'll come back to us after things are settled there."

The window was sheened with the glare of the room, but I stepped close to it and bent my head to the pane. I could see the bright helix of fireflies still out there. ". . . I don't know. I don't know anymore."

Handful

The night before I went to the City Arsenal to steal a bullet mold, me and Goodis crept up to the empty room over the carriage house—the same one where me and mauma used to sleep—and I let him do what he'd been wanting to do with me for years, and I guess what I'd been wanting to do with him. I was twenty-nine years old now, and I told myself, if I get caught tomorrow, the Guard will kill me, and if they don't, the Work House will, so before I leave the earth, I might as well know what the fuss is about.

The room was empty except for a straw mattress Sabe had laid on the floor for Minta and him, but the place still had the same old fragrance of horse shit. I looked down at the grungy mattress, while Goodis spread a clean blanket cross it, smoothing out every little wrinkle just-so, and seeing the care he took with it, I felt tenderness to him pour through me. He wasn't old, but most of his hair was gone. The lid over his wandering eye drooped, while the other lid stayed up, so he always looked like he was half asleep, but he had a big, easy smile and he kept it on while he helped me out from my dress.

When I was stretched out on the blanket, he gazed at the pouch round my neck, stuffed fat with scraps of the spirit tree.

"I don't take that off," I said.

He gave it a pinch, feeling the hard lumps of bark and acorns. "These your jewels?"

"Yeah. Those are my gemstones."

Pushing the pouch to the side, he held my breasts in his hands and said, "These ain't big as two hazelnuts, but that's how I like 'em, small and brown like this." He kissed my mouth and shoulders and rubbed his face against the hazelnuts. Then he kissed my bad foot, his lip following the snarled path of scars. I wasn't one to cry, but tears leaked from the sides of my eyes and ran behind my ears.

I never spoke a word the whole time, even when he pushed inside me. I felt like a mortar at first and he was the pestle. It was like pounding rice, but gentle and kind, breaking open the tough hulls. Once he laughed, saying, "This what you thought it'd be?" and I couldn't answer. I smiled with the tears seeping out.

The next morning, I was sore from loving. At breakfast, Goodis said, "It's a fine day. What you think, Handful?"

"Yeah, it's fine."

"Tomorrow gon be fine, too."

"Might be," I said.

After the meal, I found Nina and asked her could I have a pass for the market—Sabe wasn't in a granting mood. I told her, "Aunt-Sister says molasses with a little whiskey would do your mauma a world of good, might calm her down, but we don't have any."

She wrote the pass and when she handed it to me, she said, "Any time you need . . . molasses or anything like that, you come to me. All right?"

That's how I knew we had an understanding. Course, if she knew what I was about to do, she never would've signed her name on that paper.

I walked to the Arsenal with my rabbit cane, carrying a basket of rags, cleaning spirits, a feather duster, and a long broom over my shoulder. Gullah Jack had been watching the place for a good while now. He said on the first Monday of the month, they opened it up for inspection and maintenance, counting weapons, cleaning muskets, and what-not. A free black girl named Hilde came those days to sweep it out, dust, oil the gun racks, and clean the privy out back. Gullah Jack had given her a coin not to show up today.

Denmark had drawn me a picture of a bullet mold. It looked like a pair of nose pliers, except the nose came together to form a tiny bowl on the end where you poured the lead to make the musket ball. He said a bullet mold wasn't much bigger than his hand, so get two if I could. The main thing, he said, was don't get caught.

That was my main thing, too.

The Arsenal was a round building made out of tabby with walls two foot thick. It had three skinny windows high up with iron bars. Today, the shutters were thrown back to let the light in. The guard by the door wanted to know who I was and where was Hilde. I wound through the story about her getting sick and sending me for the stand-in. He said, "You don't look like you could lift a broom."

Well, how you think this broom got on my shoulder? All by itself? That's what I wanted to say, but I looked at the ground. "Yessir, but I'm a hard worker, you'll see."

He unlocked the bolt on the door. "They're cleaning muskets today. Stay out of their way. When you're done, tap on the door and I'll let you out."

I stepped inside. The door slammed. The bolt clicked.

Standing there, trying to get my bearings through the gloom, I sniffed mold and linseed oil and the rancid smell of cooped-up air. Two guards were on the far side with their backs to me, taking a musket apart under one of the windows—all the pieces spread out on a table. One of them turned and said, "It's Hilde."

I didn't clear up the mistake. I started sweeping.

The Arsenal was a single room filled with weapons. My eyes roved over everything. Kegs of gunpowder were stacked in the middle halfway to the ceiling. Arranged neat along the walls were wooden racks filled with muskets and pistols, heaps of cannon balls, and in the back, dozens of wooden chests.

I kept the broom going, working my way round the whole floor, hoping the *swish-swish* covered the loud, ragged way my breath was coming. The guards' voices came and went in echoes.

This one could fire on the half-cock. See the mainspring on the hammer? It's gone bad.

Make sure the ramrod head is tight and there's no rust on it.

When I was blocked from their view behind the powder kegs, my breath eased up. I got out the feather duster. One by one, I brushed the tops of the wooden chests, pausing each time to look over my shoulder before lifting the lid to peek inside. I found cow horns with leather straps. A tangle of iron hand cuffs. Bars of lead. Pieces of thin rope I guessed to be fuses. But no bullet molds.

Then I noticed an old snare drum propped up against the wall, and behind it was another chest. Picking my way over to it, my lame foot upset the drum, and *whamblam,* it hit the floor.

Here came the boots stomping. I grabbed the duster and the feathers twitched and shook in my hand like they'd come alive.

The guard yelled at me. "What was that racket?"

"This drum right here fell over."

He narrowed his eyes. "You're not Hilde."

"No, she turned sick. I'm filling in."

He had a long piece of metal in his hand from the musket. He pointed it at the drum. "We don't need that sort of carelessness in here!"

"Yessir, I'll take care."

He went back to work, but my heart had been beat to butter.

I opened the chest where the drum had leaned and there must've been ten bullet molds inside. I pulled out two, slow so they wouldn't clink, and stuck them in my basket under the rags.

Then I swept the air clean of cobwebs and wiped down the gun racks with oil. When I had the place good as Hilde would've done it, I gathered my stuff and tapped on the door.

"Don't forget the latrine," the guard at the door said, thumbing toward the rear of the Arsenal.

I headed back there, but I walked right past it and kept going.

That night in my room, I found a little piece of cobweb in my hair. I took a towel and rubbed myself clean, then lay down on top of the story quilt, remembering the smile on Denmark's face when I'd showed up and pulled a bullet mold from my basket. When I drew out the second one, he'd slapped his leg and said, "You might be the best lieutenant I got."

I waited for sleep, but it didn't come. After a while, I went and sat on the back porch steps. The yard was quiet. I eyed the room over the carriage house and wondered if Goodis had looked for me after supper. He would be asleep now. Denmark, too. I was the only one up, worrying about the bowl on the end of the bullet mold, the place they pour the lead. How many people would those musket balls kill? I might've passed one of them on the street today. I might pass one tomorrow. I might pass a hundred people who would die cause of me.

The moon was round and white, sitting small at the top of the sky. It seemed the right size to sit in the bowl on the bullet mold. That was what I wished. I wished for the moon instead of lead.

Sarah

I arrived in Charleston wearing my best Quaker frock, a plain gray dress with a flat white collar and matching bonnet, the picture of humility. Before leaving Philadelphia, I'd been officially accepted into the Quaker fold. My probation had ended. I was one of them.

Upon seeing me for the first time in over a year, Mother received my kiss on her cheek and said, "I see you've returned as a Quaker. Really, Sarah, how can you show your face in Charleston dressed like that?"

I didn't like the garb either, but it was at least made from wool, free of slave labor. We Quakers boycotted Southern cotton. *We Quakers*—how strange that sounded to me.

I tried to smile and make light of Mother's comment, not yet grasping the full reason for it. ". . . Is that my welcome home, then? Surely you've missed me."

She was sitting in the same spot where I'd last seen her, in the fading gold brocade wingchair by the window, and wearing the same black dress, holding her infernal gold-tip cane across her lap. It was as if she'd been sitting there since I left. Everything about her seemed unchanged, except she appeared more dilapidated around the edges. The skin of her neck folded turtle-like onto her collar and the hair at her forehead was fraying like an edge of cloth.

"I've missed you, dear, of course. The entire household suffered because of your desertion, but you can't go about dressed like that—you would be taken at once for a Quaker, and their anti-slavery views are well known here."

I hadn't thought of this. I ran my palms down the sides of my skirt, feeling suddenly fond of my drab outfit.

A voice came from the doorway. "If *that's* what this hideous dress of yours means, I'll have to get one myself."

Nina. She looked like a whole new creature. She was taller, standing inches above me with her sable hair swept back, her cheeks higher, her brows thick and her eyes black. My sister had become a darkly beautiful woman.

She threw her arms around me. "You are never to leave again."

As we clung to each other, Mother muttered, as if to herself, "For once, the child and I agree on something."

Nina and I laughed, and then astonishingly, Mother laughed, and the sound the three of us made together in the room created a silly joy inside of me.

"... Look at you," I said, cupping Nina's face in my hands.

Mother's eyes flitted from my collar to my hem and back. "I'm quite serious about the dress, Sarah. One of the Quaker families here had their home pelted with eggs. It was reported yesterday in the *Mercury*. Tell her, Nina. Explain to your sister that Charlestonians are in no mood to see her parading around like this."

Nina sighed. "There are rumors in the city of a slave revolt."

"... A revolt?"

"It's nothing but twaddle," Mother said, "but people are overwrought about it."

"If you believe the stories," Nina said, "the slaves are going to converge on the streets, kill the entire white population, and burn the city."

The skin on my arms prickled.

"After the killing and burning, supposedly they will plunder the state bank and then raid the horses in the city stable or else board ships in the harbor and sail off to Haiti."

A small scoff escaped Mother's throat. "Can you imagine them devising such an elaborate plan?"

I felt a sort of plummeting in my chest. I could, in fact, imagine it. Not the part about the slaughter—that, my mind couldn't fathom. But there were more slaves living in Charleston than whites, why shouldn't they conceive a plot to free themselves? It would have to be elaborate and bold in order to succeed. And it couldn't help but be violent.

Reflexively, I pressed my palms together beneath my chin, as if praying. "... Dear God."

"But you can't take it seriously," Nina said. "There was a similar situation in Edgefield, remember? The white families were certain they would be murdered in their beds. It was simple hysteria."

". . . What's behind it? How did the rumor start?"

"It started with Colonel John Prioleau's house slave. Apparently, he heard news of a revolt at the wharves and reported it to the colonel, who went to the authorities. The Guard tracked down the source—a slave named William Paul, who's well known, apparently, for being a braggart. The poor man was arrested and is being held at the Work House." Nina paused, shuddering. "I can't bear to think what they've done to him."

Mother rapped the floor with her cane. "The mayor-intendent has dismissed the matter. Governor Bennett has dismissed the matter. I want no further talk of it. Just take heed, Sarah, the climate is a tinderbox."

I longed to dismiss the possibility of a revolt, too, but I felt it inside of me now like a tidal pull.

Seeking out Handful the next morning, I found her sitting on the kitchen house steps beside Goodis with a needle in her hand and a brass thimble on her pushing finger, hemming what looked like an apron. The two of them were snickering as I approached, giving each other affectionate little jabs. Seeing me, they ceased.

Goodis leapt to his feet and the top of his coveralls flopped down on one side. Seized by a sudden ripple of nerves over how Handful would respond to me, I pointed to where his button was missing. ". . . You'll have to get Handful to repair that for you," I said, and regretted it instantly. It sounded bossy and condescending. It was not how I'd wanted to reunite with her.

"Yessum," he said, and with a glance at Handful, left us.

I bent over and embraced her, looping my arms about her shoulders. After a moment, she raised her arms and patted me on the sides of my ribs.

"Nina said you were coming back. You staying put now?"

". . . I might." I took a seat beside her. ". . . We'll see."

"Well, if I was you, I'd get back on the boat."

I smiled at her. A strip of dark blue shade draped over us from the eave, darkening as we fell silent. I found myself staring at the distorted way her foot hooked inward, at the soughing rhythm of her hands, at her back curved over her work, and I felt the old guilt.

I plied her with questions: how she'd fared since I left, how Mother had treated her, how the other slaves had held up. I asked if perhaps she had a special friendship with Goodis. She showed me the scar on her forehead, calling it Mother's handiwork. She said Aunt-Sister's eyesight was failing and Phoebe did most of the cooking, that Sabe couldn't hold a candle to Tomfry, and Minta was a good soul who took the brunt of "missus' nastiness." At the subject of Goodis, she merely grinned, which gave her away.

"... What do you know about rumors of a slave revolt?" I finally asked.

Her hand grew still for a moment. "Why don't you tell me what *you* know about it?"

I repeated what Nina had said about the slave, William Paul, and his claims of an uprising. "... The officials are telling the public they're untrue," I added.

She laid the apron down. "They are? They don't believe it's true?" Her face was flooded with such relief I got the feeling the revolt was not only real, but that she knew a great deal about it.

"... Even if they believe such a plan exists, they would deny it," I told her, wanting her to understand the danger. "I doubt they'd acknowledge it publicly. They wouldn't want to cause a panic. Or tip their hand. If they've found the slightest evidence of a plot, believe me, they'll respond."

She picked up the needle and thread and the hush fell again, heavier this time. I watched her hand move up and down, making peaks and valleys, then the flash of her thimble, and I remembered us—little girls on the roof, her telling me about the true brass thimble. This same one, I imagined. I could see her lying against the roof tiles, squinting at the blur of sky and clouds, the teacup balanced on her tummy, her dress pocket stuffed with feathers, their ruffled ends poking out. We'd spilled all of our secrets to one another there. It was the closest thing to parity the two of us had ever found. I tried to hold the picture in my mind, to breathe it back to life, but it dissolved.

I didn't expect her to confide in me anymore. She would keep her secrets now.

Nina and I set out by foot for the tiny Quaker meetinghouse on Sunday, an exceptionally long walk that took us to the other side of the city. We strolled arm in arm as she told me about the letters that had arrived at the house for weeks after my departure, inquiring about my health. I'd forgotten about the consumption story Mother had concocted to explain my absence, and Nina and I laughed about it all the way down Society Street.

A fierce summer rain had swept through overnight and the air was cool and fresh, flooded with the scent of tea olive. Pink bougainvillea petals floated on the rain puddles, and seeing them, having Nina beside me like this on such a glorious day, I felt I might re-find my sense of belonging.

The past ten days had passed in relative quiet. I'd spent the time trying to put the household back in order and having long talks with Nina, who asked endless questions about the North, about the Quakers, about Israel. I'd hoped to avoid all mention of him, but he slipped through the tiny fractures anyway. Handful had avoided me. Gratefully, nothing out of the ordinary had transpired in the city and reports of the slave insurrection had dwindled as folks returned to the business at hand. I'd begun to think I'd overreacted about it.

On this morning I was wearing my "abolition clothes," as Mother insisted on calling them. As a Quaker, that was all I was permitted to wear, and heaven knows, I was nothing if not earnest. Earlier at breakfast, upon learning of my intention to attend the Quaker Meeting and take Nina with me, Mother had displayed a fit of temper so predictable we'd practically yawned through it. It was just as well she didn't know we'd decided to walk.

Nearing the market, we began to hear the steady clomp of thunder in the distance, then shouting. As we turned the corner, two slave women broke past us, holding up their skirts and sprinting. Marching toward us were at least a hundred South Carolina militia with their sabers and pistols drawn. They were flanked by the City Guard, who carried muskets instead of their typical truncheons.

It was Market Sunday, a day when the slaves were heavily congregated on the streets. Standing frozen, Nina and I watched them flee in panic as hussars on horseback rushed at them, shouting at them to disperse.

"What's happening?" Nina said.

I gazed at the pandemonium, oddly stunned. We'd come to a standstill before the Carolina Coffee House, and I thought at first we would duck inside, but it was locked. "We should go back," I told her.

As we turned to leave, however, a street vendor, a slave girl no more than twelve, bolted toward us, and in her fright and panic, she stumbled, spilling her basket of vegetables across our path. Instinctively, Nina and I bent to help her retrieve the radishes and cabbages and rolling potatoes.

"Step away!" a man yelled. "You!"

Lifting my forehead, I glimpsed an officer trotting toward us on his horse. He was speaking to me and Nina. We straightened, while the girl went on crawling about in the dirt after her bruised wares.

"... We're doing no harm by assisting her," I said as he reined to a stop. His attention, though, was not on the turnip in my hand, but on my dress.

"Are you Quaker?"

He had a large, bony face with slightly bulging eyes that made him look more terrorizing perhaps than he truly was, but such logic was lost to me then. Fear and dread rushed up from my throat, and my tongue, feeble creature, lay in my mouth like a slug in its cleft.

"Did you hear me?" he said calmly. "I asked if you're one of those religious pariahs who agitate against slavery."

I moved my lips, yet nothing came, only this terrible, silent mouthing. Nina stepped close and interlocked her fingers in mine. I knew she wanted to speak for me, but she refrained, waiting. Closing my eyes, I heard the gulls from the harbor calling to each other. I pictured them gliding on currents of air and resting on swells of water.

"I am a Quaker," I said, the words arriving without the jerk of hesitation that preceded most of my sentences. I heard Nina release her breath.

Sensing an altercation, two white men stopped to stare. Behind them, I saw the slave girl dashing away with her basket.

"What's your name?" the officer asked.

"I'm Sarah Grimké. Who, sir, are you?"

He didn't bother to answer. "You aren't Judge Grimké's daughter—surely."

"He was my father, yes. He has been dead almost three years."

"Well, it's a good thing he didn't live to see you like this."

"... I beg your pardon? I don't see that my beliefs are any of your concern." I had the feeling of floating free from my moorings. What came to me was the memory of being adrift in the sea that day at Long Branch while Father lay ill. Floating far from the rope.

The columns of militia had finally reached us and were passing behind the officer in a wave of noise and swagger. His horse began to bob its head nervously as he raised his voice over the din. "Out of respect for the judge, I won't detain you."

Nina broke in. "What right do you have—"

I interrupted, wanting to keep her from wading into waters that were becoming increasingly treacherous. Strangely, I felt no such compunction for myself. "... Detain me?" I said. "On what grounds?"

By now, a horde of people had joined the two leering men. A man wearing a Sunday morning coat spit in my direction. Nina's hand tightened on mine.

"Your beliefs, even your appearance, undermine the order I'm trying to keep here," the officer said. "They disturb the peace of good citizens and give unwanted notions to the slaves. You're feeding the very kind of insurgency that's going on right now in our city."

"... What insurgency?"

"Are you going to pretend you haven't heard the rumors? There was a plot among the slaves to massacre their owners and escape. That would, I believe, include you and your sister here. It was to take place this night, but I assure you it has been thoroughly outwitted."

Lifting the reins from the horn of his saddle, he glanced at the passing militia, then turned back to me. "Go home, Miss Grimké. Your presence on the street is unwanted and inflammatory."

"Go home!" someone in the crowd shouted, and then they all took it up.

I drew myself up, glaring at their angry faces. "... What would you have the slaves do?" I cried. "... If we don't free them, they will free themselves by whatever means."

"*Sarah!*" Nina cried in surprise.

As the crowd began to hurl vicious epithets at me, I took her by the arm and we hurried back the way we'd come, walking quickly. "Don't look back," I told her.

"Sarah," she said, breathless, her voice overflowing with awe. "You've become a public mutineer."

The slave revolt didn't come that night, or any night. The city fathers had indeed ferreted out the plot through the cruel persuasions of the Work House. During the days that followed, news of the intended revolt ravaged Charleston like an epidemic, leaving it dazed and petrified. Arrests were made, and it was said there would be a great many more. I knew it was the beginning of what would become a monstrous backlash. Residents were already fortifying their fence tops with broken bottles until permanent iron spikes could be installed. The *chevaux-de-frise* would soon encircle the most elegant homes like ornamental armor.

In the months ahead, a harsh new order would be established. Ordinances would be enacted to control and restrict slaves further, and severer punishments would ensue. A Citadel would be built to protect the white populace. But that first week, we were all still gripped with shock.

My defiance on the street became common knowledge. Mother could barely look at me without blanching, and even Thomas showed up to warn me that the patronage of his firm would be harmed if I persisted in that kind of folly. Only Nina stood by me.

And Handful.

She was cleaning the mahogany staircase late one afternoon in the aftermath of the event when a rock flew through the front window of the drawing room, shattering the pane. Hearing the explosion of glass all the way on the second floor, I hurried down to find Handful with her back pressed against the wall beside the broken window, trying to peer out without being seen. She waved me back. "Watch out, they could toss another one."

A stone the size of a hen's egg lay on the rug in a nest of shards. Shouts drifted from the street. *Slave lover. Nigger lover. Abolitionist. Northern whore.*

We stared at each other as the sounds melted away. The room turned quiet, serene. Light was pouring in, hitting the scattered glass, turning it into pieces of fire on the crimson rug. The sight bereaved me. Not because I was despised, but because of how powerless I felt, because it seemed I could do nothing. I was soon to be thirty, and I'd done nothing.

They say in extreme moments time will slow, returning to its unmoving core, and standing there, it seemed as if everything stopped. Within the stillness, I felt the old, irrepressible ache to know what my point in the world might be. I felt the longing more solemnly than anything I'd ever felt, even more than my old innate loneliness. What came to me was the *fleur de lis* button in the box and the lost girl who'd put it there, how I'd twice carried it from Charleston to Philadelphia and back, carried it like a sad, decaying hope.

Across the room, Handful strode into the glowing debris on the rug, bent and picked up the stone. I watched as she turned it over in her hands, knowing I would leave this place yet again. I would return north to make what life I could.

Handful

The day of retribution passed without a musket ball getting fired, without a fuse being lit, without any of us getting free, but not one white person would look at us ever again and think we were harmless.

I didn't know who was arrested and who wasn't. I didn't know if Denmark was safe or sorry, or both. Sarah said it was best to stay off the streets, but by Wednesday, I couldn't wait anymore. I found Nina and told her I needed a pass to get some molasses. She wrote it out and said, "Be careful."

Denmark was in the bedroom of his house, stuffing clothes and money in a knapsack. Susan led me back there, her eyes bloodshot with crying. I stood in the doorway and breathed the heavy air, and thought, *It all came to nothing, but he's still here.*

There was an iron bed against the wall covered with the quilt I'd made to hide the list of names. The black triangles were laid out perfect on the red squares, but they looked sad to me now. Like a bird funeral.

I said to him, "So, where're you going?"

Susan started to cry, and he said, "Woman, if you're going to make all that noise, do it somewhere else."

She pushed past me through the door, sniffling, saying, "Go on to your other wife then."

I said, "You leaving for another wife?"

The curtain had been yanked closed on the window, leaving a crack on the side where a piece of brightness came in. It pointed at him like a sundial. "It's a matter of time before they come looking for me here," he said. "Yesterday they picked up Ned, Rolla, and Peter. The three of them are in the Work House, and I don't doubt their fortitude, but they'll be tortured till they name names. If our plans live to see another day, I have to go."

Dread slid down my back. I said, "What about my name? Will they say my name for stealing the bullet mold?"

He sat down on the bed, on top of the dead blackbird wings, with his arms dangling by his knees. When the recruits used to come to the house, he'd shout, *The Lord has spoken to me,* and he'd look stern and mighty as the Lord himself, but now he just looked cast down. "Don't worry," he said, "they're after the leader—that's me. Nobody will say your name."

I hated to ask him the question, but I needed to know. "What happened to the plans?"

He shook his head. "The thing I worried about was the house slaves who can't tell where they end and their owners begin. We got betrayed, that's what happened. One of them betrayed us, and the Guard put spies out there."

His jaw tightened, and he pushed off the bed. "The day we were set to strike, the troops were built up so heavy our couriers couldn't get out of the city to spread the call. We couldn't light the fuses or retrieve the weapons." He picked up a tin plate with a candle stuck to it and hurled it at the wall. "Goddamn them. Goddamn them to hell. *God—*" His face twisted.

I didn't move till his shoulders dropped and I felt the torment leave him. I said, "You did what you could. Nobody will forget that."

"Yeah, they will. They'll forget." He peeled the quilt off the bed and draped it in my arms. "Here, you take this with you and burn the list. Burn it straightaway. I don't have time."

"Where will you be?"

"I'm a free black man. I'll be where I'll be," he said, being careful in case Rolla and them said my name after all, and the white men came to torture me.

He picked up the knapsack and headed for the door. It wasn't the last time I'd see him. But those words, *I'll be where I'll be,* were the last words he ever spoke to me.

I burned the list of names in the stove fire in the kitchen house. Then I waited for what would be.

Denmark was caught four days later in the house of a free mulatto woman. He had a trial with seven judges, and before it was over and done, every person in the city, white and black, knew his name. The hearsay from the trial flooded the streets and alleys and filled up the drawing rooms and the work yards. The slaves said Denmark Vesey was the black Jesus and even if they killed him, he would rise on the third day. The white folks said he was the Frozen Serpent that struck the bosom that sheltered him. They said he was a general who misled his own army, that he never had as many weapons as the slaves thought he did. The Guard found a few pikes and pistols and two bullet molds, but that was all. Maybe Gullah Jack, who managed to stay free till August, made the rest of the arms disappear, but I wondered if Denmark had pulled the truth like taffy the way they said. When I opened the quilt so I could burn the list, I counted two hundred eighty-three names on it, not six thousand like he'd said. Nowadays, I believe he just wanted to strike a flame, thinking if he did that, every able-body would join the fight.

On the day the verdict came, Sabe had me on my hands and knees rolling up carpets and scrubbing floors in the main passageway. The heat was so bad I could've washed the soap off the floor with the sweat pouring down my face. I told Sabe floor-scrubbing was winter work and he said, well good, you can do it next winter, too. I swear, I didn't know what Minta saw in him.

I'd just slipped out to the piazza to catch a breeze when Sarah stepped out there and said, "... I thought you would want to know, Denmark Vesey's trial is over."

Course, there wasn't a way in the world the man was getting free, but still, I reached back for the bannister, weak with hope. She came close to me and laid her hand on my soaked-through dress. "... They found him guilty."

"What happens to him now?"

"... He'll be put to death. I'm sorry."

I didn't let on anything inside me, the way sorrow was already singing again in the hollow of my bones.

It didn't cross my mind yet to wonder why Sarah sought me out with the news. She and Nina both knew I left the premises sometimes for reasons of my own, but they didn't know I went to *his* house. They didn't know he called me daughter. They didn't know he was anything special to me.

"... When they gave the verdict, they also issued an edict," she said. "... A kind of order from the judges."

I studied her face, her red freckles burning bright in the sun and worry gathered tight in her eyes, and I knew why she was out here on the piazza with me—it was about this edict.

"... Any black person, man or woman, who mourns Denmark Vesey in public will be arrested and whipped."

I looked away from her into the ornament garden where Goodis had left the rake and hoe and the watering pot. Every green thing was bowed down thirsty. Everything withering.

"... Handful, please, listen to me now, according to the order, you cannot wear black on the streets, or cry, or say his name, or do anything to mark him. Do you understand?"

"No, I don't understand. I won't never understand," I said, and went on back inside to the scrub brush.

On July 2 before the sun rose, I wriggled through the window in my room, braced my back against the house and my good leg against the wall, and shimmied up and over the fence the way I used to do. To hell with begging for a pass. White people signing their names so I could walk down the street. Hell with it.

I hurried through the city while I still had the darkness for cover. When I got to Magazine Street, the light broke wide open. Spying the Work House, I stopped dead in my tracks, and for a minute my body felt like it was back inside there. I could hear the treadmill groaning, could smell the fear. In my head, I saw the cowhide slap the baby on its mauma's back, and I felt myself falling. The only way I kept from turning back was thinking about Denmark, how any minute they'd bring him and his lieutenants out through the Work House gate.

The judges had picked July 2 for the execution day, a secret everybody in the world knew. They said Denmark and five others would be put to death early in the morning at Blake's Lands, a marshy place with a stand of oaks where they hung pirates and criminals. Every slave who could figure a way to get there would show up, and white people, too, I reckoned, but something told me to come to the Work House first and follow Denmark to Blake's Lands. Maybe he'd catch sight of me and know he didn't travel the last mile of his life alone.

I crouched by the animal sheds near the gate, and soon enough four horse-drawn wagons came rolling out with the doomed men shackled in back, sitting on top of their own burial boxes. They were a swollen, beat-up lot—Rolla and Ned in the first wagon, Peter in the second, and two men I never had seen in the third. The last one held Denmark. He sat tall with his face grim. He didn't see me get to my feet and limp along behind them on the side of the road. The Guard was heavy in the wagons, so I had to stay well back.

The horses plodded along slow. I trailed them a good ways with my foot aching inside my shoe, working hard to keep up, wishing he'd look at me, and then a strange thing happened. The first three wagons turned down the road toward Blake's Lands, but the fourth one with Denmark turned in the opposite direction. Denmark looked confused and tried to stand, but a guard pushed him down.

He watched his lieutenants rumble away. He yelled, "Die like men!" He kept on yelling it while the distance grew between them and the dust from the wheels churned, and Rolla and Peter shouted it back. *Die like men. Die like men.*

I didn't know where Denmark's wagon was headed, but I hurried behind it with their cries in the air. Then his eyes fell on me, and he turned quiet. The rest of the way, he watched me come along behind, lagging way back.

They hung him from an oak tree on an empty stretch along Ashley Road. Nobody was there but the four guards, the horse, and me. All I could do was squat far off in the palmetto scrub and watch. Denmark stepped quiet onto the high bench and didn't move when they tugged the noose over his head.

He went like he shouted to the others, like a man. Up till they kicked the bench out from under his legs, he stared at the palm leaves where I hid.

I looked away when he dropped. I kept my eyes on the ground, listening to the gasps that drifted from the tree. All round, the hermit crabs skittered, looking at me with their tiny stupid eyes, sliding in and out of holes in the black dirt.

When I looked again, Denmark was swaying on the limb with the hanging moss.

They took him down, put him in the wood coffin, and nailed the lid. After the wagon disappeared down the road, I eased out from my hiding place and walked to the tree. It was almost peaceful under there in the shade. Like nothing had happened. Just the scuff marks in the dust where the bench had fallen over.

There was a potter's field nearby. I knew they'd bury him there and nobody would know where he was laid. The edict from the judges said we couldn't cry, or say his name, or do anything to mark him, but I took a little piece of red thread from my neck pouch and tied it round one of the twigs on a low, dipping branch to mark the spot. Then I cried my tears and said his name.

PART FIVE

November 1826–November 1829

Handful

It was long about November when Goodis caught a chest cough and I headed to the stable with some horehound and brown sugar for his throat, thinking it's another dull-luster day in the world. One more stitch in the cloth.

Up in the house missus and Nina were bickering. One minute it's the way missus treats us slaves, next it's Nina refusing to go back to society. Without Sarah here to separate them, they kept a fight going all day. Phoebe was in the kitchen house cooking a stew meat, getting more suggestions from Aunt-Sister than she needed. Minta was hiding out someplace, probably the laundry house, and Sabe, if I had to guess, was in the cellar, smoking master Grimké's pipe. Now that the liquor was gone, I smelled pipe smoke all the time.

I slowed down by the vegetable garden to see if Goodis planted it for the winter. It was nothing but dirt clods. The ornament garden was in a shamble, too—the rose vines choking the oleander and the myrtle spurting in twenty wrong directions. Missus said Goodis gave shiftless a bad name, but the man wasn't lazy, he was sick to the back teeth of forcing himself to care about her squashes and flowers.

While I was studying the dirt and worrying about him, I got the feeling somebody was watching me. I looked first at missus' window, but it was empty. The stable door was open, but Goodis had his back to me, rubbing down the horse. Then, from the edge of my eye, I saw two figures at the back gate. They didn't move when I looked their way, just stood there in the sharp light—an old slave woman and a slave girl. What'd they want? There was always a slave ready to sell you something, but I'd never seen one come peddling to the back gate. I hated to shoo them off. The old woman was bent and frail-looking. The girl was holding her by the arm.

I walked back there, stepping with my cane, my fingers round the rabbit head, feeling how it was smoothed to the grain from all the years of holding. The woman and the girl didn't take their eyes off me. Coming closer, I noticed their head scarves were the same washed-out red. The woman had yellow-brown skin. All of a sudden, her eyes flared wide and her chin started to shake. She said, *"Handful."*

I came to a stop, letting the sound flutter through the air and settle over me. Then I dropped the cane and broke into a run, the closest I could get to one. Seeing me come, the old woman sank to the ground. I didn't have a key for the gate, just flew over it, like crossing the sky. Kneeling down, I scooped her in my arms.

I must've been shouting cause Goodis came running, then Minta, Phoebe, Aunt-Sister, and Sabe. I remember them peering over the gate at us. I remember the strange girl saying, "Is you Handful?" And me on the ground, rocking the woman like a newborn.

"Sweet Lord Jesus," Aunt-Sister said. "It's Charlotte."

Goodis carried mauma to the cellar room and laid her on the bed. Everybody crowded in and stared at her like she was a specter. We were deer in the woods, froze to stillness, afraid to move. I felt hot, the breath gone from me. Mauma's lids rolled back and I saw the white skins of her eyes had started to yellow like the rest of her. She looked thin as thread. Her face had turned to wrinkles and her hair had gone salt-white. She'd disappeared fourteen years ago, but she'd aged thirty.

The girl hunkered next to her on the bed with her eyes darting face to face, her skin dark as char. She was big-boned, big-handed, big-footed with a forehead like the full moon. She looked just like her daddy. *Denmark's girl.*

I told Minta, get a wet rag. While I rubbed mauma's face, she started to groan and twist her neck. Sabe hauled off running to fetch missus and Nina, and by the time they showed up, mauma's eyes were starting to open to the right place.

The smell of unwashed bodies hung round the bed, making missus draw back and cover her nose. "Charlotte," she said, standing back a ways. "Is that you? I never thought we would see you again. Where on earth have you been?"

Mauma opened her mouth, trying to speak, but her words scratched in the air without much sense.

"We're glad you're back, Charlotte," Nina said. Mauma blinked at her like she didn't have the first inkling who was saying it. Nina must've been six or seven when mauma disappeared.

"Is she in her right mind?" missus asked.

Aunt-Sister set her hands on her hips. "She's wore-out. What she need is food and a good long rest." Then she sent Phoebe for the stew broth.

Missus studied the girl. "Who's this?"

Course, that's what everybody wanted to know. The girl drew up straight and gave missus a look that could cut paper.

"She's my sister," I said.

The room went silent.

"Your *sister*?" said missus. "As I live and breathe. What am I supposed to do with her? I can barely keep the rest of you fed."

Nina tugged her mother toward the door. "Charlotte needs rest. Let them see to her."

When the door closed behind them, mauma looked up at me with her old smile. She had a big ugly hole where her two front teeth used to be. She said, "Handful, look at you. Just look at you. My girl, all grown."

"I'm thirty-three now, mauma."

"All that time—" Her eyes watered up, the first tears I'd ever seen her shed in my life. I eased down on the bed beside her and put my face to hers.

She said low against my ear, "What happen to your leg?"

"I took a bad fall," I whispered.

Sabe sent everybody to their chores while I fed mauma spoonfuls of broth and the girl gulped hers straight from the bowl. They slept side by side through the afternoon. Time to time, Aunt-Sister stuck her head in the door and said, "Yawl all right?" She brought shortbread, castor oil boiled in milk, and blankets for a floor pallet that I reckoned would be my bed for the night. She helped me ease off their shoes without waking them, and when she saw their feet festered over with sores, she left soap and a bucket of water by the door.

The girl roused once and asked for the chamber pot. I led her out to the privy and waited, watching the leaves on the oak tree drop, the soft way they floated down. *Mauma's here.* The wonder of it hadn't broken through to me yet, the need to go down on my knees. I couldn't stop feeling the shock of what she looked like, and I was worried what missus might do. She'd looked at them like two bloodsuckers she wanted to thump off her skin.

When the girl came out of the privy barefoot, I said, "We need to wash your feet."

She looked down at them with her mouth parted and the pink tip of her tongue poking out. She couldn't be but thirteen. *My sister.*

I sat her down on the three-legged stool in the yard in the last warm spot from the sun. I brought the bucket and soap outside and stuck her feet in the water to soak. I said, "How many days did you and mauma walk to get here?"

She had barely spoken since this morning at the gate, and now the backwash of words rushed from her lips and wouldn't stop. "I ain't sure. Three weeks. Could be more. We come all the way from Beaufort. Massa Wilcox place. We travel by night. Use the foot paths the traders take and stay to the creeks. In the daytime, we hide in the fields and ditches. This the fourth time we run, so we learn which-a-way to go. Mauma, she rub pepper and onion peel on our shoes and legs to muddle the dogs. She say this time we ain't going back, we gon die trying."

"Wait now. You and mauma ran off *three times* before this and got caught every time?"

She nodded and looked off at the clouds. She said, "One time we get to the Combahee River. Another time to the Edisto."

I lifted her feet from the bucket one at a time and rubbed them with soap while she talked, and that was something she liked to do—talk.

"We carry parched corn and dried yams with us. But that run out, so we eat poke leaves and berries. Whatever we find. When mauma'd get where she can't go no more, I'd put her on my back and carry her. I'd go a ways, then rest and carry her some more. She say, if something happen to me, keep on till you find Handful."

The things she told me. How they drank from puddles and licked drops off sassafras leaves, how they climbed trees in the swamp and tied themselves to the limbs and slept, how they wandered lost under the moon and stars. She said one time a *buckruh* came by in a wagon and didn't see them laying right beside him in a ditch. Came to find out, she spoke Gullah, the language the slaves used on the islands. She'd picked it up natural from the plantation women. If she saw a bird, she'd say, there's a *bidi*. A turtle was a *cooter*. A white man, a *buckruh*.

I dried her feet good in my lap. "You didn't tell me your name."

"The man who work us in the rice field call me Jenny. Mauma say that ain't no name. She say our people use to fly like blackbirds. The day I was born, she look at the sky and that's what she call me. Sky."

The girl didn't look like her name. She was like the trunk of a tree, like a rock in a field you plow round, but I was glad mauma had given it to her. I heard Goodis coughing in the stable and the horse whinny. When I stood, she peered up at me and said, "When we was lost, she tell me the story 'bout the blackbirds, I don't know how many times."

I smiled at her. "She used to tell me that story, too."

My sister wasn't much to look at, and to hear her talk, you'd think she was too simple to learn, but I felt the toughness of mauma inside her from the start.

I came awake that night on the floor pallet and mauma was standing in the middle of the room with her back to me, not moving, gazing at the high-up window. The darkness was tucked round her, but her kerchief had slipped off and her hair was shining like fresh polish silver. Over on the mattress, Sky was snoring loud and peaceful. Hearing me stir, mauma turned round and spread open her arms to me. Without making a sound, I got up and went to her. I walked right into her arms. That's when she came home to me.

The next time I woke, early light had settled and mauma was sitting up in bed, looking at her story quilt. She'd been sleeping under it all night and didn't know it.

I went over and patted her arm. "I sewed it all together."

The last time she'd seen the quilt, it was a jumble-pile of squares. Some of the color had died out from them, but her story was all there, put together in one piece.

"You got every square in the right place," she said. "I don't know how you did that."

"I went by the order of what happened to you is all."

When Phoebe and Aunt-Sister brought breakfast, mauma was still hunched over the quilt, studying every stitch. She touched the figure on the last square, the one I knew to be Denmark. It pained me to think I might have to tell her what happened to him.

The air in the room had turned frigid during the night, so I got bathwater from the laundry house where Phoebe kept it good and scalding. Sky went over in the corner and washed her thick body, while I undid mauma's dress buttons. "We gonna burn this dress," I said, and mauma laughed the best sound.

The pouch I'd made for her hung shriveled from her neck with a new strap cut from a piece of hide. She pulled it over her head and handed it to me. "Ain't much left in it now."

When I opened it, a moldering smell drifted out. Digging my finger inside, I felt old leaves ground to powder.

Mauma sat low on the stool while I pulled her arms out of the dress sleeves and let the top drop to her waist, showing the grooves between her ribs and her breasts shrunk like the neck pouch. I dipped the rag in the basin, and when I stepped round to wash her back, she stiffed up. She had whip scars gnarled like tree roots from the top of her back down to her waist. On her right shoulder, she'd been branded with the letter *W*. It took me a minute before I could touch all that aching sadness.

When I finally set her feet in the basin, I asked, "What happened to your teeth?"

"They fell out one day," she said.

Sky made a sound like *hmmmf*. She said, "More like they got knocked out."

"You don't need to be talking, you tell too many tales," mauma told her.

The truth was Sky would tell more tales than mauma ever knew. Before the week was out, she'd tell me how mauma set loose mischief on the plantation every chance she got. The more they whipped mauma, the more holes she'd cut in the rice sacks. She broke things, stole things, hid things. Buried the threshing sickles in the woods, chopped down fences, one time set fire to the overseer's privy house.

Over in the corner, Sky wouldn't let go of the story about mauma's teeth. "It happen the second time we run. The overseer say, if she do it again, she be easy to spot with her teeth gone. He took a hammer—"

"Hush up!" mauma cried.

I squatted down and stared her in the eyes. "Don't you spare me. I've seen my share. I know what the world is."

Sarah

Israel came to call on me wearing a short, freshly grown Quaker beard. We were seated side by side on the divan in the Motts' parlor, and he stroked the whiskers constantly as he talked about the cost of wholesale wool and the marvels of the weather. The beard was thick as velvet brush-fringe and peppered with gray. He looked handsomer, sager, like a new incarnation of himself.

When I'd returned to Philadelphia after my disastrous attempt to resume life in Charleston, I'd rented a room in the home of Lucretia Mott, determined to make some kind of life for myself, and I suppose I'd done that. Twice weekly, I traveled to Green Hill to tutor Becky, though my old foe, Catherine, had recently informed me that my little protégée would be going away to school next year and my tutoring would end at the first of the summer. If I was to stay useful, I would have to seek out another Quaker family in need of a teacher, but as yet, I hadn't made the effort. Catherine was kinder to me now, though she still drew herself up tight as a bud when she saw Israel smile at me at Meeting, something he never failed to do. Nor did he fail in his visits to me, coming twice each month to call on me in the Motts' parlor.

I looked at him now and wondered how we'd gotten ourselves stranded on this endless plateau of friendship. One heard all sorts of rumors about it. That Israel's two eldest sons opposed his remarriage, not on general principle, mind you, but specifically to *me*. That he'd promised Rebecca on her deathbed he would love no one but her. That some of the elders had counseled him against taking a wife for reasons that ranged from his unreadiness to my unprovenness. I was not, after all, a birthright Quaker. In Charleston, it was being born into the planter class that mattered, here it was the Quakers. Some things were the same everywhere. "You're the most patient of women," Israel had told me once. It didn't strike me as much of a virtue.

Today, except for the newness of his beard, Israel's visit gradually began to seem like all the rest. I twiddled with my napkin as he talked about merino sheep farms and wool dyes. There was the clink of teacups when the silence came, children's voices overhead mingled with racing footsteps on creaking floors, and then, abruptly, without preface, he announced, "My son Israel is getting married."

The way he said it, quiet and apologetic, embarrassed me.

"... Israel? ... Little Israel?"

"He's not so little now. He's twenty-two." He sighed, as if something had passed him by, and I wondered absurdly if there was a Quaker law forbidding fathers to marry after their sons. I wondered if the beard was not so much a new incarnation as a concession.

When it was time to say goodbye, he took my hand and pressed it against the dark whorls of hair on his cheek. He closed his eyes, and when he opened them, I felt he was about to say something. I lifted my brows. But then, releasing my hand, he rose from the divan and whatever errant thought had wriggled from his heart returned to it, repentant and undeclared.

He walked uncertainly to the door and let himself out, while I remained seated, seeing things with terrible clarity: the passivity, the hesitation about the future. Not Israel's—mine.

As Lucretia and I sat in the tiny room she called a studio, winter rain pricked the windowpane, turning to ice. We'd pulled our chairs close to the hearth where the fire was snapping and popping, zinging like harp strings. Lucretia was opening a small packet of mail that had arrived in the afternoon. I was reading a Sir Walter Scott novel banned by the Quakers, which somehow made it all the more enjoyable, but now, drowsy with heat, I lowered the book and stared into the flames.

It was my favorite part of the day—after the children were put to bed and

Lucretia's husband, James, had retired to his study, and it was just the two of us gathered here in her odd little nook of a room. A *studio*. It was comprised of nothing more than two stuffed chairs, a large leafed table, a fireplace, wall shelves, and a wide window that looked out over a copse of red mulberries and black oaks behind the house. The room was not for cooking or sewing or childcare or entertaining. Scattered with papers and pamphlets, books and correspondence, art palettes and squares of velvet cloth on which she pinned the bright luna moths she found lifeless in the garden, this room was just for her.

I don't know how many evenings we'd spent in here talking, or like tonight, sitting quietly like two solitudes. Lucretia and I had formed a bond that went beyond friends. And yet I felt the difference between us. I noticed it at Meetings when I saw her on the Facing bench, the only female minister among all those men, the way she rose and spoke with such fearless beauty, and every morning when I went downstairs and there were her children sticky with oat gruel. I would get a faintly vacuous feeling in the pit of my stomach, not from envy that she had a profession, or these little ones, or even James, who was not like other men, but of some unknown species, a husband who beamed over her profession and made the oat gruel himself. No, it wasn't that. It was the belonging I envied. She'd found her belonging.

"Why, this letter is for you," Lucretia said, thrusting it toward me. It was Nina's stationery, but not Nina's script. The handwriting on the front was childlike and crude. *Miss Sarah Grimké.*

> *Dear Sarah*
>
> *Mauma's back. Nina said I could write you myself with the news. She ran away from the plantation where she'd been kept all this time. You should see her. She has scars and a full head of white hair and looks old as Methusal, but she's the same inside. I nurse her day and night. She brought my sister with her named Sky. I know that's some name. It comes from mauma and her longings. She always said one day we'd fly like blackbirds.*

Missus stays mad at Nina most all the time. Nina started some troubles at the presbyterry church where she goes. Some man came last week to punish her on something she said. Mauma and Sky are the one bright hope.

It has taken too long to write this. Forgive my mistakes. I don't get to read any more and work on my words. One day I will.

Handful

"I hope it isn't bad news," Lucretia said, studying my face, which must've been a confusion of elation and heart-wrench.

I read the letter aloud to her. I hadn't spoken much about the slaves my family held, but I had told her about Handful. She reached over and patted my hand.

We fell quiet as the ice turned back to rain, coming in a dark, drowning wash on the window. I closed my eyes and tried to imagine the reunion between Handful and her mother. The sister named Sky. Charlotte's scars and white hair.

"... Why would God plant such deep yearnings in us ... if they only come to nothing?" It was more of a sigh than a question. I was thinking of Charlotte and her longing to be free, but as the words left my mouth, I knew I was thinking of myself, too.

I hadn't really expected Lucretia to respond, but after a moment, she spoke. "God fills us with all sorts of yearnings that go against the grain of the world—but the fact those yearnings often come to nothing, well, I doubt that's God's doing." She cut her eyes at me and smiled. "I think we know that's men's doing."

She leaned toward me. "Life is arranged against us, Sarah. And it's brutally worse for Handful and her mother and sister. We're all yearning for a wedge of sky, aren't we? I suspect God plants these yearnings in us so we'll at least try and change the course of things. We must try, that's all."

I felt her words tear a hole in the life I'd made. An irreparable hole.

I started to tell her that as a child I'd yearned for the entire firmament. For a profession completely untried among women. I didn't want her to think I'd always been content to be a tutor when I had little passion for it, but I pushed the confession aside. Even Nina didn't know about my aspiration to be a lawyer, how it'd ended in humiliation.

"... But you did more than try to become a minister ... You accomplished it ... I've often wondered whether one must feel a special call from God to undertake that."

Quaker ministers were nothing like the Anglican or Presbyterian clergy I was used to. They didn't stand behind a pulpit and preach sermons: they spoke during the Silence as inspired by God. Anyone could speak, of course, but the ministers were the most verbal, the ones who offered messages for worship, the ones whose voices seemed set apart.

She pushed at the messy bun coiled at her neck. "I can't say the call I felt was special. I wanted to have a say in things, that's what it came down to. I wanted to speak my conscience and to have it matter. Surely, God calls us all to that."

"... Do you think ... I could become a Quaker minister?" The words had been tucked inside of me for a long time, perhaps since the moment on the ship when I first met Israel and he told me female ministers actually existed.

"Sarah Grimké, you're the most intelligent person I know. Of course you could."

Propped in bed, wearing my warmest woolen gown, my hair loosed, I bent over the bed-desk and pewter inkstand I'd recently indulged in buying and tried to answer Handful's letter.

19 January 1827

Dear Handful,
  What joyous news! Charlotte is back! You have a sister!

I lowered the pen and stared at the procession of exclamations. I sounded like a chirping bird. It was my fifth attempt at a beginning.

Strewn about me on the bed were crumpled balls of paper. *How happy you must be now,* I'd written first, then worried she might think I was implying all her miseries were over now. Next: *I was euphoric to receive your news,* but what if she didn't know the word *euphoric*? I couldn't write a single line without fear of seeming insensitive or condescending, too removed or too familiar. I remembered us, as I always did, on the roof drinking tea, but that was gone and it was all balled-up paper now.

I picked up the sheet of stationery with the glib exclamations and crushed it in my hands. A smear of ink licked across my palm. Holding my hand aloft from Lucretia's white eiderdown, I lifted the bed-desk from across my legs and went to the basin. When soap failed to remove the stain, I rummaged in the dresser drawer for the cream of tartar, and there, lying beside the bottle, was the black lava box containing my silver *fleur de lis* button. I opened it and gazed down at the button. It was darkly silvered, like something pearling up from beneath the water.

The button had been the most constant object in my life. I'd thrown it away that once, but it'd come back to me. I could thank Handful for that.

I returned to the warmth of the bed and placed the button on the bed-desk, watching the lamplight spill over it. I lay back on the pillow, remembering my eleventh birthday party at which Handful had been presented to me, how I'd woken the next day with the overpowering sense I was meant to do something in the world, something large, larger than myself. I brushed my finger across the button. It had always held this knowing for me.

In the room, everything magnified: cinders dropping on the hearth, a tiny scratching at the baseboard, the smell of ink, the etch of the *fleur de lis* on the button.

I took a clean sheet of stationery.

19 January 1827

Dear Handful,

My heart is full. I try to imagine you with Charlotte and a new sister, and I can't dream what you must feel. I'm happy for you. At the same time, I'm sad to know of the scars your mother *bears, all the horrors she must have lived through. But I won't focus on that now, only on your togetherness.*

Did you know once, when we were girls, Charlotte made me vow that one day I would do whatever I could to help you get free? We were out by the woodpile where the little orphaned barn owl lived. I remember it like yesterday. I confess now, that's why I taught you to read. I told myself reading was a kind of freedom, the only one I could give. I'm sorry, Handful. I'm sorry I couldn't keep the vow any better.

I still have the silver button you rescued after I tossed it out. As I write you now, it sits beside the inkwell, reminding me of the destiny I always believed was inside of me, waiting. How can I explain such a thing? I simply know it the way I know there's an oak tree inside an acorn. I've been filled with a hunger to grow this seed my whole life. I used to think I was supposed to become a lawyer, perhaps because that's what Father and Thomas did, but it was never that. These days, I feel inspired to become a Quaker minister. Doing so will at least provide me a way to do what I tried to do on my eleventh birthday, that day you were cruelly given to me to own. It will allow me to tell whoever might listen that I can't accept this, that we can't accept slavery, it must end. That's what I was born for—not the ministry, not the law, but abolition. I've come to know it only this night, but it has always been the tree in the acorn.

Tell your mother I'm glad she has found you again. Greet your sister for me. I've failed in many things, even in my love for you, but I think of you as my friend.

Sarah

Handful

That winter mauma sat idle by the fire in the kitchen house. She got a little weight back on her, but sometimes she had spells when she couldn't keep down her food and we'd be back where we started. Mauma said every time she saw me, I was coming at her with a piece of biscuit.

We had plenty of vacant slave quarters, but the three of us stayed on together in the cellar room. Goodis brought in a little bed from the nursery, and we wedged it beside the big bed and slept three peas in a pod underneath the quilt frame. Sky asked one time what was all that wood nailed on the ceiling, and I said, "You never saw a quilt frame?" and mauma said, "Well, you ain't never seen a rice field, so yawl even."

Mauma still wouldn't talk about what'd happened to her. She'd say, "What's done's done." Most nights, though, she'd wake up and pace the room, and it didn't seem done at all. I realized the best curing thing for her was a needle, a thread, and a piece of cloth. One day, I told her I needed some help and handed her the mending basket. When I came back, the needle was a hummingbird in her fingers.

The hardest part was finding work for Sky. She couldn't do the laundry to save her life. I got Sabe to try her in the house cleaning and serving tea with me and Minta, but missus said she didn't look the part, and put off the guests. After that, she went to work in the kitchen house, but she drove Aunt-Sister crazy with her chatter, stories about rabbits out-tricking foxes and bears. She usually ended up on the porch, singing in Gullah. *Ef oona ent kno weh oona da gwuine, oona should kno weh oona dum from.* That same song, over and over. *If you don't know where you're going, you should know where you came from.*

One morning on the tail end of winter, the knocker clacked on the front door and in came Mr. Huger, the solicitor, stomping the cold off his feet. He handed me his hat while Sabe went to get missus.

I found Nina in her room, readying for the class she taught at church. I said, "Quick, you need to come see what your mauma's up to. Mr. Huger's down there—"

She flew from the room before I could finish off the sentence.

I dawdled outside the closed drawing room doors, but I couldn't make out much they were saying—just passing words. *Pension . . . Bank . . . Cotton crash . . . Sacrifice.* The clock bonged ten times. The sound filled the house, turning it heavy, and when it stopped, I heard missus say the word *sky*. Maybe she was talking about the blue roof that hung over the world but I knew it was my sister.

I flattened my ear to the door. Let Sabe find me and chase me off, I couldn't care.

"She's thirteen years old, without any perceivable domestic skills, but she's strong." That was missus talking.

Mr. Huger mumbled about going rates, selling in the spring when the planting started on the plantations.

"You can't separate Sky from her mother," Nina cried. "It's inhuman!"

"I don't care for it either," missus said. "But we must face reality."

My breath clutched at my ribs like grabbing hands. I closed my eyes, tired of the sorry world.

When I found mauma in the kitchen house, she was alone with the mending basket. I sank beside her. "Missus plans to sell Sky in the spring. We got to find a way for her to earn her keep."

"Sell?" She looked at me with stun, then pinched her eyes. "We ain't come this far so she can sell my girl. That's for damn sure."

"There must be *something* in the world Sky's good at doing." The way I said it, like my sister was slow in the head, caused mauma to flare at me.

"Don't you talk like that! Your sister has the smart of Denmark in her." She shook her head. "He's her daddy, but I guess you figure that."

"Yeah, I figured." It seemed like the time to finally tell her. "Denmark, he—"

"There ain't a slave living who don't know what happen to him. We heard it all the way to Beaufort."

I didn't tell her I'd watched him dangle on the tree, but I told her everything else. I started with the church where we'd sung *Jericho*. I told her about the Work House, falling off the treadmill and crippling my foot. I told her the way Denmark took me in and called me daughter. "I stole a bullet mold for that man," I said.

She pushed her fingers hard against her eyelids, trying to keep them from spilling over. When she opened them, there was a map in her eyes of broken red lines.

"Sky ask me one time who her daddy is," she said. "I told her he was a free black in Charleston, but he's dead. That's all she know."

"How come you don't tell her?"

"Sky's got a child's way of talking out of turn. The minute you tell her 'bout Denmark, she'll tell half the world. That ain't gon help her."

"She needs to know about him."

"What she need is to keep from getting sold. The thing she know best is the rice fields. Put her to work in the yard."

Sky took the ornament garden and brought it back to its glory. It came natural to her—how deep to bury the jonquil bulbs, when to cut back the roses, how to trim the hedges to match the drawings in a book Nina showed her. When Sky planted the vegetables, she shoveled horse shit from the stable and mixed it in the dirt. She dug straight furrows for the seeds and covered them with her bare foot like she'd done with the rice. She sang Gullah songs to the plants when she hoed. When the beetles came, she picked them off with her fingers.

Wouldn't you know, the crookneck squash came up the size of drinking gourds. The heads on the peonies were big pink soup bowls. Even missus came out special to see them. As soon as the jonquils came up and turned the air choking sweet, she threw a garden tea for her friends that left them suffering with envy.

Summer came, and Sky was still with us.

"Where you keep the scrap cloth?" mauma said. She was rummaging through the lacquer sewing table in the corner of the cellar room. There was a basket on the floor beside her feet heaped with spindles of thread, needle bags, pins, shears, and a measure tape.

"Scrap cloth? The same place it always was. In the patch bag."

She reached for it. "You got some red and brown cotton in here?"

"Always got red and brown cotton."

I followed her to the spirit tree, where the crows hid up in the branches. She sat on Aunt-Sister's old fish-scaling stool with her back against the trunk and went to work. She cut a red square, then took the shears to the brown cloth and clipped the shape of a wagon.

I said, "Is that the wagon the Guard hauled you off in the day you disappeared?"

She smiled.

She was picking up with the rest of her story. She wouldn't say what happened to her with words. She would tell it in the cloth.

Sarah

When autumn came, Lucretia and I attended the women's meeting at Arch Street where we found ourselves standing in a crowded vestibule beside Jane Bettleman, who glared pointedly at the *fleur de lis* button I'd sewed at the throat of my gray dress. Granted, the button was ornate and expensive, and it was large, the size of a brooch. I'd freshly polished the silver, so there in the bright-lit atrium, it was shining like a small sun.

Reaching up, I touched the engraved lily, then turned to Lucretia and whispered, "My button has offended Mrs. Bettleman."

She whispered back, "Since you keep Mr. Bettleman upset a great amount of the time, it seems only fair you should do the same for his wife."

I suppressed a smile.

Arguably the most powerful figure at Arch Street, Samuel Bettleman criticized Lucretia and me on a weekly basis. During the past few months, the two of us had spoken out frequently in Meetings on the anti-slavery cause, and afterward he would descend on us, calling our messages divisive. None of our members favored slavery, of course, but many were aloof to the cause, and they differed, too, on how quickly emancipation should be accomplished. Even Israel was a gradualist, believing slavery should be dismantled slowly over time. But what most rankled Mr. Bettleman and others in the meeting was that *women* spoke about it. "As long as we talk about being good helpmates to our husbands, it's well and good," Lucretia had told me once, "but the moment we veer into social matters, or God forbid, politics, they want to silence us like children!"

She gave me courage, Lucretia did.

"Miss Grimké, Mrs. Mott, how are thee?" a voice said. Mrs. Bettleman was at my elbow, her eyes flickering over my extravagant button.

Before we could return the greeting, she said, "That's an unusually decorative item at your collar."

"... I trust you like it?"

I think she expected me to be apologetic. She rolled up her pale white lips, bringing to mind the fluted edges of a calla lily. "Well, it certainly matches this new personality of yours. You've been very outspoken in Meetings lately."

"... I only try to speak as God would prompt me," I said, which was far more pious than true.

"It *is* curious, though, that God prompts you to speak against slavery so much of the time. I hope you'll receive what I'm about to say for your own edification, but to many of us it appears you've become overly absorbed by the cause."

Undaunted even by Lucretia, who took a step closer to my side, Mrs. Bettleman continued. "There are those of us who believe the time for action has not yet come."

Anger seared through me. "... You, who know nothing of slavery... nothing at all, *you* presume to say the time has not come?"

My voice sailed across the vestibule, causing the women to cease their conversations and turn in our direction. Mrs. Bettleman caught her breath—but I wasn't finished. "If you were a slave toiling in the fields in Carolina... I suspect you would think the time had *fully* come."

She turned on her heel and strode away, leaving Lucretia and me the object of shocked, silent stares.

"I need to find some air," I said calmly, and we walked from the meetinghouse onto the street. We kept walking past the simple brick houses and charcoal vendors and fruit peddlers, all the way to Camden Ferry Slip. We strolled past the ferry house onto the quay, which brimmed with passengers arriving from New Jersey. At the far end of the dock, a flock of white gulls stood on the weathered planks, facing the wind. We stopped short of them and stared at the Delaware River, holding on to our bonnets.

Looking down, I saw that my hands were shaking. Lucretia saw it, too. She said, "You won't look over your shoulder, will you?" She was referring to the altercation, to the terrible inclination we women sometimes had to scurry back to safety.

"No," I told her. "I won't look back."

---

16 February 1828

Dear Beloved Sister,

You are the first and only to know: I've lost my heart to Reverend William McDowell of Third Presbyterian Church. He's referred to in Charleston as the "young, handsome, minister from New Jersey." He's barely past thirty, and his face is like that of Apollo in the little painting that used to hang in your room. He came here from Morristown when his health forced him to seek a milder climate. Oh, Sister, he has the strongest reservations about slavery!

Last summer, he enlisted me to teach the children in Sabbath School, a job I happily do each week. I once remarked on the evil of slavery during class and received a cautionary visit from Dr. McIntire, the Superintendent, and you should've seen the way William came to my defense. Afterward, he advised me that when it comes to slavery, we must pray and wait. I'm no good at either.

He calls on me weekly, during which we have discussions about theology and church and the state of the world. He never departs without taking my hand and praying. I open my eyes and watch as he creases his brow and makes his eloquent pleas. If God has the slightest notion of how it feels to be enamored, he'll forgive me.

I don't yet know William's intentions toward me, but I believe he reciprocates my own. Be happy for me.

Yours,
Nina

When Nina's letter arrived, I carried it to the bench beneath a red elm in the Motts' tiny backyard. It was a warm day for March. The crocuses were breaking through the winter crust and the grasshoppers and birds were out making a rapturous commotion.

After tucking a small quilt over my knees, I arranged my new spectacles onto the end of my nose. Lately, words had begun to transform themselves into blurred squiggles. I thought I'd ruined my eyes from excessive reading—I'd been unrelenting in my studies for the ministry over the past year—but the physician I'd consulted ascribed the problem to middle age. I slit the letter, thinking, *Nina, if you could see me now with my old-lady lap throw and my spectacles, you would think me seventy instead of half that.*

I read about her Reverend McDowell with what I imagined to be a mother's satisfaction and worries. I wondered if he was worthy of her. I wondered what Mother thought of him, and if I would return to Charleston for the wedding. I wondered what kind of clergy wife Nina would make and if the Reverend had any idea what sort of Pandora's box he was about to open.

It will always be a quirk of fate that Israel arrived at this particular moment. I was folding the letter into my pocket when I looked up and saw him coming toward me without his coat or hat. It was the middle of the afternoon.

He'd never mentioned the episode with Jane Bettleman. He undoubtedly knew of it. Everyone at Arch Street knew of it. It had divided the members into those who thought I was haughty and brazen and those who thought I merely impassioned and precipitate. I assumed he was among the latter.

As he took a seat beside me, his knee pressed against my leg and a tiny heat moved across my chest. He still had his beard. It was well-clipped, but longer with more silver. I hadn't seen him in weeks except at Meeting. There'd been no explanation for his absence. I'd told myself it was the inevitable way of things.

I removed my glasses. "... Israel ... this is unexpected."

There was an exigency about him. I felt it like a disturbance in the air.

"I've wanted to speak to you for some time, but I've resisted. I worried how you might receive what I have to say."

Surely this wasn't about the hubbub with Mrs. Bettleman. That had been months ago.

"... Is there some difficult news?" I asked.

"I imagine this will seem abrupt, Sarah, but I've come determined to speak and let things fall or stand as they will. For five years now, I've struggled with my feelings concerning you."

I felt my breath suddenly leave me. He looked off toward the bare-bone trees at the perimeter of the yard. "I've grieved Rebecca, perhaps too long. It became a habit, grieving her. I've been enthralled to her memory to the exclusion of too many things."

He bowed his head. I wanted to reassure him it was all right, but it had never been all right, and I remained quiet.

"I've come to say I'm sorry," he said. "It seemed unfair to ask you to be my wife when I felt so tied to her."

It was an apology then, not a proposal. "... You don't need to apologize."

He went on as if I'd said nothing. "Some weeks ago, I dreamed of her. She came to me, holding the locket, the one Becky insisted you wear that time. She placed it in my hand. When I woke, it felt as if she'd released me."

I'd been staring miserably at my hands, but I gazed up at him, aware of how palpable the word *released* had been in his voice, how the moment was rearranging itself.

"You must know I care deeply for you," he said. "A man is not meant to be alone. The children are growing, but the younger ones still need a mother, and Green Hill is in need of a mistress. Catherine has expressed a wish to move back to her house in town. I'm saying it poorly. I'm asking—I'm hoping you'll be my wife."

I'd imagined this moment: I would feel an outpouring of joy. I would close my eyes and know that my life had truly begun. I would say, *Dearest Israel, yes.* Everything in the world would be *yes*.

It was not like that. What I felt was quiet and strange. It was happiness defiled by fear. For an imperishable minute I couldn't speak.

My silence distressed him. "Sarah?" he said.

"... I want to say yes... and yet, as you know, I've set my course for a vocation. The ministry... What I mean to say is... could I be your wife *and* a minister?"

His eyes widened. "I hadn't imagined you would want to continue with your ambition after we married. Would you really want that?"

"I would. With all my heart."

His face furrowed. "Forgive me, I only thought you chose it because you'd given up on me."

He thought my ambition was a consolation? Reflexively, I stood and took a few steps.

I thought of the knowing that had come to me about my mission on the night I wrote to Handful. It was pure as the voice that had brought me north. When I'd sewed the button on my dress, I knew it couldn't be undone.

I turned back to him and saw he was on his feet, waiting. "I can't be Rebecca, Israel. Her whole life was for you and the children, and I would love you no less than she did, but I'm not like her. There are things I must do. Please, Israel, don't make me choose."

He took my hands and kissed them, first one, then the other, and it came to me that I'd spoken of love, but he had not. He'd spoken of caring, of need—his, the children's, Green Hill's.

"Wouldn't I, wouldn't we be enough for you?" he said. "You would be a wonderful wife and the best of mothers. We would see to it that you never missed your ambition."

It was his way of telling me. I could not have him and myself both.

Handful

I spread a pallet under the tree and set my sewing basket on it. Missus had decided she needed new curtains and covers for the drawing room, which was the last thing she needed, but it gave me a reason to come out here and sew with mauma.

She sat under the tree every day, working her story onto the quilt. Even if it drizzled, I couldn't budge her—she was like God mending the world. When she came to bed at night, she brought the tree with her. The smell of bark and white mushrooms. Crumbs from the earth all over the mattress.

Winter had packed and gone. The leaves had wriggled out on the tree branches and the gold tassels were falling from the limbs like shedding fur. Settling on the pallet next to mauma, I wondered about Sarah up north, if her pale face ever saw the sun. She'd written me a while back, first letter I ever got. I carried it in my pocket most of the time.

Thomas' wife had given missus a brass bird that fastened cloth in its beak, what they called a sew bird. I stuck one end of the curtain panel in its mouth while I measured and cut. Mauma was cutting out the appliqué of a man holding a branding iron in the fire.

"Who's the man?" I said.

"That's massa Wilcox," she said. "He brand me the first time we run off. Sky was 'bout seven then—I had to wait on her to get old enough to travel."

"Sky said yawl ran four times."

"We run the next year when she's eight, and then when she's nine, and that time they whip her, too, so I stop trying."

"How come you tried this last time then?"

"When I first get there, before Sky was born, massa Wilcox come down to see me. Everybody know what he want, too. When he put his hand on me, I take a scoop of red coals off the fire and toss 'em. Burn the man's arm clean through his shirt. I got my first whipping, but it's the last time he try that with me. When Sky turn thirteen last year, here he come back, sniffing round her. I tell her, we leaving, and this time we gon die trying."

I couldn't measure words against any of that. I said, "Well, you made it. You're here now."

Our needles started back. Over in the garden, Sky was singing. *Ef oona ent kno weh oona da gwuine, oona should kno weh oona dum from.*

Sky had never set foot past the Grimké walls since she got here. Missus didn't have owner papers on her and Nina said it was dangerous business out there. Since Denmark, the codes had got stricter and the *buckrahs* had got meaner, but the next market day, I told Nina, "Write Sky a pass, just do it for me. I'll watch after her."

I tied a fresh scarf on Sky's head and wrapped a pressed apron round her waist. I said, "Now, don't be talking too much out there, all right?"

On the street, I showed her the alleys to duck in. I pointed out the guards, how to walk past and lower her eyes, how to step aside for the whites, how to survive in Charleston.

The market was busy—the men carrying wood slats piled with fish and the women walking round with vegetable baskets on their heads the size of laundry tubs. The little slave girls were out, too, selling peanut patties from their straw hats. By the time we passed by the butcher tables with the bloody calf heads lined up, Sky's eyes were big as horse hooves. "Where all this stuff come from?" she said.

"You're in the city now," I told her.

I showed her how to pick and choose what Aunt-Sister needed—coffee, tea, flour, corn meal, beef rump, lard. I taught her how to haggle, how to do the money change. The girl could do numbers in her head quicker than me.

When the shopping was done, I said, "Now we going somewhere, and I don't want you telling mauma, or Goodis, or anybody about it."

When we came to Denmark's house, we stood on the street and looked at the battered whitewash. I'd come by here a few months after they lynched Denmark, and a free black woman I'd never seen answered the door. She said her husband had bought the house from the city, said she didn't know what came of Susan Vesey.

I said to Sky, "You're always singing how we should know where we come from." I pointed to the house. "That's where your daddy lived. His name was Denmark Vesey."

She kept her eyes on the porch while I told her about him. I said he was a carpenter, a big, brave-hearted man who had wits sharper than any white man. I said the slave people in Charleston called him Moses and he'd lived for getting us free. I told her about the blood he'd meant to spill. Blood I'd long since made peace with.

She said, "I know 'bout him. They hung him."

I said, "He would've called you daughter if he'd had the chance."

We hadn't blown out the candle five minutes when mauma's voice whispered cross the bed. "What happen to the money?"

My eyes popped open. "What?"

"The money I saved to buy our freedom. What happen to it?"

Sky was already sleeping deep with a wheeze in her breath. She rolled over at our voices, mumbling nonsense. I raised on my elbow and looked at mauma laying in the middle between us. "I thought you took it with you."

"I was delivering bonnets that day. What would I be carrying all that money in my pocket for?"

"I don't know," I whispered. "But it ain't here. I looked high and low for it."

"Well, it's right under your nose the whole time—if it was a snake, it'd bite you. Where's that first quilt you made—has red squares and black triangles?"

I should've known.

"I keep it on the quilt frame with the other quilts. Is *that* where you put it?"

She whipped back the cover and climbed from bed, me fumbling behind her, lighting a candle. Sky sat up in the hot, sputtering dark.

"Come on, get up," mauma told her. "We fixing to roll the quilt frame down over the bed."

Sky lumbered over to us, looking confused, while I grabbed the rope and brought it down, the pulley wheels begging for oil.

Mauma dug through the pile on the frame and found the quilt near the bottom. When she shook it out, the old quilt smell filled the room. She slit the backing and sent her hand rooting inside. Grinning, she pulled out a thin bundle, then five more, all wrapped in muslin and tied with string so rotted it came apart in her hands. "Well, look here," she said.

"What you find?" Sky asked.

After we'd told her about the hiring-out mauma used to do, and we'd danced round and pored over the riches, we laid the money on the frame, and I winched it back to the ceiling.

Sky went on back to sleep, but me and mauma lay wide-eyed.

She said, "Tomorrow, first thing, you tie the money up fresh and sew it back inside the quilt."

"It's not enough to buy all three of us."

"I know that, we just gon hold on to it for now."

The night drew on, and I started to drift, floating to the edge. Just before I went over, I heard mauma say, "I don't spec to get free. The only way I'm getting free is for you to get free."

Sarah

13 April 1828

Dearest Nina,

Last month, Israel proposed marriage, declaring himself at long last. You'll be surprised to learn I turned him down. He didn't want me to go on with my plans for the ministry, at least not as his wife. How could I choose someone who would force me to give up my own small reach for meaning? I chose myself, and without consolation.

You should have seen him. He couldn't accept that a faded-looking woman in middle age would choose aloneness over him. Respectable, handsome Israel. When I delivered my answer, he asked if I felt ill, if I was myself. He explained the gravity of my mistake. He said I should reconsider. He insisted I speak with the elders. As if those men could ever know my heart.

People at Arch Street can't conceive of my refusal any more than Israel. They think I'm selfish and misguided. Am I, Nina? Am I a fool? As the weeks pass without his visits, and I feel inconsolable, I fear I've made the worst mistake of my life.

I want to tell you I'm strong and resolute, but in truth, I feel afraid and alone and uncertain. I feel as if he has died, and I suppose in some way it's true. I'm left with nothing but this strange beating in my heart that tells me I'm meant to do something in this world. I cannot apologize for it, or for loving this small beating as much as him.

> *I think of you and your Reverend McDowell with hope and blessings.*
>
> > *Pray for your loving sister,*
> > *Sarah*

I laid down the pen and sealed the letter. It was late, the Mott house asleep, the candle a nub, the night impervious on the window. For weeks, I'd resisted writing to Nina, but now it was done, and it seemed a turning point, an abdication of what I'd always been to her: mother, rescuer, exemplar. I didn't want to be those things anymore. I wanted to be what I was, her fallible sister.

When Lucretia handed me Nina's letter, I was in the kitchen making biscuits the way Aunt-Sister made them, with wheat flour, butter, cold water, and a spoonful of sugar. I wasn't inclined toward baking, but I did try to be of help now and then. I opened the letter, standing over the bowl of flour.

> *1 June 1828*
>
> *Dearest Sister,*
>   *Take Heart. Marriage is overvalued.*
>   *My own news, though not as dire as yours, is similar. Some weeks ago, I went before a meeting at church and requested the elders give up their slaves and publicly denounce slavery. It was not well-received. Everyone, including Mother, our brother Thomas, and even Reverend McDowell, behaved as if I'd committed a crime. I asked them to give up a sin, not Christ and the Bible!*
>   *Reverend McDowell agrees with me in spirit, but when I pressed him to preach publicly what he says to me in private, he refused. "Pray and wait," he told me. "Pray and act," I snapped. "Pray and speak!"*
>   *How could I marry someone who displays such cowardice?*

*I have no choice now but to leave his church. I've decided to
follow in your steps and become a Quaker. I shudder to think of the
gruesome dresses and the barren meetinghouse, but my course is set.*

*Fine riddance to Israel! Be consoled in knowing the world
depends upon the small beating in your heart.*

*Yours,
Nina*

When I finished reading, I pulled a chair from the pine table and sat. Motes of flour-dust were drifting in the air. It seemed an odd convergence that Nina and I would both taste this pain only weeks apart. *Fine riddance to Israel,* she'd written, but it wasn't fine. I feared I would love him the rest of my life, that I would always wonder what it would've been like to spend my life with him at Green Hill. I longed for it in that excruciating way one has of romanticizing the life she didn't choose. But sitting here now, I knew if I'd accepted Israel's proposal, I would've regretted that, too. I'd chosen the regret I could live with best, that's all. I'd chosen the life I belonged to.

I'd struggled for nearly two years to be acknowledged as a minister, without success, and I bore down now on my efforts, performing charitable work at the children's asylum in order to win over the Quaker women and spending so many evenings reading texts on Quaker thought and worship I smelled perpetually of paraffin. The crucial factor, though, was my utterances in Meeting, which were completely dismal. My nervousness about speaking always made my stammer worse, and Mr. Bettleman complained loudly about my "incoherent mumblings." It was said that rhetorical polish wasn't required for the ministry, but the fact was all the ministers on the Facing bench were appallingly eloquent.

I sought out the doctor who'd provided my spectacles, in hope, finally, of a cure, but he terrified me with talk of operations in which the root of one's tongue was sliced and the excess tissue removed. I left, vowing I would never return. That night, unable to sleep, I sat in the kitchen with warm milk and nutmeg, repeating *Wicked Willy Wiggle* over and over, the little tongue exercise Nina had once insisted I do when she was a child.

---

8 October 1828

My Dear Sarah,

I am to be publicly expelled from Third Presbyterian Church. It seems they do not take well to my attending Quaker meetings these past few months. Mother is appalled. She insists my downfall began when I refused confirmation into St. Philip's. According to her, I was a twelve-year-old marionette whose strings you pulled, and now I'm a grown marionette of twenty-four whose strings you're manipulating all the way from Philadelphia. How skilled you are! Mother also felt compelled to add that I'm an unmarried marionette, thanks to my pride and my opinionated tongue.

Yesterday, Reverend McDowell visited, informing me I must return to "the fold of God's elect" or be summoned before the church session to stand trial for broken vows and neglect of worship. Have you ever? I spoke as calmly as I could: "Deliver your document citing me to appear in your court, and I'll come and defend myself." Then I offered him tea. As Mother says, I'm proud, proud even of my pride. But when he departed, I fled to my room and gave way to tears. I am on trial!

Mother says I must give up my Quaker foolishness and return to the Presbyterians or bring public scandal upon the Grimkés. Well, we've endured them before, haven't we? Father's impeachment, that despicable Burke Williams, and your aweing "desertion" to the North. It's my turn now.

I remain firm. Your Sister,
Nina

Over the next year, my letters to Nina were the nearest thing to a diary I'd written since Father's death. I told her how I practiced saying *Wicked Willy Wiggle*, of the fear my voice would keep me from realizing my largest hopes. I wrote of the anguish of seeing Israel each week at Meetings, the way he avoided me while his sister, Catherine, warmed to me considerably, a *volte-face* I couldn't have imagined when I first returned here.

I sent Nina sketches I drew of the studio and recounted the talks Lucretia and I had there. I kept her abreast of the livelier petitions that circulated in Philadelphia: to keep free blacks from being turned out of white neighborhoods, to ban the "colored bench" in meetinghouses.

"It has come as a great revelation to me," I wrote her, "that abolition is different from the desire for racial equality. Color prejudice is at the bottom of everything. If it's not fixed, the plight of the Negro will continue long after abolition."

In response, Nina wrote, "I wish I might nail your letter onto a public post on Meeting Street!"

The thought of that was not at all unpleasant to me.

She wrote of her battles with Mother, the dryness of sitting in the Quaker meetinghouse, and the rampant ostracism she faced in Charleston for doing so. "How long must I remain in this land of slavery?" she wrote.

Then, on a languid summer day, Lucretia placed a letter in my hands.

12 August 1829

Dear Sarah,

Several days ago, in route to visit one of the sick in our Meeting, I was standing on the corner of Magazine and Archdale when I encountered two boys—they were mere boys!—escorting a terrified slave to the Work House. She was pleading with them to change their minds, and seeing me, she begged more tearfully, "Please missus, help me." I could do nothing.

I see now that I can do nothing here. I'm coming to you, Sister. I will quit Charleston and sail to Philadelphia in late

October after the storms. We shall be together, and together nothing shall deter us.

With Abiding Love,
Nina

I'd been expecting Nina for over a week, keeping vigil at the window of my new room in Catherine's house. The November weather had been spiteful, delaying her ship, but yesterday the clouds had broken.

Today. Surely, today.

On my lap was a slender compendium on Quaker worship, but I couldn't concentrate. Closing it, I paced back and forth in the narrow room, an unadorned little cell similar to the one that awaited Nina across the hall. I wondered what she'd think of it.

It had been hard to leave Lucretia's, but there was no guest room there for Nina. Israel's daughter-in-law had taken over Green Hill, allowing Catherine to move back to her small house in the city, and when she'd offered to board the both of us, I'd accepted with relief.

I went again to the window and peered at the outcroppings of blue overhead and then at the river of elm leaves in the street, brimming yellow, and I felt surprised suddenly at my life. How odd it had turned out, how different than I'd imagined. The daughter of Judge John Grimké—a Southern patriot, a slaveholder, an aristocrat—living in this austere house in the North, unmarried, a Quaker, an abolitionist.

A coach turned at the end of the street. I froze for a moment, arrested by the *clomp clomp* of the chestnut horses, the way their high stride made eddies in the leaves, and then I broke into a run.

When Nina opened the door of the coach and saw me rushing toward her without a shawl, my hair falling in red skeins from its pins, she began to laugh. She wore a black, full-length cloak with a hood, and tossing it back, she looked dark and radiant.

"Sister!" she cried and stepped off the carriage rung into my arms.

PART SIX

July 1835–June 1838

Handful

I stood by the bed that morning, looking down on mauma still sleeping, the way she had her hands balled under her chin like a child. I hated to wake her, but I patted her foot, and her eyes rolled open. I said, "You feel like getting up? Little missus sent me out here to get you."

Little missus was what we called Mary, the oldest Grimké daughter. She'd turned a widow the first of the summer, and before they got her husband in the ground good, she'd handed off the tea plantation to her boys, said the place had kept her cut off from the world too long. Next we know, she showed up here with nine slaves and more clothes and furniture than we could fit in the house. I heard missus tell her, "You didn't need to bring the entire plantation with you." And Mary said, "Would you prefer I'd left my money behind, too?"

Just when missus had got where she couldn't swing the gold-tip cane with the strength of a three-year-old, here came little missus, ready to pick up the slack. She had lines round her eyes like dart seams and silver thread in her hair, but she was the same. What we remembered most from when Mary was a girl was the bad way she treated her waiting maid, Lucy—Binah's other girl. On the day Mary got here with her procession, Phoebe bolted from the kitchen house, shouting, "Lucy. Lucy?" When nobody answered, she rushed up to little missus and said, "You bring my sister Lucy with you?"

Little missus looked stumped, then she said, "Oh, her. She died a long time ago." She didn't see Phoebe's broken face, just her kitchen apron. "I don't know what time you serve the midday meal," she said, "but from now on it will be at two."

The slave quarters were busting seams. Every room taken, some sleeping on the floor. Aunt-Sister and Phoebe yowled about the mouths to feed, and little missus had me and mauma sewing new livery coats and house dresses for everybody. Welcome to the Grimkés'. She hadn't brought a seamstress with her, but she'd brought everybody else and their second cousin. We had a new butler, a laundress, little missus' personal chamber maid, a coachman, a footman, a groomsman, new help for the kitchen, the house, and the yard. Sabe got demoted back to the gardens with Sky, and Goodis, poor Goodis, he sat in the stable all day, whittling sticks. Me and him even lost the little room where we still went sometimes to love each other.

Now, here in the cellar room, mauma didn't raise her head off the pillow. She didn't have a use for little missus. She said, "What she want with me?"

"We got that big tea to put on today and she wants the ribbons sewed on the napkins. She acts like you're the only one can do it. She's got me fixing the tables."

"Where's Sky?"

"Sky's washing the front steps."

Mauma looked so tired. I knew the pains in her stomach had got worse cause she'd picked at her food all week. She pushed herself up slow, so thin her body looked like a stem growing up from the mattress.

"Mauma, you lay on back down. I'll get those ribbons done."

"You a good girl, Handful, you always was."

The story quilt was folded on the foot of the bed where she liked to keep it close. She spread it open cross her legs. It was July, a hot, sticky day, and for one tick of the clock, I wondered if she was feeling that cold you get toward the end. But then she turned the quilt till she found the first square. "This is my granny-mauma when the stars fall and she gets sold away."

I sat down next to her. She wasn't cold, she just wanted to tell the story on the quilt again. She loved to tell the story.

She'd forgot about the ribbons, and there could be trouble for me lingering, but this was mauma, and this was the story. She went through the whole quilt, every square, taking her time on the ones she'd sewed since she was back. Her being taken away in the wagon by the Guard. Working the rice fields with a baby on her back. A man branding her shoulder with the left hand and hammering out her teeth with the right. Running away under the moon. Finally, she came to the last square, the fifteenth one—it was me, mauma, and Sky with our arms woven together like a loop stitch.

I got to my feet. "Go back to sleep now."

"No, I'm coming. I be on up there in a while."

Her eyes glowed like the paper lanterns we used to set out for the garden parties.

I stood in the dining room, facing the window, stuffing big crystal horns with fruit, everything in the larder that wasn't rotten, when I spotted mauma shuffling toward the spirit tree at the back of the yard. She had the story quilt clutched round her shoulders.

My hands came still—the way she slid one foot, rested, then slid the other one. When she reached the tree, she steadied her hand on the trunk and lowered herself to the ground. My heart started to beat strange.

I didn't look to see if little missus was near, I hurried out the back door. Fast as I could, fast as the earth would pass beneath me.

"Mauma?"

She lifted her face. The light had gone from her eyes. There was only the black wick now.

I eased down beside her. *"Mauma?"*

"It's all right. I come to get my spirit to take with me." Her voice sounded far off inside her. "I'm tired, Handful."

I tried not to be scared. "I'll take care of you. Don't worry, we'll get you some rest."

She smiled the saddest smile, letting me know she'd get her rest, but not the kind I hoped. I took hold of her hands. They were ice cold. Little bird bones.

She said it again. "I'm tired."

She wanted me to tell her it was all right, to get her spirit and go on, but I couldn't say it. I told her, "Course, you're tired. You worked hard your whole life. That's all you did was work."

"Don't you remember me for that. Don't you remember I'm a slave and work hard. When you think of me, you say, she never did belong to those people. She never belong to nobody but herself."

She closed her eyes. "You remember that."

"I will, mauma."

I pulled the quilt round her shoulders. High in the limbs, the crows cawed. The doves moaned. The wind bent down to lift her to the sky.

Sarah

We arrived at the meetinghouse in the swelter of an August morning with every intention of going inside and sitting on the Negro pew.

"... Are we certain we want to do this?" I asked Nina.

She halted on the browned grass, a harsh amber light falling out of the cloudless sky onto her face. "But you said the Negro pew was a barrier that must be broken!"

I *had* said that, just last night. It had seemed like a stirring idea then, but now, in the glare of day, it seemed less like breaking a barrier and more like a perilous lark. So far, the Arch Street members had put up with my anti-slavery statements the way you abide swarming insects in the outdoors—you swat and ignore them the best you can—but this was altogether different. This was an act of rebellion and it probably wouldn't help my long struggle to become a Quaker minister. The idea to sit on the Negro pew had come after reading *The Liberator,* an anti-slavery paper Nina and I had been smuggling home in our parcels and, once, folded inside Nina's bonnet. It was published by Mr. William Lloyd Garrison, possibly the most radical abolitionist in the country. I was sure if Catherine found a single copy in our rooms, she would promptly evict us. We kept them hidden beneath our mattresses, and I wondered now if we should go home and burn them.

The truth was none of this was safe. Pro-slavery mobs had been on a reign of terror all summer, and not in the South, but *here* in the North. They'd been tossing abolitionist printing presses into the rivers and burning down free black and abolitionist homes, nearly fifty of them in Philadelphia alone. The violence had been a shock to me and Nina—it seemed geography was no safeguard at all. Being an abolitionist could get you attacked right on the streets—heckled, flogged, stoned, killed. Some abolitionists had bounties on their heads, and most everyone had gone into hiding.

Standing there, seeing the disappointment on Nina's face, I wished for Lucretia. I wished she would appear next to me in her white organdy bonnet with her fearless eyes, but she and James had moved to another Meeting, finding Arch Street too conservative. I'd thought to follow her until Catherine made it clear Nina and I would have to seek other lodging, and there were few, if any, suitable places two spinster sisters could board together. Sometimes I thought back to that day by the Delaware when I'd told Lucretia I wouldn't look back, and I had carried on the best I could, but there were always compromises to be made, so many little concessions.

"You don't have cold feet, do you?" Nina was saying. "Tell me you don't."

I heard Israel's voice cut through the crowd, calling for Becky, and glancing up, I caught sight of his back disappearing into the meetinghouse. I stood a moment smelling the heat on the horse saddles, the stink of urine on the cobblestone.

"... I always have cold feet ... but come on, they won't stop me."

She slid her arm through mine, and I could barely keep up with her as she towed me to the door, her chin raised in that defiant way she'd had since childhood, and for a second, I saw her at fourteen, sitting on the yellow settee before Reverend Gadsden with her chin yanked up just like this, refusing to be confirmed into St. Philip's.

Soon after Nina had arrived in Philadelphia, the Quakers had made her a teacher in the Infant School, a job she despised. Our requests for another assignment had been ignored—I believe they thought there was some pride to be knocked out of her by diapering babies. The eligible men, including Jane Bettleman's son, Edward, trampled over one another to assist her from the carriage, then loitered close by in case she dropped something they might retrieve, but she found them all tedious. When she turned thirty last winter, I began to quietly worry, not that she was becoming another Aunt Amelia Jane like me—indeed I told her if she got Mrs. Bettleman for a mother-in-law we would both have to drown ourselves in the river. No, my worry was that she would find herself forty-three like me, and still burping Quaker babies.

The Negro pew was in the low-slung spot beneath the stairs that led to the balcony. As usual, it was guarded by one of the men to ensure no white person sat on it by accident and no colored person passed beyond it. Noticing Edward Bettleman was the guard today, I sighed. We were doomed, it seemed, to make fresh enemies of his family over and over.

Sarah Mapps Douglass and her mother, Grace, sat on the bench in their Quaker dresses and bonnets. Typically the only Negroes among us, Sarah Mapps, close in age to Nina, was a teacher in the school for black children she'd founded, and her mother was a milliner. They were both known for their abolitionist leanings, but as we stepped toward them, I wondered for the first time if they would mind what Nina and I were about to do, if it would implicate them in any way.

As the thought crossed my mind, I hesitated, and seeing me pause, no doubt worrying again about the temperature of my feet, Nina strode quickly to the bench and plopped down beside the older woman.

I remember a blur of things happening at once—the exhale of surprise that left Mrs. Douglass' lips, Sarah Mapps turning to look at me, comprehending, Edward Bettleman lunging toward Nina, saying too loudly, "Not here, you can't sit here."

Ignoring him, Nina stared bravely ahead, while I slipped beside Sarah Mapps. Edward turned to me. "Miss Grimké, this is the Negro pew, you'll have to move."

"... We're comfortable here," I said, noticing that entire rows of people nearby were twisting about to see the trouble.

Edward departed, and in the quiet that followed, I heard the women take up their fans and the men clear their throats, and I hoped the disturbance would die down now, but across the room on the Elders' bench, there was a spate of whispering, and then I saw Edward returning with his father.

The four of us instinctively slid together on the bench.

"I ask you to respect the sanctity and tradition of the meeting and remove yourselves from the pew," Mr. Bettleman said.

Mrs. Douglass began to breathe fast, and I was stabbed with fear that we'd put them in jeopardy. Belatedly, I recalled a free black woman who'd sat on a white pew at a wedding and had been forced to sweep the city streets. I gestured toward the two women. "... They're not part of—" I'd almost said, *part of our dissidence*, but stopped myself. "... They're not part of this."

"That's not so," Sarah Mapps said, glancing at her mother, then up at Mr. Bettleman. "We are fully part of it. We sit here together, do we not?"

She slipped her hands into the folds of her skirt to hide the way they trembled, and I was filled with love and grief at the sight.

He waited, and we didn't move. "I'll ask one final time," he said. He looked incredulous, incensed, certain of his righteousness, but he could hardly remove us forcibly. Could he?

Nina drew herself up, eyes blazing. "We shall not be moved, sir!"

His face reddened. Turning to me, he spoke in a tightly coiled whisper. "Heed me, Miss Grimké. Rein in your sister, and yourself as well."

As he left, I peered at Sarah Mapps and her mother, the way they grabbed hands and squeezed in relief, and then at Nina, at the small exultation on her face. She was braver than I, she always had been. I cared too much for the opinion of others, she cared not a whit. I was cautious, she was brash. I was a thinker, she was a doer. I kindled fires, she spread them. And right then and ever after, I saw how cunning the Fates had been. Nina was one wing, I was the other.

Nina and I were summoned from our rooms by Catherine ringing the tea bell on what we thought was a restful September afternoon. She often rang the bell when a letter arrived for one of us, a meal was served, or she needed help with some household task. We plodded downstairs without a trace of wariness, and there they were, the elders sitting ramrod straight in the chairs in Catherine's parlor, a few left to stand along the wall, Israel among them. Catherine, the only woman, was grandly installed on the frumpy velvet wingchair. We had stumbled into the Inquisition.

Neither of us had bothered to tuck up our hair. Mine hung in limp red tassels to my waist, while Nina's floated about her shoulders, all curls and corkscrews. It was improper for mixed company, but Catherine didn't send us back. She pursed her lips into something sour that passed for a smile and gestured us into the room.

Three weeks had passed since we'd first sat on the Negro bench and refused to get up, and except for Mr. Bettleman, no one had said an admonishing word to us. We'd returned to sit with Sarah Mapps and Grace the following week and then the next, and no effort had been made to stop us. I'd been lulled into thinking the elders had acquiesced to what we'd done. Apparently, I'd been wrong.

We stood side by side waiting for someone to speak. The windowpanes burned with sunlight, baking the room to a kiln, and I felt a streak of cold sweat dart between my breasts. I tried to meet Israel's gaze, but he leaned back into the shadow from the cornice. Turning then to Catherine, I saw the newspaper lying on her lap. *The Liberator.*

My stomach caught.

Holding one corner between her thumb and forefinger, she lifted the paper as if it were a dead mouse she'd found in a trap and held by the tip of its tail. "A letter on the front page of the most notorious anti-slavery paper in the country has come to our attention." She adjusted her glasses—the lenses were thick as the bottom of a bottle. "Allow me to read aloud. *30 August, 1835, Respected Friend—*"

Nina gasped. "Oh Sarah, I didn't know it would be published."

I squinted at her frantic eyes, trying to comprehend what she was saying. As it dawned on me, I tried to speak, yet nothing came but a spew of air. I had to strip the words like wallpaper. ". . . . . You . . . wrote to . . . Mr. Garrison?"

A chair scraped on the floor, and I saw Mr. Bettleman stride toward us. "You want us to believe that you, the daughter of a slaveholding family, penned a letter to an agitator like William Lloyd Garrison, thinking he wouldn't publish it? It's exactly the sort of inflammatory material he spreads."

She was not remorseful, she was defiant. "Yes, perhaps I did think he would publish it!" she said. Then to me, "People are risking their lives for the cause of the slave, and we do nothing but sit on the Negro pew! I did what I had to do."

It did feel, all of a sudden, that what she'd done was inevitable. Our lives would never go back to the way they'd been, she'd seen to it, and I both wanted to pull her into my arms and thank her, and to shake her.

Their faces were all the same, grim and accusing, frowning through the glaze of light, all but Israel's. He stared at the floor as if he wished to be anywhere but here.

As Catherine resumed reading, Nina fixed her eyes on the far wall, on some high, removed place above their heads. The letter was long and eloquent, and yes, highly flammable.

"If persecution is the means by which we will accomplish emancipation, then I say, let it come, for it is my deep, solemn, deliberate conviction that this is a cause worth dying for. Angelina Grimké." Catherine folded the paper and laid it on the floor.

News of her letter would reach Charleston, of course. Mother, Thomas, the entire family would read it with outrage and disgrace. She would never go home again—I wondered if she'd thought of that, how those words slammed shut whatever door was left there.

Just then Israel spoke from the back of the room, and I closed my eyes at the gentleness in his voice, the sudden kindness. "You are both our sisters. We love you as Christ loves you. We've come here only to bring you back into good standing with your Quaker brethren. You may still return to us in full repentance, as the prodigal son returned to his father—"

"You must recant the letter or be expelled," Mr. Bettleman said, terse and plain.

Expelled. The word hung like a small blade, almost visible in the brightness. This could not happen. I'd spent thirteen years with the Quakers, six pursuing the ministry, the only profession left to me. I'd given up everything for it, marriage, Israel, children.

I hastened to speak before Nina. I knew what she would say and then the blade would fall. ". . . Please, I know you're a merciful people."

"Try and understand, Sarah, we looked the other way while you sat on the Negro pew," Catherine said. "But it's gone too far now." She laced her fingers beneath her chin and her knuckles shone white. "And you have to consider, too, where you'll go if you don't recant. I care for you both, but naturally you couldn't stay here."

Panic arched into my throat. "... Is it so wrong to write a letter? ... Is it so wrong to put feet to our prayers?"

"Matters like this—they aren't the work of a woman's life," Israel said, stepping from the shadowed place along the wall. "Surely you're not blind to that." His voice was mired in hurt and frustration, the same tone he'd had when I turned down his proposal, and I knew he was speaking about more than the letter. "We have no choice. What you've done by declaring yourself in this manner is outside the bounds of Quakerism."

I reached for Nina's hand. It felt clammy and hot. I looked at Israel, only Israel. "... We cannot recant the letter. I only wish I'd signed it, too."

Nina's hand tightened on mine, squeezing to the point of pain.

Handful

4 August

Dear Sarah

Mauma passed on last month. She fell into a sleep under the oak tree and never roused. She stayed asleep six days before she died in her bed, me beside her and Sky too. Your mauma paid for her to have a pine box.

They put her in the slave burial ground on Pitt Street. Missus let Goodis carry me and Sky over there in the carriage to see her resting place and say goodbye. Sky has turned 22 now and stands tall as a man. When we stood by the grave, I didn't come up to her shoulder. She sang the song the women on the plantation sing when they pound rice to leave on the graves. She said they put rice there to help the dead find their way back to Africa. Sky had a pocketful from the kitchen house and she spread it over mauma while she sang.

What came to me was the old song I made up when I was a girl. Cross the water, cross the sea, let them fishes carry me, carry me home. I sang that, then I took the brass thimble, the one I loved from the time I was little, and I left it on top of her grave so she'd have that part of me.

Well, I wanted you to know. I guess she's at peace now.

I hope this letter makes it to you. If you write me, take care cause your sister Mary watches everything. The black driver from her plantation named Hector is the butler now and he does her spying.

Your friend
Handful

I wrote Sarah's name and address on the front by the light of the candle, copying missus' handwriting as close as I could manage. Missus' penship had fallen off so bad I could've set down any kind of lettering and passed it off for hers. I closed the letter with a drop of wax and pressed it with missus' seal-stamp. I'd stole the stamp from her room—let's say, borrowed it. I planned to take it back before it was missed. The stationery, though, was just plain stolen.

Cross the room, Sky was sleeping, thrashing in the heat. I watched her arms search the spot on the mattress where mauma used to lay, then I blew out the flame and watched the smoke tail away in the dark. Tomorrow I'd slip the letter in the batch going to the post and hope nobody took a hard look.

Sky sang out in her sleep, sounded like Gullah, and I thought of the rice she'd sprinkled on mauma's grave, trying to send her spirit to Africa.

Africa. Wherever me and Sky were, that's the only place mauma would be.

Sarah

I woke each day to a sick, empty feeling. Catherine had given us until the first day of October to pack our things and leave, but we could find no one who'd take in two sisters expelled by the Quakers, and Lucretia's house was packed with children now. The streets had been flooded with hand fliers—they were tacked on light posts and buildings and strewn on the ground—the headline screaming out in the salacious way these street rags did: *OUTRAGE: An Abolitionist of the Most Revolting Character is Among You.* Below that, Nina's letter to *The Liberator* was printed in full. Even the lowliest boardinghouses wouldn't open their doors to us.

I'd reached the borders of despair when a letter came with no return name or address on the envelope.

29 September 1835

Dear Misses Grimké,
If you are bold enough to sit with us on the Negro pew, perhaps you will find it in yourself to share our home until you find more suitable lodging. My mother and I have nothing to offer but a partially furnished attic, but it has a window and the chimney runs through the middle of it and keeps it warm. It is yours, if you would have it. We ask that you not speak of the arrangement to anyone, including your present landlord Catherine Morris. We await you at 5 Lancaster Row.

Yours in Fellowship,
Sarah Mapps Douglass

We departed our old life the next day, leaving no forwarding address and no goodbye, arriving by coach at a tiny brick house in a poor, mostly white neighborhood. There was a crooked wooden fence around the front with a chain on the gate, which necessitated us dragging our trunks to the back door.

The attic was poorly lit and gauzy with cobwebs, and when a fire blazed below, the room filled with stultifying heat and smelled bitter with wood smoke, but we didn't complain. We had a roof. We had each other. We had friends in Sarah Mapps and Grace.

Sarah Mapps was well educated, perhaps more than I, having attended the best Quaker academy for free blacks in the city. She would tell me that even as a child she'd known her only mission in life was to found a school for black children. "Few understand that kind of emphatic knowing," she said. "Most people, including my mother, feel I've sacrificed too much by not marrying and having children, but the pupils, they are my children." I understood far better than she realized. Like me, she loved books, keeping her precious volumes inside a chest in their small front sitting room. Each evening she read to her mother in her lovely singsong voice—Milton, Byron, Austen—continuing long after Grace had fallen asleep in her chair.

There were hats everywhere in various stages of construction, hanging on tree racks throughout the house, and if not actual hats, then sketches of hats scattered on tables and wedged into the frame of the mirror by the door. Grace made big, wild-feathered creations which she sold to the shops, creations that, as a Quaker, she never could've worn herself. Nina said she was living vicariously, but I think she simply possessed the urgings of an artist.

Our first week in the attic, we cleaned. We swept out the dust and spiders and shined the window glass. We polished the two narrow bed frames, the table and chair, and the creaky rocker. Sarah Mapps brought up a hand-braided rug, bright quilts, an extra table, a lantern, and a small bookshelf where we set our books and journals. We tucked evergreen boughs under the eaves to scent the air and hung our clothes on wall hooks. I placed my pewter inkstand on the extra table.

By the second week we were bored. Sarah Mapps had said we should be careful to conceal our comings and goings, that the neighbors would not tolerate racial mixing, but slipping out one day, we were spotted by a group of ruffian boys, who pelted us with pebbles and slurs. *Amalgamators. Amalgamators.* The next day the front of the house was egged.

The third week we became hermits.

When November arrived, I began to pace the oval rug as I reread books and old letters, holding them as I walked, trying not to disappear into the melancholic place I'd visited since childhood. I felt as if I was fighting to hold my ground, that if I stepped off the rug, I would fall into my old abyss.

Before we'd left Catherine's, a letter had arrived from Handful telling us of Charlotte's death. Every time I read it—so many times Nina had threatened to hide it from me—I thought of the promise I'd made to help Handful get free. It had plagued me my whole life, and now that Charlotte was gone, instead of releasing me, her death had somehow made the obligation more binding. I told myself I'd tried—I *had* tried. How many times had I written Mother begging to purchase Handful in order to free her? She'd not even acknowledged my requests.

Then one morning while my sister used the last of our paints to capture the bare willow outside the window and I walked my trenchant path on the rug, I suddenly stopped and gazed at the pewter inkstand. I stared at it for whole minutes. Everything was in shambles, and there was the inkstand.

"... Nina! Do you remember how Mother would make us sit for hours and write apologies? Well, I'm going to write one ... a true apology for the antislavery cause. You could write, too ... We both could."

She stared at me, while everything I felt and knew offered itself up at once. "... It's the South that must be reached," I said. "... We're Southerners ... we know the slaveholders, you and I ... We can speak to them ... not lecture them, but appeal to them."

Turning toward the window, she seemed to study the willow, and when she looked back, I saw the glint in her eyes. "We could write a pamphlet!"

She rose, stepping into the quadrangle of light that lay on the floor from the window. "Mr. Garrison printed my letter, perhaps he would print our pamphlet, too, and send it to all the cities in the South. But let's not address it to the slaveholders. They'll never listen to us."

"... Who then?"

"We'll write to the Southern clergy and to the women. We'll set the preachers upon them, and their wives and mothers and daughters!"

I wrote in bed on my lap desk, wrapped in a woolen shawl, while Nina bent over the small table in her old, fur-lined bonnet. The entire attic ached with cold and the *scratch-scratch* of our pens and the whippoorwills already calling to each other in the gathering dark.

All winter the chimney had steeped the attic with heat and Nina would throw open the window to let in the icy air. We wrote sweltering or we wrote shivering, but rarely in between. Our pamphlets were nearly finished—mine, *An Epistle to the Clergy of the Southern States,* and Nina's, *An Appeal to the Christian Women of the South.* She'd taken the women, and I the clergy, which I found ironic considering I'd done so poorly with men and she so well. She insisted it would've been more ironic the other way around—her writing about God when she'd done so poorly with him.

We'd set down every argument the South made for slavery and refuted them all. I didn't stutter on the page. It was an ecstasy to write without hesitation, to write everything hidden inside of me, to write with the sort of audacity I wouldn't have found in person. I sometimes thought of Father as I wrote and the brutal confession he'd made at the end. *Do you think I don't abhor slavery? Do you think I don't know it was greed that kept me from following my conscience?* But it was mostly Charlotte who haunted my pages.

Below us in the kitchen, I heard Sarah Mapps and Grace feeding wood into the stove, an ornery old Rumford that coughed up clouds of smut. Soon we smelled vegetables boiling—onions, parsnips, beet tops—and we gathered our day's work and descended the ladder.

Sarah Mapps turned from the stove as we entered, sheaves of smoke floating about her head. "Do you have new pages for us?" she asked, and her mother, who was pounding dough, stopped to hear our answer.

"Sarah has brought down the last of hers," Nina said. "She wrote the final sentence today, and I expect to complete mine tomorrow!"

Sarah Mapps clapped her hands the way she might've done for the children in her class. Our habit was to gather in the sitting room after the meal, where Nina and I read our latest passages aloud to them. Grace sometimes grew so distressed at our eyewitness accounts of slavery she would interrupt us with all sorts of outbursts—*Such an abomination! Can't they see we are persons? There but for the grace of God.* Finally, Sarah Mapps would fetch the millinery basket so her mother could distract herself by jabbing a needle into one of the hats she was making.

"A letter came for you today, Nina," Grace said, wiping dough from her hands and digging it from her apron.

Few people knew of our whereabouts: Mother and Thomas in Charleston, and I'd sent the address to Handful as well, though I'd not heard back from her. Among the Quakers, we'd informed no one but Lucretia, afraid that Sarah Mapps and Grace would suffer for consorting with us. The handwriting on the letter, however, belonged to none of them.

I gazed over Nina's shoulder as she tore open the paper.

"It's from Mr. Garrison!" Nina cried. I'd forgotten—Nina had written him some weeks ago, describing our literary undertaking, and he'd responded with enthusiasm, asking us to submit our work when it was finished. I couldn't imagine what he might want.

21 March 1836

Dear Miss Grimké,
  I have enclosed a letter to you from Elizur Wright in New York. Not knowing how to reach you, he entrusted the letter to me to forward. I think you will find it of utmost importance.
  I pray the monographs you and your sister are writing will

reach me soon and that you will both rise to the moment that is now upon you.

God Grant You Courage,
William Lloyd Garrison

Nina looked up, her eyes searching mine, and they were filled with a kind of wonder. With a deep breath, she read the accompanying letter aloud.

2 March 1836

Dear Miss Grimké,
I write on behalf of the American Anti-Slavery Society, which is soon to commission and send forth forty abolition agents to speak at gatherings across the free states, winning converts to our cause and rousing support. After reading your eloquent letter to The Liberator *and observing the outcry and awe it has elicited, the Executive Committee is unanimous in its belief that your insight into the evils of slavery in the South and your impassioned voice will be an invaluable asset.*

We invite you to join us in this great moral endeavor, and your sister, Sarah, as well, as we have learned of her sacrifice and staunch abolitionist views. We believe you may be more amenable to the mission if she accompanies you. If the two of you would consent to be our only female agents, we would have you speak to women in private parlors in New York.

We would expect you the sixteenth of next September for two months of rigorous agent training under the direction of Theodore Weld, the great abolitionist orator. Your circuit of lectures will commence in December.

We ask for your prayerful deliberation and your reply.
Yours Most Sincerely,
Elizur Wright
Secretary, AASS

The four of us stared at one another for a moment with blank, astonished expressions, and then Nina threw her arms around me. "Sarah, it's all we could've hoped and more."

I could only stand there immobile while she clasped me. Sarah Mapps scooped a handful of flour from the bowl and tossed it over us like petals at a wedding, and their laughter rose into the steamy air.

"Think of it, we're to be trained by Theodore Weld," Nina said. He was the man who'd "abolitionized" Ohio. He was said to be demanding, fiercely principled, and uncompromising.

I muddled through the meal and the reading, and when we slipped into bed, I was glad for the dark. I lay still and hoped Nina would think me asleep, but her voice came from her bed, two arm-lengths away. "I won't go to New York without you."

"... I-I didn't say I wouldn't go. Of course, I'll go."

"You've been so quiet, I don't know what to think."

"... I'm overjoyed. I am, Nina... It's just... I'll have to speak. To speak in the most public way... among strangers... I'll have to use the voice in my throat, not the one on the page."

All evening, I'd pictured how it would be, the moment when the words clotted on my tongue and the women in New York shifted in their chairs and stared at their laps.

"You stood in Meetings and spoke," Nina said. "You didn't let your stutter stop you from trying to become a minister."

I stared at the black plank of rafter over my head and felt the truth and logic of that, and it came to me that what I feared most was not speaking. That fear was old and tired. What I feared was the immensity of it all—a female abolition agent traveling the country with a national mandate. I wanted to say, *Who am I to do this, a woman?* But that voice was not mine. It was Father's voice. It was Thomas'. It belonged to Israel, to Catherine, and to Mother. It belonged to the church in Charleston and the Quakers in Philadelphia. It would not, if I could help it, belong to me.

Handful

I was down near Adgers Wharf on an errand when the steamboat left the harbor and it was something in this world, the paddle thundering, the smokestack blowing, and people lined up on the top deck waving handkerchiefs. I watched it till the spume settled on the water and the boat dropped over the last blue edge.

Little missus had sent me to get two bottles of import scotch, and I hurried now not to be late. I was the one who did most of her bidding these days. When she sent her plantation slaves to fetch something, they'd come back with the basket empty or still holding the note they were supposed to deliver. They didn't know the Battery from Wragg Square, and she'd make them go without supper if they were lucky, and if they weren't, it was five lashes from Hector.

Last week Sky made up a rhyme and sang it in the garden. *Little missus Mary, mean as a snake. Little missus Mary, hit her with the rake.* I told her, don't sing that cause Hector has ears to hear, but Sky couldn't get the song off her tongue. She'd ended up with the iron muzzle latched on her mouth. It was used for when a slave stole food, but it worked just as good for a slave mouthing off. It took four men to hold Sky down, work the prongs inside her mouth, and clamp the contraption at the back of her head. She screamed so loud I bit the side of my cheek till blood seeped and the copper taste filled my mouth. Sky couldn't eat or talk for two days. She slept sitting up so the iron wouldn't cut her face, and when she woke groaning, I worked a wet rag under the edge of the gag so she could suck the water.

Coming out from the scotch store, I was thinking about the torn places on the sides of her mouth, how she hadn't sung a tune since all that happened. Then I heard shouts and smelled the smoke.

A black billow was rising over the Old Exchange. The first thing that sprang in my head was Denmark, how the city was finally on fire like he wanted. I hitched up my skirt and jabbed the rabbit cane into the cobblestone, trying to make my leg go faster. The scotch bottles clanked in the basket. Pain jarred to my hip.

At the corner of Broad Street, I stopped in my tracks. What I thought was the city burning was a bonfire in front of the Exchange. A mob circled round it and the man from the post office was up on the steps throwing bundles of paper on the flames. Every time a packet landed, the cinders flew and the crowd roared.

I didn't know what they were so stirred up about, and the last thing you want is to wade out in the middle of somebody else's trouble, but I knew little missus doled out whippings for being late the same as she did for getting lost.

I was weaving my way, keeping my head down, when I saw one of the papers they were trying to burn laying on the street trampled underfoot, and I went over and picked it up.

It was singed along the bottom. *An Epistle to the Clergy of the Southern States by Sarah M. Grimké.*

I stood stock-still. Sarah. *Sarah M. Grimké.*

"Give that to me, nigger!" a man said. He was old and bald and smelled sour in the summer heat. "Hand it over!"

I looked at his red, watering eyes and poked the booklet inside my pocket. This was Sarah's name and these were her words inside. They could burn the rest of the papers, but they weren't burning this one.

Come later this night, Sky and Goodis would come to my bed and say, *Handful, what was you thinking? You should've give that to him,* but I did what I did.

I didn't pay any heed to what he said. I turned my back and started walking off, getting away from his stink and his grabbing hand.

He caught hold of the handle on my basket and gave it a jerk. I yanked back, and he held on, swaying on his feet, saying, "What you think? I'm gonna let you walk off with that?" Then he looked down, that half-drunk fool, and saw the bottles of scotch in the basket, the best scotch in Charleston, and his gray tongue came out and wiped his lips.

I said, "Here, you take the liquor and I'll take the booklet," and I slid the basket off my arm and left him holding it. I limped off, me and that sly rabbit on the cane, disappearing in the crowd.

I kept going past Market Street. The sun was dripping orange on the harbor, the green shadows falling off the garden walls. Up and down the street, the horses were hightailing home.

I didn't hurry. I knew what was waiting on me.

Near the Grimké house, I saw the steamboat landing and the whitewash building with a sign over the door, *Charleston Steamship Company*. A man holding a pocket watch was locking the front door. When he left, I wandered down to the landing and sat hidden behind the wood crates, watching the pelicans dive straight as blades. When I took the booklet from my pocket, little charred flakes came off in my hand. I had to work hard at some of the words. If one tripped me up, I stared at the letters, waiting for the meaning to show itself, and it would come, too, like pictures taking shape in the clouds.

> *Respected Friends,*
> *I address you as a repentant slaveholder of the South, one secure in the knowledge that the Negro is not chattel to be owned, but a person under God . . .*

Little missus had me whipped by the light of the moon.

When I showed up late at the gate without her import scotch or the money she gave me to buy it, she told Hector to take care of me. It was dark out, the black sky full of sharp-edge, tin-cut stars and the moon so full Hector's shadow lay perfect on the ground. He had the bullwhip wound up, hanging off his belt.

I'd always taken my hope from mauma and she was gone.

He lashed my hands to a post on the kitchen house. The last time I was whipped was for learning to read—one lash, a taste of sugar, they said—and Tomfry had tied me to this same post.

This time, ten lashes. The price to read Sarah's words.

I waited with my back to Hector. I could see Goodis crouched in the shadows by the herb garden and Sky hidden up next to the warming kitchen, the flash of her eyes like a small night animal.

I let my eyelids fall shut on the world. What was it for anyway? What was any of this for?

The first strike came straight from the fire, a burning poker under my skin. I heard the cotton on my dress rip and felt the skin split. It knocked the legs from me.

I cried out cause I couldn't help it, cause my body was small without padding. I cried out to wake God from his slumber.

The words in Sarah's book came fresh to me. *A person under God.*

In my head, I saw the steamboat. I saw the paddle turning.

Next day, I was measuring little missus for a dress, a walking costume made of silk taffeta, just what everybody needs, and her pretending nothing happened. Being obliging. *Handful, what do you think about this gold color, is it too pale? . . . Nobody sews like you do, Handful.*

When I stretched the measure tape from her waist to her ankle, the tore-up skin on my back pinched and pulled and a trickle ran between my shoulders. Phoebe and Sky had laid brown paper soaked in molasses on my back to keep the raw places clean, but it didn't turn the pain sweet. Every step I took hurt. I slid my feet on the floor without picking them up.

Little missus stood on the fitting box and turned a circle. It made me think of the old globe in master Grimké's study, the way it turned.

The clapper went off on the front door and we heard Hector's shoes slap down the hallway to the drawing room where missus was taking tea. He called out, "Missus, the mayor's here. He say for you to come to the door."

Mary stepped off the fitting box and stuck her head out to see what she could see. Missus was old now, her hair paper-white, but she got round. I heard her cane fast-tapping and then her toady voice drifted into the room. "Mr. Hayne! This is an honor. Please, come, join me for tea." Like she'd caught the big fly.

Little missus started scrambling to get her shoes on. She and missus were always bragging on the mayor. Mr. Robert Hayne walked on Charleston water. He was what they called a nullifier.

"I'm afraid this isn't a social call, Mrs. Grimké. I'm here on official business regarding your daughters, Sarah and Angelina."

Little missus went still. She edged back to the doorway, one shoe on, one shoe off, and I eased over there, too.

"I regret to inform you that Sarah and Angelina are no longer welcome in the city. You should inform them if they return for a visit, they'll be arrested and imprisoned until another steamer can return them to the North. It's for their own welfare as much as the city's—Charleston is so enraged against them now they would undoubtedly meet with violence if they showed their faces."

It fell silent. The old bones of the house creaked round us.

"Do you understand, madame?" the mayor said.

"I understand perfectly, now you should understand *me*. My daughters may hold unholy opinions, but they will not be treated with this sort of insult and indignity."

The front door banged, the cane tapped, then missus was standing in the doorway with her lip trembling.

The measure tape slipped from my fingers. It curled on the floor by my foot. I wasn't likely to see Sarah ever again.

Sarah

Seated on the platform, I watched the faces in the audience grow more rapt as Nina spoke, the air crackling about their heads as if something was effervescing in it. It was our inaugural lecture, and we weren't tucked away in a parlor somewhere before twenty ladies with embroidery hoops on their laps like the Anti-Slavery Society had first envisioned. We were here in a majestic hall in New York with carved balconies and red velvet chairs filled to overflowing.

All week the newspapers had railed against the unwholesome novelty of two sisters holding forth like Fanny Wrights. The streets had been papered with handbills admonishing women to stay home, and even the Anti-Slavery Society had grown nervous about moving the lecture to a public hall. They'd come close to canceling the whole thing and sending us back to the parlor.

It was Theodore Weld who'd stood and castigated the Society for their cowardice. They called him the Lion of the Tribe of Abolition, and for good reason—he could be quite forceful when he needed to. "I defend these ladies' right to speak against slavery anywhere and everywhere. It's supremely ridiculous for you to bully them from this great moment!"

He had saved us.

Nina swept back and forth across the stage, lifting her hands and sending her voice soaring into the balconies. "We stand before you as Southern women, here to speak the terrible truth about slavery . . ." She'd splurged on a stylish, deep blue dress that set off her hair, and I couldn't help wondering what Mr. Weld would think if he could see her.

Even though he'd led the training sessions for Nina and me and the thirty-eight other agents, schooling us in the skills of oration, he'd never seemed sure how to advise the two of us. Should we stand motionless and speak softly as people expected of a woman or gesture and project like a man? "I leave it to you," he'd told us.

He'd taken what he called a brotherly interest in us, visiting us often at our lodgings. It was really Nina he'd taken an interest in, of course, and I doubted it was brotherly. She wouldn't admit it, but she was drawn to him, too. Before arriving in New York, I'd pictured Mr. Weld as a stern old man, but as it turned out, he was a young man, and as kindly as he was stern. Thirty-three and unmarried, he was strikingly handsome, with thick brown curling hair and biting blue eyes, and he was color-blind to the point he wore all sorts of funny, mismatched shades. We thought it endearing. I was fairly sure, however, it wasn't any of these qualities that attracted Nina. I suspected it was that saving speech of his. It was those five words, *I leave it to you.*

"The female slaves are our sisters," Nina exclaimed and stretched her arms from her sides as if we were encompassed by a great host of them. "We must not abandon them." It was the final line of her speech, and it was followed by a thunderclap in the hall, the women coming to their feet.

As the handclapping went on, heat washed up the sides of my neck. Now it was my turn. Having listened to me practice my speech, the Society men had decided Nina would go first and I would follow, fearing if the order was reversed, few would persevere through my talk to hear her. Getting to my feet, I wondered if the words I planned to say were already retreating

When I stepped to the lectern, my legs felt squishy as a sponge. For a moment, I held on to the sides of the podium, overwhelmed by the realization that I, of all people, was standing here. I was gazing at a sea of waiting faces, and it occurred to me that after my tall, dazzling sister, I must've been a sight. Perhaps I was even a shock. I was short, middle-aged, and plain, with a tiny pair of spectacles on the end of my nose, and I still wore my old Quaker clothes. I was comfortable in them now. *I'm who I am.* The thought made me smile, and everywhere I looked, the women smiled back, and I imagined they understood what I was thinking.

I opened my mouth and the words fell out. I spoke for several minutes before I looked at Nina as if to say, *I'm not stammering!* She nodded, her eyes wide and brimming.

As a child, my stutter had come and gone mysteriously just like this, but it had been with me for so long now I'd thought it permanent. I talked on and on. I spoke quietly about the evils of slavery that I'd seen with my own eyes. I told them about Handful and her mother and her sister. I spared them nothing.

Finally, I peered over my glasses and took them in for a moment. "We won't be silent anymore. We women will declare ourselves for the slave, and we won't be silent until they're free."

I turned then and walked back to my chair while the women rose and filled the hall with their applause.

We spoke before large gatherings in New York City for weeks before holding a campaign in New Jersey, and then traveling on to towns along the Hudson. The women came in throngs, proliferating like the loaves and fishes in the Bible. In a church in Poughkeepsie, the crowd was so great the balcony cracked and the church had to be evacuated, forcing us to deliver our speeches outside in the frost and gloom of February, and not one woman left. In every town we visited, we encouraged the women to form their own anti-slavery societies, and we set them collecting signatures on petitions. My stutter came and went, though it kindly stayed away for most of my speeches.

We became modestly famous and extravagantly infamous. Throughout that winter and spring, news of our exploits was carried by practically every newspaper in the country. The anti-slavery papers published our speeches, and tens of thousands of our pamphlets were in print. Even our former president, John Quincy Adams, agreed to meet with us, promising he would deliver the petitions the women were collecting to Congress. In a few cities in the South, we were hung in effigy right along with Mr. Garrison, and our mother had sent word we could no longer set foot in Charleston without fear of imprisonment.

Mr. Weld was our lifeline. He wrote us joint letters, praising our efforts. He called us brave and stalwart and dogged. Now and then, he added a postscript for Nina alone. *Angelina, it's widely said you keep your audiences in thrall. As director of your training, I wish I could take credit, but it's all you.*

On a balmy afternoon in April, he appeared without prior notice at Gerrit Smith's country house in Peterboro, New York, where Nina and I were spending several days during our latest round of lectures. He'd come, he said, to discuss Society finances with Mr. Smith, the organization's largest benefactor, but one could hardly miss the coincidence. Each morning, he and Nina took a walk along the lane that led through the orchards. He'd invited me as well, but I'd taken one look at Nina's face and declined. He accompanied us to our afternoon lectures, waiting outside the halls, and in the evenings, the three of us sat with Mr. and Mrs. Smith in the parlor, as we debated strategies for our cause and recounted our adventures. When Mrs. Smith suggested it was time for the women to say good night, Theodore and Nina would glance at one another reluctant to part, and he would say, "Well then. You must get your rest," and Nina would leave the room with painful slowness.

The day he departed, I watched from the window as the two of them returned from their walk. It had started to rain while they were out, one of those sudden downbursts during which the sun goes right on shining, and he was holding his coat over their heads, making a little tent for them. They walked without the least bit of hurry. I could see they were laughing.

As they came onto the porch, shaking off the wetness, he bent and kissed my sister's cheek.

In June we arrived in Amesbury, Massachusetts, for a two-week respite at the clapboard cottage of a Mrs. Whittier. We were soon to begin a crusade of lectures in New England that would last through the fall, but we were ragged with fatigue, in need of fresh, more seasonal clothes, and I had an airy little cough I couldn't get rid of. Mrs. Whittier was cherry-cheeked and plump, and fed us rich soups, dosed us with cod liver oil, refused all visitors, and forced us to bed before the moon appeared.

It was several days before we discovered she was the mother of John

Greenleaf Whittier, Theodore's close friend. We were sitting in the parlor, having tea, when she began to speak of her son and his long friendship with Theodore, and we understood now why she'd taken us in.

"You must know Theodore well then," Nina said.

"Teddy? Oh, he's like a son to me, and a brother to John." She shook her head. "I suppose you've heard of that awful pledge they made."

"Pledge?" said Nina. "Why, no, we've heard nothing of it."

"Well, I don't approve. I think it too extreme. A woman my age would like grandchildren, after all. But they're men of principle, those two, there's no reasoning with them."

Nina sat up on the edge of her chair, and I could see the brightness leave her. "What did they pledge?"

"They vowed neither of them would marry until slavery was abolished. Honestly, it will hardly be in their lifetimes!"

That night I was awakened by a knock on my door long after the moon set. Nina stood there with her face like a seawall, grim and braced. "I can't bear it," she said and fell against my shoulder.

That summer of 1837, New Englanders came by the thousands to hear us speak, and for the first time men began to appear in the audiences. At first a handful, then fifty, then hundreds. That we spoke publicly to women was bad enough—that we spoke publicly to men turned the Puritan world on its head.

"They'll be lighting the pyres," I said to Nina when the men first showed, trying to slough it off. We laughed, but it became not funny at all.

I suffer not a woman to teach, nor to usurp authority over the man, but to be in silence. Was there ever a more galling verse in the Bible? It was preached that summer from every pulpit in New England with the Grimké sisters in mind. The Congregational churches passed a resolution of censure against us, urging a boycott of our lectures, and in its wake, a number of churches and public halls were closed to us. In Pepperell we were forced to deliver our message in a barn with the horses and cows. "As you see, there's no room at the inn," Nina told them. "But, still, the wise men have come."

We tried to be brave and stalwart and dogged, as Theodore had described us in his letter, and we began using portions of our lectures to defend our right to speak. "What we claim for ourselves we claim for every woman!" That was our rally cry in Lowell and Worcester and Duxbury, indeed everywhere we went. You should have seen the women, how they flocked to our side, and some, like the brave ladies of Andover, wrote public letters in our defense. My old friend Lucretia got a message to us all the way from Philadelphia. It contained four words: *Press on, my sisters.*

Without intending to, we set the country in an uproar. The matter of women having certain rights was new and strange and pilloried, but it was suddenly debated all the way to Ohio. They renamed my sister Devilina. They christened us "female incendiaries." Somehow we'd lit the fuse.

The last week of August we returned to Mrs. Whittier's cottage as if from battle. I felt tired and beleaguered, uncertain if I could continue with the fall lectures. The last teaspoon of fight had been scraped out of me. Our final meeting of the summer had ended with dozens of angered men standing on wagons outside the hall, shouting "Devilina!" and hurling rocks as we left. One had hit my mouth, transforming my lower lip into a fat, red sausage. I looked a sight. I wasn't sure what Mrs. Whittier would say to all this, if she would even give us shelter—we were pariahs now—but when we arrived, she pulled us into her arms and kissed our foreheads.

On the third day of refuge, I returned from a stroll along the banks of the Merrimack to find Nina canting sharply against the window as if she'd fallen asleep, her head pressed to the glass, her eyes closed, her arms dropped by her sides. She looked like a spinning top that had come to rest.

Hearing my footsteps, she turned and pointed to the tea table where the *Boston Morning Post* lay open. Mrs. Whittier took care to hide the editorials, but Nina had found the paper in the bread box.

> August 25
>
> The Misses Grimké have made speeches, written pamphlets, and exhibited themselves in public in unwomanly ways for a while now, but they have not found husbands. Why are all the old hens abolitionists? Because not being able to obtain

husbands, they think they may stand some chance for a Negro, if they can only make amalgamation fashionable...

I couldn't finish it.

"If that's not enough, Theodore will be arriving this afternoon along with Elizur Wright and Mrs. Whittier's son, John. Their letter came while you were out. Mrs. Whittier is in there making mince pies."

She hadn't spoken of Theodore all summer, but she was sick with longing for him, it was plain on her face.

The men arrived at three o'clock. My lip was almost back to its normal size, and I could speak now without sounding as if my mouth was stuffed with food, but it was still sore and I remained quiet, waiting for them to come to their purpose, remembering the way Theodore defended us before—*It is supremely ridiculous they should be bullied from this great moment.*

Today he was wearing two shades of green that made one wince. He walked to the mantel and picked up a piece of scrimshaw and inspected it. His eyes went to Nina. He said, "There has not been a contribution to the anti-slavery movement more impressive or tireless than that of the Grimké sisters."

"Hear, hear," said dear Mrs. Whittier, but I saw her son lower his eyes, and I knew then why they had come.

"We commend you for it," Theodore went on. "And yet by encouraging men to join your audiences, you've mired us in a controversy that has taken the attention away from abolition. We've come, hoping to convince you—"

Nina interrupted him. "Hoping to convince us to behave like good lapdogs and wait content beneath the table for whatever crumbs you toss to us? Is that what you hope?" Her rebuke was so swift and scathing I wondered if it was in reaction to his marriage pledge as much as anything.

"Angelina, please, just hear us out," he said. "We're on your side, at heart we are. I of all people support your right to speak. It's downright senseless to keep men away from your meetings."

"... Then why do you quibble?" I asked.

"Because we sent you out there on behalf of abolition, not women."

He glanced at John, whose heavy brows and lean face made me feel the two could've been actual brothers, not just figurative ones.

"He only means to say the slave is of greater urgency," John added. "I support the cause of women, too, but surely you can't lose sight of the slave because of a selfish crusade against some paltry grievance of your own?"

"Paltry?" Nina cried. "Is our right to speak paltry?"

"In comparison to the cause of abolition? Yes, I say it is."

Mrs. Whittier drew up in her chair. "Really, John! As a woman, I didn't think I had a grievance until you began speaking!"

"Why must it be one or the other?" Nina asked. "Sarah and I haven't ceased to work for abolition. We're speaking for slaves and women both. Don't you see, we could do a hundred times more for the slave, if we weren't so fettered?" She turned to Theodore, casting on him the most beautiful, imploring look. "Can't you stand side by side with me? With us?"

He drew a long breath and his face gave him away—it was twisted with love and distress—but he'd come on a mission, and as Mrs. Whittier had said, he was a man of principle, right or wrong. "Angelina, I think of you as my friend, the dearest of friends, and it tortures me to go against you, but now is the time to stand with the slave. The time will come for us to take up the woman question, but not yet."

"The time to assert one's right is when it's denied!"

"I'm sorry," he told her.

Outside, the wind swirled up, churning the leaves in the birch. The sound and smell of it loomed through the open window, and I had a sudden fleeting memory of playing beneath the oak in the work yard back home, forming words with my brother's marbles, *Sarah Go,* and then the slave woman is dragged from the cow house and whipped. I don't scream or make a sound. I say nothing at all.

The older Mr. Wright had begun his piece, coming to the crux of it. "It saddens me, but your agitation for women harms our cause. It threatens to split the abolition movement in two. I can't believe you want that. We're only asking you to confine your audiences to women and refrain from further talk about women's reform."

Hushing up the Grimké sisters—would it never stop? I looked at Mr. Wright, sitting there rubbing his arthritic fingers, and then at John and Theodore—these good men who wished to quash us, gently, of course, benignly, for the good of abolition, for our own good, for their good, for the greater good. It was all so familiar. Theirs was only a different kind of muzzle.

I'd spoken but once since they'd gotten here, and it seemed to me now I'd spent my entire life trying to coax back the voice that left me that long-ago day under the tree. Nina, clearly furious, had stopped arguing. She looked at me, beseeching me to say something. I lifted my fingers to my mouth and touched the last bit of swollenness on my lip, feeling the uprush of indignation that had sustained me through the summer, and, I suppose, my whole life, but this time, it formed into hard round words. "How can you ask us to go back to our parlors?" I said, rising to my feet. "To turn our backs on ourselves and on our own sex? We don't wish the movement to split, of course we don't—it saddens me to think of it—but we can do little for the slave as long as we're under the feet of men. Do what you have to do, censure us, withdraw your support, we'll press on anyway. Now, sirs, kindly take your feet off our necks."

―

That night I began writing my second pamphlet, *Letters on the Equality of the Sexes,* working into the hours before dawn. The first line had arranged itself in my head while I'd sat listening to the men try and dissuade us: *Whatsoever it is morally right for a man to do, it is morally right for a woman to do. She is clothed by her Maker with the same rights, the same duties.*

Handful

It was springtime when all the heavy cleaning and airing-out was going on in the house and every night me and Sky would come back to the cellar room after being with the bristle-brush all day, and fall on the bed, and the first thing I'd see was the quilt frame, the one true roof over my head. I'd think about everything hidden up there—mauma's story quilt, the money, Sarah's booklet, her letter telling me about the promise she'd made to get me free—and I'd fall asleep glad they were safe over my head.

Then one Sunday morning, I rolled the frame down. Sky watched me without a word while I ran my hand over the red quilt with the black triangles, feeling the money sewed inside. I peeled the muslin cloth from round Sarah's booklet and gazed on it, then wrapped it back. Next, I spread the story quilt cross the frame and we stood there, looking down at the history of mauma. I laid my palm on the second square—the woman in the field and the slaves flying in the air over her head. All that hope in the wind.

We didn't hear little missus outside the door. The lock mauma used to have on the door was long gone, and little missus, she didn't knock. She flounced on in. "I'm going to St. Philip's, and I need my claret cape. You were supposed to mend it for me." Her eyes wandered past me to the quilt frame. "What's all this?"

I stepped to block her view. "That's right, I forgot about your cape." I was trying to fan the moth from the flame, but she brushed past me to see the pinks, reds, oranges, purples, and blacks on the quilt. Mauma and her colors.

"I'll be straight over to mend the cape," I said and took the rope off the hook to hike the frame up before she figured out what she was looking at.

She put up her hand. "Hold on. You're in an awful big hurry to hide this from me."

I fastened the rope back, the high-flutter coming in my chest. Sky started humming a thin nervous tune. I started to put my finger to my lip, but ever since she had that muzzle in her mouth, I couldn't bear to hush her. We looked back and forth to each other while little missus squinted from one square to the next like she was reading a book. Everything done to mauma—there it was. The one-legged punishment, the whippings, the branding, the hammering. Mauma's body laid on the quilt frame in pieces.

The muslin cloth with Sarah's booklet inside was in plain sight, and beside it, the quilt with the money inside. You could see the shape of the bundles laying in the batting. I wanted to tuck everything from view, but I didn't move.

When she turned to me, the morning glare fell over her face and the black in her eyes pulled into knots. She said, "Who made this?"

"Mauma did. Charlotte."

"Well, it's gruesome!"

I never had wanted to scream as bad as I did right then. I said, "Those gruesome things happened to her."

A dark pink color poured into her cheeks. "For heaven's sakes then, you would think her whole life was nothing but violence and cruelty. I mean, it doesn't show what she did to warrant her punishments."

She looked at the quilt again, her eyes darting over the appliqués. "We treated her well here, no one can dispute that. I can't speak for what happened to her when she ran away, she was out of our care then." Little missus was rubbing her hands now like she was cleaning them at the wash bowl.

The quilt had shamed her. She walked to the door and took one look back at it, and I knew she'd never let it stay in the world. She'd send Hector to get it the minute we were out of the room. He'd burn mauma's story to ash.

Standing there, waiting for little missus' steps to fade, I looked down at the quilt, at the slaves flying in the sky, and I hated being a slave worse than being dead. The hate I felt for it glittered so full of beauty I sank down on the floor before it.

Sky's hair was a bushel basket without her scarf and when she bent over to see about me, the ends of it poked my face and smelled like the bristle-brush. She said, "You all right?"

I looked up at her. "We're leaving here."

She heard me, but she couldn't be sure. She said, "What you say?"

"We gonna leave here or die trying."

Sky pulled me to my feet like plucking a flower, and I saw Denmark's face settle into hers, that day he rode to his death sitting on a coffin. I'd always wanted freedom, but there never had been a place to go and no way to get there. That didn't matter anymore. I wanted freedom more than the next breath. We'd leave, riding on our coffins if we had to. That was the way mauma had lived her whole life. She used to say, you got to figure out which end of the needle you're gon be, the one that's fastened to the thread or the end that pierces the cloth.

I lifted the quilt from the frame and folded it up, thinking of the feathers inside it, and inside the feathers, the memory of the sky.

"Here," I said, laying the quilt in Sky's arms. "I got to go mend that woman's cape. Put the quilt in the gunny sack and take it to Goodis and tell him to hide it with the horse blankets and don't let anybody near it."

Mending her cape was not all I did. I took little missus' seal-stamp right off her desk while she was standing in the room and I dropped it in my pocket.

I waited till dark to write my letter.

23 April 1838

Dear Sarah

I hope this makes it to you. Me and Sky will be leaving here or die trying. That's how we put it. I don't know how we're doing it, but we've got mauma's money. All we need is a place to come to. I have the address on this letter. I hope I see you again one day.
Your friend
Handful

Sarah

The wedding took place in a house on Spruce Street in Philadelphia on May 14 at two o'clock in the afternoon—a day full of glinting sunlight and pale blue clouds. It was the sort of day that seemed sharply real and not real at all. I remember standing in the dining room watching it unfold as if from a distance, as if I was climbing up from the bottom of sleep, coming up from the cool sheets to a new day, one life ending and another beginning.

Mother had sent a note of congratulation, which we hadn't expected, begging us to send a letter describing the wedding in detail. *What will Nina wear?* she'd asked. *Oh, that I could see her!* Naturally, she'd conveyed how relieved she was that Nina had a husband now and she hoped we would both retire from the unnatural life we'd been living, but despite that, her letter was plaintive with the love of an aging mother. She called us her dear daughters and lamented the distance between us. *Will I see you again?* she wrote. The question haunted me for days.

I gazed at Nina and Theodore standing now before the window about to say their vows, or as Nina had phrased it, whatever words their hearts gave them at the moment, and I thought it just as well Mother was not here. She would've expected Nina to be in ivory lace, perhaps blue linen, carrying roses or lilies, but Nina had dismissed all of that as unoriginal and embarked on a wedding designed to shock the masses.

She was wearing a brown dress made from free-labor cotton with a broad white sash and white gloves, and she'd matched up Theodore in a brown coat, a white vest, and beige pantaloons. She clutched a handful of white rhododendrons cut fresh from the backyard, and I noticed she'd tucked a sprig in the button hole of Theodore's coat. Mother wouldn't have made it past the brown dress, much less the opening prayer, which had been delivered by a Negro minister.

When the Philadelphia newspaper announced the wedding, alluding to the mixed-race guests expected to attend, we'd worried there might be demonstrators—slurs and shouts and rocks whizzing by—but mercifully, no one had showed up but those invited. Sarah Mapps and Grace were here, along with several freed slaves with whom we were acquainted, and we'd timed the wedding to coincide with the Anti-Slavery Convention in the city so that some of the most prominent abolitionists in the country were in the room: Mr. Garrison, Mr. and Mrs. Gerrit Smith, Henry Stanton, the Motts, the Tappans, the Westons, the Chapmans.

It would become known as the abolition wedding.

Nina was speaking now, her face turned up to Theodore's, and I thought suddenly, involuntarily of Israel and a tiny grief came over me. Every time it happened, it was like coming upon an empty room I didn't know was there, and stepping in, I would be pierced by it, by the ghost of the one who'd once filled it up. I didn't stumble into this place much anymore, but when I did, it hollowed out little pieces of my chest.

Gazing at Nina, radiant Nina, I pictured myself in her place, Israel beside me, the two of us saying vows, and the idea of such a thing cured me. It was the truth I always came back to, that I didn't want Israel anymore, I didn't want to be married now, and yet the phantom of what might've been, the terrible allure of it could still snatch me.

Closing my eyes, I gave my head a shake to clear the remnants of longing away, and when I looked back at the bride and groom, there were dragonflies darting beyond the window, a green tempest, and then it was gone.

Nina promised aloud to love and honor him, carefully omitting the word *obey,* and Theodore launched into an awkward monologue, deploring the laws that gave control of a wife's property to the husband and renouncing all claim to Nina's, and then he coughed self-consciously, as if catching himself, and professed his love.

We'd put the confrontation in Mrs. Whittier's cottage behind us, not that Theodore ever fully conceded his position, but he'd softened his rhetoric after that day, as any man in love would. The abolition movement *had* split into two camps just as the men predicted, and Nina and I became even worse pariahs, but it had set the cause of women in motion.

I'd been present when Nina opened the letter containing Theodore's proposal. It had come late last winter during a long reprieve in Philadelphia with Sarah Mapps and Grace, as we'd prepared for a series of lectures at the Boston Odeon. Reading it, she'd dropped the pages onto her lap and broken into tears. When she read it to me, I cried too, but my tears were a mix of joy and wretchedness and fear. I wanted this marriage for her, I wanted her happiness as much as my own, but where would I go? For days I couldn't concentrate on the lecture I was trying to write or hide the bereft feeling I carried inside. I couldn't bear to think of life without her, life alone, but neither did I want to be the burdensome relative living in the back room, getting in the way, and I couldn't imagine Theodore would want me there.

Then one day Nina came to me, plopping on the footstool beside my chair in Sarah Mapps' front room. Without a word she opened her Bible and read aloud the passage in which Ruth speaks to Naomi:

Entreat me not to leave thee, or to return from following after thee: for whither thou goest, I will go; and where thou lodgest, I will lodge; thy people will be my people, and thy God my God. Where thou diest, will I die, and there will I be buried. The Lord do so to me, and more also, if ought but death part thee and me.

Closing the Bible, she said, "We can't be separated, it isn't possible. You must come and live with me after I'm married. Theodore asked me to tell you that my wish is also his wish."

Theodore had bought a small farm in Fort Lee, New Jersey. We would make an odd trinity there, the three of us, but I would still have Nina. We could go on writing and working for abolition and for women, and I would help with the house, and when there were children, I would be auntie. *One life ending, another beginning.*

In the dining room, the minister was offering a prayer, and for some reason I didn't close my eyes as I always did, but watched Nina reach for Theodore's hand. We'd made a plan that I would give the married pair two weeks of privacy and then join them in Fort Lee, but I thought now of Mother and the question in her letter, *Will I see you again?* It seemed more than the elegiac pondering in an old woman's heart, and I wondered if I shouldn't seize the break in our work and go to her.

"What do you know, we are husband and wife," Nina said when the prayer ended, pronouncing it herself.

The dining table sat out in the garden laid with a white linen cloth strewn with platters of sweets and fresh-picked flowers—foxglove, pink azalea, and feathery fleabane petals. The confectioner had iced the wedding cake with frothed egg whites and darkened the layers with molasses in keeping with Nina's brown and white theme, and there was a large bowl of sugared raspberry-currant juice where all of the teetotaler abolitionists were lined up, pretending it hadn't fermented. I'd consumed a sloshing cup of it too quickly and my head was floating about.

I walked among the guests, some forty or fifty of them, searching for Lucretia, for Sarah Mapps and Grace, thinking, a little tipsily, *Here are our friends, our people, and thank God no one is speaking today about the cruelties in the world*. I came upon Mrs. Whittier's son John, whom I'd not seen since our head-to-head last August. He was amusing everyone with a poem he'd written that skewered Theodore for breaking his vow not to marry. He compared him to the likes of Benedict Arnold. When he saw me, he greeted me like a sister.

Lucretia found me before I could find her. It had been years. Beaming, she pulled me to the edge of the garden beside the blooming rhododendron where we could be alone. "My dear Sarah, I can scarcely believe what you've managed to accomplish!"

A blush crept to my face.

"It's true," she said. "You and Angelina are the most famous women in America."

". . . The most notorious, you mean."

She smiled. "That, too."

I pictured Lucretia and me in her little studio, talking and talking all those evenings. That fretful young woman I'd been, so stalled, so worried she would never find her purpose. I wished I could go back and tell her it would turn out all right.

Glancing up, I caught sight of Sarah Mapps and Grace across the garden, striding toward us. Nina and I had traveled almost constantly for the past year and a half, and except for our visit last winter, we'd seen little of them. I wrapped my arms around them, along with Lucretia, who'd known them back at Arch Street.

When Sarah Mapps pulled a letter from her purse and handed it to me, I recognized Handful's writing immediately, though it bore my sister Mary's seal. Unable to wait, I ripped it open and read Handful's brief message with a sinking feeling. There were reports of runaways beginning to find their way across the Ohio River from Kentucky, or to Philadelphia and New York from Maryland, but rarely from that far south. *We're leaving here or die trying.*

"What's the matter?" Lucretia said. "You look shaken."

I read them the letter, then folded it back, my hands trembling visibly. "... They'll be caught. Or killed," I said.

Sarah Mapps frowned. "They must know what they're attempting. They're not children."

She'd never been to Charleston. She had no idea of the laws and edicts that controlled every moment of a slave's life, of the City Guard, the curfew, the passes, the searches, the night watch, the vigilante committees, the slave catchers, the Work House, the impossibility, the sheer brutality.

"They're coming to us," Grace said, as if it had just sunk in.

"And we'll welcome them," Sarah Mapps added. "They can live in your old room in the attic. They can help out at the school."

"They'll never make it this far," I said.

It occurred to me that Handful and Sky might already have left, and I opened up the letter again to look at the date: *23 April*.

"It was written only three weeks ago," I said more to myself than to them. "... I doubt they've left by now. There may still be time for me to do something."

"But what could you possibly do?" Lucretia asked.

"I don't know if I can do anything, but I can't sit here on my hands . . . I'm going back to Charleston. I can at least try and convince my mother to sell them to me so I can set them free."

I'd asked before, but this time I would beg her in person.

She had called me her dear daughter.

Handful

Upstairs in the alcove, I peered out the window at the harbor, remembering when I was ten years old seeing the water for the first time, how tireless and far it traveled, making up that little song, prancing round, and now I was coming on forty-five and my feet didn't dance anymore. They just wanted to be gone from here. Little missus hadn't let me out since the whipping, but every free chance I slipped up here. Sometimes like today, I brought my hand sewing and spent the morning on the window seat with the needle. Little missus didn't care as long as I did my work, kept my tongue, bobbed my head, said *yessum, yessum, yessum*.

Today, it was hot, the sun eyeing straight in. I opened the window and the wind blew stiff, dredging up the smell of mudflats. From my perch, I could see the steamboat landing down on East Bay. I'd learned plenty watching the world come and go from that dock. A steamer came most every week day. I'd watch the snag boat ply ahead of it, clearing the way, then I'd hear the paddle on the steamer roar and the tug boats huff and the dock slaves holler back and forth, making haste to grab the ropes and put down the plank.

When it was time for it to leave again, I'd watch the carriages pull up at the whitewash building with the Steamship Company sign, and people would go inside and wait for a spell. Down on the landing, the slaves would unload trunks and goods and bags of mail onto the ship. When ten o'clock came, the passengers crossed the street and the slaves helped the ladies over the gangplank. The boat never left till the Guard showed up. Always two of them, sometimes three, they passed through the ship—first deck, second deck, pilot house, bottom to top. One time they opened every humpback trunk before it went onboard. That's when I knew they were searching for stowaways, for slaves.

The Thursday boat went all the way to New York, and then you got on another one going to Philadelphia—I'd learned that from reading the *Charleston Post and Courier*, which I'd swiped from the drawing room. It printed all the schedules, said the tickets cost fifty-five dollars.

Today, the steamboat landing was empty, but I wasn't up here in the alcove to watch the boat, I was up here to figure a way to get on it. All these weeks I'd been patient. Careful. *Yessum, yessum.* Now I sat here with the palmettos clacking in the wind and thought of the girl who bathed in a copper tub. I thought of the woman who stole a bullet mold. I loved that girl, that woman.

I went over everything I'd seen out there on the harbor, everything I knew. I sat with my hands still, my eyes closed, my mind flying with the gulls, the world tilting like a birdwing.

When I stood up, every one of my limbs was shaking.

The next week when Hector was handing out duties for the day, he told Minta, go strip the bedding in the house and take it out to the laundry house. I thought quick and said, "Oh, I'll do that, poor Minta's back is hurting her." She looked at me curious, but didn't argue. You take a rest whatever way you can get it.

In the alcove that day, a picture had sprung in my head—*dresses*. I saw the black dresses the missuses had worn to mourn their husbands. I saw their spoon bonnets with the thick black veils and their black gloves. These things came to me clear as the bright of day.

When I got to missus' room, I tugged off the bed linens, listening for footsteps on the stairs, for a cane poking its way, then I opened the last drawer of her linen press. I'd folded away missus' mourning dress, her bonnet and gloves my own self all those years back. I'd packed them in linen with camphor gum to keep out the moth eggs and laid them in the bottom drawer. Reaching back there, I worried they were long gone, that what warded off the moths had drawn the rats, but then my fingers brushed against the linen.

I peeked inside the parcel. It was still the grandest dress I'd ever made— black velvet stitched with hundreds of black glass beads. Some of them had come loose and were scatter-rolling in the linen folds. The veil on the bonnet had two spider tears that would have to be fixed, plus I'd forgot the gloves were fingerless mitts. I'd have to sew fingers on them. I whisked everything into the bed sheets, bundled it up, and tied a topknot. Leaving it outside the door, I hurried into little missus' room.

Her funeral outfit was stored nearly the same way in her bureau but with cedar chips instead of camphor. I didn't know how we'd air out all these rowdy smells. When I got her dress, hat, and gloves rolled tight in the sheets, I threw both of the bed bundles over my back and went down the stairs with my cane, straight to the cellar room.

That night after me and Sky had dragged the bed over to block the door, she tried on missus' black velvet dress and stood there with the buttons undone. Thick-waist as missus was, I'd still have to let the bodice out for Sky, add six inches to the length and two to the sleeves. She was her daddy's girl, all right.

Little missus was normal size, but there was enough room inside her dress for two of me.

The only thing we didn't have was shoes, proper shoes. What we had was slave shoes and that would have to do.

I started to work that night. Sky fetched threads and shears for me and watched every stitch. She sang the Gullah song she liked best, *If you don't know where you're going, you should know where you come from.*

I told her, "We know where we're going now."

"Yeah," she said.

"We'll be ready when the steamer leaves Thursday eight days from now."

She picked up her apron draped on the rocker and dug in the pocket, pulling out two little bottles like the kind Aunt-Sister used for tinctures. "I boiled us some white oleander tea."

A quiver ran from my neck to my fingers. White oleander was the most deadly plant in the world. A bush had caught fire on Hasell Street and a man dropped dead just breathing the smoke. The brown liquid in Sky's bottle would curl us on the floor retching till the last breath, but it wouldn't take long.

"We leaving or die trying," Sky said.

Sarah

I arrived in Charleston during a thunderstorm. As the steamer groaned into the harbor, lightning tore rifts in the sky and rain pelted sideways, and still, I stepped out beneath the roof of the upper deck so I could watch the city come into view. I hadn't seen it in sixteen years.

We churned past Fort Sumter at the harbor's mouth, which didn't look much further along in its construction than when I'd sailed away. The peninsula loomed up like an old mirage rising from the water, the white houses on the Battery blurred in the gray rain. For a moment I felt the quiet hungering thing that comes inside when you return to the place of your origins, and then the ache of mis-belonging. It was beautiful, this place, and it was savage. It swallowed you and made you a part of itself, or if you proved too inassimilable, it spit you out like the pit of a plum.

I'd left here of my own will, and yet it seemed the city had banished me in much the same way I'd banished it. Seeing it now after so long, seeing the marsh grass pitching wildly around the edges of the city, the rooftops hunkered together with their ship watches and widow walks, and behind them, the steeples of St. Philip's and St. Michael's lifted like dark fingers, I was not sorry for loving Charleston or for leaving it. Geography had made me who I was.

Wind swept my bonnet off the back of my head, the sash catching at my neck, and turning to grab it, I saw the menacing couple through the window of the salon. Traveling home after socializing in Newport, they'd recognized me shortly after we'd left New York. I'd tried to keep aloof from everyone, but the woman had stared at me with unrelenting curiosity. "You're the Grimké daughter, aren't you?" she said. "The one who—" Her husband took her arm and steered her away before she could finish. She'd meant to say *the one who betrayed us.*

They glared at me now, at my wet skirt and fluttering bonnet, and I felt certain the man would report my arrival to the authorities as soon as we landed. Perhaps returning had been a terrible mistake after all. I moved away from them to the bow of the boat as a crack of thunder broke overhead, becoming lost in the noise of the engine. Charleston would forgive its own many things, but not betrayal.

I found Handful within an hour of my arrival. She was sewing in the upstairs alcove, of all places. When she saw me standing there, she leapt up, stumbling a little with her infirm leg, dropping the slave shirt on the floor along with the needle and thread. I reached to catch her as she righted herself and found myself embracing her, feeling her embrace me back.

"I got your letter," I told her, softly, in case there were listening ears somewhere.

She shook her head. "But you didn't come back cause of that, cause of me."

"Of course I did," I said. I picked up the shirt and we sat down on the cushioned window seat.

She was wearing her customary red scarf and seemed barely changed. Her eyes were still large as bowls, the golden color darkened somewhat, and she was tiny as ever. Not frail or insubstantial, but distilled, concentrated.

There was a cane propped between us with a fanciful carving of a rabbit on the handle. Moving it to the side, she said, "You didn't come to try and stop us, did you?"

"It's dangerous, Handful . . . I'm afraid for you."

"Well, that may be, but I'm more scared of bowing and scraping to your mauma and your sister the rest of my days."

Speaking barely above a whisper, I told her about my plan to try and convince Mother to sell the two of them to me.

She laughed a bitter sound. *"Uh huh."*

I hadn't expected that. I looked past her, scanning the harbor, noticing the steamer in the distance rinsed clean by the rain.

She shifted herself on the cushion and I heard the breath leave her. "I just don't see missus doing one thing favorable for me, that's all. But here you are, all this way—nobody else would've done that for me—so it's worth a try, and if she's willing to sell us, I'll pay you back everything I got, four hundred dollars."

"There would be no need—"

"Well, I ain't doing it any other way."

We stopped talking as Hector, the butler Mary had installed, came up the stairs with my trunk, his gaze lingering longer than was comfortable. I stood. "I should get settled."

"You go on and talk to her then," Handful whispered. "But don't be waiting too long."

I waited four days. It seemed imprudent to make the request before that—I wanted Mother to believe I'd returned solely to see her.

I broached the matter on Tuesday afternoon while we sat in the drawing room, Mother, Mary, and I, swishing our fans at the vaporous heat. A languid silence had fallen that none of us seemed willing to break. We'd exhausted all the harmless subjects: the rainy weather, the spectacular wonder of the railroad that ran from Charleston to Savannah, an expurgated version of Nina's wedding, news of my siblings, the nieces and nephews I'd never met. If I had any chance at securing freedom for Handful and Sky, we couldn't speak of my scandalous adventures, which had been in all the papers. Nor of abolition, slavery, the North, the South, religion, politics, or the fact I'd been outlawed in the city the previous summer.

"People are talking, Sarah," Mary said, breaking the lull. She exchanged a look with Mother, and I glimpsed how in step they were with one another, how alike. An echo of loneliness reverberated from my girlhood, and I felt again like the odd-child-out. Even now. I heard Binah's voice somewhere in my memory, *Poor Miss Sarah*. These irrational childish feelings, where had they come from suddenly?

"Rumors are running rampant that you've returned," Mary was saying.

"It's only a matter of time before the sheriff arrives to inquire about it, and if you're here, I'm not sure what you expect us to say. We can hardly hide you like a fugitive."

I turned to Mother, watching her eyes veer away toward the piazza. The windows were open and the chocolaty smell of the oleander streamed in, sickeningly thick.

"You wish me to leave?"

"It's not a matter of what we wish," Mother said. "If the authorities come, I wouldn't give you over to them, of course not. You're my daughter. You're still a Grimké. We only suggest it would be easier all around if you cut your visit short."

To my surprise, her eyes filled. She was plump now with thinned white hair and one of those ancient faces that's deeply cobblestoned. She peered at me as the tears started to spill, and I left my chair and went to her. Bending down awkwardly, I put my arms about her.

She clung to me an instant, then straightened. Instead of returning to my seat, I paced toward the window and back, gathering my bravery.

"I won't put you at risk, I'll leave on the next steamer, but before I go, I have a request. I would like to purchase Hetty and her sister, Sky."

"Purchase them?" Mary said. "But why? You hardly barter in slaves."

"Mary, for heaven's sake, she means to free them," Mother said.

"I'll offer you any amount." I walked to Mother's side. "Please. I would consider it a great kindness to me."

Mary rose and came to the other side of Mother's chair. "We can't possibly do without Hetty," she said. "There are few seamstresses in Charleston to match her. She's irreplaceable. The other one is expendable, but not Hetty."

Mother stared at her hands. Her shoulders moved up and down with her breath, and I began to feel a prick of hope.

"There are laws that make it difficult," she said. "Emancipating them would require a special act of the legislature."

"Difficult, but it could be done," I responded.

Something inside of her seemed to bend, to arch toward me. Mary sensed it, too. She placed her hand on our mother's, linking the two of them. She said, "We can't do without Hetty. And we must think of her, as well. Where will she go? Who will take care of her? She has a home here."

"This is not her home, it's her prison," I said.

Mary stiffened. "We don't need you to come here and lecture us about slavery. I won't stand here and defend it to you. It's our way of life."

Her words infuriated me. I wondered for a moment if holding my tongue would help my cause with Mother. Was it ever right to sacrifice one's truth for expedience? Mother would do what she would do, wouldn't she? I wondered how it was possible I'd found my words out there in the world, but could lose them in the house where I was born.

It gave way inside of me—years of being here, co-existing with the untenable. "*Your way of life!* What does that justify? Slavery is a hell-concocted system, it cannot be defended!"

Small red wafers splotched along Mary's neck. "God has ordained that we take care of them," she said, flustered now, spluttering.

I took a step toward her, my outrage breaking open. "You speak as if God was white and Southern! As if we somehow owned his image. You speak like a fool. The Negro is not some other kind of creature than we are. Whiteness is not sacred, Mary! It can't go on defining everything."

I doubt anyone had ever spoken to her in such a manner, and she turned away from me, taken aback.

I couldn't explain that rising up, this coming fully to myself, the audacity and authority my life had found. It took me aback, as well, and I closed my eyes, and I blessed it. It was like arriving finally in the place I'd left, and I felt then I would never be an exile again.

Mother lifted her hand. "This has tired me," she said and struggled to her feet with her old gold-tip cane. She walked to the door, then turned back, leveling her eyes on mine. "I won't sell Hetty or Sky to you, Sarah. I'm sorry to disappoint you, but I *will* compromise."

In the darkness of the cellar, the sound of my knocking seemed lost and swallowed up. It was past midnight. I'd waited until now to find Handful, slipping down here when the house was asleep, still wearing my sleeping clothes. The lantern swayed in my hand, swiveling the shadows, as I rapped again on Handful's door. *Come on, Handful, wake up.*

"Who's out there?" Her voice sounded alarmed and muffled behind the door.

"It's all right. It's me, it's Sarah."

She made a slit in the door, then let me inside. She held a candle that flickered beneath her chin. Her eyes appeared almost luminous.

"I'm sorry to wake you, but we must talk."

Across the room, Sky was sitting up in her bed, her hair splayed out like a great dark fan. I sat the lantern down and nodded at her. Soon after my arrival, I'd seen her in the ornamental garden, down on her knees, digging with a trowel. The garden had been turned into a kind of wonderland, a cloister of colorful blooms, groomed shrubberies, and winding paths, and I'd gone out there as if to take a stroll. Sky hadn't waited for me to approach her, but pushed to her feet and strode over to me, smelling of fresh dirt and green plants. She didn't look like Handful, or Charlotte either for that matter. She was strapping. She looked feral and cunning to me. She said, "You Sarah?" When I said I was, she grinned. "Handful said you the best of the Grimkés."

"I'm not sure that's saying a great deal," I answered, smiling at her.

"Maybe not," she said, and I liked her instantly.

I glanced about the cellar room, a little more crowded now with two beds. They'd shoved them together side by side beneath the window.

"What is it?" Handful said, but before I could speak, I saw it dawn on her. "Your mauma won't sell us, will she?"

"No, I'm sorry. She refused. But—"

"But what?"

"She did agree to free both of you upon her death. She said she would have the paper drawn up and added to her will."

Handful stood with the light puddling around her and stared at me. It was not what any of us wanted, but it was something.

"She's seventy-four," I said.

"She'll outlive the last cockroach," Handful said. She looked at Sky. "We'll be leaving here day after tomorrow."

I was relieved and terrified in the same moment. I studied the compact defiance that made up so much of who she was. I said, "Tell me how I can help."

Handful

The night before we were to take our leave, me and Sky scurried in the dark, collecting everything together. We stole out to the stable to get mauma's quilt from the horse blankets, trekking cross the work yard with the stars pouring down. We climbed up to Sarah's room from the cellar to the second floor, three trips, carrying quilts, black dresses, hats, veils, gloves, and hankies. Up and down, me and my lame foot, passing right by missus' and little missus' doors. We went in stocking feet, taking soft steps like the floor might sink.

On the last trip, Sarah locked the door behind us, and I had a tarnish memory of her screening the keyhole while she taught me to read, how we whispered by the lamplight like we were doing now. I hung our dresses in her wardrobe. They fit us tailor-made. The veils were pressed perfect, and I'd sprinkled the velvet and crepe with missus' lavender water so they had a white lady scent. I'd sewed pockets on the inside of the dresses to hold our money, along with Sarah's booklet, mauma's red scarf, and the address in Philadelphia where we hoped to end up.

Sky said the rabbit was outfoxing the fox.

Sarah opened her steamer trunk and I rested mauma's story quilt on the satin lining at the bottom. I'd brought the quilt with red squares and black triangles, hoping to pack it, too—the first blackbird wings I ever sewed—but now that I saw how little the trunk was, I felt bad for taking up the precious space. I said, "I can leave this behind."

Sarah took it from me and laid it in the trunk. "I would rather leave my dresses—they're not worth much."

I knew the perils of what she was doing same as she did. I read the papers.

Twenty years in prison for circulating publications of a seditious nature. Twenty years for assisting a slave to escape.

I watched her fold her few belongings on top of the quilts and thought, *This ain't the same Sarah who left here.* She had a firm look in her eye and her voice didn't dither and hesitate like it used to. She'd been boiled down to a good, strong broth.

Her hair was loose, dangling along the sides of her neck like silk vines, like the red threads I used to tie round the spirit tree, and I saw it then, the strange thing between us. *Not love, is it? What is it?* It was always there, a roundness in my chest, a pin cushion. It pricked and fastened. Those girls on the roof with the tea gone cold in the cup.

She brought the lid down on the trunk.

I told Sky, go on down to the cellar and rest and I'll be there in a while—I had one task left to do by myself. Then I eased down the stairs, out the back door, and loped off with my cane to the spirit tree.

Under the branches, the moonlight splatted on me from the leaves. I felt the owls blink and the wind draw a breath. When I looked back at the house, there was mauma in the upstairs window looking down, waiting to throw me a taffy. She was standing out in the ruts of the carriageway with her leg hitched up behind her and the strap round her neck. She sat quiet against the tree trunk with sewing in her lap.

I bent down and gathered up a handful of clippings from the tree—acorns, twigs, a tired, dog-eared leaf—and stuffed them inside my neck pouch. Then I took my spirit.

Next morning, we acted same as always. Sky went to the vegetable garden with the picking basket and plucked the ripe tomatoes and lettuce tops. Missus had me rubbing her ivory fans with sandpaper to scrub off the yellow tint. I worked in the alcove with the scrape of the paper, eyeing the steamship. The water on the harbor was ruffling like dress flounces.

Sarah was down the hallway in the withdrawing room with missus having her last goodbye. She wouldn't see her mauma again. She knew that, and missus knew that. The air in the house sounded like a long note on the harpsichord. Downstairs, Sarah's trunk was locked and ready by the front door, everything inside—mauma's story, the flock of blackbirds.

The chiming clock sang out, and I counted the notes, nine of them, and Sarah came out of the withdrawing room with her eyes stinging bright. I set down the ivory fans and followed her to her room, leaving the rabbit cane behind, leaning against the window.

Sarah was wearing a pale gray dress with a big silver button at the collar, that same button from when she was a girl, pinning all her hopes on it. Stepping out through the jib door to the piazza, she peered over the rail at Sky in the ornament garden and gave her a wave. That meant, *Leave your plants and flowers and come inside. Pass by the house slaves. If little missus stops you, say, Sarah summoned me.*

When Sky tapped on the door, I was already in my dress, my face patted with white flour gum. She smiled. She said, "You look like a haint."

"Was anyone about?" Sarah asked.

"Nobody but Hector. He say to tell you Goodis gon bring the carriage now."

I did up the back of Sky's dress and helped her paint her face, and nobody spoke a word. Sarah's brow was furrowed tight. She walked to and fro cross the room, a drawstring purse swinging on her arm.

We tugged on our gloves. We fixed on our hats. We drew the veils down to our waists. The tiny bottles of oleander juice, we tucked inside our sleeves—Sarah didn't need to know about that.

From behind the veil, the room looked faint like the haze before daybreak.

I heard the horse clop along the side of the house, coming from the work yard, and my stomach tipped. I'd tried not to set my heart too high, tried not to think about the free black women up north wanting to take us in, the attic in their house with the chimney running through it, but I couldn't hold back anymore. We could help them with their school and with making their hats. I could sew quilts to sell. Sky could make a garden.

Sarah handed me her mauma's gold-tip cane. Then she looked us over and said, "I wouldn't know you on the street."

We went swift down the staircase. If little missus happened by, then she happened by. Keep going was all. Don't stop for nobody. Reaching the bottom rung, I saw the empty place where the steamer trunk sat earlier, and then Hector by the door, boring two holes in us with his eyes.

Sarah spoke to him. "Mother asked me to provide her visitors with a ride to their home. You may go. Goodis will assist us from here."

Hector eased off down the passageway. *That way he looked at us—did he know?* Little missus was nowhere to be seen.

We stepped through the front door and the world rushed up. I looked back at Sky and saw a trace of whiteness float behind her veil.

When Goodis drew the carriage up to the Steamboat Company sign, the heat had gathered thick under our veils. Sweat rivered down our necks. Sky lifted the gullies of her skirt for some air and the smell of lavender and body stench drifted out.

Helping me from the carriage, Goodis whispered, "Lord, Handful, what you doing?"

We hadn't fooled him, and for what I knew, Hector might've figured it out, too. I peered back to see if he was charging down East Bay in the Sulky with little missus.

I said, "Goodis, I'm sorry, but we're leaving. Don't give us away."

He pressed his lips together and I felt the places on me they'd touched. He was the best man I knew. Without meaning for it, my heart had got tangled with his.

He squeezed my hand, his face dim through the dark curtain. He said, "You take care yourself, girl."

We waited for the tickets, waited to board the ship, waited for somebody to say, *Who're you?*

When we walked cross the gangplank, the breeze lifted and the boat rocked. I thought about missus and her devotions. We'd been through the Bible and back with that woman. Now we were Jesus walking on water.

We climbed past the trunks, barrels, bales, and crates, past the boiler to the second deck, and sat down on a bench in the salon to wait for the Guard to pass through. The room was painted white with tables alongside the windows, all of them nailed to the floor. People stood in twos and threes, in their best clothes, in clouds of pipe smoke, and now and then they glanced our way, curious about the black grief we wore. Sarah sat a short space apart from us and kept her head tucked low inside her bonnet.

When the two guards lumbered in, I heard Sky's breath pick up. One guard patrolled the left side, one the right. They nodded at folks, making talk here and there. Looking down, I saw the toes of Sky's slave shoes sticking out from under her fine dress. The scrabble brown shoes, the scraped-up sadness of them.

He stopped before us. He said, "Where're you traveling to?" Talking to me.

My slave tongue would be like the tip of Sky's shoes, giving us away. I lifted my head and looked at him. His guard cap was cocked sideways on his head. He had new blond whiskers and green eyes. Behind him, through the smudged window, I saw the water shimmer.

"Mam?" he said.

Sarah shifted on the bench. I worried she was winding up to say something, that Sky would start humming now, that the fright spring-coiled inside me would break loose. Then I remembered the widow dress I was wearing. I made a sound with my lips like I was trying to give him an answer, but choking on the words, seized by my grief, and I didn't have to pretend that much. I felt sorrow for my life, for what I'd lived and seen and known, for what was lost to me, and the weeping turned real.

A soft wail came from inside me and he took a step back. He said, "I'm sorry for your loss, mam."

As he moved on, a white drop fell from my chin, flour plopping on my skirt.

The engine caught and a shudder ran through the bench. Then came the smell of oil and spewing smoke. The passengers left the salon for the deck to wave their hankies farewell, and we went, too, out where the wharf slaves were tossing the heavy ropes. Far off, the church bells rang on St. Michael's.

We stood at the bow, the three of us, holding the rail tight, waiting. The gulls wheeled by, and the steamer lurched, pitching forward. When the paddles started to roll, Sarah put her hand on my arm and left it there while the city heaved away. It was the last square on the quilt.

I thought of mauma then, how her bones would always be here. People say don't look back, the past is past, but I would always look back.

I watched Charleston fall away in the morning light.

When we left the mouth of the harbor, the wind swelled and the veils round us flapped, and I heard the blackbird wings. We rode onto the shining water, onto the far distance.

AUTHOR'S NOTE

In 2007, I traveled to New York to see Judy Chicago's *The Dinner Party* at the Brooklyn Museum. At the time, I was in the midst of writing a memoir, *Traveling with Pomegranates*, with my daughter, Ann Kidd Taylor, and I wasn't thinking about my next novel. I had no idea what it might be about, only a vague notion that I wanted to write about two sisters. Who those sisters were, when and where they lived, and what their story might be had not yet occurred to me.

The Dinner Party is a monumental piece of art, celebrating women's achievements in Western civilization. Chicago's banquet table with its succulent place settings honoring 39 female guests of honor rests upon a porcelain tiled floor inscribed with the names of 999 other women who have made important contributions to history. It was while reading those 999 names on the Heritage Panels in the Biographic Gallery that I stumbled upon those of Sarah and Angelina Grimké, sisters from Charleston, South Carolina, the same city in which I then lived. How could I have not heard of them?

Leaving the museum that day, I wondered if I'd discovered the sisters I wanted to write about. Back home in Charleston, as I began to explore their lives, I became passionately certain.

As it turned out, I'd been driving by the Grimké sisters' unmarked house for over a decade, unaware these two women were the first female abolition agents and among the earliest major American feminist thinkers. Sarah was the first woman in the United States to write a comprehensive feminist manifesto, and Angelina was the first woman to speak before a legislative body. In the late 1830s, they were arguably the most famous, as well as the most infamous, women in America, yet they seemed only marginally known, even in the city of their origins. My ignorance of them felt like both a personal failing and a confirmation of Chicago's view that women's achievements had been repeatedly erased through history.

Sarah and Angelina were born into the power and wealth of Charleston's aristocracy, a social class that derived from English concepts of landed gentry. They were ladies of piety and gentility, who moved in the elite circles of society, and yet few nineteenth-century women ever "misbehaved" so thoroughly. They underwent a long, painful metamorphosis, breaking from their family, their religion, their homeland, and their traditions, becoming exiles and eventually pariahs in Charleston. Fifteen years before Harriet Beecher Stowe wrote *Uncle Tom's Cabin,* which was wholly influenced by *American Slavery As It Is,* a pamphlet written by Sarah, Angelina, and Angelina's husband, Theodore Weld, and published in 1839, the Grimké sisters were out crusading not only for the immediate emancipation of slaves, but for racial equality, an idea that was radical even among abolitionists. And ten years before the Seneca Falls Convention, initiated by Lucretia Mott and Elizabeth Cady Stanton, the Grimkés were fighting a bruising battle for women's rights, taking the first blows of backlash.

As I read about the sisters, I was drawn more and more to Sarah and what she'd overcome. Before stepping onto the public stage, she experienced intense longings for a vocation, crushed hopes, betrayal, unrequited love, loneliness, self-doubt, ostracism, and suffocating silence. It seemed to me she had invented her wings not so much in spite of these things, but because of them. What compelled me as much as her life as a reformer was her life as a woman. How did she become who she was?

My aim was not to write a thinly fictionalized account of Sarah Grimké's history, but a thickly imagined story inspired by her life. During my research, delving into diaries, letters, speeches, newspaper accounts, and Sarah's own writing, as well as a huge amount of biographical material, I formed my own understanding of her desires, struggles, and motivations. The voice and inner life I've given Sarah are my own interpretation.

I've attempted to remain true to the broad historical contours of Sarah's life. I've included in these pages most of her significant events and formative experiences, along with an enormous amount of factual detail. Occasionally

I've used Sarah's own words from her writings. Her letters in the novel, however, are my own invention.

The most expansive and notable way that I've diverged from Sarah's record is through her imaginary relationship with the fictional character of Hetty Handful. From the moment I decided to write about Sarah Grimké, I felt compelled to also create the story of an enslaved character, giving her a life and a voice that could be entwined with Sarah's. I felt I couldn't write the novel otherwise, that both of their worlds would have to be represented here. Then I came upon a tantalizing detail. As a girl, Sarah was given a young slave named Hetty to be her waiting maid. According to Sarah, they became close. Defying the laws of South Carolina and her own jurist father who had helped to write those laws, Sarah taught Hetty to read, for which they were both severely punished. There, however, ends the short narrative of Hetty. Nothing further is known of her except that she died of an unspecified disease a short while later. I knew right away that hers was the other half of the story. I would try to bring Hetty to life again. I would imagine what might have been.

In addition, I've created and extrapolated numerous other events in Sarah's life, grafting fiction onto truth in order to serve the story. It's well-recorded, for example, that Sarah was a poor public speaker and struggled to express herself verbally, but there's no indication she ever had a speech impediment, as I've portrayed. Sarah did return to Charleston in the months before the Denmark Vesey plot, as I've written, most likely trying to escape her feelings for Israel Morris, and while there, she made her anti-slavery views public, inciting confrontations, but her volatile encounter on the street with an officer of the South Carolina militia is all my doing. And while Sarah knew Lucretia Mott, attending the same Arch Street Meetinghouse and finding inspiration in Mott's life as a Quaker minister, she never boarded in Mott's house. The same is true of Sarah Mapps Douglass, who also attended Arch Street Meetinghouse. The two Sarahs became lasting friends, but Sarah and Angelina did not take refuge in Sarah Mapps' attic after Angelina's incendiary letter was published in *The Liberator*. No longer comfortable or welcome in the home of Catherine Morris, they found a place with friends in Rhode

Island and elsewhere. I fabricated the attic primarily to create a future sanctum for Handful and Sky. These are just a few of the ways I've blended fact and fiction.

Here and there, I've taken small liberties with time. The treadmill inside the Work House upon which I imagined Handful becoming crippled was all too real, but I've predated the treadmill's installation there by seven years. The raid on the African church in Charleston that radicalized Denmark Vesey took place in June 1818, a year earlier than I've depicted it. I also predated the alphabet song, which I described Sarah singing to the children in Colored Sunday School, where she did in fact teach. And while Angelina's letter to the abolitionist newspaper was indeed the fulcrum that propelled the sisters into the public arena, Sarah did not come to terms with her sister's public declaration right away, as I've suggested. Sarah was often slower with her turning points than a novelist would wish. It took her a full year before finally letting go and throwing herself into the revolutionary work that would become her great flourishing. I also feel compelled to mention that Sarah and Angelina were not immediately expelled from their conservative branch of the Quakers, but Angelina's letter did create condemnation, reprimands, and threats of disownment by the committee of Overseers. The sisters were actually expelled some three years later—Angelina for marrying a non-Quaker and Sarah for attending the wedding.

The strange and moving symbiosis that began when Sarah became her sister's godmother at the age of twelve makes me think they wouldn't mind too much that occasionally I've borrowed something Angelina said or did and given it to Sarah. One of the more glaring examples of this has to do with the anti-slavery pamphlets they wrote appealing to the women and clergy of the South. Angelina came up with the idea first, not Sarah, and she wrote her pamphlet a year ahead of Sarah. Nevertheless, once Sarah dived into composing her own essays, she became the more accomplished theoretician and writer, while Angelina went on to become one of the most luminous and persuasive orators of her day. Sarah's daring feminist arguments in *Letters on the Equality of the Sexes,* published in 1837, would inspire and impact women such as Lucy Stone, Abby Kelley, Elizabeth Cady Stanton, and Lucretia Mott.

Further, it was Angelina's pamphlets that were publicly burned by the Charleston postmaster, prompting a warning to Mrs. Grimké that her daughter should not return to Charleston under threat of arrest. Let it be said, though, Sarah had no welcome in the city either.

I've abridged and consolidated events in the sisters' public crusade that took place from December 1836 to May 1838, offering only a telescoped look at the attacks, censure, hostility, and violence they encountered for speaking out as they did. They shook, bent, and finally broke the gender barrier that denied American women a voice and a platform in the political and social spheres. During the furor, Angelina quipped, "We abolition women are turning the world upside down." Sarah's jibe, which I included in the novel, was more pointed: "All I ask of our brethren is that they will take their feet from off our necks."

As for what became of the sisters after the narrative in the novel ends, they retired from the rigors of public life following Angelina's wedding, in part due to Angelina's fragile health. Together, they raised Angelina and Theodore's three children and remained active in anti-slavery and suffrage organizations, tirelessly collecting petitions, and giving aid to a number of Grimké family slaves, whom they helped to set free. Their powerful document, *American Slavery As It Is*, sold more copies than any anti-slavery pamphlet ever written up until *Uncle Tom's Cabin*. Sarah continued to write throughout the rest of her life, and I found it moving that she eventually published her translation of Lamartine's biography of Joan of Arc, the female figure of courage whom she so greatly admired. The sisters started more than one boarding school and taught the children of many leading abolitionists. While teaching in the school of Raritan Bay Union, a cooperative, utopian community in New Jersey, they came in contact with reformers and intellectuals such as Ralph Waldo Emerson, Bronson Alcott, and Henry David Thoreau. I was amused to read that Thoreau found gray-haired Sarah to be a strange sight going about in a feminist bloomer costume.

My favorite event in Sarah's later history occurred in 1870, a few years before she died in Hyde Park, Massachusetts, when she and Angelina led a procession of forty-two women to the polls amid a town election. They marched through a driving snowstorm, where they dropped their illegal ballots into a symbolic voting box. It was the sisters' last act of public defiance. Sarah lived to be eighty-one. Angelina, seventy-four. Despite sisterly conflicts from time to time, the unusual bond that tethered them was never broken, nor were they ever separated.

Besides Sarah and Angelina, I've included other historical figures in the book, rendering them through my own elucidations of their history: Theodore Weld, the famous abolitionist, whom Angelina married; Lucretia Mott, another famous abolitionist and women's rights pioneer; Sarah Mapps Douglass, a free black abolitionist and educator; Israel Morris, a wealthy Quaker businessman and widower who proposed marriage to Sarah, twice. (Her diary suggests she loved him quite deeply, despite turning him down. She maintained that she was bound to her vocation to become a Quaker minister, perhaps believing she could not have marriage and independence both.) There is also Catherine Morris, Israel's sister and a conservative Quaker elder, with whom Sarah and Angelina boarded; William Lloyd Garrison, editor of the radical abolitionist newspaper *The Liberator;* Elizur Wright, secretary of the American Anti-Slavery Society; and the poet John Greenleaf Whittier, Theodore Weld's friend, who along with Theodore made a vow not to marry until slavery was ended, a vow Theodore broke. I might add that both men were supporters of women's rights, and yet in letters to Sarah and Angelina, they strongly pressured the sisters to desist from the cause of women for fear it would split the abolitionist movement. Some of the more salient words that Angelina wrote back to Theodore are included in the imagined scene in which the men arrive at Mrs. Whittier's cottage and order the sisters to stop their fight for women. Sarah and Angelina defied the men, and indeed as historian Gerda Lerner pointed out, they were the ones who attached the cause of women's rights to the cause of abolition, creating what some saw as a dangerous split and others as a brilliant alliance. Either way, their refusal to desist played a vibrant part in propelling the cause of women into American life.

I've tried to represent the members of the Grimké family with a fair amount of accuracy. Sarah's mother, Mary Grimké, was by all accounts a proud and difficult woman. According to Catherine Birney, Sarah's earliest biographer, Mrs. Grimké was devout, narrow, undemonstrative in her affections to her children, and often cruel to her slaves, visiting on them severe and common punishments. She did not, as far as I know, inflict the one-legged punishment on her slaves, but it was an actual punishment, one that Sarah herself described in detail as being used by "one of the first families in Charleston." My representation of Sarah's father, Judge John Grimké, and of the events in his life, are reasonably close to the record, as is the account of Sarah's favorite brother, Thomas. I have no doubt that I deviated with Sarah's older sister Mary ("little missus"), whose history is mostly unknown. Though I found one source that referred to her as unmarried and others that listed her spouse as unknown, I married her to a plantation owner and later had her return home as a widow. She did, however, remain committed to the cause of slavery and unapologetic about it until her death in 1865, a detail I built upon.

It was a thrill for me to visit the Grimkés' house on East Bay Street. Though the house can be dated only to circa 1789, it may have come into John Grimké's possession at the time of his marriage in 1784. It remained in the family until Mrs. Grimké died in 1839. Today, it's well preserved and occupied by a law firm. It is likely that some of the house's original layout and interiors remain the same, including the fireplaces, cypress panels, Delft tiles, pine floors, and moldings. Wandering through the house, I could picture Handful in an alcove on the second floor, gazing out at the harbor, and Sarah slipping down the staircase to her father's library as the slaves lay asleep on the floor outside the bedroom doors. I was even permitted into the attic, where I noticed a ladder leading to a hatch in the roof. I can't say whether the hatch was always there, but I could envision Sarah and Handful climbing through it as girls, an idea that would prompt the scene of their having tea on the roof and telling one another their secrets.

The Historic Charleston Foundation was of great help to me and provided me with a document that contained an inventory and appraisement of all "the goods and chattels" in John Grimké's Charleston house soon after his death in 1819. While poring over this long and meticulous list, I was stunned to come upon the names, ages, roles, and appraised values of seventeen slaves. They were recorded between the Brussels carpet and eleven yards of cotton and flax. The discovery haunted me, and eventually it found its way into the story with Handful unearthing the inventory in the library and finding hers and Charlotte's names inscribed on it along with their supposed worth.

All of the enslaved characters in the novel are conjured from my imagination, with the exception of Denmark Vesey's lieutenants, who were actual figures: Gullah Jack, Monday Gell, Peter Poyas, and Rolla and Ned Bennett. All but Gell were hanged for their roles in the plotted revolt. Vesey himself was a free black carpenter, whose life, plot, arrest, trial, and execution I've tried to represent relatively close to historical accounts. I didn't concoct that odd detail about Vesey winning the lottery with ticket number 1884, then using the payoff to buy both his freedom and a house on Bull Street. Frankly, I wonder if I would've had the courage to make such a thing up. In public reports, Vesey was said to have been hanged at Blake's Lands along with five of his conspirators, but I chose to portray an oral tradition that has persisted among some black citizens of Charleston since the 1820s, which states that Vesey was hanged alone from an oak tree in order to keep his execution shrouded in anonymity. Vesey was said to have kept a number of "wives" around the city and to have fathered a number of children with them, so I took the liberty of making Handful's mother one of these "wives" and Sky his daughter.

Some historians have doubts about whether Vesey's planned slave insurrection truly existed or to what extent, but I have followed the opinion that not only was Vesey more than capable of creating such a plot, he attempted it. I wanted this work to acknowledge the many enslaved and free black Americans who fought, plotted, resisted, and died for the sake of freedom. Reading about the protest and escapes of various actual female slaves helped me to shape the characters and stories of Charlotte and Handful.

The story quilt in the novel was inspired by the magnificent quilts of Harriet Powers, an enslaved woman from Georgia who used African appliqué technique to tell stories about biblical events and historical legends. Her two surviving quilts are archived at the National Museum of American History in Washington, D.C., and the Museum of Fine Arts, Boston. I made a pilgrimage to Washington to see Powers' quilt, and after viewing it, it seemed plausible that enslaved women, forbidden to read and write, could have devised subversive ways to voice themselves, to keep their memories alive, and to preserve the heritage of their African traditions. I envisioned Charlotte using cloth and needle as others use paper and pen, creating a visual memoir, attempting to set down the events of her life in a single quilt. One of the most fascinating parts of my research had to be the hours I spent reading about slave quilts and the symbols and imagery in African textiles, which introduced me to the notion of black triangles representing blackbird wings.

If you're inclined to read further about the historical content in the novel or about Harriet Powers' quilts, you might want to explore this sampling of very readable books:

The Grimké Sisters from South Carolina: Pioneers for Women's Rights and Abolition, by Gerda Lerner.
The Feminist Thought of Sarah Grimké, by Gerda Lerner.
Lift Up Thy Voice: The Grimké Family's Journey from Slaveholders to Civil Rights Leaders, by Mark Perry.
The Politics of Taste in Antebellum Charleston, by Maurie D. McInnis.
Denmark Vesey: The Buried Story of America's Largest Slave Rebellion and the Man Who Led It, by David Robertson.
Africans in America: America's Journey Through Slavery, by Charles Johnson, Patricia Smith, and the WGBH Series Research Team.
To Be a Slave, by Julius Lester, with illustrations by Tom Feelings (Newberry Honor book).
Stitching Stars: The Story Quilts of Harriet Powers, by Mary Lyons (ALA Notable Book for Children).
Signs & Symbols: African Images in African American Quilts, by Maude Southwell Wahlman.

In writing *The Invention of Wings,* I was inspired by the words of Professor Julius Lester, which I kept propped on my desk: "History is not just facts and events. History is also a pain in the heart and we repeat history until we are able to make another's pain in the heart our own."

ACKNOWLEDGMENTS

My deepest thanks to...

Ann Kidd Taylor, an exceptionally gifted writer and author, who read and reread this manuscript in progress, offering me invaluable comments and endless believing.

Jennifer Rudolph Walsh, my amazing agent and dear friend.

My terrific editor, Paul Slovak, and Clare Ferraro, and the extraordinary team at Viking for their boundless support.

Valerie Perry, Aiken-Rhett House museum manager at Historic Charleston Foundation, who gave so generously of her time and efforts and offered tremendous help with my research.

Carter Hudgens, director of preservation and education at Drayton Hall in Charleston, for his time and insights into the life and history of enslaved people.

The following institutions, which, along with Historic Charleston Foundation and Drayton Hall, served as resources: the Charleston Museum, the Charleston Library Society, the College of Charleston's Addlestone Library and the Avery Research Center, the Charleston County Public Library, the South Caroliniana Library, the Aiken-Rhett House Museum, the Nathaniel Russell House Museum, the Charles Pinckney House, the Old Slave Mart, Magnolia Plantation and Gardens, Lowcountry Africana, Middleton Place, and Boone Hall Plantation.

Pierce, Herns, Sloan & Wilson, LLC of Charleston, which allowed me to explore to my heart's content the historic house that once belonged to the Grimké family (named the Blake House for its original owner).

Jacqueline Coleburn, rare book cataloger at the Library of Congress in Washington, D.C., for her enormous assistance in providing me with a treasure trove of letters, newspapers, Anti-Slavery Convention proceedings, and other documents related to Sarah and Angelina Grimké and early-nineteenth-century history.

Doris Bowman, associate curator and specialist, Textile Collection at the National Museum of American History in Washington, D.C., for welcoming me into the Smithsonian archives to view Harriet Powers' *Bible Quilt* and for supplying me with a wealth of information about it.

The New-York Historical Society for making available documents related to the Grimké sisters and Denmark Vesey, including official reports of Vesey's insurrection and trial.

The National Underground Railroad Freedom Center in Cincinnati, which awed and educated me with its exhibits and interactive experiences on slavery and abolition.

Marilee Birchfield, librarian at the University of South Carolina, for aid with research questions.

Robert Kidd and Kellie Bayuzick Kidd for being willing and able research assistants.

Scott Taylor for providing patient and expert technical help, especially the week my computer crashed.

There were many primary sources, books, essays, and articles about the Grimkés, Denmark Vesey, slavery, abolition, quilts and African textiles, and early-nineteenth-century history that became the bedrock of my research, but I would like to especially mention my indebtedness to Dr. Gerda Lerner, whose scholarship and writings about the Grimké sisters greatly influenced me, particularly her biography *The Grimké Sisters from South Carolina: Pioneers for Women's Rights and Abolition*. I'm also indebted to the research and writing of Mark Perry in his book *Lift Up Thy Voice: The Grimké Family's Journey from Slaveholders to Civil Rights Leaders;* H. Catherine Birney in *The Grimké Sisters;* David Robertson in *Denmark Vesey: The Buried Story of America's Largest Slave Rebellion and the Man Who Led It;* and Maurie D. McInnis in *The Politics of Taste in Antebellum Charleston*. I want to acknowledge an American black folktale, from which I drew inspiration, about people in Africa being able to fly and then losing their wings when captured into slavery. The story is beautifully told by Virginia Hamilton and magnificently illustrated by Leo and Diane Dillon in the ALA Notable Children's Book *The People Could Fly: American Black Folktales*.

I'm immensely grateful to the wonderful group of friends who listened to me recount the pull, challenges, and joys of writing this novel, and who never ceased to encourage me: Terry Helwig, Trisha Sinnott, Curly Clark, Carolyn Rivers,

Susan Hull Walker, and Molly Lehman. I'm grateful, too, for Jim and Mandy Helwig, who along with Terry have long been part of my extended family.

I was sustained every single day by the love and support of family: my parents Leah and Ridley Monk; my son Bob Kidd and his wife, Kellie; my daughter Ann Kidd Taylor and her husband, Scott; my grandchildren Roxie, Ben, and Max; and my husband, Sandy, who has journeyed with me since college and whose bravery during the past year both inspired and deepened me. No words can ever express my gratitude for each of them.